ISBN 978-1-330-82914-1
PIBN 10110865

1 MONTH OF
FREE
READING

at

www.ForgottenBooks.com

By purchasing this book you are eligible for one month membership to ForgottenBooks.com, giving you unlimited access to our entire collection of over 700,000 titles via our web site and mobile apps.

To claim your free month visit: www.forgottenbooks.com/free110865

English
Français
Deutsche
Italiano
Español
Português

www.forgottenbooks.com

Mythology Photography **Fiction**
Fishing Christianity **Art** Cooking
Essays Buddhism Freemasonry
Medicine **Biology** Music **Ancient**
Egypt Evolution Carpentry Physics
Dance Geology **Mathematics** Fitness
Shakespeare **Folklore** Yoga Marketing
Confidence Immortality Biographies
Poetry **Psychology** Witchcraft
Electronics Chemistry History **Law**
Accounting **Philosophy** Anthropology
Alchemy Drama Quantum Mechanics
Atheism Sexual Health **Ancient History**
Entrepreneurship Languages Sport
Paleontology Needlework Islam
Metaphysics Investment Archaeology
Parenting Statistics Criminology
Motivational

THE KINNEYS

[See p. 40

"'I GUESS NOT,' AND HE KISSED HER"

SAMPSON ROCK

OF WALL STREET

A Novel

BY

EDWIN LEFÈVRE

AUTHOR OF
" WALL STREET STORIES "
" THE GOLDEN FLOOD," ETC.

ILLUSTRATED

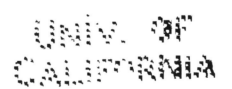

NEW YORK AND LONDON
HARPER & BROTHERS PUBLISHERS
MCMVII

SAMPSON ROCK

OF WALL STREET

A Novel

BY

E D W I N   L E F È V R E

AUTHOR OF
" WALL STREET STORIES "
"THE GOLDEN FLOOD," ETC.

I L L U S T R A T E D

NEW YORK AND LONDON
HARPER & BROTHERS PUBLISHERS
M C M V I I

TO MY FRIEND
NATHAN MUNROE FLOWER

ILLUSTRATIONS

SAMPSON ROCK
OF WALL STREET

I

THE stock-ticker in Sampson Rock's private office had been whirring away half an hour when Rock's cashier entered the room to lay on the desk a bulky letter. It was marked in one corner, "*Personal— Important*," heavily underscored. For additional emphasis there was a rough drawing of a hand, the dexter finger rigidly pointing cornerward; all of which gave the cashier no concern—he was accustomed to seeing *Personal* and *Urgent* and *Important* on envelopes addressed to Mr. Sampson Rock. What he was not accustomed to was the empty room at half-past ten.

"I wonder what's keeping the Old Man?" he muttered. He approached the ticker and looked over the tape with a desultory interest. "H'm! 61! I wonder if I hadn't better—"

"How's the market?" said a voice, sharply. Mr. Rock threw a bundle of newspapers on a chair and took the tape which Valentine silently held out to him. Nothing that Valentine could say would be as illuminative as three or four inches of the little paper ribbon.

A foot was a book; a yard, a history. Valentine couldn't read the tape that way, but he knew Rock did.

"Surface cars—blocked an hour on Broadway!" explained Rock, irritably. He came upon a quotation of the stock of the guilty Cosmopolitan Traction Company. It made him say to Valentine, savagely: "Sell a thousand Cosmopolitan at the market. . It's 165. Wretched service!"

"Yes, sir." Valentine turned to go, thinking a shade enviously of the ways in which a rich man could gratify revenge against offending corporations—to wit, by selling their stocks short—when Rock said, "Send for Dunlap, and get me the last Cosmopolitan Traction annual report."

He had not stopped looking over the tape, reading backward, until he had seen how the market had gone from the opening. After a final glance at the very last quotation or two which the little machine had printed while he was studying the beginning, he walked, frowning, to his desk. The long blue envelope marked *"Personal—Important"* lay on the top of the mound of the morning's mail. He opened it and read the type-written pages with the closest attention. It was a copy of the report which an expert railroad accountant had made on the financial and physical condition of the Virginia Central Railroad for a committee of English bondholders, who were fearful that the optimism of Colonel Robinson, the president of the road, was too American for British consumption.

Rock, for some months, had been so nearly certain that he needed the Virginia Central to round out his own Roanoke system, that he had sent out experts to report in great detail on the physical condition of the property, and to determine the feasibility and cost of a connecting line, while others were analyzing the company's annual reports for years back, supplementing the official figures with confidential information obtained from one of the underpaid book-keepers of the Virginia Central. Williams, the accountant, unaided and alone, doubtless hindered at every step by a management conscious of its own shortcomings, had learned as much as Rock's experts had with the aid of the bribed book-keeper, and, moreover, he had taken precisely the same view of the grossly mismanaged road and of its great possibilites that Rock did. Therefore Williams must be bought and paid for. He had succumbed to the Old Man's insidious flattery and had sent him the report, in order that the Old Man might realize that Williams was the best man in his line in the country. He could not be cheap, for he was not only intelligent, but, to boot, honest. However, no price would be too high to pay the man who had saved Rock months of valuable time by makng the great captain of finance realize definitely now that Williams was a wonder, and also that the Virginia Central must be benevolently assimilated by the Roanoke. The Virginia Central and its owners did not yet know it.

Rock's friends often spoke of his habit of thinking in lightning flashes, of the marvellous quickness with which he abandoned old and settled on new policies, and, at the same time, of the systematic, von Moltke-like manner in which he planned some of his market campaigns. In their heart of hearts they sometimes doubted that any human mind could think so much and so quickly, or see so far and so clearly. Their minds did not. Therefore they half thought that Rock often closed his eyes, jumped, and landed safely on a golden feather - bed, compelling fortune's smiles by sheer audacity. But it was not difficult for Rock to know, in the twinkling of an eye, what to think or what to vision to himself and why. His untiring patience in the conduct of the subsequent campaign, and his final success so deliberately led up to, alone shook his friends' confidence in the "blind plunge" theory.

And this particular plunge was not blind. Williams, in addition to telling in how poor a condition, physical and financial, the Virginia Central was, proceeded to show how the one hope of the English bondholders' committee lay in building an extension; not to Biddleboro; to connect with the Roanoke, as Rock planned, but to Franklyn, to connect with the South Atlantic branch of the Great Southern—the Roanoke's powerful rival. The stock had been strong lately, and the Street listlessly thought that possibly President Robinson expected to succeed in raising the needed capital in London. But Rock had taken pains that it should not be active enough to make it an attractive gamble. Men should help their fellows, and Rock felt that poor, harassed Robinson might spare himself further anxiety about that English capital and the Virginia Central. He decided to take Robinson's burden of care and worry on his own broad shoulders. Ungrateful Robinson, when Robinson should discover the philanthropy!

Sampson Rock leaned back in his chair. His eyes were half closed. The accountant's report was on the desk before him, open at the last page, but he did not see it. The ticker was tinklingly promising golden coins, but he did not hear it. What he saw was a range of hills; there were some black holes—mouths of tunnels leading into rich bituminous mines that were not half busy enough; what he heard was the rumble of a train of loaded cars that was not half long nor half

• 4

heavy enough—the unexploited mineral wealth of a vast section of territory and the criminal negligence of a mismanaged railroad. Beyond the range of hills was a system of veritable Himalayas of limestone, and beyond them huge deposits of iron ore. With a little more heat and a little closer proximity to the limestone and to the coal the iron almost would have smelted itself into high-grade pigs—only the pigs in Virginia Central were also asses. The control of the road, an extension to Biddleboro to connect with his own Roanoke & Western subsidiary companies to exploit the mineral and agricultural territory thus far untapped, a merger, a first-class system controlled by Sampson Rock, a big bull campaign in the stock-market, permanently establishing the credit of his own securities on an investment plane, and—

He awoke. His eyes, wide open now, took on a curious, alert look.

"H'm! It bears out Morson"—his chief expert, who had been studying the same proposition from Rock's more practical, or, possibly, more piratical, point of view. He must turn Morson loose again—this time to secure options on iron-mines and coal-lands and quarries and water-rights, in the interest of the yet unborn Old Dominion Development Company. The Roanoke & Western would guarantee the Development Company bonds, thereby making them easily vendible. That would supply the necessary capital. The Development stock would be called water; but it was Rock's wager on the future growth of industrial Virginia, and sixty per cent. of that water would be Rock's; also, all the credit, later, for the modern miracle of turning water into gold. But that was merely a "side issue." The deal itself would at once enhance the value of his Roanoke holdings. That meant more millions—real millions—and more work; and more power.

Rock pushed one of a row of buttons on his desk. While he waited for Valentine he looked over the rest of his correspondence, reading the letters at a glance. Most of them he threw into the waste-paper basket— one he tore into bits before so doing; two he laid aside, writing undermost; the remainder he initialled, or scribbled on them a word or two, and placed them on the top of the desk to be answered and filed. No business literature was ever allowed to accumulate. Even the letters from beggars and cranks were promptly answered by the secretary, or by him referred to the proper man for reply. Rock never dictated any letters until after ticker hours. But when he left for the day not a scrap of paper remained on his desk. And he never philosophized about it.

Valentine entered.

"Telephone to Walter Williams to come over at once. Take him into the last room. Tell Dunlap to come over in five minutes. I'll see him after I'm done with Williams."

The last room was at the end of the corridor—No. 888—the last of the suite occupied by Rock. It was the next but one to the private office. It was there that Rock received callers whom he did not wish any one else in the office to see. His best friends never went into any other room. His worst enemies also had called at 888 on occasion.

"Yes, sir. Here's the Cosmopolitan report, and a telegram."

"From whom?"

Valentine handed the telegram in silence and laid the report on the desk. Rock read the message.

"It's from Sam. His boat's at Quarantine."

"That's nice." Valentine looked pleased. Rock looked instead at his watch.

. "She ought to dock in a half-hour. H'm!" His only son was returning from a trip around the world after an absence of eighteen months. Rock saw the smile on his cashier's face. It struck him that he ought to smile too. This made him frown. He said, impatiently, "Tell Morson to meet Sam at the dock, American Line, and bring him up here." He added, with a curious, half-defiant, half-apologetic air. "I must see Williams at once."

It did not occur to Valentine that Rock, who had not seen his only son in a year and a half, should be apologetic about a few minutes more or less. He went out quickly to carry out the Old Man's commands.

Rock walked to the ticker. As he looked the tape over he saw "1000 CT 164¾." It was possibly the one thouand shares of Cosmopolitan Traction he did not own but had spitefully sold because of his delay that morning. There are profits and profits; the more the merrier. It reminded him of the annual report on his desk. He sat down again and read it, frowning. The revenge should be profitable, otherwise he would forgive. As he finished, his brow cleared and a good-humored look replaced the frown. It was as he had thought. The stock was too high. The brazen manipulation of his semi-occasional friend Judson, the street-railway magnate, had put up the price, but the road itself was not gaining. It had, quite obviously to Rock, whose expert eye could read between the lines of the report, reached the limit of its prosperity by reaching the limit of its facilities. It was a physical impossibility to do more business. But its operating expenses and fixed charges had gone soaring, owing to losing lines which the inside crowd had bought cheap and sold dear—to their own company. These lines must be "modernized." That would mean more graft, and more graft would tell on the stock in the end, however skilfully Judson manipulated it now, in trying to unload before the community discovered the outrageous over-capitalization. Judson was unintelligently optimistic; his version of Lincoln's aphorism was that he could fool all the people all the time. Therefore Rock smiled—if it had not been for the delay on Broadway he never would have thought of selling the stock short—and rang for Valentine. There were half a dozen telephones on a long table at one end of the room; those were for his confidential brokers, and went to their offices, according to the rules, but were so arranged that they could be switched on to the lines that went to the Board Room — the "floor" of the Stock Exchange. Ordinary orders in ordinary stocks he let Valentine give out for him to the office's routine brokers, as Dunlap called them.

"Valentine, sell four thousand Cosmopolitan more, at the market. It may take some months, but we'll buy it back at 125. Keep track of it." He had no bear campaign in mind. It was merely an investment on the short side, and he immediately dismissed it from his thoughts. If, on the way to the big gold-mine, he saw a few coins on the path, he picked them up—it did not delay or distract—and walked on.

"Yes, sir." Valentine decided that the Old Man was still angry at the delay. Somehow the Old Man had a habit of turning even his anger into dollars— fancy a drunkard getting paid for getting drunk! Lucky people, these stock-gambling captains of finance, thought Valentine, with keen regret that the Old Man had said it would take months to cash in. If he had said days, or even weeks, Valentine himself would have sold short one hundred shares. To get rich is pleasant; to get rich quick is heaven, but takes capital. There were many Valentines in Wall Street, also in the United States. They thought the same thing—no brains and no expert knowledge needed, only money and patience. Lacking capital, patience was slow death, unless there was luck. Even then, Rock would be lucky merely because Rock had money. His short sale of Cosmopolitan Traction, so obviously prompted by nothing but petulant spite, would make two hundred thousand dollars walk by themselves into Rock's pocket, to pay for the twenty minutes lost on Broadway. Ten thousand dollars a minute that would be, because Rock was rich—Valentine was logical.

A moment afterwards the cashier announced that Mr. Williams was in the secret room, which a facetious accomplice of Rock's had once dubbed the pool-incubator and scheme-hatchery.

The best railroad accountant in the United States was a short, slim man, utterly bald, with a Vandyke beard and sharp gray eyes. Habitually he looked angry, as if the incompetence of book-keepers annoyed him. Moreover, the devices some railroad financiers adopted to mislead the public were so transparent as to be an insult to the eagle eye of Mr. Walter Williams, licensed public accountant, forty years old, and not yet a millionaire. But with visions—visions!

"Good-morning, Williams," said Rock, with an affability that was not excessive. He could be very affable at times, even to newspaper reporters. His face, however, was expressionless as he went on: "I

9

have read the report. It is a good piece of work; but—"

Williams's face became at once defiant. He allowed no "buts," and he half repented now having been persuaded to send the copy of the masterpiece to Rock.

"But you cannot send it to London." Rock spoke very evenly, very dispassionately. His eyes looked neither alert nor sleepy—the eyes of an ordinarily intelligent man speaking to a friend about an everyday matter regarding which both were of the same mind. Further discussion would absurdly exaggerate the importance of it.

On Williams's face the defiance rose to anger, and he said, scowling:

"Why not?"

He was bitterly sorry that he had been unfaithful to his employers in allowing this stock - gambler, masquerading as a railroad magnate, to see the report as soon as it had been completed. The Old Man had admired his work—which tickled his artistic vanity—and had, moreover, promised to turn Williams loose on the books of the so-called "Rock roads," which would help the bank account. Williams sincerely thought his mission in life was to teach corporations how to conduct their business and keep their books honestly, but above all scientifically. Brooding on the obvious designs of a higher power Walter Williams had chloroformed his sense of humor.

"Because I think it would be well to wait a little." Rock's voice and manner had not changed.

"*I* don't," retorted Williams, brusquely.

Rock smiled a trifle as he said: "Williams, it's going to make them feel so good, when they do get it, that a few weeks' delay won't hurt." His voice was full of good-humor.

"They expect me to mail it this week."

"Cable that you need to verify some figures."

"My figures never need verification, Mr. Rock." His manner was coldly austere.

"That's why I am here trying to do you a good turn. You must wait." Mr. Rock's look now was full of friendliness. He did not yet know the accountant's price, but was reading the quotations on the accountant's vanity. He did not despise the accountant for having it, because Williams also had the peculiar ability of the expert to a remarkable degree, and he understood scientific railroading in the abstract. Rock could utilize his critical and analytical gifts, and would gladly pay for them. Sometimes theorists' suggestions could be carried out with profit. This theorist must make no suggestions to Rock's competitors. Like charity, the profit should begin at home.

"Impossible!" said Williams. There was finality in his tone. Few people spoke that way to Rock. It would have made a saint angry, also a sinner, but not Rock. Yet Rock deliberately asked:

"To how many people have you shown the report, Williams?"

The accountant flushed angrily. "Only you," he growled, "and I'm sorry I've—"

"I'm not, and you won't be either. How much of the stock have you bought?"

"Why must I have bought any?" Williams sneered.

But Rock, who was looking at him meditatively, saw the merest gleam of a fleeting uneasiness in the accountant's sharp gray eyes, and he answered, calmly: "You wouldn't be human if you hadn't, knowing what

you do. Now, let me give you some friendly advice, Williams. You sell what you have bought,
and—"

"How do you—" began Williams, still stubbornly
defiant.

"My suspicious nature, I suppose," said Rock, with
a touch of resignation in his voice "Look here,
Williams"—there was an air of conscious patience
about him as he went on—"that stock is going down."
Williams could be of use to him in several ways. He
saw what position the accountant could fill. Frankness now was merely an advance payment.

"But it won't stay down. You can't keep it down.
Why, if Robinson wasn't such an ass—"

Rock interrupted the accountant

"Does he know what your report—"

The accountant interrupted Rock: "No, we didn't
get on. The London people don't love him, and he
knows it, and he thinks I will make my report unfavorable in order to please my clients who don't trust
him. He tried to put obstacles in my way. The
ass! Why, if he knew how to run a railroad, that
stock—"

"Precisely. But he doesn't." Into Rock's eyes
came a look alert, aggressive, that sparkled with a
living intelligence, the look of a man who both thinks
and fights, who both dreams and does. Williams,
whose fear that he had made a mistake in his purchase
of Virginia Central stock made him sharp-eyed, saw it,
and the frown on his face disappeared. Rock went
on, his voice not less kindly but more commanding, because he had estimated the accountant's price and the
value of services present and prospective: "Sell that
stock at once. I'll tell you when to buy it back. It's

going down, and going down fast. That report is merely delayed in transmission—see? Don't argue. When the time is ripe you can buy five thousand shares in this office. Don't worry about the margin. This is a personal matter between you and me. But that report is not mailed until I tell you."

Some things lose nothing by repetition. The exact amount of the bribe is one of them. Rock added, aiming straight at the breach in the fortifications: "The day you mail it you buy five thousand shares. I guarantee that the price will be lower than it is to-day. That same day you start on the books of the Roanoke & Western at your own price. I'll have a good deal of work for you all this year and next."

A flash burned in Williams's eyes. He saw at a glance what Rock's scheme would be—to acquire the control of the Virginia Central in the open market. To do this cheaply he would depress the price of the shares. That was as $2+2=4$. Then the price would rise as he bought it in bulk; and then, once the control was in his possession, the price would rise still more, just before Mr. Sampson Rock, the daring individual speculator, sold the entire block to Mr. Sampson Rock, the conservative chairman of the executive committee of the Roanoke & Western Railroad. That was as $4+4=8$. Efficiency was Williams's monomania, and Rock, he saw with sympathetic enthusiasm, was highly efficient. Also, being an expert accountant, Williams, in less than three seconds, figured that he himself stood to win one hundred thousand dollars on that deal; and more, if he could be useful to Rock later. He was an honest man —that was why Rock had not dreamed of asking him to "doctor" the report—and with praiseworthy enthusiasm, but too quick at ticker arithmetic for his own good. He controlled his exultation and abjectly apologized to himself for what he was going to do by saying, with a carefully calculated shake of the head and a dubious tone of voice, "Well, Mr. Rock, I—"

"Yes, Williams: it's all right. I'll give you five minutes to sell your Virginia Central. You need not go short—if you don't *wish* to." Rock said this very deliberately. He knew what Williams would wish, therefore he finished, "Not too much of it; just enough for pocket-money."

Williams was human. He said: "I'm very much obliged, Mr. Rock. I—"

"Don't mention it. Remember, in five minutes Virginia Central begins to decline. If you've told any of your friends it was a good thing, it might be only fair to warn them to get out." It was a very nice touch. Williams felt that the Old Man had a heart. The Old Man knew Williams would think so; he also knew that if he did not advise Williams to tell his friends, Williams, being a decent chap, still would do it. And after a judicious pause Rock added: "But be discreet. No details to anybody. And *quick*, Williams." It takes genius to advise a man who is in a hurry to get rich to make haste about it.

"Thank you, Mr. Rock," repeated the accountant, his burning desire to run out of the room making his voice sound husky as if with grateful emotions. Sampson Rock considerately held the door open for the ticker-stricken man, and said: "Any time you have anything you think I ought to know, come and see me. And remember, Williams, I trust you," he finished sternly, yet not unkindly.

Rock did not so much think that every man had his price as that devotion, personal and impersonal, like everything else in this world, must be paid for. He was not yet rich enough to have lost the sense of proportion. He made money for others in order that he might make money for himself. He was a highly intelligent man.

II

STILL looking as if he trusted Williams, Sampson Rock went to the front office. He approached the ticker and gazed intently on the printed letters and numbers of the tape—so intently that they ceased to be numerals and became living figures. Williams was ten million leagues away, and Rock's vision leaped from New York to Richmond, from Richmond to Biddleboro, from Biddleboro back to the glittering marble-and-gold Board Room of the Stock Exchange. The tape-characters were like little soldier-ants, bringing precious loads to this New York office, tiny gold nuggets from a thousand stockholders, men and women and children, rich and poor, to the feet of Sampson Rock. It may be there would be shrieks and sobs, pain-squeals and imprecations; but they would not reach the ears of a man whose soul had soared so high that the entire State of Virginia was spread before him in miniature, like an outrolled map, glowing and glittering poly-chromatically in a flood of sunshine. And through this map ran a line, not a ticker-tape, with towns instead of abbreviations or bridges instead of dashes, but a vein; and it was not a vein of human blood or of human tears, but of human sweat, a living thing, born of work, stretching tentacle-like arms everywhither, reaching to every corner of the State of Virginia, to the great Atlantic; and more faintly, the same net-work of life-giving and life-creating veins extending to the Great River and the Great Lakes, and perhaps—if Sampson Rock lived long enough to realize the dream of every railroad emperor—even unto the golden remote Far West and the blue Pacific—from ocean to ocean.

But how to bring all that to him? . . . Those little' soldier-ants on the tape must be trained to march, gold-laden, Sampson Rockward. They would, little by little, make a vast mountain, and that mountain would turn the dreams into realities—not gold, but life, would Sampson Rock give to his fellow-men. The gold he would keep—gold meant so little to them who only dreamed, so much to one who dreamed and also did!

Order out of chaos, a definite plan unravelled from the tangled sunbeams—it would not be difficult. He knew exactly what he wished to do. That was a great deal to start with; it was about ten million dollars' worth more than the disorganized and leaderless mob who still owned the Virginia Central knew. And so, the Virginia sunshine dimmed, and the visions faded, and in the place of the poet that had been dreaming in the office—the poet whose numbers were of railroad tonnage—there returned to the side of the ticker a calculating machine, all steel—thoughts and desires and purpose all of the temper of steel. It was good advice a great man had given to an expert accountant in bidding him sell out his Virginia Central stock, not because it was too dear, but because it was too cheap!

He walked into the customers' room. Rock made his "headquarters" with the firm of Daniel G. Dunlap & Co., having separate though adjoining offices, and keeping his own set of book-keepers. The Roanoke & Western offices were on the floor below. What he said was law, however, whether Mr. Dunlap was present or not, and the Street, as well as the office, so understood. The firm did a good business because it was strong and was supposed to be "next to Rock." But it really had outgrown a general commission business because Rock and his pools insured prosperity. Dunlap was courteous enough to the small customers, and gave them good·service, but seldom gave what they really wanted, which was tips. But the small customers hoped on; some day, perhaps, they would be repaid for waiting. And so they waited, in the mean time getting their daily tips elsewhere, even taking them from the newspapers.

Rock sought Valentine, who was employed by both Dunlap and himself and received salaries from both. He asked:

"Has the Wall Street News Agency man been around to-day?"

"Who? Gilmartin?"

"Yes."

"No, sir; not yet."

"If he comes, send him in to me." And Rock walked back to his private office. The eyes of Dunlap's customers who sat before a huge quotation-board followed him yearningly. If only they had X-ray sight to pierce through the Old Man's skull and read in the Old Man's brain what was good to buy, what was good to sell! It never struck them that it was a particularly well-shaped head. A demoralizing thing, this practice of holding the tape within six inches of the eyes; all they could see after a while was a financial Moses smiting a rock with a rod of gold, and a stream of dollars gushing out. Looking to see exactly where to place the bag in order to fill it quickly—that strained the eyes also.

Rock was looking at the ticker when Dunlap entered.

"Good - morning, Sampson. Want to see me?" Dunlap was tall, stout, gray-haired, with a small mustache that drooped like a mandarin's. He was frowning. That meant nothing. He always frowned, even when he made money. He was somewhat myopic, but would not wear glasses; the frown had become habitual from his efforts to see. He was an excellent broker, with a sort of rudimentary imagination.

"Yes. Virginia Central is pretty high." Rock did not raise his eyes from the tape.

"How do you mean high?" asked Dunlap. He had been buying the stock for the Old Man unostentatiously for some weeks. The Old Man, therefore, couldn't have been bearish on it very long. And even now the voice was not bearish; it could not mean that he really wished to sell the stock, that he had abandoned the campaign.

"H-i-g-h," spelled Rock, looking up. He was in a cheerful mood.

Dunlap arched his eyebrows, let the corners of his mouth drop, and posed for the statue of resignation. At length he said, mournfully:

"Shoot ahead."

"It's forty-eight," said Rock.

"Yep."

"Well, it would look better at thirty-eight by the end of the week."

"This is Wednesday."

"Precisely. That gives you plenty of time. And if you're real clever, Dan, you'll have more stock at thirty-eight than you have now."

"How much more?"

"I'd begin buying on balance from forty-two down. I want all there is floating around. Let somebody else clear for you. The stock in the office goes out with a becoming blare of trumpets. See?"

"Ay, ay, sir!" Dunlap smiled. It was the kind of an order he liked—the War Office saying to the general in the field: "Go in and win!"—no handicapping with useless instructions, no hampering with unnecessary admonitions from bureaucrats who thought nobody else knew anything. "Go in and win;" that was all! It called for the exercise of those qualities of which he was, mistakenly, the proudest. He rather overestimated them as he underestimated the fact that much of his success as a stock manipulator was due to the great fortune of Sampson Rock, which kept him always in ammunition, and to the guiding mind, always suggesting, tactfully, moves and counter-moves, more vigor here, less dash there, feeling for weak spots everywhere and finding them and concentrating the attack on those points. The brain was Rock's always; but Dunlap was a good corps-commander, and Rock knew his strength and his weakness and made the most of the one and protected himself against the other.

Dunlap said "Anything more?" so briskly, yet so obviously looking for a negative reply, that Rock smiled slightly:

"No, Dan; I leave the details to you."

Dunlap hurried out of the office as if he feared Rock would change his mind. He was at the door when the Old Man's voice made him pause, a frown on his face:

"I say, Dan!"

"Yes?"

"Not too violently at first."

"All right." And Dunlap was off to the Board Room

to distribute selling orders. Rock began once more to watch the tape. He was now on the march. His vision was not in Virginia. He saw no life-giving, life-creating railroad. His mind had taken a calm judicial attitude. He would see, coldly, critically, how Dunlap would carry out his orders, ready to prevent mistakes and to check inartistic excesses. No zeal, no fire; only intelligence, dispassionate as mathematics. The game was indeed one of pure mathematics just now. At the proper time the game would pass the mathematical stage and attain the psychological. And then Dunlap would get his orders in words of one syllable, to insure their execution exactly as given by the real commander-in-chief. Ethics? In that environment?

The door opened and a short, pudgy, red-haired man partly entered. He was clean-shaven and somewhat careless as to dress.

"Good-morning, Mr. Rock," he said, not advancing an inch beyond the threshold. He was ready to retreat if Rock's face made it prudent. A few days before Gilmartin had so retreated.

"Hello, Gilmartin! Come in. I won't eat you."

Gilmartin entered, all smiles. "No," he said, "I guess I'm getting too tough for that, living in this neighborhood. Anything new, Mr. Rock?"

Mr. Rock shook his head. "N-no," he answered, doubtfully, as if he really were trying to remember something to tell to the reporter. It was a subtle compliment, the admission of a certain degree of intimacy and willingness to help. Gilmartin's news-slips went to all the offices in the Street and the newspapers regularly cribbed from them. Rock was accessible to all the financial writers, but he distributed impressions through the news-slips. It saved him time.

SAMPSON ROCK OF WALL STREET

The suggestion in Rock's manner of personal good-will made Gilmartin feel better, and he approached the ticker by the window. It symbolized the democracy of the money-makers. All men had the same heart-interest in the little machine—the actual millionaire and the would-be, the piker and the plunger; and all being, therefore, equally entitled to a look, any one might read the tape over another's shoulder and not be deemed rude; only human. Perhaps this is because the ticker lifts to eminence to-day the pauper of yesterday, and can turn the ingratiating smiles of to-day into the derisive laughter of to-morrow. Or it simply may be the democracy of the betting-ring.

"H'm," observed Gilmartin, really to make talk and to show that he knew Rock liked him, "Virginia Central is 47⅓. It was 48¼ a minute ago."

Rock turned to the tape with an air of novelty, almost as if it were the first time that morning he had glanced at it, and said, a trifle correctly: "It's now 47; 6⅞; ¾. Rather active, isn't it? You might say it's in a melting mood, eh?"

"I wonder what makes it so weak?" asked Gilmartin, ignoring the play of words. He looked at Mr. Rock interrogatively. Rock laughed.

"Don't look so accusingly at me, Gilmartin. Come; what's on your mind?"

"I thought you had some," confessed Gilmartin, looking at the Old Man's face; it was now impassive, perhaps too impassive; and Gilmartin continued: "And I wondered if—" Gilmartin had no business even to suspect such a thing. Realizing this, he ceased to speak. The Old Man could not wish anybody to know it. But ignorance is as difficult to keep dark in Wall Street at times as knowledge. Rock did not show his displeasure. He asked, with a sort of careless kindness:

"Have you any?"

Mr. Rock's face, it burst joyfully upon Gilmartin, now looked distinctly philanthropic. It made Gilmartin very promptly look dejected, however dithyrambic his soul might be. It was the psychological moment—to get at one and the same time a good tip and the facts; that is, to make money out of the tip, which was nice, and to get news for his slips, which was his duty. In the human order of niceness, first the gamble, then the other. He answered:

"Yes, sir. I'm sorry to say that I have." He hesitated and took another look at the tape. What he saw there made him say, angrily: "Yes, sir, I'm decidedly sorry to say I have. The pup is now 46⅜." By this time he almost believed his lie and was on the verge of mourning his loss. A rich man's sympathy, if artistically aroused, can do pleasing things. He hoped Rock was making money. That would make him very sympathetic. And so little to Rock meant so much to Gilmartin!

"H'm!" grunted Rock, who was watching the little paper-ribbon intently. The grunt did not have a particularly philanthropic sound.

"Yes, sir," almost wept Gilmartin.

"H'm!" again came from Rock, who was not listening to anything but the ticker.

"I've got two hundred shares," wailed Gilmartin, hesitating between a self-reproachful frown at his stupidity, and the visible expression of an unbearable pain at his misfortune.

"Eh? Ah!" Rock turned to the reporter. "What did you say you had?"

"Two hundred Virginia Central. Holy smoke!" excitedly, "it's 46!" He remembered himself, and said, very bitterly: "It cost me 48⅓." To lose six hundred dollars would make a very poor man bitter. And Gilmartin was even poorer.

"Well, why don't you—er—" Rock stared vacantly at Gilmartin's red hair. His thoughts were across the street with Dunlap.

"Yes, sir?" said Gilmartin, eagerly. Rock blinked his eyes. The vacant look disappeared. In its place was indifference—nothing gained by the change!

"Er—do something." And Rock turned to the ticker again.

"Why don't you tell me what to do?" retorted Gilmartin, with precisely the degree of indignation he thought he might safely permit himself. He meant Mr. Rock to imagine that his loss made him talk that way. The fear of death will make even rabbits desperate. Gilmartin hoped the Old Man might think of an inoffensive rabbit who wrote for a living.

"You get all the news. You ought to know what to do." The tone of the voice was non-committal, narrowly escaping being sarcastic; which was bad. Then: "What do you hear about it?" The voice was again friendly. One wing of hope fluttered.

"I heard," answered Gilmartin, emphasizing the past tense to show that out of loyalty to Rock he no longer believed it, "that the London people were waiting for some kind of a report before they bought a block of treasury stock Colonel Robinson is trying to sell them. I thought Colonel Robinson might get somebody to put up the stock to lure them on."

"Well, I guess the Englishmen will get it cheap enough," said Rock, calmly.

"Robinson going over?"

"Don't ask me questions," said Rock, sharply, looking at Gilmartin straight in the yes. "How do I know what he is going to do?"

"*I* am telling *you*." Gilmartin spoke with the dignity of a man who is rebuffed while being good. "He is, or was, to sail on the third of next month." His heart suddenly fluttered with fear. He could not tell whether the Old Man would blame him for Robinson's actions or for his ignorance of them. The uncertainty being reducible to dollars, not to know whether the sign in Rock's mind was a *plus* or a *minus* sign was to be stricken unto death; and he a writer with a family.

"Are you sure?"

"Yes, sir." Then he placed the blame on others; he added, "Hubbard and Stillwell said so."

On Rock's face there was nothing that Gilmartin could read. But the captain of finance said, reflectively:

"They are easy-folks in London to deal with. He'd better make haste."

"Do you think—" Gilmartin's eager voice told so plainly his fears, which were prompted by his hopes, that Rock smiled, and answered:

"Oh, it's a mighty fine road. It has a great fuchah, by gad, suh!" Rock was plagiarizing from Colonel Robinson, who was a very southern Southerner. It made Gilmartin say, impetuously:

"Do you really think it's rotten?"

Rock laughed.

"Nonsense, Gilmartin; you are becoming prejudiced and slangy. It's a fine road. Hasn't it kept out of bankruptcy — so far?" The speaker, it was quite obvious, did not wish to be nasty to a competitor, but neither did he wish his reporter friend to be fooled. In the tie-vote between friendship and duty, the ticker usually casts the deciding ballot. Gilmartin gratefully asked:

"Do you think there is any danger of a receivership for the Vir—"

"Look here, Gilmartin, you mustn't talk that way. There is a law against the circulation of malicious lies calculated to injure a corporation's credit." The sternness was of a friend who is wise towards a friend who is indiscreet.

"I know; but—" began the unabashed Gilmartin.

"Well, there are good times coming for all. If Robinson can land the English again for another ten million or so and gets a few up-to-date railroad men to show him how the road ought to be run, I think he'll pull through," This was gospel truth.

"Mr. Rock," asked Gilmartin, tremblingly, "do you think the stock is going still—"

"It is not still. It keeps moving. It's now 45¾," observed Rock, the tape between his fingers.

"Somebody on the inside is selling out. The report must be unfavorable."

"Don't jump at conclusions, Gilmartin," quizzed Rock. "Maybe it's only a drive to get cheap stock." That also was an eternal verity

"Drive? That's long stock coming out. Just look at it!" retorted Gilmartin, with indignant scepticism. Mr. Rock's face did not permit itself to smile. Dunlap, like every professional trader, actually rejoiced when he had a chance to "whack" a stock. If a man is in a hurry to reach a place on foot, it is nice to be able to walk down-hill. He was happy now. So were the professional traders, who were blithely selling it because somebody else was. They knew nothing about Virginia Central, but the unknown somebody else probably did.

"Tut, tut, man!" said Rock, just a trifle impatiently. There was something in the way Rock was looking at the tape that made Gilmartin say, determinedly—it was no time for play-acting:

"Mr. Rock, do you think it's going much lower?"

"Is this for your paper?" Rock looked at the reporter with a sort of indecisive benignity.

"No, it's for Gilmartin," answered Gilmartin, thrilled. The ticker began to sing, goldenly, *Haste! haste!* and then, *the cash! the cash!*

"I think," said Rock, very deliberately—and Gilmartin, listening with his very soul, heard the words tinkle like coins dropping into a cup slowly, one by one, all of gold, each an embodied hope—"I think that the price is more than likely to go down. In fact, Gilmartin, I think the entire market will work lower. And the Virginia Central stock, I should say, might very possibly be the leader. It depends on whether Robinson can raise the money he needs or not."

"I bet he won't get a cent," interjected Gilmartin. He had made up his mind. The Virginia Central was doomed. The doom was also reducible to dollars and cents. He still waited, in the hope of getting more information. That was common-sense. Moreover, with additional data he could reckon more closely his probable profits. He might then tell his wife exactly what needed things she would be able to buy in a few short and happy days. He loved his family. For their sake he now loved the ticker. A year's salary in one week—what did that mean? Heaven! The ticker would open the shining gates; Gilmartin would let his wife and children enter first. He was not selfish.

"I haven't said anything for publication, you understand?"

"Do I ever quote you unless you specifically say I may?" asked Gilmartin, reproachfully.

"No; that's why I talk to you," said Rock, dismissingly. "And, Gilmartin"—as the reporter turned to go—"tell Valentine I said you were good for a couple of hundred shares, whether you want to buy or sell—"

"Thank you, Mr. Rock. It will be Virginia Central, and it won't be to buy," said Gilmartin, ingratiatingly; "unless," he added, prudently, "you think there is some other stock that I'd better—" His hopes did not intoxicate him utterly; he still thought of his family's welfare.

"It's your funeral," laughed Rock. "Pick your own winner. If you hear anything of interest. let me know, will you?"

"You bet," replied Gilmartin, with hasty gratitude, before he almost ran out to sell two hundred shares of Virginia Central in Dunlap's office, without having to put up any margin. Mr. Rock had not asked him to circulate false statements about the road nor about the stock, and had not bribed him, but left everything to Gilmartin's susceptibility to impressions. If Gilmartin wished to sell Virginia Central short, and allowed his gambling to bias his judgment and influence his writings, it was of his own doing. Mr. Rock had merely been generous in lending money to a poor chap to gamble with, that a poor chap might make a year's salary in a week — a glorious, workless week — which would buy clothes for three red-haired little boys in Flatbush. Rock did not tell lies, deliberately or accidentally. He considered it unnecessary, which, indeed, it was—in Wall Street. Gilmartin inevitably would sell that tip to people who would gamble on it and give him a share of the winnings; and then he would give it, free of charge, to as many people as would listen to him—so that they too would sell the stock short. Each of the recipients of the tip, which was a very good tip, would in turn tell his friends; for, naturally, if the friends took it and passed it on to their friends, it would mean selling, and that would help the price to go down, and that would help the third and second and first generation of tip - givers; and that would help Gilmartin, and that would help Rock, and that would give work to railroad - builders in Virginia. The philosophy of the truthful, and therefore intelligent, "inside tip" at a certain stage of the manipulation is the fascinating philosophy of the endless chain.

III

ROCK turned to the table where eight or ten telephone instruments stood. He must discourage not only Colonel Robinson, but the English bondholders as well. He would cable to his London brokers later in the day. Other stocks than the Virginia Central ought logically to go down. In order to divert suspicion he must not attack Virginia Central alone. If the weakness was general, the decline of any one stock would look "natural," and naturalness is the first essential of really skilful manipulation, since naturalness and convincingness are synonymous. In the last vigorous attacks of the campaign, Virginia Central would bear the brunt of the pounding, as it was proper it should. It would be safe to do so by that time. He took one of the several desk-telephones on the long table.

"Tell Mr. Dunlap to come to the 'phone, please."

He put down the instrument and walked to the ticker, studying the tape. Presently a bell rang. Rock took the same telephone.

"Dan?—Yes.—What's the last Virginia? 45½?— How easily does the real article come out?" (He meant actual stock, not traders' contracts.) "Good.—Well, let up now, but see that the price doesn't get back above 46½ on any rally; and pound it again just before the close if it doesn't go down of its own accord.—I'll

attend to London.—You can let Cross sell.—Cross—yes.
—Let Cross sell five thousand Roanoke at the market.
Not too eagerly.—Understand?—And distribute a few
five-hundred-share lots.—Reduce the supporting orders
in Roanoke." (The orders he had given out to buy his
own stock in case others tried to sell.) "And you, personally, buy five hundred every eighth down, as loudly
as you please, Dan." (That would show that poor
Rock was "supporting" his own "specialty," and was
suffering like other magnates from the general selling
movement.) "If you think it advisable, you might
also sell a few other stocks.—Catch the idea? Yes.—
Good-bye.—Hello!—Don't lose any more Virginia Central than you can help.—That's all."

Rock was obliged to be very explicit, and to volun-
teer answers to the questions he knew Dunlap would
have asked if sharp-eared telephone clerks in that particular row of booths on the Exchange were not sur-
rounding him. They knew that when Dunlap telephoned it was to Rock, and they knew Rock was a
gold-mine in an active market. Rock also knew it.
He sometimes sold bricks from his gold-mine to the
clerks' employers—without paying commissions to the
clerks. Genius is an infinite capacity for taking pains.
Rock took pains. He was very rich.

He rang the bell for Valentine. The cashier came
in. Before Rock could ask any questions, Valentine
said: "Morson says the St. Louis is just docking."
The news of young Sam Rock's return had excited the
front office far more than the private office.

Rock, still unexcited by the news, said: "Aha!"
And then: "Telephone Rosenstein to quote thirty-day
puts in London on ten thousand shares of Virginia
Central. As soon as he answers cable orders to sell

five thousand shares about two o'clock, their time, to-morrow. You'll have to be down early to-morrow morning. If Ismay cables for news, say it looks to us like lower prices."

"Yes, sir."

An office-boy entered.

"There's a lady to see you, Mr. Rock."

"Huh?" Rock looked at the boy with a frown of non-comprehension.

"She said her name was Mrs. Collyer," went on the boy, transferring the blame with the effect of dropping a hot poker. "She said she knew you were busy, but she would only take half a minute," the boy continued, accusingly.

"Very well," said Rock. "Show her into the next room. That's all, Valentine."

"I've warned Willie always to say—" began the cashier, apologetically.

"Oh, well," said Rock, with a smile, and went into the adjoining room "Of course, I am always in to Mrs. Collyer."

Mrs. Collyer was the widow of his best friend. He and Jack Collyer had been chums as school-boys and at college, and their wives had been chums as school-girls. Minnie Rock had died first. Sampson Rock had been the executor of Jack's estate. At first he used to dine at Mrs. Collyer's every Wednesday. Of late years he had dropped out of the habit. The children kept it up. Sam was five years older than Fanny Collyer; she was ten years wiser than he, Sampson Rock had once told Miss Fanny in Sam's hearing. It was when Sam came home from the football field, a seven-columned hero — newspaper — with bruises and limps and aches and an air!

In the next room Mrs. Collyer was speaking to Fanny. She was stout and hated it. In hot weather she could hardly breathe, having illusions as to dressmakers. She was white-haired with a youngish face, which looked more florid than it really was because of the contrast with the snowy whiteness of the hair and the resolute expression she habitually wore. It pleased her for some reason to think she could think. Often when she indulged in small talk she looked distrait, as though her real mind were thinking of serious things even while her auxiliary, or society, mind was forced by the exigencies of the situation to stoop to trifles. She had nice manners when she was not interested in the stock-market; but even when she was gambling, if she was inattentive to another's impressive remarks, she often discovered it in time and apologized: "My dear, I'm perfectly impossible, I know. I was thinking about some investments. I really don't know what's come over me in my old age unless it is that the cost of living increases so every day." Her family connections made it possible for her to refer to her insufficient income with impunity. She had a rather nice smile at times. Also, she sometimes had common-sense, even though she sought to get something for nothing in the stock-market. She rather feared Rock because his advice to her was always to invest, and she had so little to invest that at four per cent. per annum it meant practically nothing. Just now she was counting on her fingers, a frown on her face, her eyes on the centre electrolier, and her lips moving silently.

"Mamma, what in the world are you—" Fanny began.

"Hush!" hissed Mrs. Collyer, waving the uncounting hand at her daughter.

Fanny persisted. "It makes me uncomfortable to see you there, muttering and—"

"How do you do, Marie?" said Rock. "And Fanny! My, this is nice!" He had always been fond of her. It showed in his speech.

"How do you do, Sampson?" said Mrs. Collyer, nodding, but without ceasing to count mechanically. "I came down to see Wilson & Nesbit" (her lawyers, in the same office building, who took care of the two small houses she owned) "about some leases, and I thought I might as well see you about—" She was again counting, counting!

"Well, Uncle Sam," hastily interjected Fanny, with a very friendly smile to offset the counting, "you are looking so well that I fancy the bears—or the bulls, is it?—must be feeling pretty ill."

"No complaint; everybody satisfied," laughed Rock. "But as I get a good look at you it strikes me some young man must be feeling pretty uncomfortable, I'll bet."

"Only five. When's Sam due?"

"Is he the sixth?"

"The first, Uncle Sam." She was rather a serious-minded girl. Her sense of humor was national rather than individual, and her flippancy came from a half-conscious imitation of the habitual speech of her friends.

"Expect him any minute. His boat's at the dock now."

The girl's face brightened. "Oh, is it? Won't it be jolly if he finds us here! I would have gone to the pier to meet him if I'd known it was to-day. I'll wait here; may I?"

For some reason Rock looked towards Mrs. Collyer,

who was counting, counting! She caught his look and said: "What was that, Sampson? I was figuring how much—"

"Sam's back!" cried Fanny. Her face wore a look of mingled pleasure and annoyance—Sam was in New York, and her mother was in Wall Street.

"Isn't that nice! He's been away a long time, hasn't he? Sampson, you know that one thousand Roanoke I bought last week?"

"No, I don't," answered Rock, with a polite frown, as if he did not forgive himself for his ignorance.

"You don't? Why, you told me yourself to do it."

"I did? I haven't seen you in two months, Marie."

"Yes, but you told me then."

"It was around seventy at the time."

"Well, I forgot all about it," said Mrs. Collyer, very impressively, "until I heard one of the Van Courtlandt-Joneses—I think it was Frank—say the other day it was very strong and looked like going higher. I telephoned Mr. Valentine to buy a thousand shares for me and he did. I have the report at home," she finished, as if clinching an argument. Of course Rock must remember now.

He nodded.

"What did you pay for it?"

"Seventy-eight. What is it now?"

"Seventy-five."

"Sampson Rock!"

"My dear Marie, if you wanted to invest seventy-eight thousand dollars why didn't you find—"

"But I don't want to *invest* any money at all. Do you think I carry seventy-eight thousand dollars around for a pocket-piece? I wanted to speculate." She spoke as though making a confession, but also as though some one else were to blame for the things she confessed.

"Well, then, speculate. As long as you stick to one-thousand-share lots you can't lose very much." Rock felt certain that Roanoke would eventually sell higher. But if it went down he would see to it that Mrs. Collyer was not sold out. That was why he had made Dunlap & Co. her brokers. But he never told her; she would have lived in the office had she known his intentions.

"I can't? Sampson, this dealing in mythical millions"—Rock could see that the alliteration pleased her, she exuded so much visible wisdom—"that you Wall Street men call operations, completely destroys your sense of relative values. I can lose a thousand dollars a point, can't I?" She defied, Ajax-like, the lightning of contradiction.

"Mother, think of your only child!" implored Fanny, with a pained look. It was in jest. But, also, she did not wish Rock to be vexed with the Collyers. And though she believed in his business infallibility, because she was very fond of him and because she read the newspapers, she did not relish the possibility of loss. It always made her mother unamiable.

"And I only wanted to make vacation money and not lose half a year's income." Mrs. Collyer's voice had an accusing ring. She never before had speculated so heavily. But there were so many things she wished to buy! And now Sampson Rock deliberately—

"Do you mean to say that in your mad plunge you have—" began Fanny, in exaggerated alarm. She was intensely unhappy whenever her mother had anything to do with stocks. It made her count, count!

Rock laughed. "Well, Marie, cheer up. It's only down three points, and—"

"Three!" Mrs. Collyer's alarm was quite real.

"It's seventy-five now and you bought it at seventy-eight—"

Mrs. Collyer resumed her counting, aloud, and not so calmly as before. "Seventy-eight, seventy-nine, eighty—" It was the way she loved to count; it had become an ascending habit.

"The other way, mother, dear; it's down," said Fanny, sweetly spiteful because it seemed retribution and also might have educational value.

Rock laughed.

Mrs. Collyer indignantly, but doggedly, began to count on her fingers: "Seventy-five, seventy-four, seventy—"

"You've lost three thousand dollars," interrupted Fanny, unsympathetically. "Hasn't she, Uncle Sampson?"

"I have not," retorted Mrs. Collyer, sharply, before Rock could answer. "Fanny, I wish you wouldn't interrupt me when I'm thinking."

"There's no loss—yet," began Rock, slowly.

"I knew—"

"And there won't be any if you have patience."

"Oh, I'll be patient enough!" said Mrs. Collyer, amicably. Then her face clouded with doubt and suspicion. Gambling and jealousy have some things in common.

"H'm!" muttered Fanny with a resigned look.

Her mother shot a rebuking glance at her.

Rock interjected, quickly: "Marie, Roanoke is going to sell higher—"

"When?" interrupted Mrs. Collyer. To a gambler, patience is the suggestion of an unintelligent fiend recommending the pursuit of the unattainable.

"Before long. I think it will go to par."

"That means—" said Mrs. Collyer, with a smile that

showed she knew, but preferred Rock to put it tersely for Fanny's benefit.   Men are so good at definitions!

"A hundred dollars a share."

As by magic, Mrs. Collyer began counting, counting! She gave it up between eighty-five and ninety.

"How much will I make?" she said, with an air of arithmetical surrender combined with strictly business-like curiosity.

"Twenty thousand," answered Rock.

She beamed on him.

"Sampson, you are a genius! I always said you were, and nobody is gladder of your success than I. Oh, if our poor—"

Rock frowned slightly.   He knew she was about to mention his wife's name, and he did not like to be reminded of his loss, even after these many years.   A knock at the door made him seize the opportunity avidly.   He said, "Excuse me," very quickly, and opened the door.   It was Valentine, who told him Dunlap wanted him on the 'phone.

Rock was suggesting certain attacks when the door opened and five messenger boys entered, laden with valises, hat - boxes, bundles of rugs and canes, and a heavy piece of iron that looked like some part of a machine.   Behind them was a small, wiry, swarthy man in an automobile cap, who stood very straight, with an expression of haughty ennui.   Sampson Rock, the receiver still held to his ear, took in the messenger boys and then looked sharply at the Frenchman—there was no mistaking his nationality.   The man returned the stare coolly, as befitted a world-renowned scorcher, but old Rock's eyes took on such an expression that the Frenchman's hand went up to his cap.   He did not remove the headgear, but he looked at the floor and mumbled. The messenger boys, like bubbles drawn together by capillary attraction, grouped themselves about a bundle of canes and alpenstocks as about a May-pole, and looked expectant, as though the final chapter was yet to be written. Wall Street was good graft.

"Yes, yes. Do as you say, Dan," Rock said to the telephone and hung up the receiver.

"Sam's beginning to arrive," muttered Rock, a trifle impatiently. Sam evidently had not changed. Then Rock heard the sound of voices in the front office— jovial shouts and laughter—and he was walking thither when the door opened and his son entered.

"Hello, Dad!" shouted Sampson Rock, Jr., and held out his hand.

"How do you do, Sam?" said Sampson Rock, Sr.

They shook hands.

Sampson Rock, Jr., was twenty-five, and looked younger. His eyes were blue-gray and a trifle restless, with a suggestion of impatience and, withal, carelessness. The brow, the nose, and the chin were the brow and the nose and the chin of Sampson Rock. But, possibly because of his youth, he was a more athletic and a cleaner-cut Sampson Rock. The mouth, inherited from the mother, was different, as though laughter came more easily to him. The father's eyes were grayer than the son's; not more intelligent so much as more purposeful. The elder Rock looked as if he always knew what he was doing; the younger as if he knew what he was not doing and did not care. He was heavily sun-tanned.

Sam scrutinized his father with a sort of quizzical affection.

"You don't look as if my absence had affected your appetite, Dad," he said. "Business must be good."

"And you look as always." Rock said this kindly enough; but, as he glanced at the luggage strewn all about the office, he added, with a shade of impatience, "Only more so."

Sam laughed. "Well, some men accumulate love-letters, others debts. I'm great on luggage." He waved his hand towards the messenger boys and their burdens. "All mine, and more at the dock. Wait until you see the crime of the century—one hundred horse-power, and the duty—"

"H'm!" grunted Rock, unenthusiastically. Sam was still a motor-maniac. "Mrs. Collyer and Fanny are in the next room."

Sam's troubles over automobiles and duties vanished and his face brightened. "Where, Dad?" he asked, eagerly, and Rock pointed to the door. Sam hurried to meet them.

"How do you do, Aunt Marie?" he said, joyfully. "Hello, Fan!" he shouted.

"My boy, you're looking splendid," said Mrs. Collyer. She wasn't his aunt, but he had always called her so. He threw an arm about her and smacked her resoundingly on the cheek. Then he hastened towards Fanny.

Her color had risen and her eyes were very bright.

"Welcome back, Sam," she said, and held out her hand. He looked very brown—a strong and good-looking chap, very healthy and very glad to see her.

"What?" said Sam, indignantly ignoring the hand. "I guess not, my child," and he kissed her. He was the same Sam, she decided. She was a year and a half older than when she had last seen him. But he was not. He did not look it and did not act it.

"I tell you," he said, generally, "it makes a man feel like something to be back."

"You've been pretty much everywhere, haven't you, Sam?" said Mrs. Collyer, absently. She began to count on the fingers of her right hand, but caught herself, and thereupon gave Sam a rather formal smile. She really was very fond of him. But he was interrupting her golden calculations. The human heart has room for many affections; but for passions, only one at a time. She was not a rich woman, and life was so short! There was no time to lose. Fanny needed so many things, and the stock-market was nice at times. This time . . .

"Yes. And if I had known you were looking so well I'd have cut short my sight-seeing and hurried back. No sight to equal this anywhere. Has Fanny been a dutiful child?"

"No," said Fanny.

"Well, I'm back now," he menaced. He laughed again. "My, my, it's good to be back! Your house for mine to-night."

"We're going to—" began Mrs. Collyer, explanatorily.

"That's all right. I'll go, too," said Sam, with an air of overlooking an unintentional mistake.

"Do you know them?—the Van Courtlandt-Joneses?"

"What? Frank Jones? That little shrimp? I guess he ought to be glad to see me, considering I saved his life at college. If it hadn't been for me he'd have killed himself studying. Ask him. I was an usher at his wedding, don't you remember?"

"So you were," agreed Mrs. Collyer. Her acquiescence sounded perfunctory. To prove she had not forgotten what she had never thought of remembering, she added: "I remember now." Woman - like, she clinched it. "Of course!"

Sampson Rock entered.

"Sampson," said Mrs. Collyer, "he looks very well." She assumed Rock could have but one "he" to interest him in life. Fanny smiled acquiescently and almost felt like the chorus.

Sampson Rock looked at Sam critically, whereupon Sam arose, inflated his chest, and said, in a deep voice, "Yes!"

Sampson Rock laughed and approached his son. On his face was a look of satisfaction, almost of pride. He was not thinking of the Virginia Central. He felt Sam's biceps, and Sam obligingly doubled up his arm. He was hard as nails.

"Gad, what couldn't I do with this and a good digestion!" Rock exclaimed, in mock regret.

"Don't forget the brains," laughed Sam. "Keep in training, and don't make too much money." He made a motion as if to throw his arm around his father's neck, but Rock, unaware of it, walked away. Fanny felt a vague sense of embarrassment, as if her outstretched hand had been deliberately ignored. Sam was too young for his years—too careless. That was the trouble with being an only son, and motherless, when the father was a very busy man. Sam was just Sam. . . .

"Sampson," observed Mrs. Collyer, with an air of business-like determination, "if Roanoke is going to par, why can't I buy another thousand?" If there is a heap of gold pieces within reach, why not use a shovel?

"You, too, Aunt Marie?" interjected Sam, mournfully.

"Yes. Isn't it dreadful?" said Fanny. Sam looked at her with mock sympathy, but his eyes suddenly took on an interested look; she had grown into a very pretty girl in his absence. He had never before in his life thought about her looks. But she was the first New York girl he had seen in months. Fanny felt his stare, and, unpleasantly conscious of it, ended it by laughing: "She's always studying the market quotations. That's all she gets the newspapers for. She sometimes doesn't lose."

"My dear Marie," Rock answered Mrs. Collyer, with the merest suspicion of impatience, "nobody can tell with absolute certainly what a stock may or may not do."

"Can't *you?*" asked Mrs. Collyer, with a flattering incredulity. She smiled, to let him see that she knew *he* could tell, of course. She had risked more than she could afford to lose, convinced of his infallibility.

"No, I can't," answered Rock, so decisively that Sam stared at him, and after a pause said:

"Well, I always imagined it was your business to know and to keep the other fellow from finding out."

The gold pieces in the distance seemed to Mrs. Collyer to grow tarnished, until they did not look like gold. Then they grew bright and beautiful again, because, of course, Rock knew she would win. Of course! For scouring tarnished gold, use hope.

It annoyed Rock. No thought, no study, no work—sure-thing gambling; that was what they thought he did. It was the same thing the ignorant masses thought. Not the faintest suspicion of the struggle and the competition, the planning and the fighting, the never-absent danger of disaster. Did they know that he sometimes risked his financial life? That he had no monopoly of brains or courage? That there was more to the game he played than the gamble? That he was other than a money-making machine? Nothing—they

4   43

knew nothing; and his only son, who should know all, knew nothing.

"Well, I don't, and it's about time you—" He hesitated. Fanny could not help looking as she felt—uncomfortable. She divined rather than understood his annoyance.

Sam frowned and asked, "I what, Dad?"

Rock turned it off with a laugh. He replied:

"Buy Roanoke to hold for par, and see if it's so certain."

"Sampson," hastily put in Mrs. Collyer, in a spasm of common-sense prompted by fear—which again tightly bandaged Hope's eyes—"if you think there's any danger, perhaps I'd better sell out mine before I lose anything." She did not wish to lose a little in preference to losing all. All she wished was that she would not lose a penny, but make thousands. It was the woman in business—conventional words of wisdom and the irrepressible heart's desire. Business—woman.

"But you've already lost three thousand dollars," observed Fanny.

"I have not," said Mrs. Collyer, determinedly. How could that be when she did not wish it to be?

"What's the price now?" asked Sam, hopefully. "It was thirty-five when I left." The bare knowledge of it was the extent of his interest in his father's business.

"Seventy-five," said Fanny, quickly. Great changes had been in stocks in eighteen months, but Sam had not read the market reports.

"Whew!" whistled Sam. "Bull market; and here I've been economizing—"

"Maybe it's gone up since we came," suggested Mrs. Collyer, so hopefully that Rock laughed. Mrs. Collyer thereupon beamed gratefully upon him. No man laughs at a funeral, and she had begun to fear her speculation would end in one. She was on the point of thanking him for laughing at her when Sam said:

"I'll see." He started towards the private office to look at the ticker, saying, "Come, Fanny."

"No," said Fanny, because she felt the impropriety of playing at business in this office. "I want to be here when you break the news."

At the door Sam paused and asked:

"What's the blooming abbreviation for Roanoke?"

"The same as it always has been," answered Rock, sharply. The boy was the same—he knew nothing about his father's business; not even the two letters on the tape that should have interested him if for no other reason than because they told how much he was to inherit. That his own flesh and blood did not know what was a part of him almost killed the sense of kinship. Rock finished impatiently, "RK."

From the other room Sam called out in triumph, "Here it is—*five hundred!*"

Mrs. Collyer jumped electrically. "It—can't—can't be—p-possible—" she murmured, tremulously. Could a human being make a half million in three minutes and not quake before emitting the exultant whoop? Rock roared. Fanny half smiled. She did not under stand.

"Five hundred shares at 73⅝," shouted Sam. "Some body's swatting it for keeps."

"Seventy-three and five-eighths!" almost shrieked Mrs. Collyer. The fingers on her right hand began to count, tapping feverishly on her thumb. The fraction bothered her. How much was five-eighths of a thousand dollars? How much was even one-eighth?

Rock said, seriously:

"The whole market's very weak. But Roanoke will come out all right, Marie. If it goes any lower—"

"You—don't—think—it's—going—*lower?*" whispered Mrs. Collyer. She had been a tippler of the wine of gambling, intoxicating herself with counting and spending the money the marvellous and kindly ticker would surely—oh yes, surely!—make for her. Usually it was only a hundred shares. This time she had plunged—this time of all times! Plunged, and the abyss was bottomless!

"It might. And then we'll buy you another thousand—"

"But—" Mrs. Collyer began, in consternation. To lose; that is to say, to stop the heart's action by means of a vise of frozen steel, and yet survive! Man or woman, hero or craven, there is no intellect about it, only the squeezed heart and the icy numbness.

"And then you stand to win fifty thousand. And you will, too," finished Rock. He looked absolutely confident.

"Very well," said Mrs. Collyer, doubtfully. Fifty thousand! She began to count on her right hand, with each motion of her fingers loosening the clutch of the frozen steel vise, passing from doubt to delight. She took a deep draught of the wine. It went to her head in a second. "That will be fine, Sampson. We'll have a nice celebration—won't we?—when Roanoke goes to par!" Her voice rang triumphantly and her eyes grew misty as she smiled entrancedly at Fanny, at Sam, at Sampson Rock, at all the world! . Oh, she would make them all happy with the money! That blessed money was made to be spent in happiness. Nothing would be extravagant. That was the surpassing beauty of that kind of money. Everything that she could not now afford, that was what she would buy when Roanoke went to par!

"How funny that sounds—*when Roanoke goes to par!*" said Fanny.

"That's the office slogan," smiled Sampson Rock.

"You don't understand business, my dear," mildly snubbed the mother. "Come," she added, regretfully, "we must be going." And she rose, looking as though she would like to be contradicted. She would have liked to have seen the actual minting of the dollars that could not be spent extravagantly, whatever they might be used to buy.

They went out, all talking at the same time, and Rock returned to the private office to the watch of the ticker. The general, while the battle was waging, had been without a telescope. Now he could see how his lieutenants were fighting.

IV

THE battle was not going as planned. Prices had begun to rally ahead of time. They should not have shown resistance to the bear attack until Rock himself, with his wise lack of precipitancy, had helped the recovery. It was not a "drive" he had in mind, but a campaign of depression.

Gilmartin, who had duly sold his tip to a half-dozen gamblers, and then had impressively told it in confidence to a half-hundred more, had written and sent out the following through his news agency:

"The selling of Virginia Central, which is the feature of the market, has every appearance of being by the inside party. It is understood that the recent investigation into the affairs of the company in the interest of an English syndicate has been disappointing to the friends of the property. This will make it difficult to float the ten million dollars of stock authorized by the stockholders some time ago, but not yet issued. It is confidently expected in well-informed circles that lower prices for the stock will be seen."

That item, and the inevitable verbal variations of it in the Board Room, had helped Virginia Central to go down; but other financiers were not quite ready to let their own specialties decline just then, and their support had steadied the market. This in turn frightened some of the shorts in Virginia Central, and they began to buy back the stock they had sold earlier in the day.

.48

The price was rising once more. It was 46½—the figure which Rock had told Dunlap must be the limit of the recovery. Among others, Cosmopolitan Traction was particularly strong.

Sam returned smiling. His father said, shortly: "Send those things away." He pointed to the luggage and the statufied messengers.

Sam stared at his father; then he smiled and answered: "Very well, Dad. This is a breechlock of one of the Spion Kop guns, supposed to have killed nobody knows how many Englishmen." He patted the piece of steel caressingly. There was a story to it—and to the way he secured it. It had cost money, and insidious persuasion, and there had been the risk of a patriotic Boer bullet or two.

But his father said, curtly, "Send it home." Not so much the luggage, but the presence of the messenger boys and the chauffeur destroyed his feeling of privacy and annoyed him.

"I wanted to talk to you," remonstrated Sam.

"You don't need all that truck to talk, do you? Send it to the house. You can follow later." It was not especially unpleasant, the old man's manner; rather it was a sort of impersonal irritation. He was frowning.

Sam could see that it was at something in the market. The effect was as of listening to a voice without seeing the speaker's face. The madly whirring ticker was discharging psychic waves into the atmosphere of this office, filling it with something unseen but most curiously felt. Sam knew that every stroke printed a letter or a figure that meant something to thousands of watching eyes; and even as this thought came to him he could almost feel the unblinking stare of the hungry eyes which he now remembered the ticker fiends had. Whatever it was, that something was visible and audible and disturbing to his father. Dollars were being won and being lost, because somewhere, in other offices, in other States, in other countries, human brains were working —planning, scheming, attacking, defending, hoping, fearing—somewhere, everywhere. To many, the ticker might be a roulette-wheel, the marker of chance and its caprices. But to a chosen few, the handful who fought against the mob, it meant far more—the success or the failure of great plans, the exact tonnage the tireless railroads were carrying or were not carrying, or expected or did not expect to carry, the tonnage that could not increase or decrease without the ticker telling of it. The pulse-beats of the working world, that was what the ticker-strokes were. And yet in the whirring and the clicking of the little wheels there rang the same metallic note, the money-monotone, the sound of clashing dollars, as if a cloud of coins were rising and falling, blown this way and that, to and from pockets; and that part of it was the least interesting. Less than thoughts, Sam's mind for a few seconds recorded merely fleeting impressions, in seeking to establish the connection between the ticker's message and his father's ill-humor and his own aloofness from both. There stirred within him a vague feeling of uncomfortable inactivity, of being a spectator at a battle between his countrymen and a foreign foe. What was his father doing?

Sam turned suddenly to the chauffeur he had brought back with him, and spoke some words in French. The man nodded carelessly, whereupon Sam, whose mood no longer was careless, said two words sharply, and the man touched his cap with his forefinger, said "Oui, monsieur," and picked up a ridiculous French valise and a small kit of tools. To the messenger boys Sam said: "Pick up those things, boys, and go with this man to 14 East Seventy-third Street. Here's a dollar. Divide it even. The cab is waiting down-stairs." He followed them, and at the door said: "Say, Val, pay these chaps, will you?" and returned to his father. But the interruption had made his heart cease to beat in tune with the pulse of the ticker.

Rock was watching the tape. The tide was rising when it should have ebbed. Virginia Central had sold up to 46⅞, notwithstanding his instructions to Dunlap. Other stocks were rising. He walked quickly to the long table and picked up Dunlap's telephone.

"Hello!" he said, sharply.—"Mr. Dunlap, at once!" and waited, frowning. Presently: "Yes—Dan, this won't do.—Is that it?—Well, deny it; it isn't true.—I want the rally checked. You attend to Virginia Central.—I'll do the rest.—Sell ten thousand.—No!—No! —Virginia Central.—Reduce the support in Roanoke. —Make it two hundred every quarter down and two thousand at seventy-three; twenty-five hundred at seventy-two and five thousand at seventy-one, if it should go there.—No use to wait till the close."

He turned and picked up another telephone.

"Hello?—Mr. Kirby, please.—Well, then, Mr. Higgins.—Hello?—Higgins?—Rock.—Sell five thousand St. James—No, short.—Account R.—Very well.—Send them to Valentine." He took up a third transmitter and said: "Number four, please, in a hurry." He waited, frowning—not in anger, but in thought. "Willie? Listen carefully.—Sell five thousand each of Great Southern preferred, Broomstick common, Allegheny Central, and Mohawk Valley.—Give it out to Meighan & Cross and Rivers & Dolliver.—It's supposed to be very good selling. I'm glad you understand.—No, no, borrow it privately.—Yes; I think the market is going down.—Don't tell them until after you have sold out mine.—What?—Immediately!—I want to see you.— No hurry; after three will do."

He rose and returned to the watch of the ticker.

His father's words meant less to Sam than his father's look and his father's voice. They impressed him mysteriously, inarticulately, more as though the spirit which animated this man somehow had the power to set a-quivering those little nerves that cause thrills in us; and they made him wonder if his father were not, after all, the lord of the ticker, so that the ticker obediently repeated the message that the master said should go forth to the thousands of well-dressed men with hungry eyes. To speak to the world and to have the world listen—and shiver or exult as the speaker willed—that was worth while. The man could be greater than the ticker.

"I say, Dad," began Sam, admiringly. He stopped because he saw that Rock did not hear. His commands were being executed, and he was noting the effect. Great Southern preferred of all others was resisting over well. It ought to be the chief loser if Rock secured the Virginia Central and turned it over to the Roanoke. The stock should reflect the loss. There was not any loss yet; but when it came those who had taken time by the forelock—"discounting" it, Wall Street calls it—would profit.

Back to the telephone-table.

"Hello?—Mr. Cross?—Yes.—Cross?—Rock.—Sell ten thousand Great Southern preferred.—At the market. —Give it out in one-thousand-share lots.—At once.— You ought to get it off without breaking eighty.—No, not below eighty.—Borrow it.—No, as openly as you can.—They'll think it's surely long stock if you are anxious to make them think it's short stock. At once!"

Back to the ticker, one elbow leaning on the corner of the ticker-stand, tense, immobile, watching the cascading tape intently, his soul and mind and body merged into a pair of unblinking eyes to which every printed character was full of meaning, surcharged with significance, eloquent in its directness. The first volley had been fired by Dunlap; now Higgins; Willie was obeying orders; Cross and his artillery had arrived; and . . .

The market began to go his way. Blood was being shed, and it was golden blood, and he was unscathed. There might be a day of reckoning later, perhaps to-morrow; to-day there should be one—for the bulls. He was a leader, and the unattached soldiers of fortune —the "traders"—gathered under his flag and, without knowing it, fought for him, fought madly for dollars— more dollars—even as Rock fought for railroads, more railroads

In the big marble Board Room the air was filled with the exultant whoops of the bears who were winning, the maddened shrieks of the bulls who were losing and would not lose more—the primal passions made audible in the discordant chorus of the dollar-hunters, made visible about the various "posts" in a sea of heads that broke into a foam of fists clinched and defiant—with, here and there, the quivering, outstretched fingers of a drowning man. And beside the man who had said, "Let there be storm," out of sight and out of hearing of the money-mad mob, under its protecting glass dome, as though it were a fragile plant, the little ticker in this office was impassively ticking, ticking, ticking!—singing its marvellous song of triumph and defeat in one;

ticking very fast because it must keep time to the heart-beats of the mob, and the heart-beats were very fast—not because men were losing and men were winning, but because the world cannot stand still, but must work. And because men must live by the sweat of their brow, one man would give to men, to thousands of men, the chance to sweat. That and nothing more was what Sampson Rock would have said he was doing if he had philosophized about it. It is the autohypnotism of the great captains who do not count their dead, of the other captains who, on the battle - field of industry, count nothing but results—results—results! Efficiency, spelled in dollars, because dollars are the measure of men's work, and therefore of the men themselves. Above everything, efficiency—the great world's progress and the eyes unwaveringly fixed on the individual star.

Sam was again filled with an exasperating sense of uselessness as he gazed on his father—an elbow resting on one corner of the ticker-stand, tense, immobile, something less than human, something more than human about him, his eyes fixed hypnotically on the tape—little soldier-ants bearing tiny burdens to lay at the feet of Sampson Rock, the characters had been an hour before; but now they were shot-scars on a fortress, that told whether the golden projectiles discharged by a human cannon had hit or had missed. If a miss, there were more projectiles to fire; if a hit, one obstacle had been removed from the path of the Virginia Central Railroad on its way to efficiency, with Sampson Rock at the throttle. At least five miles of the Biddle-boro division already had been built. For the price of Virginia Central had yielded. Soon Dunlap would begin to buy it, quietly, circuitously, untraceably, loving it greatly even while cruelly bludgeoning it.

Great Southern preferred was going down; now eighty-three—eighty-two—eighty-one. The last order had been just the finger-touch needed to push the bowlder over the edge of the cliff. Eighty now! Cross could not have sold the ten thousand shares; it had taken less than that to break it; so much ammunition saved.

It was a very weak, not a panicky market, the difference between fear and blind terror. There was no ugly confusion of ruin. A gambling foundation that had taken two weeks' hard work to upbuild had been razed in two hours by a man who risked a fraction of his fortune. The effort of the morrow, for that man, would be to keep the recovery from being too rapid or too violent. And then, sentiment being unsettled by the market's "ominous lack of recuperative power," it would be easy, by a series of drives against Virginia Central, to push the price of that stock of stocks down —the newspapers would help unwittingly by printing the vaporings of fools whose fears made them garrulous. And then . . .

Then the tape-characters again would become little soldier - ants, gold - laden, bringing the spoils, grain by grain, to Sampson Rock; and Sampson Rock, his eyes fixed steadfastly on the future, would be extending one railroad, consolidating two into a great, a strong system, transforming a wilderness not into a beautiful garden, but better—into pierced mountains and stabbed hill-sides and furrowed valleys under smoke-clouded skies, the abode of grimy miners and iron-workers and of their food-providers and clothes-makers, bringing to Virginia the gift of life and to these men the gift of work, whereby they might fill their bellies and clothe their nakedness, and, also, love and multiply, to the greater glory of God. And to the self-hypnotized Sampson Rock bringing—

His only son was before him.

Sam looked inquiringly at Sampson Rock as Sampson Rock looked at his son, until his mind, torn suddenly away from the battle-scenes of the ticker, wondered: What if Sampson Rock died suddenly? To-morrow? Next week? Next year? Die he must, and there was Sam, the same Sam he had always been—the same boy without any thought of the morrow, without the vision of a life of work, without the ears to heed the message of the Rock destiny; who had accomplished nothing; who might accomplish—what?

Sampson Rock had used the brain that had been given to him, animated by the spirit that had been born in him—a spirit that, with the march of the years, had moved steadily in one direction as inexorably as the years themselves moved towards eternity. Sam had been his joy and his wife's, the proof and reminder of their love. But with her death the child had failed to hold his father's blind adoration. The loss of her was too vast a void for Sam to fill, and to Sampson Rock work, at first a solace, became a fixed habit. To work was to think, to think was to live. His affection for his son was enough to supply the little *boutonnière* of love, and that was all the garden Rock needed or had time to think of. In his half-conscious search after an excuse for the exclusion of other human and humanizing desires he found it in efficiency. It became the sole goal, the excuse, the yardstick of his life. If a certain type of man can't use his heart he must overwork his head or die.

Never before had Rock cared poignantly that Sam did not care for his business. Some day Sam would.

Some day some men will make their wills. In gradually becoming less interested in the fluctuations of railroad stocks and more in the railroads themselves, Rock had himself grown marvellously, especially in the last five years of his fifty-five; for in the "hard times" his brain and his courage had found an opportunity, and with the ending of the commercial depression, the opportunity had burst into full blossom, as he had expected. In the stock-market, while his wife was alive, he had found an easy means of livelihood. But he had come to see in it merely the means to an end, until his enemies reluctantly called him a reformed gambler. And because of his own changed point of view towards business and therefore towards life, he came to realize the brevity of the individual span. Having founded a dollar-dynasty, he desired permanency, a work that should endure, his only immortality. And now, thinking of his only son as a possible successor, he was not comfortable. His mind, enmeshed in coils of ticker-tape, still wrapped in the acquisition and scientific development of the Virginia Central, could not solve in an instant this poignant problem of his heir—the heir not to his money but to his work, the work that was his soul and should live and wax greater after him. He could not expect Sam, a boy for all his five-and-twenty years, inexperienced for all his occasional visits to this office, uninterested because ignorant, to become at one jump the intelligent lieutenant of a captain of industry; nor that a trip around the world should teach him business sense and Wall Street methods and the comprehension of the work his father had done, was doing, and hoped to do. Nevertheless, because he had thought of Sam as the future master of the Roanoke and the pilot of its destinies, he was disappointed. There was so much to do that he could not do it all; he did not wish so much to do it himself, but that it should be done. Sam ought to complete the work. And·Sam—

"Damn it!" said Sampson Rock, aloud. He was speaking to himself. He had been alone a great deal.

The Lord of the Ticker was a human being, after all. The exclamation made Sam laugh. He asked his father as he might have asked a chum:

"Market going against you?"

It was asking it with a carelessness that was not intelligent that touched the raw spot and silenced the ticker. Rock said, very quietly:

"Sam, I wonder if you'll ever be serious?"

"Serious? Sure! Easiest thing in the world." Sam looked at his father confidently.

"Look here, Sam, we must have a long talk, you and I. You are no longer a boy." · Sam had some rejoinder on the tip of his tongue. But Rock, to prevent another cold shower from falling on his dreams of the Rock destiny, went on, quickly: "It's about time you did something—I don't care what; but something, anything. Use your brains, if you have any." Rock looked away; then he looked at Sam steadily.

Sam stared back at his father in amazement. When he answered, it was with a sort of amiable acquiescence:

"I'll have to find out about the brains. But I certainly want to do something. I met a chap at Cannes by the name of Darrell; a mining-engineer from Denver. Nice fellow; he rode with me when I tried for the Gordon Cup. He's away up in his business and—"

"What do you want to bother with mines for?" Rock interjected impatiently.

"What for? To do something, of course. It's better than doing nothing, isn't it? I'd like to go West.

Do you want me to go in for that?" He pointed to the ticker.

"It's my business. It ought to be yours." Rock's lips were pressed together. The ticker was whirring and clicking away madly—unheeded.

"Don't like it; never did," said Sam, shortly.

"You know nothing about it," retorted Rock, impatiently. "You never will, probably. But I'll be satisfied if you realize that you are no longer a boy. Do you think you do realize it?" Rock evidently was not convinced at all.

"Oh yes," said Sam, so slowly as to convey an impression of premeditation. "I realize it as well as I realize that if I went into your business I'd lose my temper too many times a minute. No, thanks. The simple life for mine."

Absence had blurred the outlines of Sam's image of Sampson Rock, making the colors softer and more beautiful—a trick that absence, like death, is apt to play with affection. The sneering incredulity of Sampson Rock, therefore, seemed so uncharacteristic as to come as an unpleasant surprise, and it stung Sam's temper into a quick rise. But the sting was not deep, and Sam smiled, a trifle forgivingly—it was the ticker game that made his father unamiable; he said, conciliatingly:

"I'm too old to begin as office-boy now. That's what you ought to have done with me, if you wanted me to become a great man. But never mind, Dad. Suppose we talk it over in words of one syllable? I'll listen."

Sam's very words betrayed the absence of genuine intimacy between father and son. Both were older; each knew it, and neither admitted it to the other in their speech.

The telephone-bell in Rock's desk rang impatiently. Sam felt that the man at the other end of the wire was in a hurry. It made him notice which telephone it was. He said: "Let me answer that for you. Try me."

"This isn't play," retorted Sampson Rock brusquely. He went swiftly to the table and took up the instrument.

"Hello!—Who?—How are you, Tuttle?—Virginia Central? I don't know anything about.—You heard *I* was selling it?—Well, you know, Dunlap has other customers besides myself.—Eight thousand shares?— What did you pay?—Oh, the deuce!—That was pretty high, but it probably will sell up there again some time. —Robinson meant well by his advice, I suppose. Are you sure you know whose stock it was you bought?— I don't mean to suggest he sold out on you, but—. I really can't say.—I don't feel like giving you any advice, Tuttle. The market looks pretty sick to me, but there ought to be a rally.—Yes, yes; I remember what you did for me last year.—Of course, if you put it that way, I'll give you my opinion. It's only my opinion, remember.—I firmly believe Virginia Central is going down.—Oh, several points!—Well, I myself haven't as much of it now as I had last week.—Don't repeat this, will you?—Good-bye, old man.—Don't mention it.—Nonsense.—Good-bye."

He put down the transmitter, hung up the receiver in the hook and ran to the long table. He took up the last instrument. Sam was watching and listening intently. He was more than eighteen now.

"Hello! Hello!" Rock said, impatiently. "Are you asleep?—Mr. Chase, at once.—Hello! Chase?—Go in and offer down five thousand shares of Virginia Central. —Pratt will buy it from you.—Wait until he gets there before you begin." He put down the telephone; took up the one next to it and spoke, sharply: "Mr. Pratt! —Yes, hurry up! Hello! Hello!" he almost shrieked in his anger. Seconds counted. "Hello, Pratt!—This is S. R.—Archie Chase has an order to sell five thousand Virginia Central as low as he can.—You buy it all and— *Listen!*—A customer of Hardwick, Bunner & Co. is going to sell eight thousand.—They'll probably sell more; they have quite a lot in their office. Take every share.—Don't let one get away from you.—Clear it yourself.—Hurry!"

He hastened to the ticker and gazed intently at the tape. Sam knew enough of the stock-market to understand what had happened. Chase would sell five thousand shares as low as he could, as though he were executing an order for a panic-stricken client, instead of a manipulative order from Sampson Rock, who would buy the same stock from himself through Pratt —Chase would see to it that of all the brokers who might be buying, it would be Pratt who got the stock— which was a violation of the Stock Exchange rules, as well as of the rules of fair play. It would depress the price so that by the time Tuttle's eight thousand shares came to be sold, Tuttle would find a weak and lower market; the stock would be sacrificed, and his father would get it cheap. There was no sense in thinking of his working in Wall Street. He would not. He might as well make it clear to his father now, once and for all. But there came to him a sudden desire to make sure first, in order to be both just and intelligent. He asked:

"Father, is this man Tuttle a friend of yours?"

Sampson Rock, not lifting his eyes from the tape, nodded. He had no time to do anything else—Chase and Pratt evidently had sprinted from the telephone booths to the Virginia Central post—the stock was breaking half a point at a time. And here came twenty five hundred shares at 44—three thousand at 43¾—two thousand at 43½. Tuttle's stock was changing ownership.

Sam saw no reason now for restraint of speech. He did not even think of such restraint. His father's acknowledgment of friendship for the man who had rung the telephone-bell so impatiently that Sam could tell by the sound he was in a hurry, made the hot disgust he had felt become cold and compact—the phenomenon of molten iron cooling. He said: "He asks your advice. You give it. *Sell out!* Your brokers hammer the price down—"

Sampson Rock held up a hand to command silence while he kept his eyes unblinkingly on the tape, unable to turn his head at that moment; but Sam went on:

"And then you rake in friend Tuttle's stock at bargain-prices. That's to pay friend Tuttle for the favor he did you last year. Great game, that! It's a sin not to make money if people throw it at you when you tell them to. But me for the mines, with my friend Darrell," he finished with a resolute look.

"Forty-two and one-half, seven-eighths; three; a quarter; three-eighths; a half! All over. They got it!" muttered Rock. He looked up, and seeing Sam's eyes gazing steadily at him, remarked, absently: "She went down fast!" His thoughts were on the stock. But of a sudden he remembered that he had heard Sam speaking to him, and then he was conscious of groping in his mind for the words that his ears had heard, until they came back to him. His face flushed slightly; and he said, with an unpleasant calmness that might have frightened a man less like himself than his son:

"The price *is* going down. I'm going to put it down and he'll save a great deal of money. He gets forty-three for it by selling now, but I'm going to make it sell at thirty before I'm done."

"The price is not going to stay at thirty, and you know it." Sam's chin was thrust forward and he looked unblinkingly at his father.

"What's that got to do with it?" Rock's voice was still unpleasantly calm. It was manifestly impossible for a stock-market general to take the entire stock-gambling world into his confidence. That was so obvious as to require no demonstration. But to Sam his father's composure was so suggestive of an utter absence of remorse that he retorted: "It's got every thing to do with it. And after you scoop it in, what's the next chapter?"

"It goes into the Roanoke & Western—"

"At thirty, of course," Sam nodded, in sarcastic self-felicitation. "That's where the philanthropy comes in."

Rock's face became livid. Sam's speech was not all; there was also Sam's exasperating ignorance.

"It's worth more to the Roanoke than to any one else and they'll gladly pay a fair price," he answered, the business end of it before his mind. Then he added: "You don't know what you are talking about. It is a bad habit of yours and the sooner you lose it the better."

"To profit as an individual first; then as one of several stockholders of the Roanoke. Yes; that's a good paying habit. I guess I'll go into mines and lose some of your money for you for a change. Or I might just keep on running over people with my new machine. I'll give 'em as much chance for their skins as if they were in Wall Street."

63

"You jackass!" said Sampson Rock, his fists clinched, his eyes burning. "Do you know what I'm going to do?" Some of the newspapers might editorialize their disapproval of his methods in Sam's words, but that wouldn't annoy him after the deal was over. To have his own son permit himself opinions born of crass ignorance angered him for many reasons.

"Yes, I know. A jackass couldn't help knowing. It's as plain as the nose on your face. You are going to make money by doing things I wouldn't do," answered Sam. The Old Man's face did not frighten him, but after he had spoken it softened his own heart. He had evidently shaken the Old Man's very soul. For that he felt sorry. It deepened his affection, but it did not weaken his conviction that it was not a square game.

"You wouldn't because you couldn't," said Sampson Rock, his voice husky with passion. His soul was flooded with a light that made him see what he sincerely thought was the truth about himself, crystallized and sharp of outline, as many men see it only when they feel themselves misjudged. It was not the practical dreamer, not the stock-gambler nor the railroad-builder that spoke, but a man with a ruling passion goaded into defending himself and his steady march towards a goal, driven into an audible soliloquy.

"You wouldn't because you couldn't," he repeated. "I am going to get control of that railroad because it's feeble, stunted by lack of brains, mismanaged by incompetents. This world has no room for incompetents. The weak must go to the wall that the strong may live and grow stronger!"

"Why must they?" interjected Sam, sharply. In his father's face he saw a ruthlessness so unreasonable that

he clinched his fists and felt like fighting for the weak
—an appeal from Philip drunk to Philip sober rather
than unfilial hostility.

"Why?" Sampson Rock's echoing monosyllable
was almost a snarl; the upper lip rose, exposing the
teeth. "Because they are useless; they are the dogs
in the manger of this world. They obstruct progress.
They interfere. They have no right to live if it means
to stand in the way and keep others from working.
Dogs in the manger!"

"Tough on the dogs. I suppose they interfere with
that?" Sam pointed to the ticker. "They keep other
people from making money. Off with their heads!
They're in the way!"

Making money—that was the crime the mob always
imputed to the men who did good work. Rock almost
shouted: "Do you think it's only on the Stock Exchange that my work shows?—or in my bank account
alone? What do I care for *that!* But I tell you—
you!—that it is going to show in Virginia, in the coal-
mines that I shall buy and the manufacturing towns
that I'll develop and the seaports that I'll open. I'm
going to make money—lots of it. And I'll pay for it
by giving to Virginia better and cheaper transportation
than she has now, or ever has had; and that will mean
growth, business, more wages to more people—there,
in Virginia, and here and in Europe and all over the
world. It won't mean that I — *your* father — have
cheated people out of some stock, but that Sampson
Rock, with his brains, has done something to make his
country richer and greater, to make his fellow-men—
thousands of them, hundreds of thousands of them—
earn a better living. The making of money is nothing.
The doing of the thing—that's the thing! And I'll

do it because it's my duty, because I can do it and they can't! Bet on fluctuations? I *make* them in order to carry out my plans. And if stock-gamblers are crushed and incompetents are killed, it is because the world must go forward. It's the survival of the fittest, and *I* am the fittest! I'll get that road and I'll extend it, and I'll merge it with mine, no matter who stands in the way, because I'll use it better than he can, and I know it. What's this man's eight thousand shares alongside the bread-and-butter of eighty thousand people? Make money? Of course I make money—for good work well done. And you? How much have *you* earned all your life? How much can you earn? What work can you do? The next time you talk to me about my business," he finished, with the usual anticlimax of real life, "get *facts !*"

Sam's face was pale, and his eyes, wide open with amazement, stared at his father. The resistless energy of the Old Man's words almost gave him a sense of physical fatigue. The glimpse of a naked soul had startled him even while his kinship with that soul— the soul of a fighter—had made him glow with a vague feeling of admiration, in the wake of which came a certain uneasiness at possibly having misread and misjudged. He was certain his father had told the truth as he saw it, but somewhere, he also felt, there was an undetermined fallacy. The frank ruthlessness of a strong man was not pleasant. A man need not be an idealist, but neither need he be a mucker. Every man could be square. The world must go forward without regard to the individual; but railroads didn't have to be extended over the corpses of those who were not born strong, whose financial weapons were as straws against the bludgeon of Rock's millions. A captain of finance must work and be paid; he might take, but he must also give. And this captain of finance, who glorified strength, to whom the individual was nothing and work everything, was his father, his own flesh and blood—he took and he said he gave. Was the exchange fair? Sam was now not sure that it was not.

Sampson Rock was looking at the ticker, but his mind was elsewhere; his heart was beating too fast; the tape was merely a strip of paper with meaningless figures on it. He drew in a deep breath, muttered "Bosh!" and began to pace up and down the room.

His son approached him and stood squarely before him, so that Rock had to stop. He glared at his son; but there was a resolute look on Sam's face as he held out his hand, man to man, and said, "I'll get facts before I talk to you about your business again." It was not a menacing tone, but a judicial one. It conveyed a subtle sense of conditional apology—should he have been mistaken.

Sampson Rock looked at Sam keenly. This boy was his heir; but he was more; he was *Her* son. He had *Her* mouth. And because of it the father suddenly felt the blood-relationship, with his heart as well as with his head. He shook hands and said, so very gruffly that it meant something else, "I should also have mentioned common-sense, if you can get that." In thinking only of the boy and not of the heir, Sampson Rock ceased to be an efficiency-mad captain of finance and became a father, his affection growing stronger with each breath.

Sam retorted, "Well, I ought to; I'll work hard; and then, I am your son, Dad." It was no longer man to man with Sam, but son to father, and Rock was conscious of it, and conscious that he had already forgiven the offence and the ignorance.

When Sam was a child and misbehaved his mother used to say, proudly, "Come and see what your son has done!" Rock remembered now, a sturdy little chap, full of life and whimsical child-ideas

Sampson Rock said: "And your mother's, too, Sammy. Your mother's, too."

He looked steadily at Sam, and it came to him that this was the boy she had loved so much that when she went she thought not of *his* son but of hers. On her death-bed, that gray Sabbath dawn, she had said: "My boy, my darling boy, I can't leave you! I can't! I can't!" And little Sam was not there at all while "big" Sam stood beside her, holding her hand, in plain sight of her so that she could have thought what it meant to leave him. Only of little Sam she thought, of her beautiful little son—"Come and see what *your* son is doing, Daddy!" And this was her son and his, heart of her heart, love of her love. He had her mouth, so that his smile was her smile. . . .

The tone in which his father spoke about his mother made Sam approach him, his mind silenced, his heart eloquent. But Sampson Rock, American by birth and undemonstrative by nature, disregarded the hand which his son—*his* son—penitently held out to him and instead kissed *her* son on the cheek. He moved away quickly, and said, very quietly: "Go home and see to your things, Sammy. And hunt me up at the Union Club at five, won't you?"

He walked to the ticker and began to study the tape.

Sammy closed the mouth that sheer amazement had pried open; then opened it again, and, forgetting all about the unfair game of the ticker and the self-apologies of its votaries, and thinking remorsefully of an affection greater than his own, saw only the father before him. Throwing an arm protectingly around that father, he said, reassuringly:

"You are all right, Dad!"

V

THEIR first evening together was less satisfactory than Sam had anticipated, because several of Rock's Wall Street friends at the club did what they were in the habit of doing nightly—sat down to talk with him. Rock had not thought of a special dinner in honor of Sam's return, as Sam's mother would have done, but, like Sam, he had meant to dine at home. The decision to remain at the club seemed to have been forced upon him by the intrusive friends. Sam himself had not attached a symbolical meaning to a dinner of father and son in the home that should have brought to them a sense of their blood-relationship and its sentimental obligations, but he had hoped to learn more about his father's work and plans and intentions and their possible bearing upon his own future. He resented the club dinner, which was too much like the hotel life of which he had grown weary in his travels, and was irritated by the feeling that his desired conversation with his father had been postponed by the ticker. It was the ticker that almost had parted them, that interfered even after Stock Exchange hours with the free sway of their mutual affection.

He found the Wall Street men very uninteresting; probably his irritation over their intrusion helped, but he vaguely had expected to find them unusual types. Instead they were quite as commonplace as men whose names never appeared in the newspapers. Their stories were not amusing, their observations on men and manners were not particularly profound and very decidedly not original. The human factor in the business equation, to which Sam attached a new importance since his father's speech, these men in their conversation seemed utterly to disregard, to the extent of almost making Sam feel like a theorist or a school-boy. When they spoke, in general terms, of some vast deal or another—which, to do them justice, was only at intervals—he was so impressed by the disappointing lack of mysteriousness of the procedure that he concluded that their business operations, for all their glamour, were like any other business operations, plain, simple, a matter of the mathematics of obvious common-sense, neither conceived by an inspiration nor executed with especial subtlety or adroitness, each of these men being merely the shopkeeper raised to the millionth-dollar power. The glamour came from the amount of cash involved; and if they thought nothing of risking one million, it was because they had many of them; their courage, therefore, was neither thrilling nor inspiring. And his father, Sam observed with a half-protesting amazement, was as uninteresting and unepigrammatic, as non-spectacular as the others. Was it a pose, this deadly dulness? Did these world famous capitalists, for supremely shrewd business reasons, wear a mask? Were there subtle significances to read between the lines of their speech?

Commodore Roberts, the man who had made a fabulous fortune in leather and had trebled it in industrial consolidations, and then had sextupled it in railroads until he controlled—absolutely, the newspapers averred —the third largest railway system in the world, was a short, fat man, bald, with a little gray mustache that was as a label insistently spelling commonplaceness. He had a chronic smirk and deep crow's-feet—one of those irritating fat old men who smile with their eyes also—and he laughed at his own insipid jokes. And the smiles of his punctiliously attentive hearers were not pleasant to see among social equals at the Union Club. Sam heard with pleasure his father grunt from time to time—non-committal grunts, to be sure, and not rude enough to be entirely satisfying, but, nevertheless, not smiles. The Commodore took to telling his "jokes" to that bright - looking son of Sampson Rock, and Sam laughed — at Roberts's selection of a victim—until the Commodore looked pleased at the triumph of his humor.

Of them all, Sampson Rock alone looked like a great captain of finance, and he was probably the least rich of the crowd—a good-looking chap, the governor; not so tall as Sam by an inch, nor so square of shoulders, and rounder about the waist; but his face was healthy-looking, strong, and intelligent, and his eyes were the eyes of a man who could think and who could fight. At times they seemed to film over with a curious impersonal coldness as though he saw little difference between inanimate objects and human beings.

It was the first time that Sam had tried to establish a connection between what the newspapers say a man is and what he looks. It interested him for a time, but it soon palled. Their discussion of affairs did not savor of a conspiracy; they were not loading the dice the newspapers said they used when they played the stock - market; and to escape Commodore Roberts's jokes he excused himself early and drove to the Van Courtlandt-Joneses' to see Fanny Collyer.

SAMPSON ROCK OF WALL STREET

The man whose life he had saved at college—Francis Van Courtlandt-Jones, now an active stock-broker and only a year older than Sam—to whom he had telephoned that afternoon, had implored him to come to the dinner, an informal affair—only fourteen and all old friends. But Sam had declined; it was his first night back and he would dine at home with his father; but he would be around in time for the dance. There were many questions he wished to ask his father, but he wished to ask them alone. Roberts and the others being in the way, he would do his asking on the morrow. The more he saw of Wall Street men the better he liked Darrell, the Western mine engineer.

The fourteen old friends were still at the table, but they welcomed him effusively. The host, having foreseen such a stroke of luck, as he called it, had given orders that Mr. Rock should not be allowed to wait in the drawing-room. They were all men and girls he knew well, and absence seemed to have made these fond hearts grow fonder. Sam was more interesting for having circled the world in eighteen months, just as his father had trebled his fortune in Sam's absence. They all liked him for himself and his twenty-five years. Three of them, two brokers and one female, liked him for his father and *his* fifty-five. Sampson Rock's age meant something to them since a magazine sketch appraised those fifty-five years at a half-million each. It was a gorgeous overestimate. But those colleagues of his who knew better did not enlighten the public. They themselves lived in glass houses gilded to resemble multi-millions. The overestimates helped them all. Prestige is potential cash; and cash, actual or potential, is power; and power is real cash.

These young old friends did not talk like the over-

73

estimated multi-millionaires. They had their cares and their tragedies. But as, during the Terror, the young aristocrats of France walked gracefully to the guillotine and smilingly "tipped" the executioner, so did these laugh—at punctured automobile tires and at misjudged horse-races and at offended rich aunts. That had been his life, before he started on his round-the-world trip.

He saw less of Fanny than he had intended to see. She was looking extremely pretty, he again thought. Certainly she had improved in his absence. But he could not talk to her because everybody insisted upon his telling them stories, and they listened so attentively that the mild elation he felt at interesting them made him talk well and feel very friendly towards them.

But as he went home some hours later the very dissimilarity between the two lives—his old life with these people and his father's life in Wall Street—made his thoughts recur to the ticker and the words of the ticker and the words of the men who lived by the ticker. It was a great game. There might be ways of playing it like a gentleman; of getting all the excitement without the unpleasant after-taste. He did not fully understand its functions as an adjunct to railroad improvement and to industrial development. He might learn. But the romance of the West, the life of the mining-camp, was far more alluring. It was easier to understand. The excitement of it was healthier.

Sampson Rock was already studying the ticker and scooping in Virginia Central when Sam awoke the next day. He had invited himself to luncheon at Mrs. Collyer's, and he was too busy looking after his martial bric-à-brac — poisoned daggers, wonderful old pistols, blood-rusted spears, which he had accumulated in his travels — to think about Sampson Rock's work. He had some really remarkable ivory carvings which he had picked up in Delhi for Mrs. Collyer, and two perfectly matched pearls he had bought at Aden from a Persian Gulf man who wanted to put ten thousand miles or more between himself and the fisheries. He had paid a round price for them. Darrell, his Denver friend, who was a perfect crank on gems, assured him he had not paid a tenth of what such pearls were worth in New York, but it only struck him now that the real story was the anxiety of the man who sold them to him. He had put the pearls unwrapped in his vest-pocket at Quarantine and had forgotten to "declare" them. It would please him to give the smuggled pearls to Fanny, because they were very beautiful and because they had been such a bargain.

Mrs. Collyer was delighted with Sam's gift. She handled the ivories as she had seen that eccentric old Bleecker Fish examine his own choice carvings, plagiarizing, as closely as she remembered, old Fish's learned words. Sam, who knew nothing about ivories, said, "I'm so glad you like them," from time to time, as though that had been his one hope. When the flood moderated he turned to Fanny.

"I was so rushed that I didn't have time to get what I wanted for you—"

"Excuses!" smiled Fanny "But never mind, Sam. You brought yourself back."

"I had your joy in mind all the time; that's why I was so careful of myself."

"And you brought the ivories to mamma," added Fanny, gratefully.

"Just what I wished he'd bring me," put in Mrs. Collyer, with the effect of an echo.

"But I thought you and I might play marbles again as we used to do, so I brought back these." Sam took the pearls from his vest-pocket and made a motion to toss them to her.

"Catch, Fanny!" he said; but he laid them on her out-stretched hands.

"Sam!" said Fanny, with a gasp. "Mamma, look at these. No, no, let me look at them some more! Are they really for me, Sam?"

Mrs. Collyer, being human, arose, walked over, and took the pearls from Fanny. Fanny also rose and kept looking at them in her mother's hand. Sam was very glad that she was glad.

"Perfectly beautiful," observed Mrs. Collyer, with the cold, discriminating voice of an expert. Her tone warmed as she added, "Just what I had promised to get Fanny when Roanoke went to par." The things she had promised herself to get when Roanoke went to par were all perfectly beautiful. Also, they were very numerous; for her heart beat at least five thousand times an hour. Anticipation kept the wings of her fancy buzzing like an insect's; that overstimulated gambler's fancy of hers—Roanoke, one hundred dollars a share!—which alighted on a million flowers and sipped its drop of honey from each, fresh joy upon joy, one to the heart-throb. Doubt's snow-flakes were so tiny that her soul-sunshine quickly melted them into drops of dew and made the flowers even more beautiful. *When Roanoke went to par!* That was why her eyes grew moist with gratitude.

"I'm glad I got ahead of Dad," said Sam, not thinking of Dad and the scooping in of Virginia Central which would make Roanoke sell at par.

"How can I thank you, Sam?" Fanny's look was ten million thanks.

"I don't know," answered Sam, "unless it's by keeping mum about it."

"They must have cost—" began Mrs. Collyer, coming back from the golden heavens to her house. Sam was almost as her son.

"I stole them," broke in Sam. He told them the story of the purchase, described the Persian's appearance, genealogy, Moslem aspirations, and probable ending—everything, save only the price of the pearls. And he did not say he smuggled them into his native land.

At the table he told them humorously about the outlandish dishes h⸱ had tried. They laughed a great deal. He felt happy. He was very healthy

Mrs. Collyer explained, shortly after luncheon, that she had to go over her real-estate accounts, and she left them and went up-stairs. Business cares, he opined, with a sympathetic air, were not conducive to longevity. Mrs. Collyer, replying from the stairs, was certain they were not, but who could help her carry her cross? She looked so heavy-laden that Sam promptly and sincerely said it was too bad, so that when he turned to Fanny, after poor Mrs. Collyer finished climbing the stairs, cross and all, Fanny said:

"Take off that expression, Sam, or you'll make me believe you mean it. You know perfectly well she is going to have her usual nap. If your absence has made you feel like a stranger, you might as well begin to be truthful and friendly-like."

Sam laughed. He looked at her. He ceased to laugh.

She was a very pretty girl; she had been the prettiest girl at the Jones's dinner. She had improved a great deal, he thought, in his absence. He could not have described her to a stranger and made the stranger see Fanny as pretty as Fanny was. All that he could have said was that her head was gracefully set on a beautiful neck and shoulders; that her eyes were brown and bright and expressive, without any stage effects; and her hair, golden-brown and very fine, with a wave to it; and her complexion fair, clear-skinned and delicately rosy; that she was graceful in her walk, in her gestures, in the little sudden movements of her head; nothing statuesque and nothing over-athletic, but absolutely normal and completely pleasing. In short, Fanny herself was very pretty. Also, she was barely twenty and in good health.

He had always been very fond of her; she really was the one friend to whom he always could speak frankly with the certainty of a sympathetic hearing. When he was ten and she was five they were engaged to be married. It lasted until they forgot all about it, possibly a week. After all these years he remembered it. It made him hope that she would not marry very soon.

He had a great deal to say on the subject of Sampson Rock, Jr. The more he thought about it, the more he found he would have to say to this girl who was and yet was not the girl he had always known.

"Fanny," he said, abruptly, "you have changed a great deal."

"For the worse?"

"Inartistic! Tut, tut!" he told her, with a wave of his hand. "You are better looking than you were. I can't say more intelligent, because it isn't fair to judge by the brilliancy of your conversation."

"Judging by the same, I should say you yourself had not changed beyond recognition." She leaned forward in an attitude of listening intently, as though she would not miss any of his inspired words.

He did not laugh. "No," he instead admitted, very humbly; "I'm the same idiot; only more so. But I've been thinking about it, and I've come to the conclusion it's about time I was something else." He had begun in jest and ended in earnest. The transition probably was too abrupt for her to grasp. He himself did not like subtleties or shadowings.

"Something sensible?" She smiled as a sister might smile; but he saw in her eyes an unvoiced curiosity that told him she had perceived the line of demarkation between his jesting and his seriousness. It made his mood more confidential. He was at the age when a man cannot think of himself in silence before a sympathetic woman. He brushed aside all introductory remarks, seeing no necessity for formality with Fanny, and said:

"My father and I had some words yesterday."

"You don't mean—" She paused, puzzled rather than alarmed.

"No bloodshed," he said. "Just words. He has a big deal on and I didn't like the way he proposed to go about it. I told him so."

"To hear you talk—" she began, unimpressed.

"It takes too long to explain," he broke in. "All I know is that I don't like his business."

"You never did."

"I never thought much about it, one way or the other. But now I know I don't care. He wants me to go into it, but it's a hard game—"

"And your health is so delicate—"

"Don't be Smart Alecky, my child. I meant the game itself. It's a case of loaded dice, right and left."

"I suppose it was your violent dislike of it," she said, with a coolness which carried a subtle rebuke, "that drove you around the world."

"No, the reason I went away was to have a nice time. Considering your absence, I did pretty well. But now—"

"You've decided to do something sensible. How does Uncle Sampson Rock take it?"

Her look showed a deep and approving interest. That and her words and the tone of her voice made him feel that he had not been away from New York, or from her, a day. He answered:

"He called me a jackass. It is *his* word."

"It is not a pleasant word," she said, judicially. "You must have done—"

"It's for what I haven't done that he was angry. I don't know much about his business, so I can't see much difference between a man who tells lies and one who makes the ticker tell them. Can you?" In speaking to her he was in a manner merely thinking aloud. The realization of this is sometimes called falling in love.

"There may be. I don't imagine anybody goes to the ticker to hear the truth."

"Then what's the use of my going down there and being cooped up in an office all day long? Pshaw, it's the lying for money that goes against the grain!"

"Sam," said Fanny, with conviction, "I'm sure Uncle Sampson doesn't tell lies."

"No; he doesn't. He just lets the ticker tell them so that a bunch of idiots do exactly as he wants them to. It helps the family bank-account. I don't know enough about the game to understand the fine points, so you can't get any help from me. Anyhow, if I did anything, I think I'd go into a mining scheme with a friend of mine—awfully nice chap. But that would take me away from New York." He looked at her and shook his head, as though because of her he had abandoned his trip to the West.

She frowned and said:

"In time New York might possibly become resigned to its misfortune."

He laughed. "I shouldn't like New York to run that risk."

"That means, I suppose, a return to your strenuous career of usefulness. Brain workers don't live long, and—"

"No; they don't. I'm training for old age."

"Be natural and you'll make it, Sam."

There was an undercurrent of seriousness in her voice that made him look at her carefully. This was a new Fanny. The little girl he had always known had gone and with her had departed the Cupid-proof protection of immaturity. She was not even the same Fanny he had been so glad to see in his father's office the day of his return. The old Fanny used to look up to him as a loving younger sister might. But this Fanny had a mind of her own, and could scold in sarcasms and could detect any counterfeit of affectation, so that even if he would he could not pose before her. This difference in her seemed to make his old affection, which was two-thirds habit, stronger, deeper, more grown-up, as it were.

"Fanny, how many proposals have you had this season?"

"I knew I'd win!" she exclaimed, her face clouding.

"Win what?"

"I made a bet with myself that you could not stick to one subject three consecutive minutes."

He looked at her in mock admiration "You ought to write a book, Fanny. You talk like one."

"No. But you do. If you'll speak slowly I'll jot it down word for word. *How to do Nothing—By an Expert.*"

"Better do nothing than do people, isn't it?" He was amused.

"Is that a subtle epigram or merely slang?"

"No. That's the difference between what I'm doing now and what I'd have to do if I went down to Wall Street. Honestly, Fanny, it's a tough game, I tell you." He said it seriously. She was very pretty. He could see that she was as fond of him as she had ever been. He also could see the color of her cheeks, the light in her eyes, the sudden graceful motions of her head. It made him almost glad that she disapproved of him. That was because she didn't understand him, and didn't realize that he was older, and that he had seen many curious things and curious people in his trip around the world.

"It's ridiculous to talk that way about your father's business. But even if it were all you say it is, it seems to me that, if you wished, you could play it like a gentleman." In her eyes there was a hope that he would understand her phrase to its last subtle significance. Sam was too nice a boy to be allowed to drift along idly, like so many others who had been nice boys and were not nice men. She was too fond of Sam not to be deeply interested in his future—more, indeed, than in her own.

"Fanny, it's nonsense to generalize about such things.

But I tell you nobody can play the game down there without using loaded dice. Darrell and I are going to buy a mine and—"

"That simply requires money. You won't know much more about mines after you are done than you do now. If you're lucky you'll make money. If you're not you'll lose some. But what will it do for Sam Rock? You have better opportunities—"

"It will give me something to do."

"The fact that you'll work instead of playing polo is what you wish to be congratulated on, isn't it?"

His reply was a smile. There was something amusingly motherly about her talk and she did not know how much in earnest he was. The smile made her frown. She said, a trifle impatiently: "You needn't be a philanthropist, but you need not work simply to avoid being bored by idleness. I should think you'd like to do something difficult, Sam, something useful, something—"

"Don't you feel well, Fanny?" He looked at her with mock solicitude. "Are you sure there is no unhappy love-affair that makes you so — ah — stimulating?"

"I wish I *could* stimulate you into being something more than your father's son." She spoke so earnestly that he could not resist the temptation to answer:

"Oh, Dad isn't so awful, after all."

"No. He works while you talk. He does things—"

"And people. Don't forget the proletariat."

"I feel like laughing when you talk about his business," she retorted, impatiently. "I read a magazine article about him the other day. It called him a reformed stock - gambler and the Von Moltke of the Ticker and a lot of things that weren't nice. But it also said he was a wonderful man. And he is, too. It spoke about his railroads and what he had done to improve them and how he had developed the country. Wouldn't you like to be somebody instead of somebody's son? *I* would."

Her words did not reverberate in the recesses of his soul like a clarion call to duty. That was because he was looking with such pleasure at the flush on her cheeks. Her eyes were bright with her own enthusiasm; her lips were slightly parted. She was so pretty, and looked so earnest that he said:

"You would what—like me to be somebody?"

"Yes."

"Very well. It's quite original. You never read that in novels. But never mind. I'll do it." From his look it was already done.

"Pshaw!" she said. Her disgust at what she deemed flippancy was so obvious that it forced upon him for the first time a serious mood.

"Listen, Fanny. It's very easy to work yourself into a pitch of excitement about this. But I tell you it's not so easy to decide what to do. Give me a chance to think about it—and—"

"And talk about it a year or two—"

"Could I do anything better than to talk to my father about it?"

"No. But you say his business is—"

"That's the way I think now, but I admit it may come from my ignorance. I know that his point of view and mine are not the same. Am I going to be a success in a business that I don't like? The Wall Street end of it is not for me. My father talks of the good he is going to do by improving a railroad; and deliberately proceeds to get stock as cheap as possible, no matter whose it is—" He paused, frowning.

"Business is business," she said, vaguely conscious of apologizing for Sampson Rock. Sam might not know all the reasons for his father's actions.

Her phrase aroused him instantly.

"That's what they all say: business is business. Tell the truth to nobody. Get the most you can for the least price. Friends first, then the enemies. Tell them it's for their own good and swallow 'em whole. Let everything slide but the profit. The profit makes you fat; it's good for the health three times a day, before and after meals. Hooray for the profit!"

She looked at him, with surprise not unmixed with a subtle thrill. She had not thought him capable of such feeling. He was a different Sam; he looked different; he spoke another man's words in another man's voice. It might not be difficult to spur him on into doing something worth while. She was so pleased with the thought of it that her lifelong habit of affection for him took on a subtle aspect of novelty.

"Sam," she said, a trifle Joan-of-Arc-like, "don't you see your opportunity? To do what your father is doing and do it—ah—in a way that—" She hesitated.

"An *honest* way, you mean, don't you? I don't know whether I can or not." The frown on his face made him so resemble his father that she felt all Sam needed to accomplish wonders was to be kept in that mood.

"Oh, if you only could, Sammy!" she said, thrilled with the quick vision of the new Sam—a man—her work. It rang in her voice.

"Would it please you so much, Fanny?" He looked at her curiously.

"Yes, indeed, Sam. Indeed it would."

"If it were a case of money—" he mused, thinking of the work.

"I'm sick of hearing nothing but money! money! money! all the time, as if there were nothing else in life. Everybody one meets talks stocks and how much money this man made or that man lost. It's disgusting. It makes New York unfit to live in. The men study nothing but how to make money and their wives how to spend it. People grow old so quickly in this country because of that."

"Shake, Fanny!" He extended his hand. She waved it aside impatiently.

"Be serious, Sam."

"I am," He rose. "I'm going."

"So soon?"

"Yes. You make me think too much and I'm not used to it." He took both her hands in his by a sudden impulse. There came to him a faint odor as of violets—a perfume so delicately evanescent that only at times he thought he breathed it. But the touch of her soft, warm flesh thrilled him so that he bit his lips and dropped her hands a trifle quickly.

She smiled with her bright eyes as well as with her lips, and said: "It *is* fatiguing at first, isn't it? It was very good of you to come to-day—"

"Yes, it was. To show how easy goodness comes to me, I'll drop in to-morrow night. May I?"

"To-morrow night? Let me see." She thought a moment, wondering if she had a previous engagement, and Sam was conscious of a pang. He wished to see her again, very soon. "Yes. I'll be at home, Sam. Do come."

"Look for me, then, unless I drop dead in the meantime. And if you don't mind, I'll bring Dad with me."

"Mamma will talk him black and blue about Roanoke."

"That's why I'll bring him. Good-bye, Fanny."
He again held out his hand and she shook it firmly.
The touch of her hand, warm, living, thrilling, made him unwarily voice a sudden thought.

"I wonder if—" He checked himself and frowned.

"What do you wonder?"

"If I tell you now I won't have anything to talk about to-morrow. It will keep. Good-bye."

He had wondered if they never would be more than old friends. It was so asinine a thing to say to Fanny that he looked at her to see if there was a similar query in her eyes. They looked, indeed, as though she expected a question from him.

"Good-bye," he repeated, hastily, and left her, without a look at her again.

She was not the same girl he had always loved as a sister. She was no butterfly. She had brains. If he did anything worth while it would please her. He felt a great generosity stir within him; he would like to give her everything she wished. He walked along briskly, swinging his cane, his chest inflated, his lungs full of oxygen, his soul overflowing with confidence, and his mind not very deeply concerned with the details of what he would do.

She looked after him from the window, smiling at the swinging of his cane. He was a nice boy, strong, manly, clean-cut, clean-looking, not stupidly unsophisticated. but not unpleasantly wise. He was still in his formative period. He might have inherited more of his father's abilities than anybody gave him credit for.

He lacked incentive. He needed somebody to keep at him. He did not have the spur of poverty, but neither did he have the money-madness. There was no reason why he should not develop into a fine type of man. She would love to see him become the glorious exception in his set, and Sampson Rock, the envy of other rich men with sons.

She watched him until he turned the corner, and the moment he vanished from her sight a smile came to her lips. That was because she saw him in her mind, still swinging his cane, walking springily, his shoulders squared, full of health and wholesomeness. She picked up a novel. She read the opening paragraph three times before her smile disappeared.

VI

AFTER leaving the Collyers' house, Sam, obeying a vague impulse, telephoned to the office and learned that his father would dine with some friends at the club—an engagement he could not break—but he would be glad if Sam called for him at half-after ten. Sam promised cheerfully, conscious of a gradual obliteration of their misunderstanding as to stock-market strategy. He felt more filial and withal less susceptible to sudden impulses. Although Sam still preferred mines to the ticker, he increasingly realized his ignorance of the latter. Methods obviously concerned Sampson Rock less than achievement. That was the defect of a strong man; an admirable defect in the eyes of the business world, probably. Therefore, it behooved Sam to study his father's business. The necessity of this became obvious with the inevitable thought that if anything happened to Sampson Rock, his only son should at least know how to protect himself, how to defend his father's work, and, indeed, it might well be, his father's name. To whom should he turn for advice if not to his father?

He was mindful less of the ethics of his father's business at that moment than of the knowledge of it. Intelligence and knowledge went hand in hand. Therefore he decided that he must acquire knowledge. To do this he would ask questions and he would listen to answers. He would not argue, he would not dispute. It is not easy to reason one's self into a judicial mood. Sam tried. As soon as he fancied he had succeeded he went out for his first American ride in his new one hundred horse-power machine. The long though unexciting trip quieted his nerves. He dined at the Racquet Club, won seven out of eight games of pool from young Treadwell, and shortly before eleven went to the Union for his father.

Sampson Rock, Major Roberts, and George Mellen had spent the evening discussing the market. In one corner of the big room they sat and talked—so quietly and unemotionally that not one of the men who saw them and knew who they were felt any desire to overhear the conversation. That, of course, was as it should be in a club where the members were gentlemen first of all, even if many of them were stock-gamblers afterwards. But any one who knew the difference between a stock-ticker and a-sewing-machine would have seriously strained his gentlemanliness in order to hear what it was that the "Big Three" so quietly discussed. They had agreed that their several plans would benefit by a declining market. Their decision had not made stocks less valuable; nevertheless, stocks would look it. Times were good; but times would probably be better in a few weeks, when two or three cloudlets should have vanished from the financial sky. Lower prices, by discouraging impudent attempts at booming made by reckless gamblers, would avert the nasty little flurries that, like influenza, always carried the germ of more serious troubles. Theirs was a philanthropic decision. It really would be for the Street's ultimate good. Also, it would permit the profitable repurchase of the stocks which the three head philanthropists had sold some days before. Each of them therefore promised to take care of his own stocks, with a view to the effect of such "care" on the general market and on 'each man's especial benefit. It was one of those "conspiracies" which the Street at times suspected and the newspapers guessed at: only there were no details, no statistics of profit and loss, no oath - bound pledges. Three logical minds thought as one on the same subject, and, having the same object in view, decided on the same course of action, no other being open. That was all.

Major Roberts was very affable to Sam, and George Mellen, whose younger brother was the richest man in the world, shook hands warmly with the youngster. Sam inquired after "Willie" Mellen, whom he had known intimately at college, and it was some time before Sampson Rock rose to go. They did not discuss financial matters in Sam's presence, Major Roberts insisting upon telling the appreciative young listener some new stories he had heard that day.

Rock was about to order a cab when Sam asked him to walk home, adding:

"It will do you good, Dad. I don't believe you take half enough exercise."

It was a filial speech. Sampson Rock smiled and nodded.

They walked up the avenue leisurely. Sam's father never disliked silence; it enabled him to talk with Sampson Rock. The Old Man was frowning slightly— a trick of his when he was thinking. The frown subtly checked the son's impulse to take his father's arm. Sam could not but feel that the man beside whom he walked at that moment was less his father than Sampson Rock, the animating soul of the "Rock roads" and arbiter of their stock-market destinies—a man of brain, a man of character, a man of power, known to millions of Americans who knew nothing of the man's son or the man's heart, but a great deal about the man's work. But Sam did not philosophize thrillingly about it. What he thought, in his new-born desire for wisdom, was that, if only there could be drawn out of this captain of finance all the secrets, the experience and the knowledge, the business sagacity and the ticker-strategy that made him what the world said he was, many problems would be solved at one swallow. Instead, Sam must learn little by little. There was no royal road to knowledge. How long would it take his father to learn? How much had he accomplished and how much more did he intend to do? If Sampson Rock kept his health and his strength, what and where would he be in the business world before he ceased to work?

Sam looked curiously at his father's face. It no longer wore a frown, for Rock had decided what orders Dunlap would receive on the morrow. The uninterested look had come on again. Thereupon Sam ceased to think of his father's future and considered his own.

"Dad," he said, "I've been thinking."

Rock looked up and saw that Sam was serious. But he himself was in good humor over the stock-market outlook now that he, Mellen and Roberts had agreed. Roberts and Mellen would see to it that the big banks duly helped, all of which would greatly assist Rock's Virginia Central campaign. But after all, he was an American. He asked, laughingly:

"Does it hurt, Sam?"

"N-no," answered Sam, with an effect of feeling his

"'DAD,' HE SAID, 'I'VE BEEN THINKING'"

brain for bruises, being also an American and a patron of vaudeville. "I haven't been at it long enough to be fatally injured—only since the squelching at the office the other day."

"Oh, well, Sammy," began Sampson Rock, with a tinge of compunction in his voice. It was, indeed, almost a motherly tinge and he was not smiling. Sam interjected, quickly:

"Don't apologize. I did not know I was so ignorant; nor that there were so many other idiots in the world. Amiably assuming that you were right, there is still a puzzle: What am I going to do? Have you the answer?"

"What do you wish to do, Sam?" His father's voice was kindly. Recalling Sam's conversation, he now hoped his boy had forgotten all about the Colorado mines and therefore did not mention them. He would not, indeed, have tried very hard to discourage Sam, believing it would be easier to arouse interest in railroads after mines than in railroads after automobiles.

"I'll tell you what I don't want to do, and that is, monkey with the stock-market. I'd rather start at something—easier." Sam barely caught himself at the point of saying "decent."

"How about the railroad end of it, Sammy?" Sampson Rock in Sam's place would have begun his education then and there. The consciousnes of this made Sampson Rock look at his son with a curious hopefulness in his eyes.

"I'd rather do that," answered Sam, with an absence of enthusiasm that, more than his words, replied to Rock's hopes, "than be watching the ticker all day and trying to think it wasn't a horse-race. But it seems to me," he finished with decision, "that I ought to know more about your business than I do, no matter what I may go into later. If I have any questions to ask, now is my time, when you can answer them. No matter how disappointed you may be, Dad, it stands to reason that if I don't like the business I'll never succeed at it. If I like it after I understand it better, you can do your worst in the educational line. That's fair, isn't it?"

"Do you mean it, Sam?" In his earnestness Rock was frowning.

"Yes," answered Sam.

Rock, in an utterly matter-of-fact tone, said: "Very well. You'll stay with me in the office a little while and learn by absorption as well as by long lectures. It's slow, but sure." Without the gift of patience, even when patience was torture, Sampson Rock never would have become Sampson Rock. He took his big, strong son's arm in his and finished kindly: "There are many ways in which you can help me."

Sam thought his father had spoken kindly in the belief that, being young and ignorant of business affairs, Sam needed encouragement. He said nothing. After a moment Rock spoke:

"My boy, I'll find some work for you that won't be a bore and—"

"Never mind about the bore," interrupted Sam, confirmed in his suspicions, "the thing is to learn. I'd like to do something useful, but also congenial, so that—"

"I understand," in turn, interrupted Rock. "I can't ask any more of you. To me, of course, my work is interesting enough and I think it will be to you. But let me tell you one thing, Sam: whatever you go into you must first see your way to the very end, not only that you may be sure to get there, but so that you may have no illusions about being a human automobile. You have the sense not to want to be a Napoleon of Finance, for you know so little about the stock-market that if you went into it you'd be gambling. That's stupid. You need neither the money nor the excitement. I'd rather you went in for art or for collecting postage-stamps."

"The ticker game is a form of coin-collecting, isn't it?" Sam smiled, but his father shook his head a trifle impatiently.

"The ticker game is an incident. You must read up on the theory of Exchanges—"

"And you'll tell me the practice?"

"Yes. The papers talk about the stock-gambling. As a matter of fact, the one great trouble with people in this country is not that they wish to get rich, but that they wish to get rich quickly. Of all desires that is the worst, though it's useful enough in Wall Street, when others have it. The man who wants something for nothing, who wants a comfortable leisure without the uncomfortable earning of it, is bound to have his price. When the mob that hangs around a ticker has it, it pays the intelligent capitalists' price; and after paying, the mob shouts: 'Thieves!' The philosophy of it is as plain as the nose on your face, and you can reckon on the desires of the mob with as much certainty as on the law of gravitation. Yes, Sam."

"So I had thought," said Sam, dryly.

"I'm not defending either the loser or the winner. I'm showing you the stupidity of the loser. The principle is the same in a man who wants to do it all in a minute, and *that* is something you might want to do. The work may be worth doing but it must be done well; and undue haste may make it unintelligent work; and that is dishonest work. It's like those asses who put up cheap tenements that collapse. The cheapness of the material not only is criminal but it is expensive, which is stupid. You must give the mortar time to dry. It is our national failing. Personally," he said this with a quizzical smile as if he thought the confession would please the boy, "I prefer the dashes to the slow plodding; for, after all, a man only lives when he is doing something, doing it well and doing it quickly in order to do much before he dies. But if you use your brain you will learn that there is a time to walk and a time to sprint, and why this is so and how it averages up pretty well in the end. Also, that you are not the only man on the job, and that it is almost as bad to be too far ahead as too far behind. Patience is the hardest thing to learn, but it pays, Sam; it pays because so few people in this country like to exercise it. By patience, I don't mean laziness. You under stand?"

"Yes," said Sam. "You didn't have to use words of one syllable. I realize all that."

"No, my boy, you don't. You can't. No man does, at your age, with your temperament and your habit of life. You've never had to weigh the consequences of over-impulsiveness and you must learn to do it habitually. You haven't begun to learn; but I'll remind you of it whenever I see you forgetting it. A stupid man can recognize abstract wisdom at a glance. It's like a shoe; you know that with leather, thread, a few nails and some buttons a pair of shoes may be made. To make the shoes, that is not so easy. To stop generalities: you start working for me, which means that you start working for yourself because you are my only son. You therefore begin by what most men hope to end. Your care must be to eliminate the only possibility of failure that there could be for you if I died to-morrow and you wished to take up my work where I left off. The only way you can do it is by making sure you know what you want. That is why you must take your time now and not later. If you know what you want and you work for it and for nothing else, and you love the work while you are doing it, so that you can't help doing it well because it would make you unhappy to bungle, you will get what you're after as sure as fate. Making money is nothing; it's easy; any fool can make money at times. But that only means so many pounds of gold, and it's permanent work that counts; something done, completed. Why, my boy, the only terror that Death really has is the thought of leaving something unfinished. It's like setting your heart on training your son for something and dying when he is two years old." Sampson Rock's frown relaxed and he finished with a smile: "That sounds kind of highfalutin' and long-winded, eh, Sammy?"

"No," said Sam, shortly. "I can stand more."

"Well, it's really so. Just think a minute. Everybody nowadays wants money, each man for what it means, what it can do for him. But only an utter ass would deny that health is much more than money. Yet, while the average man has good health he forgets he has what's better than money and he thinks only of what he hasn't. If you are doing big work you know that it is the work itself that gives you the greatest pleasure and not the money there may be in it; but you also may forget it. I don't want you to forget the joy of the work nor the money of it, but you must never measure results exclusively by dollars. If the work you are doing is good the dollars will come to you in such a way that you'll have to lock the door of the safe if you don't want them to walk right in. Sure as fate, Sam."

Sam answered nothing. He knew that the burden of Sampson Rock's argument was that the end justified the means; the greatest welfare of the greatest number; ethics placed on a mathematical basis, with here and there a dollar-sign. It was all a matter of the point of view, and Sam was certain his own was not the Wall Street point of view. He wanted to learn how to do good work without changing his point of view. From the fulness of knowledge would come intelligent decision.

They had reached their house, the last silence unbroken.

"I'm going straight to bed, Sammy," said Sampson Rock. "I must be down-town early to-morrow."

"Me, too," remarked Sampson Rock, Jr.

For the first time in their lives Sampson Rock and his son, by an impulse which came to both simultaneously, shook hands as they said good-night.

VII

SAM turned inevitably, almost eagerly, to the financial pages of the newspapers the first thing the next morning. In the money articles, the writers as usual gave reasons for the various market movements, but how sound those "reasons" were he could not tell and he did not care; they did not interest him. Of Virginia Central, which had been weak, and he knew why, the papers said that further liquidation was in evidence, doubtless due to knowledge of circumstances possessed by a favored few. One ventured the theory that the management was in need of money and was finding some difficulty in securing it on favorable terms, which difficulty had been duly reflected in the tape. Sam knew that, in this instance, the newspapers were mistaken, excepting the one that was only half right. It was a tribute to the adroitness of his father. It widened the gulf between those who knew and those who did not. The existence of that gulf appeared vaguely unfair, but, he was forced to admit, inevitable.

As they rode to the office together in an electric brougham, Sam began his cross-examination.

"Dad," he said, "the Virginia Central Railroad is what you are after, isn't it?"

"Yes."

"Where does it run from; where does it go to; how big a railroad is it?"

99

"It begins nowhere and ends in the same place."

"I haven't any stock to sell you," laughed Sam.

Sampson Rock had not meant to be epigrammatic. He had said what he felt, what angered him, in that ineptly managed railroad, the aimlessness of which irritated him as being so much waste, so great and so unutilized a possibility—as the sight of an idler vexes a hard-working man, or a misused engine exasperates a born mechanic. He would make a railroad of it. But Sam's scepticism pleased him because it made enlightenment easy, and he answered in the way he thought Sam would understand:

"The Virginia Central Railroad was built before the war, by Southern capitalists, at a time when nobody knew much about correct railroad building. They had little to learn from the past and they could not foresee the wonderful growth of the country. They let the road wind about like a crooked river. No town of over five hundred inhabitants was skipped, because the people were clamoring for a railroad and the builders thought the clamor meant dollars; it seemed to assure business at once. They got to Richmond. In time they hoped to get to some established port. So they waited for the port to establish itself. From the first they should have had two ends—logical, inevitable, natural ends—and they should have built an air-line— as straight a line as they could get—between these two points. If they wanted to tap sections off the main line, they could have run feeders to them. When the railroad does not go to the towns, the towns will come to the railroad. A new line must look less to the present than to the future. You don't build a railroad for a little while; you build it for all time. These Southerners were Americans enough to be thinking only of their own generation. That generation is gone, and because the road was built for it, it is not up to-date. It paid once, but not now. Virginia has tobacco, coal, iron, to send north and east; and the north and east have hats, shoes, dry-goods, hardware, to send to Virginia. The road that can carry what Virginia sells and what Virginia buys will prosper, if it carries enough. The farmer takes his produce to town in his market-wagon. If on the return home he can cart something to one of the neighbors instead of going back empty, he is making money both ways, out of his wagon and his team and other people's work as well as out of his own farming. See? We must look for markets and we must find them and develop them and keep them ours. We must keep our wagons loaded, coming and going.

"And it is by an infinite number of infinitesimal economics that we can reduce expenses and meet competition. To haul your freight after you get it, more quickly, more economically, more efficiently in short, that is the problem. It cost the Roanoke last year six hundred thousand dollars to reduce grades and straighten curves on the Riverside branch alone, which was hardly paying. But that made it possible for them to run heavy trains and as fast trains on that division as on any other part of the system. Instead of six freight-trains a day, we need only to run four to do more than the six did formerly. And we must be ready to run twelve. We save a fraction of a mill per ton per mile. But a good many thousands of tons go over the two hundred and twenty miles of that branch line in the course of a year, and as the country grows we shall be able to handle all the business likely to come for many years, and not only not increase rates, but even reduce them. We'll make up the initial expense in a little while. There will come a time when some of the increased business will be in the nature of 'velvet.' Transportation's what we have to sell. Apply the same principle that you would to any product. Do you understand?"

"Perfectly."

"Well, a railroad must gain; it must go forward all the time. There is a normal rate of increase as the country becomes more thickly populated and more intelligent in its productive work. To stand still is therefore really to go backward. It means some one else is getting the increase. We must strengthen or rebuild old bridges, double-track, and use heavier rails and more powerful locomotives and larger cars. The crew of a small train is the same as on a larger train. You see the difference in the street-cars—one conductor and one motorman and one car; but the car now carries twice as many fares as it used to—a greater earning capacity per working unit. But the increase in operating expenses is or should be—there is no reason why it shouldn't be—smaller than the increase in the earning capacity. Have you got all that down, Sam?" he finished, with a smile.

Sam nodded quickly. He was very much interested. He was getting elemental facts made comprehensible to infant ears, and he was not aware that his father was picking his words with that end in view.

"I want that road because, notwithstanding certain disadvantages, it has possibilities that the present management does not realize, and, moreover, is financially unable to develop into realities, so that Virginia is not getting what it ought to get in the way of transportation. The capital stock is thirty-five million dollars, and the bonded indebtedness is not large—not so large as it might be with benefit to the road—and safety to investors, Sam. Nobody wants to overload a property with bonds nowadays; only what we think it can stand —and stand in hard times. Do you understand that? Well, don't forget it, ever. The worst we do, and we do it because we are Americans, is to capitalize our hopes. We think this country will grow—the railroads help it more than anything else—and what some people call water to-day becomes the dividend-paying stock of to-morrow. The water, after all, is only an intelligent optimist's appraisal of the value of the equity *plus* the future. The money is made by the people who have faith in this country, by upbuilding and not by pulling down; and time will do more for all of us than the ticker. Rodney Bruce, of Chicago, said something at the club the other night to a chap who was very bearish and saw hard times ahead: '*In the last five years I myself have helped to bury thirty-seven men who bet against the United States.*' Do you understand that?"

"Yes," said Sam, impatiently. "But about Virginia Central stock?" Sampson Rock went on, with a slight smile:

"If I could get eighteen of the thirty-five millions of the Virginia Central stock at about thirty-five dollars a share it would cost only about six and one-half millions in cash. To build extensions from the main line of the Roanoke to the sections I want to develop would cost all of that and more. But it also would mean two roads going there; whereas by getting the Virginia Central and improving it out of its own earnings, there would be but one, and one that would throw the traffic our way just the same. The improvement of the Virginia Central will make it a valuable property.

The Roanoke, therefore, would profit not only by the increased traffic it would get from the Central, but by its investment in Central stock itself, of which it would hold the majority. The Roanoke could afford to pay fifteen millions for the majority of the Central stock and issue four per cent. bonds for it, which would mean six hundred thousand dollars a year, because some day the Central's stock will be paying four per cent., or even five per cent., dividends on its par value, or much more than the interest on the bonds, and in addition the Biddleboro extension alone ought to be good for two hundred thousand dollars a year net in increased business to the Roanoke proper."

"But if you buy stock for six and one-half millions and sell it to the Roanoke for fifteen—" began Sam. The work itself was good, praiseworthy, inspiring; the financing of it was not.

"I won't get fifteen for it and I won't buy it for six and one-half. No such luck. I'll probably have to pay forty or fifty dollars a share, and possibly more, and I'll have to take the Roanoke's collateral bonds in payment, and I'll have to sell them at a discount, which won't net me the fifteen millions. And besides, I'll only be one of a syndicate. I can't make millions quite as fast as that. But I'll have to get the price of Virginia Central stock down, Sam, not so much to get it cheap, but to get it at all. I must make it very active and very weak, because that will bring stock from all over the country. Holders of it will read what the newspapers say of it and they won't like the looks of things. They don't have to sell if they don't wish; I can't force them to sell, and I won't advise them to sell. But I can't tell them to buy now, can I? Wall Street says the tape never lies, and what the smart

Alecks of Wall Street say the public who listens will repeat, being sheep. If anybody has Virginia Central stock for investment and believes in the growth of his country, he will hold on. But it is neither these men nor the speculators who make the railroads prosperous. So the tape will say things which stupid people will imagine mean something that the tape doesn't mean at all. And those—the speculators—will sell their Virginia Central, Sam."

"To Sampson Rock?" His father certainly would be doing good to Virginia—over the emptied pocket-books of the ticker-listeners.

"To somebody or other who doesn't put too much reliance on what the ticker or anybody says, but has brains to do his own thinking with."

"Then, if you put the stock down to ten dollars a share—" began Sam.

"I can't." He paused. Sam thought there was a limit to the ruthlessness of business. Sampson Rock went on: "The stock has value. I'm not the only one who knows it. You might not want to pay ten thousand dollars for a house, even though it was really worth it; but you'd jump at it at five thousand dollars, even if you had to wait months or years for a ten thousand dollar buyer. The stock is really worth more to the Roanoke than to any individual, because of the traffic arrangements which would be of mutual benefit. But at a certain price it is worth while to many individuals to buy it."

"Why don't you make a fair offer to Colonel Robinson?" Sam suggested this tentatively. He had strengthened his suspicion that what seemed fair would not be practicable.

"He would know what we can afford to pay. Wait;

that isn't all."—For Sam had opened his mouth and his father had divined a conventional remonstrance, as it were. "He would add twenty-five per cent. to what really would be a fair price, in order to make sure he wasn't giving it away. I hate a man who is so ready to take advantage of the needs of others." He smiled.

"Yes," acquiesced Sam, unsmilingly. "But do you count on getting all the Virginia Central stock you want in the open market?"

"I can't tell yet, Sam. I hope so. I have a list of the stockholders, and I'm trying to find out where the stock is held. The stock paid dividends years ago, but the road has allowed competitors to grow while it has itself stood still, and during the last period of depression it narrowly escaped bankruptcy. It has not paid any dividends since. The stock is up where it is because other stocks have boomed rather than because its own future is as bright as that of the rest. But it has many stockholders. Robinson owns a large block and Robinson's friends are also heavily interested. Robinson's stock probably won't come on the market unless somebody guns for it, but I think I can do without it. Some of the others would sell if it went up a great deal, which it won't—or if it went low enough to frighten them. Some is held in England, and then there is the floating supply held by more or less speculative holders. *That* I know I'll get—that and what's knocking around the Street. If I get the bulk cheap I'll be generous enough with the balance."

"I should think Robinson—" began Sam, with a sort of wondering impatience.

"He would, if he had the brains and the money, Sam," interjected Sampson Rock; "but he thinks the New York bankers are extortionate in their terms, when, as a matter of fact, they are only intelligently prudent. ﹅ They know where the fault lies; it isn't with the road, but with the management. He will be one of Wall Street's self-elected victims. The woods are full of them, and you read about them in the newspapers. As a matter of fact, it is the human factor in the equation; it is always that, Sam. Robinson hopes the Englishmen will help him out, but before he can find out positively I hope to get what I want. You'd be surprised to know," he finished, reflectively, "how much stock comes from strong-boxes all over the country when the price breaks and stays broke." He was looking thoughtfully at the door-handle of the brougham. Perhaps he saw how much Virginia Central stock was coming from strong-boxes all over the country — a growing mound of engraved certificates, growing, growing, bringing with them the power to give to Virginia prosperity—life and the chance to work and sweat!

"It isn't a square deal, Dad," said Sam, without heat, in order to avoid offence. "They don't know that the price is going down because you are—"

"Sam," retorted Sampson Rock, impatiently, "that stock pays no dividends. It won't pay any as long as Robinson runs the road, and he'll never resign the management while he and his friends are in control. I don't want to wreck the road in order to get it for practically nothing. I'm after the control of it because I tell you, my boy, that the possible welfare of an individual must not be allowed to stand in the way of the actual welfare of hundreds of thousands of people. And I'm getting it in and through the stock-market because that is the easiest, cheapest, and best way— and perhaps the only way."

He believed his own words; nevertheless, when he

continued it was in a defensive tone: "You won't know Virginia five years after the Roanoke gets the Central. Its own mother wouldn't know it in ten. And we won't stop there. The Roanoke must go westward. Let me get this road"—Sampson Rock's eyes shone and he clinched his right hand as though the Virginia Central were a struggling eel—"let me get this miserable little road and I—" He drew in a deep breath, and came back to an electric brougham in New York after having been on the shore of Lake Michigan, the inevitable terminus of the great Roanoke system of the future.

Sam, who was watching him, asked: "And you what, father?"

"That must be your work, Sam," answered Rock, very quietly—"that is, if you care for that sort of thing."

"Yes," answered Sam, quickly, "I care. But have I the brains to think—"

"Have you the will to work? That's more to the point. There is no mystery about these things. They are perfectly obvious." The quality which makes some men leaders of men does not always go with the power to understand why the minds of the subchiefs do not always work quickly enough.

"Obvious to you," said Sam. Whatever sophistries there might be in Rock's speech, Sam could not put his finger on them. And the work *was* interesting! He could vision to himself pleasant, inspiring things in the future.

"And to you, after you have studied them and men a few years. What votes are to a political statesman dollars are to a business man. But there are other things in life than votes or dollars. You must know your own country first. You don't know it yet. Therefore you can't know your own countrymen."

"But I will. And I want to know Virginia and see for myself where and why it is going to change so much after the Roanoke gets the control." Sam felt certain he would see with his own eyes and understand.

"That's very easy. Industrial development is now held back by the lack of adequate transportation facilities. Take the Austin iron deposits. It's fine ore and makes a particularly fluid iron which is very desirable for mixing with the cheaper Alabama grades in making certain castings and for other purposes. But the railroad handicaps them. Nature gave these iron deposits to Virginia, and Virginia cannot take advantage of them because the Virginia Central doesn't develop them. But *I* will develop the Austin and the Randolph County coal-fields, and instead of two blast-furnaces there will be ten at Austin, and instead of shipping seventy-five thousand tons of excellent coal to near-by towns at rather high prices we'll be carrying a million tons, not only to Virginia people but to New England. It will be good and cheap fuel. And there are many other things. And I shall profit because the Roanoke will get more tonnage, since the Central's natural outlet will be by way of the Biddleboro extension and then through us to tide-water. That is all, without any verbal fireworks on the subject of the nobility of labor."

Sampson Rock turned to his morning papers—big and little, yellow and staid, he had them all—and read them one after another; first the stock-market articles, then the head-lines of the other pages, his glance jumping jerkily from one column to another, then quickly down the page. Then—a minute or two to each paper—he put them aside.

Sam was lost in thought. It occurred to him he

ought to buy coal and iron lands and develop them, and that now was the time. He suggested it to his father.

"Yes; you'd make money, Sammy; but it would tie up a lot, and I can do better, dollar for dollar, just now, down here. Of course we'll come in on the coal and iron, too, for I'll help to promote a big development company, and we'll have enough stock to be in on the prosperity at a relatively small cost, Sam." He smiled slightly at the thought of the smallness of the cost. Nothing could be smaller than nothing, and that was what this stock would cost. "You see, the Roanoke is anxious to help enterprises that will develop the country's resources and traffic. I'll send people out to work on that as soon as I see things coming my way."

"Have you all the Roanoke stock you want?" asked Sam, presently.

"Yes; why, Sam?"

"Will the purchase of the Central make Roanoke go up?"

"Yes—with some help. The acquisition of the controlling interest of the Central will be a great bull card. But the public will have to know the reason why, and then the tape will have to corroborate it. The tape," he added, after a pause, "will duly corroborate. It is a wonderful educational force, at times."

"Are you sure the Roanoke will buy the Central from you if you get it?" Sam had the railroad in his mind's grasp. The philosophy of the ticker did not interest him very much now.

"Oh yes."

"At what price?"

"It depends. I think the Roanoke would pay seventy-five dollars a share for fifty-one per cent. willingly enough. Some of it should not cost me more than thirty-five, but some may cost me eighty or eighty-five. The market-price will probably be about eighty-five when the deal is made, because there will be a very small supply by that time. Also by having it sell way up on the Exchange it will make the price the Roanoke pays seem cheap and silence adverse criticism. We must defer to public opinion. *My* average must be a good deal below seventy-five."

"Roanoke is no higher now than Central will be then. Isn't it worth more?"

"Yes, much more. It's a better and stronger road. Only it has more stock." He smiled. The newspapers, three years before, when Rock reorganized it, had dubbed the Roanoke the "Hydrant - headed Monster" — a felicitous allusion to its watered capital. But the boom in business had changed the water into real value, to Rock's enormous profit, for Rock had seen the boom coming when the majority were building cyclone - cellars. He went on: "Roanoke is paying four per cent. dividends now, and it will be some years before the Central does that. If things turn out as I hope, Roanoke ought easily to pay five per cent. and sell at par before the end of the year. The Roanoke's future, if it gets the Virginia Central, will be bright."

Some people would have given up their chances of eternal salvation for such an assurance from Sampson Rock; but Sam could not help recalling Mrs. Collyer's habit of savoring that phrase—Roanoke at par—and he said:

"Aunt Marie would drop dead if she thought she'd have to wait that long. She ought to buy Virginia Central instead."

"Sam"—Sampson Rock spoke sharply—"what I've told you is for your own information. An indiscreet word might spoil everything." The look on his face was not pleasant to see.

"I understand," said Sam. It was the dollar-hunter's look, the look a man should not have who is thinking of the work and not of the money. After a pause he asked:

"All you need is one hundred and eighty thousand shares of Virginia Central, isn't it?"

"Yes, just a bare majority of the capital stock."

"Why don't you take it all?"

"Don't need it; a bare majority gives control."

"How much of it have you now?"

"Not very much."

"How much, Dad?" he persisted. "I want to know the reason for everything you do."

"About thirty thousand." Sampson Rock reflected that it might really help Sam to be on the absolute "inside" of this deal. Sam was his only son.

"You'll have to work hard to get the other one hundred and fifty thousand. What do you expect the whole will average when you get it?"

"I can't tell."

"Fifty?"

"I hope less."

"Forty?"

"Probably more. It all depends on how much stock I can shake out in the next fortnight. At sixty or under I'll make enough money. It doesn't matter," he added, "whether it's lightning-rods or rubbers or railroads, Sam; the first rule of business is to buy as cheap as you can and sell as dear as you can. It will cost a lot of money to do such work as I'm doing now in the stock-market, and I may not be able to get as much stock as I want, in which event I might have to come to terms with Robinson and lose a million of profits to avoid losing two or three of my own. But I don't think I'll need his help or his stock. Still, don't run away with the idea that there is no risk. There always is risk; but the odds are in my favor."

Sam understood fully that anybody who bought Virginia Central now and held it until Sampson Rock finished his purchases on a wholesale scale would make a great deal of money—money that would not actually come out of Sampson Rock's pocket, though it would reduce his profits. The Roanoke would pay for it in the end. And in the end everybody—workers and drones—would make money by the increased prosperity. The stock was selling under forty in the open market now, and Rock would make money even if he paid fifty-five or sixty for it. To secure one hundred and seventy-five thousand shares in the open market was difficult. Even his father wasn't sure he could do it, after all his preliminary manipulation and market-rigging and the skilful campaign of depression.

His father thought Robinson's stock could not be bought cheaply. Robinson would be on his guard against Sampson Rock, who was chairman of the board of directors of the Roanoke.

But would he be on his guard against some agent of Sampson Rock, Jr., who was nothing? Sam would pay Robinson a fair price; that would be playing the game fairly. The profit would be reduced but the work would be done. The work was the thing, not the money.

On Sam's face there was a frown, because he realized that he did not yet know the game well enough to play it intelligently, and the consciousness of it closed the door on confidence. It was like playing football with the eyes bandaged. The need of knowledge meant the need of patience, and the need of patience made him impatient. The impatience made him frown. And yet he had learned two things worth millions—that he must be patient, and that it was interesting work.

VIII

THEY walked into the office together, abreast, as though they were partners. The Old Man—Rock became the "Old Man" the moment he was in the ticker district—found a dozen cablegrams from his London brokers. They were in code, but Valentine had deciphered them, writing the plain English in lead-pencil over each code word, and Rock read them aloud in chronological sequence, for Sam's benefit. For the most part they were merely reports of sales for Mr. Rock's account, but two contained requests for information—which even Sam understood were thinly disguised prayers for advice, that eager hearts across the sea might make money. Everywhere it was the same: people wished to make money. To Sampson Rock his work might mean more; to his acquaintances it seemed to mean the chance to get rich. The money end of the deal was the unpleasant part, but Sam dispassionately admitted the silliness of expecting the average man to think of the work without the money; everybody wasn't rich. He asked:

"Do you sell there for effect on this market?"

"Yes; and for effect on theirs, too," replied Rock. He rang the bell for Valentine.

In determining to learn, though he had not yet acquired the ability to analyze, Sam was developing an increasing susceptibility to impressions. Things whereof he had long known the bones now took on flesh and lived; so that he mistook them for discoveries.

In this campaign—in which Sam's future way of living was involved—the first battle was waging in New York, with dollars for soldiers and the ticker for artillery. People he did not know, but for whom he still felt an impersonal sympathy, owned bits of paper called stock-certificates, and the game was to induce them to exchange these certificates for a certain number of dollars. The ways of inducing them to do so were not the ways of a railroad expert with his gaze on the future and his heart on the prosperity of a state, but the ways of a military strategist who left nothing to chance, but at the same time was insensible to the suffering of individuals. He would get that stock, as much of it and as quickly as he could, and he would use financial fear as a goad. Some people would lose some dollars; Rock would gain some. But Virginia would gain the most, he had said. Even in London would the dollar-strategist fight skirmishes, and it was civilization, work, progress, that same progress that his father had in mind when he spoke of "progress," which now permitted so extended a battle-line because progressive men had invented banks and exchanges and telegraphs and submarine cables. A strong hand it must be and a quick and versatile brain that could grasp the situation. And, for all that it seemed hard, Sam again found something inspiring in the vital importance and magnitude of the game. It was small wonder that otherwise kindly men could convince themselves that the heart had no place in the struggle. Tears easily became insignificant, almost as meaningless as a lament against one of the natural forces. The law of gravitation had no conscience; the tempest was ignorant of ethics.

"I send them selling orders just as I do in New York. The price there comes lower unless they suspect ulterior motives. They are not asses, over there." It did not occur to Rock to add that New York, getting lower prices from London, would be sure to think that the report to the bondholders' committee was not favorable and that London speculators had advance news of it. It was self-evident. Valentine came in just then, and Rock told him:

"Cable Ismay and Israel that we look for lower prices for Virginia Central. Attitude of best bankers here towards present management not friendly."

Valentine, Sam noted, went out frowning, and Sam asked:

"Is that right?"—he corrected himself lest he be misunderstood—"I mean, are the bankers really unfriendly?" The sense of inspiration was buried beneath the sordid details of the great upbuilding plans. Even Valentine had showed by the look on his face that he did not relish his part in this work. As a matter of fact, Valentine had frowned because he was trying to remember the exact words of the message he was to send. Ethics and accuracy in figures are not twin drops of rain.

"Yes. I explained it to you." Sampson Rock turned to his mail. Some of the unfriendly bankers would be in the syndicate later, but Rock did not think of mentioning this.

Sam perceived that his father was again at his favorite practice of telling the truth because of his conviction that it would be misinterpreted. Was it ever right to tell less than the whole truth? It was impossible to exclude doubts as to the righteousness of it all; but certainty of its utter unrighteousness was quite as elusive. Sam's was not a metaphysical mind. Every time the ticker intruded, the light flickered, and the flickering made the philosophizing hazy. But at least there was no doubt that more knowledge was needed. He asked:

"What about your orders in this market?"

"Given last night." Sampson Rock did not look up as he talked. "Valentine will distribute them this morning. I wish to see what effect on the commission-houses last night's weak closing will have. We have enough stock for sale at forty to guard against too strong a rally. Then, at about half-past ten, if it looks as if pressure is needed, we'll let them have enough to do the trick."

These were elemental facts—things which Sam, being his father's son, should have known these many years. The details, the knowledge of the personal characteristics of the brokers employed, the "revelations" of the tape, the psychology of professional Wall Street and of the stock-gambling public, the ability to eliminate the inessential which made it easy to perceive when it was time to strike and when to hold off—they were as the eyes and nose and mouth of the game, that gave it a recognizable physiognomy. Sam saw these but dimly now; yet he realized—though he vaguely resisted too prompt an admission of it—that this game of the ticker, viewed from the "inside," might indeed be more than an unfair raid on a heap of dollars in the distance, more than a struggle for a potentially profit-able railroad. The little machine printed on the tape letters and figures in black ink. It printed on human souls fears and hopes; and printed them with an ink made of brains and blood and tears and gold.

Valentine re-entered to say Mr. Harding was waiting to see Mr. Rock.

"Tell him to come in," said Mr. Rock.

"Good-morning, Mr. Rock," growled Harding, of F. W. Harding & Co. He was not known to be one of Mr. Rock's brokers. The firm did a large commission business, most of it for out of town, and they had a branch office in Richmond, Virginia. Frank Harding was the most unpopular man on the Stock-Exchange, and he was aware of it. This made him even more unpopular, because he revenged himself in the only way possible — by exacting the last drop of blood wherever there was blood to be exacted. And, as he expected reprisals, he was always on his guard. He was not a gentleman, and was so unwise as to show it in little things; also in big things. But he was an experienced and alert broker and he could be trusted. Rock would use him now because Harding's Southern connections would enable him to convey certain impressions to the observant Street; and also, later in the campaign, because, having no friends in the world, Harding had the blessed gift of silence. With silence, indiscretion comes hard.

"Good-morning, Harding," said Rock. "How are you feeling?"

"All right," answered Harding, curtly. He almost sneered, from force of habit, when he suddenly remembered that more was expected of him in this office, where there were no reasons for hostility. He added: "How are you?"

"Not well, not well," answered Rock, half crossly. Sam stared at his father in amazement. Then he stared with displeasure to see why the Old Man was not well in that tone of voice.

Harding grudgingly reassured him: "You look all right."

"Ah!" said Rock, with a shrug of mingled recklessness and resignation. Then he went on: "I want you to sell some Virginia Central for me. But you must use discretion."

Harding nodded.

"Ten thousand shares," went on Rock. Sam was not sure he guessed why his father looked almost guiltily uneasy. He did not know that Rock knew what Harding would be sure to think.

It was a good order. Harding merely nodded again, and asked:

"What price?"

"Wait and see if it rallies. It closed at thirty-eight and a quarter to three-eighths last night. It ought to rally a point or a point and a half."

"Don't think so myself; but *you* ought to know."

"I don't. Sell it at thirty-nine and a half or better. If the market has not rallied that much by half after ten, sell the lot as well as you can." Rock hesitated. After a pause he continued with the air of a man who is taking chances but trusts his friend: "You'll have to borrow it. There's no harm in telling you, Harding, that it's a short sale."

Harding had suspected that it was short stock when Rock first spoke. But of course now he was certain it was not. He remembered that Dunlap had been quietly picking it up for some days, presumably for Sampson Rock. Very obviously Sampson Rock was now selling that same stock. Sampson Rock was taking a very fair loss on this operation and that was a sign the stock was going lower, which was a sign that whoever bought it from him would lose. This last nearly made Harding cheerful, and he said, briskly:

"Very well, Mr. Rock."

"See Valentine if you want a check now." Harding turned to go.

"Good-morning, Harding," said Rock, very politely.

"Good-morning," answered the unpopular man, without turning his head, and he left the room.

"Why all that, Dad?" asked Sam, impatiently. He was not aware that he was frowning.

"He has a branch office in Richmond and does considerable business for people there. The Virginia Central general offices are in Richmond."

"And people here will therefore assume that he is selling for the home crowd!" Sam said this quickly. Harding had gathered impressions from his father and his father again had not lied; and people would gather impressions from Harding's selling; and his father had not lied. In thinking, Rock probably would say, everything is in knowing how and what to think. Sam himself was beginning to think what his father would think.

Rock rang for Valentine.

"Valentine, take these orders: Virginia Central at the opening."

Valentine took a lead-pencil and a small pad from his pocket.

"Meighan & Cross; sell five thousand; to be distributed among ten men; let them use commission-houses. Wilkins, buy ten thousand himself, at the opening; let them clear it." This meant the transactions would be put through the clearing-house in the brokers' own names and nobody save themselves could tell who the principal was. Many principals would be suspected.—"That's all for the present."

"Why do you buy more than you sell, if you want the price to go down?" asked Sam.

"I want the price to rally a little, so that Harding's order will have the proper effect. It will look as if, had it not been for the mysterious and persistent selling—this time from Virginia—the stock would naturally have rallied. There will be more selling then, by Meighan & Cross's ten selling-brokers. Wilkins's ten thousand shares take care of my own five thousand, which I gave out merely to make the stock active, and will offset an additional five thousand shares of outside selling. I don't think there will be more outside selling than that at the opening, as most people will prefer to wait and see what tendency the stock will show. If it rallies they won't sell at all. There will be probably some buying by room-traders when they see Wilkins taking ten thousand shares. Dunlap has men with orders to buy one thousand shares every eighth of a point down—five men, each taking two hundred— so that it won't look as if anybody in particular were accumulating it on the decline. That stock will be salted away, though we'll lend it freely enough to the shorts if they want it. The stock must be kept active and I must get the price down without losing stock. The newspapers will talk about it, and as it goes down they will print nothing but the sad news they get from the people who speculate in it. In order to accumulate twenty thousand shares, I'll have to sell eighty thousand or one hundred thousand shares and buy one hundred thousand or one hundred and twenty thousand, because—"

"I see!" said Sam. It was always the same—the master of the ticker against the slaves of the ticker, the man who knew against the mob that guessed. He would wait—and study.

The ticker began to whir and click. Sam approached it.

"London prices," laughed his father, sympathetically, at the youthful impatience. Sam began to read the quotations. They meant something more than figures now

"V. C. is down three-quarters," he called out.

"H'm!" grunted his father, not unamiably.

"Good-morning!"—Dunlap entered with his chronic look of dissatisfaction. "Why, hello, Sam!" He shook hands and asked: "What are you doing here at this time of day? Trying to injure your health?"

"Good-morning, Dan. Look pleasant. I'm here to help you out." Dunlap was smiling now. Sampson Rock watched him. Everybody liked Sam. That would be a valuable asset, if Sam learned to be intelligently business-like.

"What orders have you to give Dan, Sam?" asked Rock.

Sam looked at his father's face. The expression there was half serious, half quizzical. He understood it was a test, playfully meant, perhaps, but the Old Man would not be displeased if it were taken seriously Sam's mind began to work, and, as he thought, the speed of his mental machinery quickened. The price was to go down. That was the main object of the campaign. But to-day, at first, it must go up a little, so that Harding's order might have the proper effect and wipe out the first rally and leave the market ripe for a further decline—unless, improbable as it now looked, unexpected opposition were met. There must be ways of doing this, and intelligent brokers to do it. He knew neither ways nor brokers, but Dunlap did, and Dunlap need not know that Sam did not know.

Sam looked at his father and said: "The newspapers say insiders must be selling because they know something about the condition of the property that the public doesn't."

His father nodded noncommittally.

Sam turned to Dunlap and said: "Dan, I don't know whether you have the brains to understand the mysteries of high finance." He shook his head dubiously; that was to gain time; he did it very well.

"When the stock sells at thirty-eight—you will let them have five thousand shares; at thirty-seven another five thousand; at thirty-six another five thousand; at thirty-five—"

"Hold on," laughed Sampson Rock.

"At thirty - five," continued Sam imperturbably, changing his plan on the instant, "you will buy as much as you can get without putting up the price above thirty-six and one-half." His father had checked him in time, and Sam had turned as though he had really meant to do so of his own accord. He felt a glow of mild excitement.

Dunlap smiled. "That's fine, Sam. You are a Napoleon of Finance."

"I am. But first, Daniel, make the stock open at least as high as thirty-nine and then get it up to thirty-nine and one-half."

"But if I get it up to thirty-nine and one-half how can I sell the five thousand at thirty-six and thirty-seven and thirty-eight and—"

"Daniel G., just get Virginia Central up to thirty-nine and a half and you can spare yourself the fatigue of thinking. We'll do the rest."

Rock laughed approvingly. High financial practices had not killed his sense of humor. Besides, the ticker was still; he had time to laugh.   Dunlap looked at him; then he looked at Sam.

"The orders go; see?" said Sam.

Dunlap turned to Rock.

"They go, Dan," laughed the Old Man.

"Dan, there are other brokers—intelligent brokers, looking for a job."   Sam pulled out his watch.

"Hey! what about the money?   You must put up some margin," said Dunlap, sternly.   To him Sam was still a boy.   Sam felt this; therefore he smiled and answered:

"Charge it to the Old Man."   He said it so naturally, as if from a lifetime's practice, that Rock and Dunlap laughed.

Sam was not laughing; he was thinking. With money many things were easy to do—good things and things not so good.   With still more money, a man could pick and choose what things to do.   Money that made more money, and money that did not have to make it, but always money—the ability to do—power. That was what money meant: power—for good or evil.

It was only a child playing with adult machinery. Nevertheless, money began to mean something to Sampson Rock, Jr.

IX

SAM'S gaze was fixed on the tape, waiting for the game to begin, for the "absorption" of Virginia Central to proceed. He looked at his father and wondered vaguely how little excited the general-in-chief was. Rock was composedly reading letters, throwing some into the waste-basket, scribbling memoranda or initials on others and laying them aside, writing undermost, on his desk.

A telephone rang. Rock looked up and said:

"Which bell was that, Sam?"

"I don't know," answered Sam. There were half a dozen on the long table. The bell rang again.

"This one," said Sam. It was the last, the farthest from him. It looked very new.

Sampson Rock took up the telephone.

"Hello! Yes.—What?—Don't be in too great a hurry. I think it ought to cross thirty-nine.—Yes.—What?—More selling than— Well, then, you'd better get it all off as early as possible.—I expect to see a lively opening; you might help.—Thanks."

To Sam's look of inquiry Rock said:

"That's Billy Graves, one of the specialists in V. C. He says he has more selling than buying orders on his books. He executes orders from the commission men who can't watch the stock all the time when their orders are away from the market. I've told him—"

"'IT OUGHT TO CROSS THIRTY-NINE'"

"Yes; but why did you tell him anything at all?" interrupted Sam.

"I suppose he makes pocket-money trading in the stock. He tells me what orders he has on his books. I can't pay him in money. But he takes the equivalent. And he won't tell anybody what I tell him." Rock finished reflectively: "The pocket-money would stop."

It sounded like bribery. But before Sam's indignation could become either deep or, indeed, concrete, his father went back to his letters, and, instead of hot disgust, there came to Sam the cold conviction that Sampson Rock was obliged to have information and reports from everybody; he needed a legion of scouts—willing hands, willing to serve and willing to be "crossed" with pieces of gold. It was all in the game; there was no blind chance about it. Knowledge was power, and power was money.

The ticker began its record. Sampson Rock took his station beside it, elbow to elbow with Sam. It printed sales and prices of a score of stocks, but no Virginia Central.

"How's this, Dad? No Virginia Central yet!" asked Sam.

"That's a good sign," answered Rock, not lifting his gaze from the tape. "It means such heavy transactions at the opening that the ticker reporters were too busy getting all the sales to telegraph it to the ticker-operator from the first one. It's very hard when there's a big crowd about the post, all buying and selling at the same time to— Ah!"

The ticker unexcitedly printed: "V. C. opened 8000 shares 38¼ to 39." Then after a few others: "V. C. 1000 39, 38⅞, 39—500. 39⅛-¼—300. ⅜."

"Ah!" echoed Sam.   He drew in his breath. "Harding will soon—"

"V. C. 1000 39¼–⅛; ¼; 39⅛."

The ticker then began to print quotations in Great Southern, Pennsylvania Central, New York Midland—stocks Sam was not interested in, but which, he could not help observing, his father studied as carefully as he did Virginia Central.

Presently Virginia Central came out once more.   "A thousand shares sold at 39, 500 at ⅛, 700 at ⅜; then 2500 at 39½, and 300 at ⅜, 200 at ¼, 100 at ⅜; then 5000 at 39½."

"Harding!" said Sam aloud, to himself.   He looked at his father for confirmation.

Rock nodded calmly.   And after a moment, his eyes still on the tape, he answered: "Probably."

The rest of the market was rising fractionally.   Then Virginia Central came out again—"1000 at 39½, 500 at 39⅝, then 2500 at 39½, 600 at ⅜, 1000 at ½, 1000 at ⅜, 1700 at ½, 1000 at ⅜, 1700 at ½."   It was plain that there was fighting between the buyers and the sellers.   That fractional fluctuation, down to three-eighths, up to one-half, thrice repeated, thrilled Sam.   Almost he saw two wrestlers locked in each other's embrace, swaying, swaying.   Presently it came: "1000 at ⅜, 4000 at ½, 500 at ⅜, 1000 at ¼, 1500 at ⅛, 5000 at 39!"   The downward pressure had overcome.   They were fighting—father's brokers and the rest of the world—and then Sam lost sight of the fight because the tape began to quote other stocks.   But he waited for the next glimpse, saying nothing, thinking of nothing but of the fight.   The ticker was talking to him; not as it talked to the mob, but as it talked to the few.

Valentine entered.   He said:

"Harding sold ten thousand Virginia Central at thirty-nine and a half."

"Very well," said Rock. "He's a very good broker, Sam. Wait a moment, Valentine." His eyes had left the tape.

"V. C. 1500 38⅞; 1000 39; 800 38⅞; 500 ¾; ⅞; ¾; ⅞; 39." The stock showed what financial writers sometimes called resiliency.

"Valentine, tell Harding to sell ten thousand more at the market and to report quickly." As Valentine closed the door Rock remarked to Sam: "He worked off the ten thousand shares easily. More pressure is needed. I won't tell him to sell the second ten thousand shares as low as possible, because he might do it too obviously. But I'll tell him to report quickly. He'll not stand on ceremony; but, at the same time, he will not sell as though he wanted to give away the stock—only to get rid of it as quickly as possible. You can't be too particular over details, Sam. If the stock is wanted by anybody else, this second lot of Harding's will show it plainly; but if it's as I think, it will help Dan. And Tuttle's peace of mind, too," he added, a trifle maliciously. "By three o'clock to-day he will have saved fifty thousand dollars." Sam frowned and said nothing. There were two sides to the Tuttle matter. He saw that; but the fight was on. There was no time to philosophize.

At that moment Virginia Central was the most active stock of all, and the activity attracted to the "post"—it was No. 11—the cream of the room-traders: the professional gamblers whose one request was not that a stock should be good or bad so that they might buy it or sell it intelligently, but that it might be active, so that they might make—or lose—their money quickly.

SAMPSON ROCK OF WALL STREET

From all over the big room they came running, their nostrils dilated quiveringly. as though they scented golden prey. For a moment their eager eyes looked at the latest price on the marker, and studied the faces of those who were offering it, or bidding for it, at the same time that their eager ears were listening to the voices of those who were selling it or buying it, taking in all the externals of the trading, receiving a thousand little impressions in a fraction of time, so that they too might buy or sell according to their logical, but unanalyzed, impulse. The relative ease with which, after selling at thirty-nine and five-eighths, the stock had gone down to below thirty-nine convinced them that the preponderance of heavy artillery was on the bear or downward side. Somebody was more anxious to dispose of the stock in bulk than anybody seemed to be to acquire it, wherefore they, too, sold, and the price yielded further. Dunlap waited a moment and then sold his first five thousand—at thirty-eight.

Immediately after, Harding came running into the crowd, to execute his second order. He heard a voice shout: "Seven - eighths for a thousand!"—and he pounced on the wildly waving hand that he thought belonged to the voice and shrieked "*Sold!*" There followed pandemonium—"*A hundred at eight!*" "*Any part of a thousand at eight!*" "*Three-quarters for two thousand!*" "*Seven - eighths for five hundred!*" To the man who bid thirty-seven and seven-eighths for five hundred, Harding sold the stock, so quickly that the man's lips had not yet closed after his shout when Harding was jotting down on a little pad the broker's name, the amount and the price. The traders who had been bidding seven-eighths for the stock divined that Harding had more to sell, divined it by their sixth—or broker's—sense and not by Harding's face, on which they could see only his chronic scowl. A commission man who was willing to pay seven-eighths for two hundred shares said so and was obliged by Harding. Then nobody bid more than thirty-seven and three-quarters. A few thousand sold at that price, Harding saying nothing, as though his authorized figure was seven-eighths. The intelligent mob, however, prudently reduced their bids to five-eighths. They did not desire to buy; they merely wished to "feel out" Harding.

Harding was a good broker. His order was to sell at the market or prevailing price. By pausing as he did, he could determine whether it was better to try to work off the balance of his order gradually, or to press it for sale. He perceived that the stock would sell much lower than thirty-seven and five-eighths if anybody gave it a push, and thought that if he didn't do it some one else would, which would mean that he would have to sell at another man's price. And so, when the others kept on bidding five-eighths, he filled their wants before they had time to change their minds, and, as the price declined, he followed, hot on their trail, selling all they were willing to take until it looked as if he were "slaughtering" his order, as if he did not care for his customers' bitter reproaches later—at thirty-seven and five-eighths, at one-half, at three-eighths, at a quarter, and the last hundred at thirty-seven and one-eighth. Those traders who had begun to sell short at thirty-eight thought there would be some buying orders at thirty-seven—it was a two and one-half points' decline and there ought to be a rally— so they began to cover at thirty-seven and one-eighth, to forestall the thirty-seven buyers. They did not know how much more was coming until Dunlap, his face convulsed as with mingled anger and terror, shrilly implored the crowd to buy five thousand from him at thirty-seven. The Harding selling, it was obvious to the Room, was for Richmond people, and Richmond people of all others should know when to sell Virginia Central. And now, on top of it, this selling by Dunlap! It meant that Old Man Rock was getting out in a hurry. That also was a "good" selling. Therefore, they followed the new lead and sold—thousands upon thousands, until, at thirty-six, Dunlap sold his second five thousand.

That clearly, unmistakably, meant that a bad break was coming—it was coming whether Rock was selling to be rid of stock he had and didn't want or whether he was selling stock he did not have but wished to buy cheaper. Then the astute mob went mad, visibly and audibly insane, and offered a car-load of Virginia Central stock at thirty-six, at thirty-five and one-half, and the commission-houses that had "stop-loss" orders at thirty-six also sold—real stock, theirs, not merely contracts—and the specialists sold and everybody sold—excepting Dunlap, his face no longer panic-stricken, but watchful. He hovered about the edge of the clamoring, swaying mob, whispering to trusty brokers to buy V. C.—one thousand shares to one, five hundred to another, twenty-five hundred to a third, any part of five thousand to a fourth, darting from one to the other, jotting down the amounts as he gave each order, until the traders realized that, if two score of people were frantically selling that particular stock, some party or parties unknown were taking the offerings in sufficient bulk to prevent it from crashing down to the zero abyss—somebody who looked like many bodies.

Thrice the bear battalions, scenting easy money, hurled themselves against that buying rampart. But it was like stabbing a ghost—there was no impact, no shock, no ominous trembling and tottering before the collapse, no sense of having touched a vital spot. They could not break through the "peg" at thirty-five. Therefore, it was time to retreat, to buy. But somebody was there before them, somebody who had taken all the stock that everybody was willing to sell below thirty-six, and in a jiffy the stock was back to thirty-six and one-half. At that price Dunlap stopped buying. The traders kept on; but they bought stock that came from belated commission-houses whose customers had been frightened but could not make up their minds fast enough to sell before, when the price was sliding downward so breathlessly, and were selling now, their fear having caught its second wind. Dunlap had sold fifteen thousand shares himself, Meighan & Cross five thousand, and Harding twenty thousand, forty thousand shares in all, in less than two hours. But Rock's brokers had bought fifty-one thousand shares, so that by the end of the day the great manipulator was the possessor of eleven thousand shares more than he had owned the day before; and Virginia Central closed at thirty-six and one-eighth. Moreover, it had become an active trading-stock.

Anybody with money enough can plunge, but it takes somebody with money and brains to plunge intelligently. To paint certain effects broadly with big blocks of stocks and to do miniatures are two different things. It is only the generals who do not count their dead that can handle big bodies of men as easily as regimental commanders handle their little companies. Whenever the Room thought of buying, Rock discouraged them by offering the entire capital stock at an eighth above the last quotation. They thereupon recognized the futility of playing for a further rally. Whenever they sought to drive it down, he bought all they sold, until, fearing a steel-trap, they desisted. He lost a little stock one moment, only to get it back very promptly the next. It made sentiment feverish, nervous; and out of the womb of uncertainty was born a multitude of rumors. Why? why? why?

The one thing obvious was that the South was selling that stock. *Why?* And who was buying it? *And why?* The financial reporters asked the brokers the same questions the brokers had been asking themselves. Some brokers had been watching Virginia Central all day. Who sold it? Probably the insiders, they said. Who bought it? Why, everybody and nobody in particular, scattering lots, covering by the traders, etc.

Not a soul suspected Rock. That was the art of it. He chose his time—and his men—well.

X

SAM, standing beside the ticker in his father's office, could not appreciate the subtler shadings of the manipulation, though he could read the turmoil and the frenzy of gamblers in the printed figures on the tape. But he realized that the objective point of the campaign had been brought nearer. His father ex plained to him why it was not possible to achieve all in one day; also, why the selling of the professionals, while helpful, was not sufficient. Those unattached soldiers of fortune, fighting under one flag to-day and another to-morrow, obeying no commands save when uttered by the desire of gain, advancing and retreating not as they were told but as they were compelled by superior force, thought only of fractions and to-day. They dealt in contracts, and Rock desired the actual stock. That would come later. Manipulation, a much-abused and much-misused word, meant advertising by means of the ticker. Some advertisements advised people to buy and to hold stocks; others urged the entire world to sell. But the effect of all advertising is cumulative. One entire page one .day and nothing more for a month was not as efficient as only a column every day; the same advertisement, the same advice —corroborated by the voice of the ticker, which does not lie.

It was when Harding had finished selling the second

ten thousand shares and the stock had begun to go down with some degree of earnestness—Sam almost could imagine the market as an invalid of a sudden sitting up very straight, the face livid and a hand pressed to the heart—that Gilmartin, of the Wall Street News Agency, came in.

"Good - morning, Mr. Rock." His pudgy, smooth-shaven face was wreathed in smiles. There was an air of assurance about him that he had not possessed before. He was almost jaunty—fearless for hours at a time. He had the confidence in himself and in a kindly disposed Providence that came from his success-ful short sales of Virginia Central—four thousand dollars in paper profits, which could be converted into real money by merely giving an order or two. The need to be any man's slave was gone; want wore no spurs. It showed on his face—the great, golden independence that glitters in the eyes of those men who are beyond vain wishes of food and raiment and a roof, and whose words, moreover, are considered precious by those people to whom those same words also carry their promise of gold.

To Gilmartin his fellow-men had grown suddenly lovable — servile, deferential, their pores exuding a pleasurable incense. For how can fellow - men listen but with their souls if in the silence following the master's speech they seem to hear the clink of coins— the coins themselves tripping on the very heels of the words?

Gilmartin's advice on Virginia Central had been a howling success, a delirium of wealth to those who had believed him and followed it, selling the stock short at forty-five. More grateful than Gilmartin was to the great Rock were these dozens of greed-stricken fellow-men to the great Gilmartin. For days they had hung on his words. They had nice paper profits; should they convert them into good hard cash? Turn an abstract pleasure into a concrete delight? Gilmartin, proudly nonchalant, profoundly sapient, had intelligently opined nay! The eyes of the golden prophet's followers had glistened and their lips had made haste to smile ingratiatingly. Gilmartin was the mouthpiece of Providence working benevolently through the medium of the ticker. Did not Gilmartin think the golden harvest yet ready for the gathering? Thrice-blessed Gilmartin—for the harvest then would be even greater. They had sown hopes and hundreds; they would reap joys and thousands. Gilmartin knew everything; their faces showed that. Gilmartin held in the hollow of his hand the destinies of the Virginia Central Railroad; *his* face showed that.

"I'll tell you when to cash in," he said, very graciously, very kindly, to those who asked. "I am not covering mine yet." That settled it. Gilmartin was not covering *his* shorts; whatever Gilmartin did, that was the wise thing to do, for he knew when; and what he did they would do—that and nothing else.

And so, because Gilmartin was to them even more than Rock was to Gilmartin, Gilmartin had taken to thinking well of Gilmartin. It showed in his walk, in the poise of his head, in his gestures, in his eyes, even in the glitter of his red hair, which was lustrous as with a varnish of gold. Only a merciful vestige of common-sense prevented complete auto-hypnotism and kept him from being Olympian in Rock's office now. His lungs might have filled to choking with the incense of his tip - following flatterers. But, as he spoke to Sampson Rock, the great and golden Gilmartin was not arrogant — he himself desired to know when to "cash in" his own paper profits. Of course, if Rock was ugly about it, Gilmartin could go away wrapped in the soothing dignity of what paper profits there were. He wished all the money he could get, but what money he already had on his deal gave him a sense of immunity that kept him from servility. He carried no chip on either shoulder. He was human; but it did not follow that he must be stupid.

"Good-morning, Gilmartin. How do you do this fine day?" said Rock, amiably, almost playfully. Harding's selling had begun to prevail.

"Finer even than the day," replied Gilmartin, delighted with the friendly reception.

"This is my son. Sam, Mr. Gilmartin is from the Wall Street News Agency."

"I am very glad to know you, Mr. Rock," said Gilmartin, boldly extending an honest hand. Sam took it and echoed the words of Gilmartin's joy.

"What's new, Gilmartin?" asked Rock.

"They're selling it for keeps," answered Gilmartin, very quickly, almost felicitatingly, as though he knew he was conveying news that must be particularly pleasing to Mr. Sampson Rock.

"Selling what?" asked Mr. Sampson Rock, very obviously not understanding Gilmartin's "it."

"Virginia Central, of course," said Gilmartin. Then he felt a slight pang of fear. Was it possible the Old Man was not the arch-villain of this rapturous break, and, therefore, not the right man to ask about the exact time to cover? The paper profit began to tremble, and with it Gilmartin's heart.

"Oh, *that!*" said Rock. "Oh yes! You are short of it, I think?" Rock laughed understandingly, sym-

138

pathetically—a kindly Rothschild listening to the ped-dler's tale of a good day in shoestrings and collar-but-tons. "Great thing, to see a stock go to pot—when you are short of it, eh? Well, what do you hear about it?"

"The Richmond crowd are selling it to beat the band. *They* know what's wrong, you bet!"

"What's wrong?" asked Rock, sharply

"Search *me.* I suspect it's the London—"

"Pshaw, that's old!"

"It may be old, but Colonel Robinson led every one to think he would get the money there. I guess he'll be busy explaining for the next ten years. He's great on explanations," finished Gilmartin, wishing to please Rock—in some vague way, half-instinct, he thought anti-Robinson talk would sound pleasantly to Rock's ears.

"He's a nice fellow," said Rock, mildly rebuking. Then he added, amicably, "*You* must have quite a profit, Gilmartin?"

"Do you think I ought to take it?" asked Gilmartin, diving into the opening like a flash. Rock's answer would mean either the caress of the gold itself, if he said to cash in, or the warm hope of still more to come by standing pat.

"I'm not running a kindergarten," answered Rock. "It's your funeral. But "—he hesitated—"a profit's a profit. No man ever got poor taking profits." That is as old as "good-morning," and as meaningless.

"Since you think I'd better take in my stock, I'll—" began Gilmartin, as he thought, adroitly.

"I haven't said a thing about it," interjected Rock, sharply. "It's your own lookout. You need a nurse. How do you know the Richmond crowd is selling?" If Rock had been angry he was over it by now.

"Why—because the selling is for them. Harding

has sold thirty or forty thousand shares." This was the usual exaggeration of the Street. "You don't think he'd dare sell that much stock short, do you?"

"You are asking me. Don't! It's a bad habit you have. Drop it! I am asking you."

"Well, I know it's for Richmond. He's got the accounts of all these Southern—"

"Oh, pshaw! You are guessing now."

"I am not," retorted Gilmartin, indignantly. "I know it's for the Richmond aggregation." He proceeded to lie to Rock, in self-defence, as he habitually lied to his tip-worshippers for his self-aggrandizement. "I'm very chummy with Harding's cashier. He as much as admitted to me a minute ago that it was for Richmond. He thinks the stock is going much lower." Perceiving that Rock seemed impressed, he went on, with the air of imparting vital information; "I myself think it's a receivership." His manner conveyed that his reasons for thinking so had twice the solidity of Gibraltar.

"That's nonsense," said Rock. "I've warned you several times to go easy with receivership talk. You'll be bankrupting the Bank of England, or me, some day. Why don't you call Robinson up on the long-distance telephone and ask him point-blank?"

"By jingo, that's just what I'll do at once!" He started to go out. At the door he turned and said to Rock, "I'll come back and tell you what he says before I publish it."

"I wish you would, my boy," said Rock.

He looked grateful, thought Gilmartin. It made Gilmartin feel the same way—towards luck—as he hurried away.

Sam looked at his father, frowning. He said:

"He thinks just as you thought they all would."

Rock nodded, said "Sheep!" and looked at the tape.

Across Sam's mind there fleeted a thought that his father had not lied; that he had very carefully not lied; that he had too carefully not lied. And yet the whole thing was a lie—and a cheap lie. The game interested him so much that this smallness annoyed him; it seemed unnecessary.

Rock rang for Valentine. The cashier came in, a bundle of papers in one hand.

"Valentine, telephone Walter Williams to come over. I'll see him here."

Five minutes later Walter Williams walked in.

"Ah, good-morning, Williams. Come here, Sam, and shake hands with Mr. Walter Williams, of whom you've heard me talk. My son."

Williams was not frowning. The ticker had smoothed out the chronic frown as a wrinkled handkerchief is smoothed by a sad-iron. He was looking particularly well pleased with Walter Williams and the rest of the misjudged world. He also glanced at the ticker—twice in six seconds—longingly. He was short of Virginia Central, the ticker was whirring away at a furious rate, and the days were sunshiny.

"Sam, Mr. Williams is the best railroad accountant in the world. If anything ever happens to me, and you are in doubt, consult him. He is a radical in some things, but if he doesn't bankrupt you in the first year you'll have a railroad."

All three laughed. It struck Walter Williams that he was one of the Rock family now. He and his friends were making money out of Virginia Central because they had followed Papa Rock's advice. He felt well-disposed towards the head of the family; he wished to make more money. There was no time like the present, for the favor of the great is like the sunshine, cheering and profitable—while it lasts. The rule about hay-making was a golden rule indeed.

"About the report, Williams—"

"Yes, sir." Almost you could have said Williams had cocked his ears, his face took on such a look of attentiveness. The Old Man had said that when he told Williams to send the report to London he would buy five thousand shares of Virginia Central for the accountant. That meant also that Walter Williams must take in his short line and warn his friends, that all might grow rich. A human being cock his ears? Rock's words would have made a stock-gambling fish cock what ought to have been its ears, expectantly.

"What about it, Mr. Rock? Time to—er—mail it?"

"N-no, not if you can wait a few days more, I think," Rock said, reflectively, exactly as though he were studying an abstract proposition instead of giving gambling instructions. "That is, if you can consistently do so, you had better wait a few days. Yes." He paused. Then he went on, still meditatively, as if he were not thinking of Walter Williams's short sales: "Virginia Central has several points to go before it touches bottom. Yes." He nodded. Williams also nodded. That was to show he had heard Rock. He had also heard the triumphant pæan of his soul. Every point meant five hundred dollars to him; there were several points more, Rock said—several times five hundred dollars. The money was walking fleetly towards Walter Williams, public accountant, railroad expert, honest man, forty years old—and not yet a millionaire! He mildly, gratefully felt that something was due Rock —a something not incompatible with the accountant's sense of duty towards his English employers. He therefore said:

"No time was specified. I can wait a few days." The delay was not criminal. His whole manner showed that he was doing nothing to hurt the London people. The London people might wonder that the stock had become so weak—but a coincidence was a coincidence.

"There's another thing," Rock went on. "Your report is too long. Were you told to make suggestions as to what might be done, or merely to report on the actual condition of the property?"

"Only on the physical and financial condition of the road. But I—"

"Yes," interrupted Rock, good-naturedly. "You could not help it. Look here, Sam," pointing towards Williams, "this Walter Williams right before you is one of the men I told you about, that I find so scarce, who always do ten times more than they are paid to do simply because they can't help doing their work thoroughly. I suppose the London syndicate paid him twenty or thirty thousand dollars—" He looked inquiringly at Walter Williams. Williams nodded confirmatively; in point of fact, he would only receive twenty-five hundred pounds for the report, but Mr. Sampson Rock knew what the job was really worth, even if the Englishmen did not — which showed that the soul-malaria of the ticker had filled Williams's system to the saturation-point—"for a piece of work worth much more. What does he do? He gives them a hundred thousand dollars, not because he loves them, nor out of charity, but because he couldn't help it. It's the artistic pride, Williams." Rock smiled good-naturedly; so did Mr. Williams. "It's in you. Now, I don't see why you should tell them what they ought to do. Just report how you found the road and its books. Why suggest that they ought to do anything more?"

Williams's face clouded. He was proud of his report; he thought it would do much for his reputation. Also, he knew why Sampson Rock did not like those suggestions about a deal with the Great Southern, the Roanoke's rival. But Sampson Rock, who had been watching Williams's face, went on, quickly:

"Pshaw, man, don't imagine I'm trying to get you to help *me*. I can take care of myself. Tell them what they paid you for. But don't *give* your brain; *sell* it to them."

Williams's soul rather than his head—it is the way the get-rich-quick microbe works—told him that Rock was right. He had shown in the report that the Virginia Central was in very poor shape. But he had demonstrated also how the same poor road could be reorganized, strengthened, made to pay; how by spending a million or two the value of the property would be doubled in four years, possibly in three, if the South grew as it surely must. It really was more than he had been asked to do.

"Report on what you were paid to report," repeated Rock, putting the accountant's thoughts into words. "Then, if you wish, write them that you can tell them how they can invest a few millions very profitably—and tell them what your terms are." Rock knew that would take time, and he wanted a clear track in Virginia—for a few weeks, only for a few weeks. But Williams must not get exaggerated notions of his own value; and Williams was intelligent—but not yet a millionaire.

"I don't know about that," began Williams, dubiously. Rock saw that he had won. He said to Sam:

"Williams and I are the only two people who saw the possibilities of this road. I saw them first. Yes, I did, Williams, because I've been at it for a year. But it took me months to find out what you did in days." Williams's frown relaxed, and Rock continued, earnestly, "Now, I think the Virginia Central belongs to the Roanoke—"

"Or to the Great Southern," Williams could not help interjecting.

"No, to the Roanoke, because I need the Roanoke, and the Roanoke needs the Virginia Central, and the Virginia Central needs Walter Williams, and Walter Williams needs Sampson Rock. There's your vicious circle, Williams. As to the report, do whatever you think best."

Williams did so; in a flash, he thought best to eliminate the valuable suggestions because they were too valuable to be given away gratis to people he was under no obligations to, as Rock had so truthfully and intelligently pointed out. Walter Williams needed Sampson Rock because Sampson Rock needed Walter Williams; nevertheless, Williams would try to *sell* his plan to the English. Rock was square and unselfish; Rock had objected only to Walter Williams not making money legitimately.

"I'll cut out the suggestions, Mr. Rock," said the accountant, decisively.

His mind worked quickly. He would write to the Englishmen about the plan he had evolved in connection with the Virginia Central, and if they paid well he would unfold it to their slow but enraptured gaze. He could go also to the Great Southern people—in case Rock was not grateful or intelligent. In either event Walter Williams would profit. Williams added, "But I give you fair warning, Mr. Rock, I'll offer to make a supplementary report on what ought to be done, if they pay for it."

"Of course, of course," acquiesced Rock, still concerned exclusively with Walter Williams's personal prosperity and aware of the leisureliness of English capitalists doing business by mail. "Get what the thing is worth. I'll remember my promise about the time to buy Virginia Central." To show Williams that he was kindly and withal not imbecile, he added: "You now stand two to one to win. Come and see me day after to-morrow, will you? About three o'clock."

"Yes. Good-morning, Mr. Rock. Good-morning, sir."

He went out. He stood two to one to win, when he bought Virginia Central.

"That man's honest, and yet—" Rock observed, thoughtfully because of the expression on Sam's face.

"Yes, alongside of Judas Iscariot. Would you really trust him, Dad?" Sam would not; his face showed it.

"With every cent I have in the world," said Sampson Rock, with decision, because he had seen Sam's look— "provided I had previously come to a full understanding with him and paid the price he asked, convincing him beforehand that he was not being cheated." He turned to the ticker.

Sam shook his head and said, with conviction:

"I can never learn to read character within hearing distance of the ticker." He felt like kicking Williams out of the room.

"Yes, you will, if you neglect none of the details. Never look for perfection. No good man is absolutely good, but neither is any man altogether bad. What will insure personal loyalty to you in a deal is not half so important to ascertain as what will make it easy for a man to keep his word. Provide for every contingency. Make your man realize that the time for gentlemen who are also cold-blooded business men to fix the price is at the very beginning, and whatever the other side may do later, when compelled to, you are willing to pay more now, without compulsion. You must implant some sustaining influence in the weak man's mind before you turn him loose to run across temptation. But men—study men, all men, all the time. If you learn to know men you need never suffer from insomnia nor bother about your bank account."

"That's all very well. But studying human nature isn't a case of learning Spanish in ten lessons."

"Study men as I have studied them. Form no preconceptions and never run away with the idea that the least important of them is altogether unimportant. Few men are exempt from doubts and vacillation, and many mistake stubbornness for courage. You will discover all this for yourself in time. But remember always that when you wish to convince a man you must not argue with yourself but with him; use the arguments which your knowledge of him tells you he himself would use, at night, in his bed, as he thought over the matter. If he thinks he is listening to his own wisdom, he is yours."

Sam shook his head. He didn't like tortuous ways. It was not by indirection that automobile races were won. His father frowned; then he laughed, for he misunderstood Sam's gesture. "It will come with time, Sammy; it 'll come with time. It is one of the acquired tastes, this thing of projecting yourself into another's personality. Never underestimate the importance of the unimportant, and do everything thoroughly, big or little. You need not cross the bridge till you come to it. But while you're crossing it examine it carefully, because you never can tell how heavy a wagon you may have to drive over it some dark night."

Sententious wisdom is usually impressive. Sam did not know what to answer, so he nodded his head twice, slowly.

The door opened and Valentine announced:

"Gilmartin says he must see you."

"Very well."

Gilmartin, still panting from his running, said:

"Mr. Rock, Colonel Robinson says Wall Street is full of liars—"

"That wasn't worth while telephoning at a dollar a minute, was it?"

Gilmartin grinned. "No. He was mad as blazes. He said the talk of a receivership is absurd, and that he'll make it hot for—"

"I told you that."

"And he says nobody in Richmond is selling." Gilmartin looked inquiringly, almost anxiously, at Rock.

Rock looked up from the ticker and said:

"What do you expect him to say—that he is selling his?"

"No," admitted Gilmartin. Of course the Robinson crowd were selling; and of course, since they were selling, the stock would go lower; and of course, if the stock went lower—

Gilmartin smiled happily; the paper profit was safe. Also, there would be more of it.

"Of course!" went on Gilmartin, talking to himself as much as to Rock. "It's a certainty Richmond was selling the stock to beat the band this morning."

"I don't know anything about the Richmond selling, but I can tell you this much—" Rock paused.

"Yes, sir?" murmured Gilmartin, trying to look concerned only with the news value of Rock's words—that is, looking attentive rather than over-eager.

"That whoever it was that sold all that stock this morning will sell more before you see the end of it."

"Do you think so, Mr. Rock?"

"Where are your eyes, man? Doesn't the tape say so as plainly as it ever said anything?"

"That's what I think, too," agreed Gilmartin, cockily. "I guess I'll stand pat." He looked at Rock's face to see if he approved the policy of masterly inactivity, whereby the paper profits were to grow. But Rock merely nodded from the ticker without looking up, and Gilmartin left, saying, "If I hear anything more, shall I come in and tell you?" It was an insidious invitation—to himself.

"Always glad to see you, Gilmartin, when I'm not too busy." But, as Rock's tone was not unkindly, the reporter did not mind the last words.

Gilmartin, on the way to his office, ran across two or three of his followers, who asked him the same question he had asked Rock. He replied with much decision: "Cover? *Now?* If you have cold feet, why, then, the best thing's to run. You've got a profit? Then take it; you won't go broke if you do that. But all *I* know is that whoever is selling that stock isn't done selling yet. I don't have to be told that. I can see it on the tape as plain as the nose on your face; and the tape's good enough for me. *I* am standing pat."

He could see the words sinking in and then spread in

waves over the listeners' faces. Of course, they too would stand pat; that was the part of wisdom; and because Gilmartin felt a sense of responsibility towards those of his fellow-men who had followed his tip and whose profits he expected to share, he wrote and sent out on his slips:

"*President Robinson, of the Virginia Central Railroad, stated exclusively to a representative of the Wall Street News Agency that neither himself nor any of his associates in the company has sold any of their holdings. He says he knows of absolutely no reason why anybody should sell Virginia Central stock at these prices. This, it will be remembered, is the same thing Colonel Robinson said some time ago, when the stock was ten dollars a share higher.*"

It was a scorpion paragraph—the sting was in the tail. Wilfully or unconsciously, the other financial writers would be influenced by it. The afternoon papers, lacking the time to verify it, would do their duty— that is, they would rewrite the item, leaving the sting for piquancy's sake. The morning newspaper men, having leisure, would elaborate — along Gilmartin's lines—and lengthen the venomous tip of the tail. Rock knew how financial news was gathered. That was why he allowed the red-headed writer to form impressions of his own. When one of his own acknowledged stocks was concerned, Rock impartially told all the financial editors precisely what he wished them to print. It was always "inside information"; nevertheless, it was always true. But the Virginia Central was not yet his. He was a rank outsider in the eyes of the Street, and he desired to remain so, for publication, a few weeks longer.

As Sampson Rock, Jr., left the office that day, the

sum total of his education was that Sampson Rock, Sr., was buying and selling Virginia Central in his manipulation, but always buying a little more than he sold—"accumulating it on the way down," the Street would have called it. The price would go lower—that was certain, though not as low as Sam in his ignorance had at first feared. It was plain to the veriest tyro that a way to make sure money was to buy Virginia Central stock at once, without waiting for the bottom. Not even his father knew when the bottom would be reached; but that the price would rise later was as certain as anything could be. Ten thousand shares at, say, thirty-three. At forty-three, that would mean $100,000; at fifty-three, $200,000; at sixty-three, $300,000. By the time Sampson Rock had fifty-five per cent. of the capital stock it would be sixty-three; possibly even seventy-three, which would mean $400,000 in cold cash. Money won by Sam, earned by Sam, to do with as he saw fit; to do good work with; to invest ungambler-like and make more; to give away to poor children, to cheer crippled paupers, to "stake" deserving "hard-luckers." Money. . . . Knowledge was power, and power was money; therefore knowledge was money. And money was ten thousand things, good and bad. Eliminating the bad, there remained the good, on which to use the money. .

Did the end ever justify the means? Was this abuse of his father's confidence excusable? Was it wrong to anticipate a gift? If his father made money, Sam could have it for the asking; but if Sam made it, he need not ask; he would have it to use as he saw fit. The Virginia Central stock that was being dislodged by Sampson Rock's ticker-blows came from speculators, from gamblers who had merely bought for a rise and knew the chances they took, men who therefore deserved to make money as much as a race-track loser deserves pity or a Monte Carlo victim merits charity. None of it came from people who depended on it for their bread and butter, for the stock paid no dividends, yielded no income to the holders.

Robinson's stock: that was another matter. The president of the Virginia Central Railroad, inefficient as a manager, might be a well-meaning, honest man who might deserve consideration. He might take years where Sampson Rock took weeks, but he need not be throttled to force him to hand the reins to a better driver. But any Virginia Central that was bought now would enable Sam to do the right thing at the right time. All the subtleties of the ticker game he might not understand. But the deal itself — to put that through, or help to put it through, in a straightforward, gentlemanly way, to make a good railroad out of a poor one and do it without self-reproach—that was worth doing. There were obstacles, unseen but existent. How to acquire the knowledge to see them and to overcome them?

He thought of nothing else; but the way was not clear. The fog was thick. But as a refrain to his thoughts ran this: Money is needed; without it all is vain—vain—*vain!*

XI

SAM found that the suggestion to spend the evening at the Collyers' was received without enthusiasm by his father, but he persevered.

"I told them I'd surely bring you with me. You'd better come along quietly. What do you want me to do—the stock-market from ten to three down-town and poker from ten to three up-town? Let's be chums and respectable instead."

Sampson Rock laughed good-naturedly. The nights at the club were getting to be a habit. Now that he had his son with him—and that the market was going his way—he would take a night off occasionally. He couldn't expect to be with Sam every night. He looked at his son and found it gave him pleasure.

"All right, partner," said Sampson Rock, happily. He drew in a deep breath. He felt physically stronger, as if the mere sight of his athletic boy had imparted the vigor of youth to his own body. He dismissed the ticker and the railroads from his mind without a pang. A vacation mood, restful, pleasurable, came over him. He joked as they walked to the Collyers' house, and his light-heartedness, after the strenuous hours down-town, made Sam feel the blood-kinship to the exclusion of all else.

Mrs. Collyer exceeded Sam's wildest expectations. In less than ten minutes she took Sampson Rock to the library, where in the business-like pigeonholes of a dainty Circassian-walnut desk, she kept her "papers." Because she had irrepressibly spoken about Roanoke, Sam's mind was turned to Virginia. As soon as he was left alone with Fanny he said:

"Fanny, I've started." He looked at her not precisely expecting plaudits, but conscious of distinct pleasure that hers was a serious mind and a sympathetic. It was fully ten seconds before he rejoiced also in the attractive coloring of her face and the warming charm of its smile.

"You have?" she repeated, a trifle vacantly. "Oh!" she exclaimed, understandingly, and it seemed as if her eyes had suddenly filled with light. "Have you, Sammy?"

She smiled at him with an effect of acknowledging their joint ownership of some precious thing. It subtly strengthened their intimacy, imparting to it an element of novelty that was more than delightful to Sam. She took the place of his Other Self and kept it. She was his confidante. She was his sole audience. He felt a sense of aloofness from the rest of the world, a widening gulf between him and friends, acquaintances, even his father.

All this did not seem sudden to him.

"Yes. I've had long talks with my father. I know what he is trying to accomplish. It is big work. There's more than money in it. He is going to get a railroad which is badly run and keeps back the development of Virginia. And he is going to bring it up to date and make it prosper." He was speaking judicially. She saw that.

"Of course," she assented. "I knew he did those things. I told you he did."

"Yes, you did," he said, a trifle impatiently, because his sobriety of speech and control of his feelings and doubts had been wasted on her. "But it's the way he gets it that I don't like."

"Yes, but you are no judge of what is—"

"The easiest and quickest way to it is all that he considers. Anybody who gets in his path is eliminated by the quickest method, squeal or no squeal. Now, what I'd like to do is to see if it all couldn't be done without maiming the mob. What's the use of lying?" He paused, frowning.

"Well?" she queried. She would hear the next chapter. So far the story lacked the flesh and bones of detail.

"Well," he answered, defensively, "I'm going to see how it can be done decently."

"Is that all?" She was a trifle disappointed. There was no thrill to the *dénouement*. A soul-tragedy is interesting enough, but she saw none in Sam's effort to learn railroading and other useful things. It nettled him so that he said, determinedly:

"No. I'm going to *do* it."

She looked doubtfully at him. His business education so far could not enable him to work wonders. Her look brought him a distinct feeling of annoyance. It rang in his voice:

"Do you think it's so easy to devise methods for doing these things? My dear, please remember that I'm going to do pioneer work. That's what it comes down to — doing business without lying when you want to get something. It has all the charm of novelty."

She smiled, as an old person might smile at a boy's original discovery of the truth of some axiom. She

said, with a kindliness that did not hide the consciousness of superior wisdom and age:

"Lots of people do that."

"They don't fill Wall Street to overflowing," he retorted.

"Well, how are you going to do it?" There was
visible interest in her question.

The way he would like to do it would be by going to
Colonel Robinson and saying, frankly: "Look here,
you can't run this railroad. Let us try and we'll pay
you more than the stock is worth in the open market."
But the childishness of this was on a par with the
desire to grasp the moon. However, perhaps Robinson
was an honest and truthful man with enough common-
sense to realize regretfully, but unashamed, his own
shortcomings as a modern railroad manager; in short,
he might be a man above personal vanity. But what
Sam said to her was: "I'm going down to Virginia
to look over the field. My father has so many irons
in the fire that he stays at home and he fights here.
He uses the ticker and a host of agents who are all
practical business men, all of them trained to see
nothing but the dollars and cents to be made.
They all make money by doing as he says, and
they think he is the greatest man that ever lived.
I'm going to see the railroad and the men who
now own it and find out whether they will sell
their stock at a fair price—more than my father
would pay. As it is, there will be money in the
deal; but it's the work itself and not the money that
interests me."

She did not know what she could intelligently say.
She told him, with a touch of sympathy rather close to
motherliness:

"It's the only way to get experience, and that's what you chiefly need."

"You don't think a man can do business intelligently and at the same time like a gentleman unless he is an old—" he began, challengingly.

"Of course he can. I've always assumed that. It's the only way you ought to do anything. What I don't like about you is your attitude. You've just caught a little glimpse, and it seems so hard and cruel that you imagine you stand in solitary grandeur on a pedestal of unusual honesty and cleverness. You must hustle—"

"The race is not always to the swiftest."

"Not always; not more than ninety-nine times out of a hundred."

"Well, just you watch the hundredth." He did not say it vaingloriously. But for all that, his confidence seemed boyish to her.

"Are you sure you won't upset any plan of Uncle—"

"No. I ought to help him, instead. And I'm going to study railroading—the practical end of it—and then I'll know what to do in New York. But—" He paused.

"Yes?"

"It's the money."

"Do you mean—"

"I mean, not having it, not having enough to be independent of everybody. Fanny, it isn't hard to make money. Anybody can make it."

"You've never made any."

"I never had to. If I merely wished to make money, I could make a heap now."

"How?"

"In the stock-market."

"You think so, Sammy." She smiled. "But gambling isn't—"

"Betting on a sure thing isn't gambling; it's plain business. There's half a million lying there waiting to be picked up." He saw the picking-up process; it was like falling off a log, for difficulty.

She smiled incredulously. It was too easy. Sam, who knew nothing about business, make money like that!

Her scepticism made him say, seriously:

"If I don't, my father will. It's part of the deal."

"Well, then, why don't you make it, and then do something—"

"There's this about it: I don't know whether it's fair to my father to take advantage of what he has told me in confidence. He told me because he wanted me to understand this deal from A to Z. Now, if I start on my own hook to make money out of his information—"

"Would it make him lose?" There was, in the tone of her query, a desire to hear a negative answer.

"No. It merely would reduce his profit by exactly as much as I made. I would simply be taking advantage of what he is doing. As a matter of fact, my dear girl, it's perfectly plain that whatever he makes out of this will come to me some day, in some shape or other, and—"

She frowned, and was about to speak when he went on, with a smile:

"I'm not thinking of poisoning him to inherit his money. What I mean is that I'm sure he'd never give me a half-million to experiment with—"

"Certainly not," she said, with conviction.

"But if I made it myself and I did what I wanted with it—"

"You'd lose it."

"Very well. What of it? Think of the educational value of the loss. It would be cheap if I found out there was no use in my trying to go to work."

"You'll have to do something, anyhow, whether it's what you like or not. You are so wise, Sammy, and so old that—"

He was not offended. He explained, very patiently.

"I think men in Wall Street are so accustomed to using certain tools that they never think there are others that can be used."

"It is barely possible that they are guided by experience," she suggested, with mild sarcasm.

"Why, my dear girl, whenever my father wants men to guess the wrong thing, he merely tells them the truth."

"Then he can't be the monster you—"

"It isn't monstrous to tell the truth with intent to deceive; but what I object to is the callousness to the suffering of the people who can't get the results others think they should."

"Sam, I want you to do something because it's a man's duty to do it, and it should be a pleasure. But indiscriminate charity—"

"Should begin at home. I know all that. I read it in a copy-book once. But I want to do something that won't make me think of myself as a money-maker so much as a—well, I want to do useful work. I must have money to do it with, not my father's money, but my own, so that if I lose it I've only myself to blame. If I buy this stock, that I know he is going to put up—"

"Don't tell mother what it is. If Uncle Sampson won't lose anything by it and you don't interfere with his plans, I think you ought to. You've got your mind in a rut, and anything that will take it out will be good for you. It isn't the money, anyhow; it's doing something. If you give me more particulars, I might be able to judge better."

"The case is as I put it to you. I think, after it was all over and I told him what I had done, he'd laugh. The particulars wouldn't help you to judge."

As he said this, she pouted—at the thought of the unshared secret, he supposed. Instantly, business thoughts were driven out of his mind and he saw her, not as the inspiration, but as the only companion of his life. She was good to look upon—her eyes, her cheeks, the chin, the throat. . . . She exhaled good health and a sympathy so distinctly personal, an interest in him so obviously keen, that it was as though a subtle perfume had been wafted from her to him. Curious ideas began to intrude, thoughts of divers hues and of varying degrees of incoherency. He felt that without her he was desperately alone; with her near by, there were many personalities within him, all of them voluble. . . . Her perfect lips were red and the rounded throat was white; and the eyes like luminous sapphires said wonderful things, and he felt that his eyes replied. She became less a thing of flesh and blood than a radiant vision, merely to look at whom made the blood flow faster and warmer and the thoughts come more quickly, something of the effect of champagne. Within him it was as though his very soul was in a tremor.

"Fanny" — he tried to smile easily as he spoke— "I'm mighty glad I went away. It's only now that I am beginning to realize how much you mean to me."

"How much is that?" She was unconscious of her own divine metamorphosis before him.

"Don't do it again, Fanny! . . . I'm afraid of boring

you, talking of myself, and there are so many things I want to talk over with you that I can't say to anybody else. I'd feel so lonesome, if I didn't have you to talk to, that I guess I'd—" He ceased to talk. He was thinking of so many things he was not saying that it seemed useless to continue to make sounds.

"Well, dear boy," she said, encouragingly, "I can stand it. You know I'll listen with interest. I expect you to tell me." She looked at him. Whatever it was she saw made her look away uneasily.

"I'd like to—ah—talk to you forever." He spoke almost through his clenched teeth. Then there came to him the vision of their past life and the relationship as of brother and sister. It had a disagreeable effect.

"Forever is a long time." She spoke lightly. She did not look at him, but he looked at her—at a beautiful woman, young, and very near to a young and healthy man. He said:

"It would seem a minute to me."

"Oh, bosh!" She laughed, frankly. "Do you love to talk that much?"

"Did it ever occur to you that I—"

"No, it never did. And you mustn't be silly," she interjected quickly. Also she looked at him with a stern displeasure.

"Well, you have no business to look so—" He paused. The sight of her intoxicated him. He saw her face like a flower seen through a mist. There came to him a faint odor as of violets, so delicately evanescent that only at times he breathed it. . . . He could not live without Fanny—this girl who was the only living being before whom he felt absolutely no sense of reticence. The book of his soul gladly opened itself before her eyes, for her to read everything. This feeling rose in him like a surge.

"Be serious, Sam," she said, rebukingly.

"Serious?" he echoed, conscious of an effort to control his voice. "What can be more serious than—than what you will help me to do? Nothing is more serious."

"Less talk and more work—" she began, admonitorily.

"I'll work hard enough," he said, "if it will please you—"

"Of course, it will please me to see you do something else than trying for automobile records."

"That's why I'll work." Sincerity rang in his voice.

"No, Sam," she said, with much positiveness, "you'll work because it is your duty to—"

"Oh yes," he nodded twice, quickly, "to do something to make you feel proud of me."

"To make us all feel proud of you, especially your father."

She spoke as a loving mother to a headstrong youngster.

"My father does not need me, but I need you."

"What ails you, child?" she asked, in mock alarm. There was a shadow of uneasiness in her eyes. It was the worst question she could have asked him. There was but one truthful answer.

"*You!* I can't help it, Fanny," he said, very determinedly, looking at her thirstily, hungrily, his very soul in his eager eyes. "Ever since I came back I've realized it, and you might as well know it now as ever. Has it ever occurred to you that I—that I—" He floundered helplessly. She arose and said:

"What occurs to me is that it is positive cruelty to let mamma talk Uncle Sampson to death."

"Let her be," he retorted, fiercely. The more he looked at Fanny, the more he wanted her, all of her, for himself exclusively. To be alone with her on a desert island, that was heaven. He was certain of it. "Sit down and let me tell you something. You are the only soul in this world that means anything to me, and you know it. And I want you to be the only one as long as I live. Oh, my dear, I've known you all my life, and only now, when I want to become something in this world, only now I realize how much you mean to me."

"Oh, Sammy," she said, tearfully, "let me—" She felt like an older sister before a sophomore brother who has just come home—at 2.30 A.M.—and she has opened the door for him because he tried for an hour and found the key-hole elusive.

"No," he said, "you must help me, and the only way is by marrying me. Then I'll have you to myself. Why not? I've always loved you, all my life, and—"

"Not—not in that way." Her distress was evident.

"Dear girl, we were too young. It surprises you now, but you'll understand it if—if—you'll think a little and see how natural it is and how nice it is that it's natural. Listen: I'm going—"

A sweetheart was not before her. It was only Sam, her brother. And yet she was conscious that her life habit of him was gone, plucked roots and all. Sam couldn't love her—that way—and yet Sam said he did, and he looked as if he did, and it might be that he really did, and, therefore, Sam was changing before her very eyes. Already it was a different Sam who stood there. . She took more interest in Sam than in any other man, having no brothers. He always had belonged to her; there existed between them perfect frankness. He could never be as a stranger, but she could not see him in this new character. . . . Not yet.

Out of the tangled odds and ends of thoughts that seethed in her disturbed mind, one resolve rose above everything else: Sam must become a man, a useful man, a man the world would respect; and she must help him. It was her duty to him and to herself; she saw that very clearly. The readjustment of their relations, the final decision as to what they were to be to each other during the life that was before them—that could wait. Let him first become a man with definite ideals and an object in life, a man with a career. In the mean time his hopes could wait. Being a woman, she laid them on the top shelf of her soul-cupboard and locked the door.

The face she turned to him was calm and resolute. It was evident to him that she took him seriously. This brought with it hopes—and fears.

"Sam," she said to him, a trifle sternly. "Of course, I'm very sorry to hear you talk like this."

"You don't under—"

"It isn't a matter of what I do or don't. You haven't any right to—even think of such things."

"Certainly, I have. How can I help—"

"If you were not a boy, you would have helped—"

"My dear, I'm twenty-five, and I know I love—"

"Don't talk of love to me," she said, with a sort of fierce impatience. "Do you think I'm a silly little—"

"No; I know you are the—"

"Let *me* speak. You've been away two years—"

"Wasted, utterly wasted!"

She checked his speech with a frown. "It's about time you began—"

"It is," he agreed, promptly. "Therefore, I—"

"You'd better acquire common-sense."

"The most sensible thing I ever did in my life was—"

"You don't know your own mind two minutes in succession."

"I know that I—" he began, eagerly, anxious to prove her in error.

"You don't," she contradicted, vehemently. In her anger she seemed to him a goddess whose every look and every gesture was an inspiration to something noble—for her sake, for her sake alone. So thinking, he said:

"I'll make you love me. I'll—"

"Do it." In her challenge he did not—as she intended he should—detect the command to do something to deserve her, to compel her to love him by sheer force of great deeds. Nevertheless, he rose impetuously. She pointed to his chair so resolutely that he obeyed her rigid finger: he sat down.

"What right have you to ask anybody to marry you? What have you ever done to—"

"I've never asked anybody. It's only now that I've asked you."

"Don't do it again, Sam, or I'll never—"

"Yes, you will," he did not let her finish her threat. "You will, because—"

"First show that you have brains enough to—"

"Fanny," eagerly, "if I do, if I do, will you—" He rose. He saw himself accomplishing great things—all for the love of her, for her sake alone.

"Don't think of me at all. Sit down here and—"

"No, I won't." He took a step towards her. "Fanny, don't you care a little bit for me?"

"No."

"Is there somebody—"

"No; there's nobody. You know I'm fond of you and I don't want you to—"

"How can I help it?" he said, with a touch of ex-asperation. "How can I? I'm only human. I've always loved you, ever since I was a kid. Don't you remember that time we were engaged to be married and—"

"No, I don't," she said, quickly. "And besides, I was only seven and you were twelve. And you don't act one day older now."

"I'd like to act as I did then " His voice grew husky for the dryness of his throat "I—there is nothing I wouldn't do—if—if only you—" He was approaching her. His eyes were moist and he breathed quickly. He loved her—this man who was Sam and wasn't Sam—and she saw it. She put up her arm instinctively, as if to ward off a blow

"You—frighten me, Sam," she said, tremulously.

"Forgive me, dear girl," he said, quickly. He walk-ed back to his chair and sat down. He drew in a deep breath and avoided looking at her. At length he said, very quietly:

"Listen, dear. I do love you, very, very much. It was only when I began to think seriously of my life, and I looked years and years ahead, that I realized how much I needed you. I can't tell you how much that is. It—it rather overwhelms me when I think of it. I can't bear the thought that perhaps I may not have you always with me and tell you everything, and work for you and—and have you help me to make good. This seems sudden to you, but it really isn't. I know you'll never love me as much as I love you. It will come harder to you to love me like that. But I wouldn't marry you if you only loved me like a brother. Believe me, Fanny, I am going to do something, to give me the right to ask you. I'll work for you, and if, after all, you—you can't, why, I'll keep on loving you just the same. And," he finished in a low voice, "I won't frighten you again. Forgive me, dear. But if you only knew—"

"That's—that's—" she stammered. Her eyes were full of tears. Her soul was thrilled less by his words than by his voice and his attitude. A great tenderness came over her and with it a wish to protect him, motherwise. She said: "That's the way I like to hear you talk. But, oh, Sammy, why did you—"

"I always did," he said, very quietly; "but I didn't know it."

She waited for him to say more, but he was silent.

"But, Sam, now you must do something to show you are not merely your father's son. Don't you know? I was so encouraged by what you said—"

"About going to Virginia? I'm going. I'm going to make money and I'm going to do something useful. I'm going to earn the right to ask you to love me." He would make money in the stock-market, to have it in order to do better things. And then he would come back to Fanny

"And you won't talk—about other things until you—"

"Until I make good? I promise. But if I do—"

"If you do what, Sam?" asked Mrs. Collyer, benignantly, from the door. "Put up Roanoke?"

"Yes," said Sam.

"I wish you'd lose no time," said Mrs. Collyer, gayly. Sampson Rock had encouraged her to overflowing.

"I will, Aunt Marie. I'm now working as head

office-boy, but I'll keep an eye on the market. What will you give me if I make Roanoke sell at par?"

"Something very nice," smiled Mrs. Collyer. She began to count.

"You are on! You heard her, Fanny?"

"Make good first; then talk about it," she answered, lightly—for effect on the others. She did not wish them to know what had happened.

"Cash on delivery," said Mrs. Collyer with a technical look, thinking it was a Wall Street expression.

"That's the best way to do business, after all," said Sam with decision. "You were right, Fanny."

XII

SAM had been studying Darrell from memory during the last two days, recalling their joint experiences and their talks, analyzing his impressions of the Denver man. Little things to which he had attached no importance at the time came back to him, and became illuminative clews to Darrell's character, until he was certain that Darrell was an intelligent chap, who had been in deals and knew people and business, and, moreover, was a man to be trusted. They had been very friendly, taking to each other from the first. They had not called one another by their first names, but they were, he felt, intimate enough to do it in the future. Sam had put up Darrell at the club, but had seen him only once since their arrival in New York. Now that he was about to earn Fanny's love, he had no time to lose. The first thing he did in the morning was to write Darrell to dine with him.

That evening, as they sat over their cocktails at the club, Sam asked, abruptly: "I say, Darrell, how are you fixed financially?"

The Westerner looked slightly surprised—the change of conversational topics had been sudden. He was a tall, square-shouldered, athletic-looking fellow of forty, whose face told of an out-door life and who wore good clothes well. His hair was very fair and his eyes were blue and alert, calmly confident, the eyes of a man who was quick-witted but not excitable. There was that about him which conveyed an impression of habitual self-control over features and feelings without any tinge of cold-bloodedness. It required little discernment to know that he probably meant what he said, just as it did not take a very vivid imagination to feel that he would be a good man to have with you in a fight against odds. He had also the Western manner—life was too short to beat about the bush all the time.

"How do you mean? I've saved something out of the wreck. But alongside of the steel millionaires I'm in the thirty-cent class."

"You told me about some of your deals. I've got a big one myself now." Sam spoke with a sort of restrained eagerness.

"I could scrape up a few cents," smiled Darrell. "What's the deal, Colonel?"

"You know my father does things in the stock-market now and then."

"So I've heard," drawled Darrell.

Sam looked steadily at Darrell and said: "See here, Darrell, I'm going to tell you something, and I'm going to tell it to you because I like you, and because I think you have brains and experience, and I need somebody that has more of those things than I. Because I happen to be Sampson Rock's son, I've found ways of making money. I'll wait until that sinks in."

"Rock," said Darrell, "there's no need to spar for an opening. Life is too short. I like you, too, and if I had you out West with me a year, by jinks, I'd make a—" He paused.

"A man of me; I know. That's the West," laughed Sam. "Well, I've got to do the making myself, right here and now. But you can help me. Must you go West very soon?"

"No, I don't have to; but I've loafed long enough. There is always something to do in my line. I'm considering several things. But they could wait."

"I'll begin," said Sam, "by calling you Jack. My name is Sam."

Darrell extended his hand and Sam shook it cordially. The handshake cemented their friendship. Sam felt instinctively that Darrell thought the same; which was true enough.

"My father," said Sam, now calm and confident, "is buying the control of a certain railroad. But first let me go back and tell you this: He and I had some words the other day." Darrell frowned. Sam held up a warning finger—against hasty judgments—and went on: "He thought it was time I did something—work of some kind. I suggested going into some mining deals with you, like those we had talked over on the steamer, but he wanted me to go into his own business. I didn't like it, because it didn't seem a square sort of a game. You see, my father deals in pretty big things."

"From what I hear, he is a great man. I don't mind telling you that I've inquired about him. I've a friend in Wall Street, and he says your father's the ablest and the clearest-headed man of all the big guns. By the way, my friend thinks that Roanoke is going to sell at par one of these days and stay there. He wanted me to buy some." He looked inquiringly at Sam. But Sam said:

"What I want to do is to go after the same thing the Old Man wants and get it without having to lie about it " Sam hesitated. Then, being full of the one subject, he blurted: "The fact is, my girl won't have me unless I stop being my father's son."

Darrell laughed. Sam went on earnestly:

"She's the only girl I ever met who wanted me to work."

"She's a brick," said Darrell, with conviction "I hope she's poor and—"

"She's not very rich; but she is a brick just the same " Sam was grateful to Darrell and grateful to Fanny. "Now, I know how I can make money. But I want also to do something which my father says he can't do. I don't know how I'll do it, but I've got to do it."

"What is it?"

"Here's my trouble: I don't want my father to know what I'm doing. That makes it necessary for me to get my money from somebody else."

"How much will you need?" asked Darrell, curiously.

"I don't know yet. Of course, I've some money of my own. I have a million in government bonds that my mother left me, and I own the house we live in. It was hers. She left everything to me. The house is worth about two hundred and fifty thousand dollars, I guess. It's appraised for nearly that. The bonds are 'way above par, so that, all told, I've got about a million and a half."

"And you need more?" Darrell's eyes gleamed admiringly. This boy was either a chip of the old block or an ass. The alternative that the boy's inexperience suggested made the Westerner watch Sam closely as he went on:

"Maybe, before I'm done; but not now. I know if I asked my father for the bonds, or if I mortgaged the house, he'd ask questions. I can't calmly tell him I'm

going to take advantage of all he's told me in his wild
desire to teach me his business.   Therefore, I've got to
borrow the money.   I'm good for it, whether I win out
or not.   But this is safe.   I know what is going on and
what is going to happen.   I'll tell you, but you must
not tell—"

"Rock, you can tell me or not as you see fit.   But
put this in your pipe, whatever you tell me goes no
further."   He meant it.   Sam saw that.

"The first thing to do is to get a broker we can trust.
As Sampson Rock's son, I can't very well look for one.
But you can.   He must be a reliable man.   The account may have to stand in your name.   It's a lot to
ask, but think about it.   Take your time and—"

"I've got the man," interrupted Darrell.   "He's a
second cousin of mine, Albert Sydney, of Sydney & Co.
He's the man I asked about your father."

"He'd suspect the governor—"

"He doesn't know your father personally."

"Sure?"

"Absolutely.   I trade through him myself, at times.
He's our man, I tell you.   You can ask about him."

"Very well.   Now, how to raise the money?   I've
got the bonds, but I can't put them up as collateral,
and—"

"No; you can't.   But if you own your own house,
why not take out a mortgage for one hundred or one
hundred and fifty thousand dollars and don't have it
recorded?"

"Who'll lend me that?"

"I will," answered Darrell.   He hesitated.   Then
he said: "Oh, hang it, you're all right!"   Sam could
see that the hesitation was not from distrust, but because of a man's shyness about confessing affection.

Sam rose, and Darrell did likewise, each extending the right hand. Then Darrell laughed: "Say, we'll talk about the deal later. Tell me about the girl. Do you really and truly—"

"I really and truly," said Sam. He pictured to himself Fanny exhorting him to become "something." He added, with profound conviction, "I've got to make good."

"And I'll make it my business to see that you do. What a lucky dog you are, Rock!"

"Call me Sam. Yes; I'm the hero of the novel. I never thought such things happened in real life—"

"Is she light or dark?"

"Light. Now, if I begin by buying five thousand shares—"

"Holy Moses! What a lucky cuss!" Darrell sighed. He was a mining-engineer, always on the go, as an expert going to Mexico, to Oregon, to Bolivia, to Alaska; as a promoter to London or to New York; never remaining in one place longer than three months; a man with a princely income and a victim of his own ability, that made his friends implore him to examine mines and join syndicates; and all the time frantic at the mere thought of a home and a wife who called him "Jack, dear"; imagining, with despairing raptures, children calling him "Dad"; afraid of all women, not because of *gaucherie*, but because he feared not to find Her among them; and yet ready, eager, to believe the one he was talking to was She. He had thought about Her so long that She lived, somewhere. Beyond question, Sam's girl was the one he had been looking for these many years. Darrell was in love with love, and he reverenced marriage as an institution, because it represented the joys he had felt in his waking dreams.

His heaven was domesticity. He shook his head. Then he asked, eagerly:

"Say, Sam, has she a sister?" Sam's girl's sister was beyond the shadow of a doubt the girl he sought. He was all but ready to propose instant marriage by telephone, sight unseen.

"No," answered Sam, carelessly. "Why?"

"Oh, nothing." Darrell's face lost its eager look. He frowned pensively.

At dinner Sam unfolded his plans.

"I'm going to buy a few thousand shares of the railroad stock my father's after. That's why I am so careful about the broker. The slightest suspicion—"

"My boy, I appreciate your confidence in me, but I tell you that you are taking bigger chances than you ought."

"If I've made a mistake in trusting you, what's the use of doing business with anybody?"

"That's all right, but—"

"I'm betting on you and on your judgment of your broker. That little purchase of stock is to make enough money to pay for something else. If my father gets the road, he'll improve it. There are valuable coal and iron properties along the line that as soon as there are good railroad facilities—"

Darrell hastily swallowed an oyster, and interjected:

"I see! Next!" In the interruption Sam perceived Darrell's intelligent approval. This gave him confidence, and he was grateful to his friend.

"Well, I want you to see them with me so you can tell me how much I can pay for them. If I don't buy them, my father will. He's planned to form a big development company, with the bonds guaranteed by the railroad—"

"I'm on. Go ahead."

"If you say buy, I buy. See? I assume your knowledge of all kinds of mines is—"

"Absolutely."

"On that deal, if you wish, we share and share alike. Will you—"

"With both feet, Sammy boy, unless the owners are wise and ask fancy prices."

"I'm less interested in making big profits right away than in making a real success of the work. What's the use of my working just to make money? I'd like to see something grow out of this—a great big company, employing thousands of men." He looked at Darrell steadily.

"That's all right," said Darrell, soothingly. "You are young."

"That's it. I have plenty of time, and if the work is big—"

"The bigger the work, the bigger the profit," said Darrell, sententiously. Sam felt that the Westerner did not entirely understand him. He explained, a trifle deprecatingly:

"I don't wish to think of the money end of this deal."

"I'll save you the brain-fatigue at that end. You take the other."

"Darrell," said Sam, determinedly, "I mean it when I say that I'm not interested in making money so much as in playing the game fairly and squarely and—"

"Look here, son, don't be an ass. You can help it if you really try. You talk like a New England conscience in a story-book. Nobody needs to do dirty work for money. I never have, and I don't expect I ever will. I wouldn't lie even to a woman. But I'm not going to see you panhandled by any old hobo that strolls along, and I'm not going to let you pay any idiotic price for anything you may think you ought to have. You are merely playing at business now. It's a novelty to you and you are a little excited about it. What I don't understand is why you don't let your father do the instructing."

"He tells me what he wants and I see how he is going to get it. He doesn't steal or lie with his own lips. But he works through the ticker. Do you know what that means?"

"Oh yes, I know. It takes a heap of brains to do it well, and your father's one of the tiptoppers. See here, if you want me to go into this or any other deal with you, I'm with you to the limit. If you don't, and you just wish me to go along as your private secretary and professor of wisdom-toothing, I'm your huckleberry, and I'll pay my own board-bills besides. But, in the name of common-sense, don't get too blooming virtuous so early in the game! Feelings hurt?"

"Not a bit," laughed Sam. "I talk like an ass. What I really wanted to say was that I want to do a certain thing without all this cold-blooded—"

"You don't know any better. It's a common disease at your age. Wait until you stack up good and hard against the great American Hog and his brother, Fido-In-The-Oat-Bin, as well as a few millions of the Get-Rich-Quick family "

"That's what he says."

"Who?"

"My father."

"He's right."

"That's all very well. But you don't have to be

an ass to keep from certain forms of persuasion, do you?"

"My boy, every day I get dozens of letters from people who want to sell me mines, every one of them a bonanza that will make the Comstock Lode look like a cobble-stone. Some of them are sincere but ignorant, and don't know their mines are little one-man affairs. Other mines are too far from a railroad—or no timber— or something that makes them impracticable. But their owners only think of the ore they know they have. Again, others know what they've got and what it'll cost to get the stuff out, and they are willing you should make a nice thing out of your investment, something like two per cent. a century, if there are no accidents. A man who buys property of any kind runs all sorts of chances. You've got to figure on them and you mustn't cheat yourself. This game of freeze-out that you hear about so much is oftener brought on by the hoggishness of the man who is really yearning for the cold-storage. We'll go down and take a look at the coal and iron lands. Then I'll let you deliver a few more Fourth of Julys. See?"

"That's what I wish to do."

"First I'll have a mortgage drawn up, or you'll do so—"

"No, you," said Sam.

"All right; that's in case you croak. And I'll lend you a hundred and fifty or two hundred thousand dollars."

"Can you spare as much as that?"

"Yes; and my New England conscience does not vociferously demand that you should tell me the name of the stock you are going to buy."

"It's—" began Sam, impetuously. He felt both

gratitude for such confidence and pleasure that such a man lived. Darrell interrupted him, quickly:

"Don't. It wouldn't be fair to your dad. We'll make him help us on the coal proposition."

"Yes. But I also want to see if I can't get a big block of the railroad stock held by the people who are now in control that he doesn't think can be bought. The reason he thinks so is that he says their price is too high."

"You'd better let him be the judge."

"Why, man alive, I know what he is going to sell that stock for, after he gets it. I know what can be done with the old railroad if money is spent on it—"

"How do you know? Since when have you become a railroad expert?"

"I saw the report of a man my father says is the best in the country."

"Get a copy of it."

"I will. And—"

"Yes, and read it slowly fifty times, forward and backward. But, honest Injun, boy, if I were you I'd be content to play second fiddle to father for as many years as God spares his life. Leave the railroad alone and stick to the coal and iron proposition. All you need learn is how to care for your own when you will no longer have the Old Man behind you."

"No; I want to do more than that," said Sam, quietly. "I'm an ass now. But I know it. I want to learn something I don't know." He had big work to do. It was worth while to earn Fanny. That thought of *earning* her—old as love and common as misery—pleased him mightily.

"Jack," he finished, quietly, "we must not lose any time. Come over and have luncheon with me to-morrow, will you? I'll be at the office all day. I want you to meet my father."

"I'll do even more than that to oblige a friend in distress. We'll make a man of you yet. Now, let's go to the theatre and listen to other voices than our own, for a change."

XIII

SAMPSON ROCK'S programme, as Sam called it, was changed on the next day. He bought stock all around the room—that is, he bought back the various stocks he had previously sold in order to depress Virginia Central artistically and bought a little more. The market had begun to show signs of demoralization here and there. All the professionals were selling too confidently, because the truthful tape hinted at far worse things to come. It was at the very moment when it looked to them as if the safest thing in the world was to sell stocks short that he began to buy. In so doing he was in a highly profitable minority. After he had very quietly, almost meekly and quite unnoticed, bought more than he had sold, he bid for more—his brokers did—boldly, confidently, ostentatiously. The sapient sellers hesitated. He bought more. The sellers began to fear they had made a mistake. He bought still more. The market became active and strong, prices rising. Wherever the short interest was heavy, there was a scramble. Virginia Central rose like the others, reluctantly at first, then with a quick little jump to thirty-nine, at which price Rock sold to the traders what, without having, they had previously sold at thirty-seven and thirty-six. He explained to Sam—who once more realized that the game could not be learned in one day—that his opera-

181

SAMPSON ROCK OF WALL STREET

tions had created too numerous a following and that, to prevent it from hindering, it must be shaken out. After a day or two of ascending prices, when everybody would be ready to swear that prices must inevitably go very much higher—for the tape said so—he would begin to sell stocks in bulk once more. To keep people guessing facilitated the good work.

Sam understood why patience was profitable and also how it could be borne philosophically. He took advantage of the resting spell to broach the subject of a trip to Virginia to go over the Roanoke and the Virginia Central. And also he would like to look at the Austin furnaces. "Darrell is a great mining expert and he is a mighty nice fellow. I'd like to take him with me. I've told him I want to study the coal and iron mines of central Virginia. As a matter of fact, I do."

"Tired of that, Sam?"—Sampson Rock pointed to the ticker. He did not even ask Sam if he had been indiscreet in his talk with Darrell.

"No; but I know this end of the deal now—that is, I know what you are doing. Now, I want to see what Virginia is like. I'd like to go over the Roanoke first and—"

"Very well, Sam. Keep your mouth shut and your eyes open, and ask questions from the division superintendents. I'll arrange things for you. How long do you think you'll be away?"

He asked this carelessly. He would miss his son. They had spent hours together, they had talked at great length, and he was encouraged, he assured himself, because Sam listened intently and asked many questions—questions which showed utter ignorance, but also moderate intelligence. Sam could grasp elemental truths quickly enough, and he had self-confidence. He ought to acquire the habit of quick and accurate thinking at all times. Rock had not missed Sam very much while Sam was travelling around the world; but he would miss Sam a great deal while Sam was travelling in Virginia. We learn to live economically and do it for years. A little prosperity, and we no longer know how to economize—either money or affections.

"Oh," said Sam, also carelessly, "I don't know; a couple of weeks—unless you need me." He looked quizzically at his father; then he finished: "I'll miss you, Dad." He walked over and threw his arm around Rock's shoulder. He repeated: "I'll miss you like anything. But I've got to see that railroad with my own eyes. And I want to 'see the country and talk to the people down there and learn certain things for myself."

Sampson Rock was pleased to feel his son's arm about his neck. But all he said was:

"Bear in mind that you are not to talk to any one about my business affairs. You are my son, and therefore—"

"And therefore I'm an ass. I understand."

Sampson Rock laughed "Don't overdo it, Sammy, even if it comes natural."

Valentine came in.

"Sam, Mr. Darrell is here."

"I want to introduce him to you, Dad." And, as Sampson Rock nodded, Sam went to the outer office. Presently he came back with his friend:

"Father, this is my friend, John A. Darrell."

"How do you do, Mr. Darrell?" Rock spoke pleasantly, but made no motion to shake hands.

"I'm very glad to meet Sam's father," said Darrell, and bowed.

"You've done considerable work for the Heinsheimer Exploration Syndicate, I think, Mr. Darrell?" Rock's voice and manner were very polite, but his eyes were keenly studying the mining expert. The mining expert was conscious of the scrutiny without resenting it.

"Yes," he answered, calmly, "quite a little."

"Let me see. I think I saw your Blue Blazes report." Rock spoke reminiscently. "Yes, I did. It interested me very much. I thought it a highly intelligible report. How are they getting on?"

"Better than I predicted in the report, but no better than I believed personally. They'll do still better when they—"

"When they build their own railroad?" interrupted Rock.

"Yes, sir," said Darrell, with a mild look of surprise.

Rock laughed. "Of course, as long as they stick to the Central they'll help Bill Rolston more than anybody else. They'll do nothing for a year or two."

"I understood—" began Darrell.

"Talk! You don't know the rivalry between Je— between the Pacific Midland and the Denver & Southern. When the syndicate gets tired of the dog-in-the-manger business and tells both to go, to get out, you'll get your road—and not before. Your little road should connect with both."

"Oh, there is really no need—"

"Yes, there is—at Yellow Jade and at Lincolnville. It would only mean a little more expense, and look at the position of the Blue Blazes: three roads, all enemies, to pick from. Any one of them would buy out at a profit your road, once it was built, to keep the other two away, and fix rates to suit."

"I see," said Darrell, very much interested. He had quite a block of the stock.

"It will come in time. The first syndicate did pretty well. If I had known you at the time, it might have done better. Sam wants to go to Virginia, Mr. Darrell. I think he thinks he is a captain of industry."

"So he's told me. I'm afraid he'll end in one, if you don't watch out."

Sampson Rock laughed. He said· "Well, Sam, if Mr. Darrell finds some good mine or other golden op portunity in Virginia, you'd better take it. But re member, I'm not the Bank of England."

The thought came to Sam that he might use Darrell's reputation in order to raise the money he needed from Sampson Rock himself. He said, slowly: "I'll keep you to your word. Remember. Darrell and I are going to luncheon. Won't you come with us, Dad?"

"No, thanks. I have to work for a living. Mr. Darrell, I'm very glad to have met you. If I can ever be of service, drop in—with or without Sam." He extended his hand and Darrell shook it and was glad to do so. He liked Sam's father.

"So long, Dad. I'll see you at the Union Club at six?"

"No. We'll dine at home. Bring Mr. Darrell, if he hasn't better things to do." He waved his hand at them almost jovially and returned to the ticker. Five minutes later he was driving the frightened shorts before him like a flock of sheep.

After luncheon Sam and Darrell went to the office of Albert Sydney & Co., Darrell's brokers. Sam read over the mortgage. Notwithstanding his unfamiliarity with legal documents, he was certain that it was what it purported to be. Darrell had made out a check for two hundred thousand dollars to Sam's order, and Sam endorsed it over to Albert Sydney & Co. Then he talked business to Sydney. He was more concerned with not being indiscreet than with anything else in connection with the operation.

"Mr. Sydney, I'd like to buy a little stock." He paused.

"Delighted to be of any use to you, Mr. Rock."

The broker's use of the name made Sam say: "But I don't want my father to know anything about it."

In some people that same desire that Sampson Rock should know nothing about a stock deal was comprehensible for obvious reasons. In this instance the reason was also obvious to the broker—the boy feared paternal sermons on the evils of gambling. But so long as he paid his commissions and the margin was adequate, one man's money was as good as another's. Young Rock was of legal age, at all events.

Sydney explained tranquillizingly. "Our business, Mr. Rock, is altogether a confidential matter between our customers and ourselves. It is the same in any reputable office " He took it upon himself that Sam was a stranger to Wall Street methods, like other rich men's young sons.

"You'll give the reports to Darrell. I'd rather not have them mailed to me." This confirmed Sydney's theory. Still, it ought to be a good account.

"Very well, Mr. Rock."

"Virginia Central. That's around thirty-eight. It's down from around forty-eight. Don't you think it ought to go up again?"

"I don't know, Mr. Rock. I wish I did."

"Of course," Sam laughed, pleasantly. "Well, buy me a thousand shares every point down. Begin at thirty-five and—"

"It's thirty-eight now," interjected Sydney, broker-like.

"I know. But it might sell at thirty-five—" Sam became aware that he was speaking almost indiscreetly, so he went on: "It looks as if the market ought to go down. If it does, Virginia Central ought to go down, too. If it sells at thirty-five, buy me one thousand, and another at thirty - four, and if it goes lower—"

"Sell out?"

"Not much," said Sam. "Buy one thousand at thirty-five, one thousand at thirty-four, two thousand at thirty-three, and three thousand at thirty-two; and then, if—"

"That will take a lot of money, Mr. Rock," said Sydney, dubiously. "We like to keep a margin of fifteen points, or at least ten, in ordinary times."

"Oh, that's all right! If you need more money at any time, let Darrell know."

"Yes," put in Darrell, "I'm going to stay here some time."

"Frankly, Mr. Rock," said Sydney, "I shall be very glad to have your account. But I think you ought to realize thoroughly that this game, as your father would probably tell you if you asked him, is—" Sydney was one man in a thousand. Some of his friends said he was eccentric. His enemies said the same thing, differently expressed.

"My dear Mr. Sydney," broke in Sam, very pleasantly, because he saw that Sydney was honest, "I know all you are going to say. I am very grateful for your good intentions. But let me tell you this: There's only one way to learn anything, and that is by experience. All I ask is that you don't tell a soul that I'm speculating through you. And so, if you will buy Virginia Central as I said — let me see — one thousand at thirty - five, one thousand at thirty-four, two thousand at thirty-three, and three thousand at thirty-two, and four thousand at thirty-one—if it goes that low, whether it's to-day or to-morrow or next week or next month. And when it goes up, if it does go up, don't sell until I say so. Darrell and I are going out of town to - morrow. Say, you have quite a view of the river from this window, haven't you?"

He walked over to the window and looked out, over the roofs of the lower buildings, to the North River. Ferry-boats were crawling on the gray water like some sort of giant beetles, and officious little tugs were blowing white smoke-rings into the air as they puffed their way up-stream. But he did not see them. In an autohypnotic spell, his vision was several hundred miles farther south, a vision less vivid than his father's, but nevertheless it was there. This part of the big work he didn't relish. But once in Virginia. . . .

"Great Scott!" muttered Sydney to Darrell. "His father had better be rich."

"Oh, pshaw!" laughed Darrell. "He is a nice chap; only he is young. It wouldn't surprise me much if he turned out to be as bright as his father, some day."

"It would surprise me to death," answered Sydney. Then to Sam: "Very well, Mr. Rock. I'll do as you say, and I hope you make a nice thing out of it. You'll probably get the stock, all right."

"I hope so," said Sam, gently. Sydney felt very

sorry for the lad, which made the broker feel very friendly.

"Remember, please, you mustn't breathe a word to anybody about my buying this stock," finished Sam.

"I most certainly won't," Sydney assured him, earnestly. He would say nothing to hold his young customer to the scorn of the world — of the same world that did not scorn his young customer's father. "If you go out of town you had better keep in touch with us—I mean, let us know where we can reach you by wire."

"Oh yes."

XIV

SAM arranged to leave early the next day for Virginia. He would study the possibilities of industrial development along the line of the Virginia Central, he told his father, in a broad, general way, and he secured a copy of Williams's report, in which Sampson Rock had prudently substituted initials for names. Sam learned also that his father now had forty thousand shares of Virginia Central stock, which was as much as he could reasonably expect; but he would soon resume the campaign of depression in the stock-market, and the final "drive" would not be long in coming. He thought the "low price" would be thirty or a little under. Also, he gave Sam a thick package of "yellow-backs" and told him to leave his pass-book with Valentine. There was twenty-five thousand dollars at the Metropolitan National Bank to Sam's credit, and, if Sam would only keep his check-stubs accurately, he could notify Valentine to deposit more from time to time.

After dinner Sam went to see Fanny.

Her greeting was friendly; no more. He looked well, she thought, but a trifle absent-minded. She looked more than well, he thought. But he did not give up the work he was about to commence in Virginia. To *earn* this girl! . . . He forced himself to look calm.

Mrs. Collyer came towards him with outstretched hand. "How do you do, Sam? And how is Sampson?

Do you happen to know how Roanoke closed to-day?"
Before he could answer she added, half apologetically
and half in admiration at her own stoicism: "I haven't
seen the evening papers yet!"

"The entire market was very strong. Roanoke
closed at eighty, I think."

Mrs. Collyer beamed on him; she would have beamed
on the hangman if he had brought the same news; it
meant a profit of two thousand dollars. That was the
honey; the gall that, on second thought, went with it
was that she had held the stock a fortnight and the
profit ought to have been greater. How the bitter
runs with the sweet in this world!

"Eighty! That is still a long way from par." She
shook her head; and then, for decency's sake, smiled.

"Oh, it's only twenty points," laughed Sam. "You
must be patient, Aunt Marie. You can't make a
million a minute."

"It's two weeks now," she said, rebukingly, "and
anyhow, it would be only twenty-two thousand dollars
if it was par." She looked at him triumphantly—the
triumph of her own moderation in the teeth of temptation.

"Just be patient." Then he added, reassuringly:
"We'll get it there for you!"

She smiled gratefully, because she was grateful to
hear another voice than that of her soul's desire. She
yearned for a mighty chorus singing a song of promise.
Patience? She would undergo that, or any other form
of torture, if only, in the end, Roanoke sold at par.

"Patience, Sam, dear," she declared with a sort of
playful sternness—Mrs. Collyer was really posing before
Mrs. Collyer—"is the one quality I possess to an ex-
traordinary degree." She began to count on her

fingers very rapidly. If she had three thousand shares at eighty and the price went up, not even to par, only to ninety-five—

"Patience is a good thing to have, Aunt Marie," Sam acquiesced, gravely. "If you are not born with it, it is mighty hard to acquire it."

Fanny's eyes did not leave Sam's face while he was speaking. She gladly would have listened to him talking about stocks all night because she was convinced that he did not speak as a mere echo of Sampson Rock, nor, which was even more pleasing, with an air of boyish bravado, unintelligently proud of his sudden transformation; but in a matter-of-fact way, a sort of sincere sedateness. Some men had a quick adaptability, and possibly Sam—

But it was better not to expect too much too soon.

Mrs. Collyer made up her mind to buy another thousand Roanoke the next day. The reason why she did not decide on five thousand was that a satanic thought crept in through one of the still open gates: Supposing the stock went down? The vision of doom that engloomed her soul in the fraction of a second at the mere thought was enough. She shivered; a little more and she would have exuded icicles. No; another thousand shares would do. That meant forty thousand dollars profit at par. Better little and safe than much and vanishable. In the recesses of her gambler soul one of the Mrs. Collyers congratulated the other on her philosophy.

"Sam, I'm going to write a note to Mr. Valentine. Will you give it to him early to-morrow?"

"Yes, Aunt Marie. I won't forget. I'll bet it is very important."

His flippant words made her say, suspiciously: "He

must have it before ten.   Perhaps I'd better mail it.
You don't breakfast until—"

"I'm working with Dad, now.   We go down-town
together every morning."

"Very well, then." She was reassured and was
tempted to tell Sam to ask his father if it was wise to
buy the second thousand.   But Sampson Rock might
dissuade her from buying it; he might dissuade her
from winning forty thousand dollars.   These men
gambled and made millions and always preached "conservatism." She wished with all her mind and heart
and soul that Roanoke would go to par.   It was therefore inevitable that Roanoke would go there.   Why
not?

"I'll go and write it at once.   You won't forget, will
you?"

"How could I, now?"

She nodded unhumorously and went to the library.

Sam turned to Fanny.   He looked at her a moment
before speaking.   She was very beautiful.   Her hair,
the light in her eyes, the color of her cheeks, the poise
of her head—she—all—had grown more beautiful than
ever.   He said, calmly: "Fanny, I am going to Virginia to-morrow—on business."

"I'm so glad, Sam," she said, eagerly.

"Glad I'm going?"

"Yes; glad you're going on business.   What are you
going to do?"

"Do?   I hope to do something—something to earn
you!" He took a deep breath.   He had not lost sight
of his resolve to help secure the control of the Virginia
Central for the Roanoke at a fair price and to develop
the resources of Austin County.   But as he looked at
her, filling his soul with the sight of her as he filled his

lungs with air, the worst he did was to continue to think that he would do all this for her sake. It made him say, logically:

"Fanny, when I come back, you must be prepared to—"

"Don't be silly, Sam," she interrupted. If it would come to that, would it— But she refused to listen to her own answer.

"I'm not. I mean business. You need not do as I say if I don't make good. But I'll make good."

She was silent because he was not laughing, and he was not gloomy and he looked terribly self-confident. He did not notice that she was silent. He was interested in what he still had to tell her.

"Fanny, I think I now have an opportunity to do something useful. I may fail, because I'm doing it on my own hook without any help or advice from my father and without resorting to underhand methods." He could not help thinking of the way he had begun, in Sydney's office. But that was no crime. There had been no lying.

"What is it, Sam?" she asked, excitedly.

"I won't tell you now. But never mind. All you have to know is that with the first money I make through my own efforts I'll buy two rings for you; one for immediate use, and the other for—"

"Tell me more, Sam—about the work, over there, in that nice chair."

"No; I'll stay here and I'll tell you the same thing again. I love you and I love to work for you. It's nicer to work for both of us than for myself alone. Fanny, do you love me—er—yet?"

"You promised not to—"

"I didn't promise not to love you. I can't promise

that, Fanny," he whispered, huskily   "I've loved you all my life.   I'll be gone for a long time—maybe weeks, Fanny!   Will you—er—will you—"   He looked at her. In his eyes, very bright and moist, there was an entreaty; in his face, flushed and tense, there was hunger. He was leaning over her.

"Fanny," he repeated, "if you love me, won't you— ah—just one, Fanny!   Tell me if you love me, and—" He bent closer.   She drew away weakly.   "I'll be gone so long, working for you, dear girl!"

"Here's the letter, Sam," said Mrs. Collyer.   She had seen nothing, because before her mind was the tape on which the ticker of her dreams was printing: "*Roanoke*, 96, 97, 98, 99, 100!"

"I'll give it to Valentine," said Sam, composedly, "the first thing in the morning."   He walked towards her, took the letter, and placed it in his inside coat-pocket very deliberately, with an air of realizing how important the letter was.   His face was still flushed and his fingers felt stiff.   Fanny's face was also flushed, and she was glad he was not so near now;   it helped to subdue that curious nervous trembling that did not show outwardly.

"Sam's going south to-morrow, mother," said Fanny.

"Are you, Sam?   Whatever in the world are you going to do there at this time of the year?"

He almost answered that he was going down to make Roanoke sell at par very quickly.   But what he said was that he was going because he had begun to work with his father, and one of the first things he would do was to go over the Roanoke and see the improvements that were making.   He spoke seriously but not over-earnestly, Fanny thought, without the enthusiasm that would have made her fear it would not last. He plagiarized bodily from his father's dissertation on the art and science of railroading, but made it sound original by saying how interesting he had found it to learn all this and how much more there was to it than anybody suspected.

He perceived he would not have another opportunity to be alone with Fanny that night, and because of that blood-cooling fact, and also because he began to think of Robinson and his stock, he spoke calmly, judiciously, and interested them.

He shook hands with Fanny—a firm and significant grasp—as he took his leave. He was cool. He was even ready to begin a scientific, deliberate, methodical siege.

"Good-night, Fanny. Remember, when I come back!" He looked at her meaningly. His firm resolve to "make good" made his heart beat almost normally.

"Good-night, Sam. I wish you luck!"

She looked at him. She meant it!

And as Sam walked away, his soul was among the stars and his body almost soared with it, it felt so light, so buoyed with love and hope. He could not live without her, he could not work unless he worked for her. Of course he would marry her. . . .

He did not think of the work in Virginia for fully six blocks.

XV

SAM and Darrell decided to "inspect" the Virginia Central first, without waiting to see what his father's Roanoke & Western was like. Sam had read the copy of Walter Williams's report on the Robinson road so carefully and had discussed it with Darrell so often on the way that he felt almost like a railroad expert. Darrell had spent his last hours in New York collecting data on the Austin County iron deposits and coal mines in general, and on the Austin Iron Company in particular. Its shares were quoted in Richmond at from thirty-five to forty dollars a share—a "wide" quotation due to the stock's inactivity and its limited market. The capital stock was only two million dollars, because the company had been organized in dull times when it was only necessary to inject about sixty per cent. of water, instead of an ocean, as during booms. A dividend—the first in several years—had been paid in January; it was only two per cent., but it had made the stock advance about ten dollars a share. The stock had sold as high as fifty dollars at the time of the incorporation, when the organizers wished to capitalize their hopes, and as low as eighteen dollars in the next panic, when fear did the appraising.

Sampson Rock had said that the acquisition of the Austin mineral lands at this time would tie up capital that he could use to greater profit in the stock-market end of the big deal. Whoever controlled the railroad had the mine-owners at his mercy, and Sam knew his father would not allow the owners' hopes of better transportation to warp their judgment as to the value of their properties to him. But Sam thought only that to double, to treble the capacity of the iron works and the mines, to produce two, three, five tons where but one was now produced, to create something that had not existed, something tangible, real, honest — *that* would be worth doing. Indeed, as he thought about it, in his comfortable chair in the Pullman—Darrell was reading the morning papers in the smoking compartment—there came to him the American vision of bigness: a Titanic structure, like an impressionistic picture of Pittsburg at night, a Niagara of molten iron and huge smoke spirals blackening the sky, vastness and speed and life—the strenuous life of sweating puddlers and grimy miners, the soldiers of toil, picturesque and inspiring, a great army fighting the modern battle of business. He could not see the outlines of it, but he did seem to hear the roar and rumble of it, and, thrilled by the sound, was made eager to begin. It was a species of excitement rather than exaltation which filled him as he thought about it. His fingers itched to grasp some lever that would start the stupendous machinery.

But a change came over the spirit of his dream as the Pullman was switched into Virginia Central terri tory. It was a new world, and he felt more like a tourist in Virginia than he had felt in Borneo. From the Pullman window he saw things kaleidoscopically. Impression succeeded impression before the process of mental crystallization could fairly begin. Analysis was impossible. Walter Williams's report on the Virginia

SAMPSON ROCK OF WALL STREET

Central had been his Baedeker; but now he saw living pictures in lieu of mileage figures and tonnage statistics, and he could not identify the railroad of the report with the railroad over which he was travelling.

In the section which Sampson Rock already saw thickly settled, with a new population profusely sweating from its strenuous new activities, Sam beheld instead a land asleep, Rip Van Winkle counties, a territory that wore an air of comatose unkemptness. Even his freely self - admitted ignorance did not make his hopes soar. The long stretches of rusty single track looked absolutely unimprovable; the potential thrift and industry of the land were utterly invisible. He marvelled at the wizard sight of his father—granting that Sampson Rock was not mistaken—which could translate the wheezing of the decrepit locomotive and the rattling of antiquated passenger-cars into fat dividends. The room for improvement was vast, but the profitableness of it, to him, who had never thought of profits, seemed akin to the money-making power of a summer lemonade-garden at the North Pole in January. Indeed, the talk of the ticker was easier to understand, and the abstractions of stock speculations seemed concrete and comprehensible beside this railroad and this country. On the sidings and way-stations the strings of empty cars suggested not freight to come, the exchange of transportation for the shippers' cash, but rather so many hearses—such was the death-stillness whenever the train stopped and the engine's asthmatic wheezing ceased. The sweating, grimy army of toilers became an occasional negro or a malarial-looking white native.

He turned to Darrell for the relief of honest confession, and smiled as he told of his blindness. But Darrell answered, seriously:

"It's natural enough, my boy. You look, but you don't yet know how to see. It's like looking at a picture and thinking it perfect until an artist friend begins to point out where the left arm is out of drawing, or the light is doing unnatural stunts, or something else is askew; or else the fine points you've overlooked in trying to see who it was that painted the picture, and the date—"

"I know; pass on to the fine points."

⟩"Forget Broadway. This road is no blooming street-car line, but it ought to make money with half a show in the way of equipment and other improvements. This country, with good transportation facilities, will be like the Southwest after irrigation came. But it will take time and money. Study Williams's report some more. You'll have to take it for granted that beyond those hills there are hundreds of thousands of tons of freight to be had in the next few years. Making money is contagious. Prospectors flock to a new mining district on the first news of a strike, and the first thing you know thousands are there. Well, as soon as somebody picks up a dollar or two here, we'll see the mob scratching like mad for car-fare. When you hear of a manufacturing concern building a plant that will employ two thousand men, don't think of a few tons of machinery and a one-hundred-and-fifty by seventy-five brick shed. Just turn your intellect to the two thousand men and their wives and children, and the butcher-shops, and the grocery-stores, and the 'clothing emporiums,' and the carpenters and plumbers and their help, and their wives and children, and—"

"I know," interrupted Sam. Darrell was talking

like a school-teacher to a child. It was the way his father spoke.

"You don't. You can't, because you don't know local conditions. I've seen Easterners turn pale while travelling over barren stretches out West and telegraph their Wall Street brokers to go short at once of Pacific & Northern, or St. James & Manitoba, because they couldn't see how the dividends the stocks were paying could be really and truly earned. The railroad presidents must be all liars. What did the travellers know of the lumber - camps and the wheat - farms and the millions of tons of ore being dug up? Don't you worry about the Virginia Central. · Your father knows his business. Let that fact seep through the lower strata of your dome of thought. If the Austin property is as represented—and we'll mighty soon find out when we go over it—the stock is cheap at fifty, and the coal lands should not be expensive in their present undeveloped state; probably you can buy them for the price of the timber on them." He paused. "But, of course, always provided your father takes over this road and improves it."

"If he gets it he'll improve it; and he'll get it."

"Well, we'll bet on it, anyhow."

"It will be a big job," said Sam, impressed by the work once more.

"Sure, it's a big job. Aren't you looking for one, or do you sigh for cold feet?" retorted Darrell.

Sam did not answer. He was thinking of what one man might do to accomplish it, to work this miracle. It would take money—millions—and a master spirit to direct the work. It was beyond his powers now, for his ignorance was illimitable. He must take one step at a time. He would learn many things; his

father would help him. One step at a time. The first
was to buy the Austin Iron Company. After that,
Robinson's stock. And Fanny

They drove to the works in a rickety station-hack
over streets of red mud. Again the unprosperous aspect of the country made it difficult to see the inspir-
ingly rapid transformation Sam desired. Darrell trans-
lated Sam's silence and answered it as they entered
the company's property:

"What did you expect? Marble palaces, open
plumbing, hot and cold water and valet attendance
free?" He took in the building and the furnaces,
glancing everywhither, marking less the probable act-
ualities than the possibilities. At length he turned
to Sam and smiled cheerfully: "Brace up, kid, your
father's a wonder and a half." Sam looked a question,
and Darrell said: "This place was made for Sampson
Rock, Jr. All you have to do is to make your Dad
give you good transportation and you put in some
money and some brains—you can always hire *them*—
and then sit back and let the dough pile up. But wait
till we've made the acquaintance of the superintendent.
He may be willing to talk."

"You can't be sure of the real value of the company
yet," said Sam, challengingly.

"No; but in two hours I'll know whether we are
losing time or not. I'm no iron man. J. A. Darrell is
not the boy I'd pick out for the proud job of main
cheese here, but before I separate myself from six cents
I'll know what I'm paying for. You can now go to
sleep, my bonnie child."

They introduced themselves to the manager of the
works, Mr. Fletcher, as Northern tourists, and sought
permission to go over the plant, which they understood

was the best in Virginia. They were intelligent and well-informed men who wore the clothes of well-to-do New-Yorkers. The little manager thereupon became very cordial. The more well-to-do people who knew him and his great abilities the better it pleased him; for who could limit the vagaries of fortune's lightning?

Fortune had been indeed kind to Sam, for Fletcher· was one of those men whose tutelary deities are vanity and wealth. His hobby was Versatility, a legitimate enough offspring of the deities, for he regarded Versatility as the sign-patent of brains; and with brains and the fame thereof what couldn't a man do? He would put on overalls and repair an engine himself for the mere pleasure it gave him to be a Chesterfield even while greasy; and an hour later entertain American royalty at dinner, and be more courtly than any European king. Everywhere, in everything, thoroughly at home, and very decidedly looking it. He desired money ardently, but it was less for the money itself than for the conviction that it would enable him to do great things before the applauding audience that always attends the very rich. He was, indeed, what is called a naturally handy man, with a decided mechanical bent and very practical in most things; yet, an inveterate dreamer, incessantly stupefying himself with delectable visions as with the fumes of opium.

Darrell soon learned that he knew several of Fletcher's professional acquaintances and he rose in the versatility-mad little manager's estimation. But Sam soared infinitely higher. Fletcher happened to speak of Mr. Beekman Stuyvesant 3d, of the famous New York family, as "young Stuyvesant," with an irrepressible air of bravado at leaving off the servile, money-worshiping "Mister" Sam remarked casually that

"Beekie" was a well-meaning little chap. Mr. Fletcher acted as though he had social aspirations in the metropolis. He had been in New York several times and had stopped at the Waldorf twice. All Austin knew it.

Sam asked few questions, but he listened so attentively that the little manager spoke of his mines and furnaces very eloquently and of the Virginia Central most emphatically. That infernal tinpot railway alone had prevented him from making Austin the Pittsburg of the South and himself Andrew Carnegie II.

"This country is full of such things," commiserated Darrell, his eyes on the furnaces. "Everybody stacks up against a game calling for time, money, and patience."

Fletcher laughed, with an undercurrent of seriousness to show, synchronously, his sense of humor and his modesty. He then decided to be epigrammatic, after having been a handicapped maker of Pittsburgs:

"Time flies; money passes us by, and as for patience, it isn't in you when you are under thirty." He smiled. He was thirty-five; but these men did not know it; but they probably knew that Napoleon had done a great deal before he was thirty. Fletcher looked at Sam for certain encouragement and Sam smiled back. He was twenty-five, and he had no patience, and he wanted to outrace time, and he would get the money. He said:

"But you pay dividends, don't you?"

"They paid nothing when I came, eighteen months ago, but last January we paid two per cent. If the company had only given me what I asked for, I'd have paid twenty per cent."

"You've done wonders, considering the old machinery and your handicaps in handling the raw material," said Darrell, admiringly.

"I've told them that—" began Fletcher, self-defensively.

"But after all," continued Darrell, "it would have been throwing away money here, so long as the railroad couldn't handle your stuff on a big scale."

"I'd make the railroad do better!" asserted Fletcher so determinedly that he looked like five feet four inches of omnipotence. There was really a suggestion of pow er in his look. It made Sam ask:

"All you need is capital to enlarge your plant?"

"That's all." Mr. Fletcher knew what Mr. Fletcher could do.

"Well, Mr. Fletcher," said Sam with quick decision, "if you can show me how you can make the money you need here pay twenty per cent, I'll back you for any amount you say." And he looked curiously at Fletcher, trying to determine whether the little manager's air of corked-up energy came from real power or from sheer emptiness.

"Iron is an uncertain thing, Sam," cautioned Darrell, paternally.

"I can do it," said Fletcher, defiantly. Of course, the twenty per cent. was a figure of speech. Figures do not lie.

"Who owns the controlling interest?" pursued Sam, brickly.

Fletcher had more than once yearned for such a man to express such a desire—yearned for him and for it with an enthusiasm heated to incandescence in the forge of his imagination. Often he had succeeded in arousing enthusiasm almost as hot in people who had no capital—people who, unrebuked, regarded *him* as a capitalist! He had seen those greed-bitten listeners sigh regretfully that they did not own millions to place unreservedly in Mr. Fletcher's wizard hands, for in building the model iron-plant of the South Mr. Fletcher had also created untold wealth for his friends and followers. It had been one of his pet hopes. After all, it was not very expensive to make a great fortune in dreams, which glittered infinitely more goldenly for being dream - built. He saw himself rich, powerful, admired—a captain of industry, a political dictator, a patron of the fine arts, an engineer, a social lion, and an erotic poet. Rockefeller turned green, Beau Brummel double-locked his grave, and Shakespeare sighed: "What's the use?"

"The control," said Fletcher in an impressively matter-of-fact way, "is not held by any one man, but is scattered. Half a million cash would get it." He preferred the contemptuous "half a million cash" to the less humble "five hundred thousand dollars." Sam looked so interested that the little manager added: "You get up your syndicate and I'll do the rest. We could do wonders here with money." He looked to see what effect the last plural would have on the young man.

"The last quotation of the stock I saw," said Sam, musingly, "was thirty-five dollars a share. Even at forty dollars, it would only be four hundred thousand dollars for fifty-one per cent. of the stock."

It was evident the young man was not as ignorant as he looked. But Fletcher gave his surprise no time to grow into a suspicion. He said, quickly: "It would be worth twice as much after we got the control and planned to increase the plant." He could see no harm in persistently pluralizing.

"It wouldn't improve your pig-iron any to stack it up and accumulate rust until the Virginia Central began to think of moving it year after next," said Darrell.

"That's all right," retorted Fletcher. "They wouldn't earn fixed charges if they didn't move freight that dropped from Heaven."

"Do you want to do business with us, Mr. Fletcher?" asked Sam, abruptly.

"I'm not here for the benefit of my health alone," smiled Fletcher.

"Very well, if you can get me sixty per cent. of the stock of this company—" Sam paused.

"I can get it."

"I'll pay half a million dollars for it." Sam said this so calmly that Fletcher's soul began to shake with the gold-ague.

"I can handle *my* end of this deal."—And Fletcher looked challengingly at first at Sam, then at the less enthusiastic Darrell.

"My dear sir," laughed Sam, "anybody can raise money for a profitable undertaking. It's finding the opportunity that's not easy."

"You've found it right here."—And Fletcher nodded twice.

"You get an option on the stock and we'll take the stock from you at the price I named." Sam looked like a business man. It was his youth that made him try to look like one.

"Supposing we look over the plant more carefully and take a peep at the cost-sheets?" suggested Darrell.

Instantly Fletcher became sober. He had been femininely certain he could secure and sell fifty-five or sixty per cent. of the capital stock for the five hundred thousand dollars at a handsome profit—certain because he had wished it. But, as a matter of fact, he was not sure he could buy even thirty per cent. Moreover, strangers did not go about flinging half millions right and left. If the young New-Yorker thought he was investing his money at twenty per cent. interest, it would take some figuring to prove it. But it was easier to figure on prospective profits than on past returns. Who could deny that another million spent on this plant might not yield a yearly income almost as big as Fletcher had hastily promised? At all events, just now, Fletcher stood to lose an hour or two and nothing more.

"I'll show you over the works, anyhow," he told them, with a tinge of reserve. They inspected the blast-furnaces and later they drove to the iron mines. They also studied the maps of the coal-lands and the limestone quarries. It really was as Sampson Rock had told Sam—a vast unutilized possibility of profit, an exceptional combination of money-making factors such as nature sometimes throws in the way of captains of industry.

Darrell found occasion to say to Sam:

"If your father gets the Virginia Central he'll own this property as sure as fate. It wouldn't take much money to make it pay pretty well and he'd make something on the railroad end of it, too."

"He'll get the Virginia Central—with my help. Do you think Fletcher is the man to get the stock for us?"

"Do you?" asked Darrell, curiously.

"I think so. It will be to his interest; he knows everybody and he doesn't know what my father is doing. Is the property worth the price?"

"Yes, if the railroad gets a hustle on and is friendly. Of course, lots of machinery here is gravitating towards the scrap-heap, but they've got all the decent ore cinched. It's a special iron, and they ought to sell ten times more than they do. Personally, I think the iron boom is here to stay for a few years, and five hundred thousand dollars a year profit is a big return on what you'll need to spend. Of course, Sam, I can't get it down fine by a glance of my eagle eye, but—"

"Is half a million for sixty per cent. of the stock a fair bet?" interrupted Sam.

"Yes; to a man of your father's means. Tell Fletcher to get six months' options and you'll pay ten per cent. cash."

"Very well," said Sam. It was enough to know.

It was not until they were sitting in the manager's private office that Fletcher's hopes began to take on substance—that is, when Darrell began to ask questions too intelligent for ignorant tourists, or for impostors masquerading as capitalists. Why these men should so suddenly desire to buy this property was enough to arouse suspicions, and the doubts overcame the hopes enough to make Fletcher look coldly at the Westerner and say:

"That's all very well. Some of these questions I can't answer. I don't know you. Don't misunderstand me," he explained, with a benevolent, offence-removing smile. "I know you to be a gentleman, but I don't know how serious your intentions are, and neither do I know whether I'm giving away valuable information to possible competitors."

"You are giving away nothing," said Sam. "We expect to pay for everything we get." Fletcher stiffened perceptibly. Sam liked him for it, and added, amiably: "My dear chap, we are not experts in disguise. As for knowing us, we don't know *you*, and yet we are taking you at your own valuation. I think you are right, and that with more capital this property ought to do much better than it has. I'm willing to gamble on it. If you get twelve thousand shares for me for five hundred thousand dollars, I'll take it. You ought to be able to get it and make a profit. Unless I have my own way, I won't bother with it. That's why I want the majority of the stock. You ought to get options on the stock. I'll pay ten per cent. cash and the balance in six months. But unless you are sure you can get the majority of the stock, there is no use to bother any further." Sam looked frankly at the manager.

Fletcher answered politely, but without enthusiasm: "It will be hard work to get sixty per cent. at the price you've fixed."

"You were sure you could get it a moment ago."

"I'm sure of it still. But it will take a lot of time and trouble."

"Well, figure out whether it can be done" Sam desired the iron company more than ever. An echo of some aphorism of his father's came to him. He said, gently: "In working for me, Mr. Fletcher, you will be working for yourself. You are going to identify yourself with a big work, a successful work. You mustn't imagine that I merely promise. I will give you twenty-five thousand dollars in cash the moment you have the options safe. And if you can get more than the sixty per cent., I'll buy it from you at forty dollars a share. The stock is now around thirty-five, and if you can—"

"You only need fifty-one per cent., Sam," cut in Darrell. "What's the use of—"

"Never mind. I'll take all Mr. Fletcher can get over the bare majority."

"It sounds attractive," admitted Fletcher. He said it in a way that showed he had a hint in mind. "You don't know what a task it will be—"

"We think it's twenty-five thousand dollars' worth of task. That's more than I can make in a week," said Darrell, impatiently.

"It isn't a matter of a week. And, besides, for me to give you the confidential information you desire does not seem altogether fair to—"

"Don't do anything you think unfair," interrupted Sam, frowning.

"What we yearn for is the chance to buy a pig in a poke. I'm losing sleep looking for the chance." Darrell looked particularly wide awake as he said this.

"Then you'd better—" began Fletcher, in an offended tone.

"Oh, be sensible!" said Darrell. "There are brokers in Richmond who can buy the stock for us if we want it, after we get the information elsewhere."

"They couldn't buy the control, not at any such price, nor at any price." Fletcher spoke a trifle superciliously.

"Mr. Fletcher," said Sam, whom this exchange of words was beginning to annoy, "understand this once for all. If I want the stock, I'll get it. I'm giving you a chance to work for me. If you don't take it, I'll get somebody else to get what I want. It's a family trait of ours. I don't know whether you have ever heard of my father?"

"I think I have," answered Fletcher, politely prevaricating. But the young man's words suggested an obvious explanation for his reckless business methods. There were fond fathers who had millions and who often backed their sons' plunges.

"That being the case, you needn't be afraid of my not doing whatever I say I'll do. That's what we call in New York a friendly tip to you, Mr. Fletcher." It was the way in which Sam spoke that made Darrell look at him admiringly.

"Let me see," said Fletcher, frowning, as if to recollect the exact time and place of his meeting with Mr. Rock, Sr. "Your father is now—"

"He is now in New York," answered Sam.

"Where he's always been, and where he will continue to be whether his son buys your picayune works or not," supplemented Darrell, impatiently.

"You seem anxious enough to pick up any stray picayunes," said Fletcher, sarcastically.

Darrell felt sure that the little manager had not "placed" Sam's father. Since Sam had spoken about it, Fletcher might as well be told. He assented, amiably:

"We are, my dear fellow. It's not picayune to us, but it really is to Sampson Rock. His son has more time to pick up the pennies."

"Oh!" exclaimed Fletcher, involuntarily. A spasm of fright passed over his face at the narrow escape. Almost he had failed to heed Fortune's thundering knock at his door! He had not connected young Rock with the great Sampson Rock. But now everything that young Rock had said appeared in its true colors— no longer an idle whim, but a masterpiece of wisdom tinted with the superb nonchalance natural in the son of such a man. He recovered very quickly, and said, deferentially:

"Oh, I never doubted your ability to do what you said, Mr. Rock. But I felt that you did not know me, and you might think what I told you for the mere asking I'd tell any stranger who happened to stroll in. I wanted you to understand that I'm faithful to my employers, no matter what I may lose in the way of outside money." From that moment he relegated Darrell to the nineteenth place.

Sam perceived the change in the manager's manner, and felt sure that the battle was won. The struggle had not been particularly strenuous, though it might have become more exciting but for the casual mention of Sampson Rock's name. Before the dazzle of his father's prestige, this man, who had been full of doubts and suspicions, and permitted himself to be irritated by Darrell's more or less natural questions, now looked as if to be the slave of Sampson Rock's son was to live in heaven.

Marvellous power of a name!

He looked at Fletcher, whose eyes were fixed almost hypnotically on Sam's. There was nothing Fletcher could not do for this pleasant young man who no longer was an idle, sight-seeing tourist, but a bringer of cash and opportunity, a benevolent magician who carried in one hand the trumpet of fame and in the other the fairy wand that transformed golden dreams into clinking realities.

"We might settle Mr. Darrell's doubts and gratify his curiosity, Mr. Fletcher," suggested Sam, amiably, and Fletcher quickly answered, "Certainly, Mr. Rock."

Until a late hour they sat that night, Darrell asking questions and Fletcher answering them unhesitatingly, studying analyses of ores and reports of the company's mineral and timber lands, poring over the statistics of cost, production, and sales, until Darrell said:

"It's all right, Sam, provided the railroad will do its share. At present it has neither motive-power nor rolling-stock enough to handle any increase in our business here."

At Darrell's assumption that they were already in

control, Fletcher's hopes became solid. In the process of metamorphosis whereby the hopes took on the shape of coins, the manager's alert mind began to throw out the grappling-irons of sundry other profitable schemes, a luxury he had not hitherto permitted himself, as being beyond even the dreaming stage. Profit piled itself on profit automatically, and the golden mountain-top dented the rosy clouds. He must do all in his power to secure control of the Austin Iron Company to these Heaven-sent friends. Much of the stock was held by people who would have sold out in disgust long before but for Fletcher's earnest entreaties and promises of much better returns in the future. In now advising the same people to sell out, he must undo his own work. How many shares he could get he did not know even approximately, but, as he thought about it, the number grew, for this opportunity wore golden spurs, and he felt the prick of them in his soul. In order to discourage over-optimistic holders whose annoying faith in Austin's future had been strengthened by that year's unfortunate dividend, it was obvious that the company must make a bad showing—that there might be no ill-feeling, no more dividends, no more desire to hold the stock. Mathematics is one of the exact sciences. So is greed.

"Don't you worry about the railroad," Fletcher told Sam. "Of course, they'll do better by us when we have more tonnage to give and are prompter in paying our bills. We've never had working capital enough, and we've often had to close down for repairs in the middle of a busy season. All I am worrving about is to get the stock you want for the price you are willing to pay."

"It's a good price," said Darrell, shortly.

"The ore lands alone are worth ten times more, and there are eighteen hundred acres more that never have been prospected," retorted Fletcher, loyally. "I've got the best—"

"I know," said Darrell. "But what about the stock?"

"I think, if anybody ᴄan get it, I can."

Sam looked as if he were about to say something, but changed his mind and was silent. Fletcher assumed that young Mr. Rock doubted his ability to make a majority of the stockholders dispose of their shares, and he went on: "I can make them sell. My report must be turned in next week. You know the annual meeting will be held in Richmond early next month. I have an idea that, after reading it, they will fall all over themselves in the scramble to get out." He did not look particularly villanous nor, indeed, over-complacent. He was very much in earnest.

Sam, who again had been visioning to himself a great and good work here, was hurled to the earth of the ticker and disagreeably jolted. A Spanish proverb came to him—"People boil beans the world over." When business consisted of wanting to buy something that other people had to sell, the buyers, whether in Wall Street or Virginia, instinctively boiled the same kind of beans in the same kind of water, and the water boiled at 212° F. He was willing to pay a fair price, more than the market-price, and it was not a manipulated nor fictitious market-price. Yet there must be deceit. It filled him with a sort of impatient disgust.

"Mr. Fletcher," he said, "I don't care to—"

"Why, you ought not only to get the stock, but to make a nice little thing out of it," put in Darrell, very quickly. Sam was certain his friend had spoken in order to check words that conceivably might have made the deal impossible; for Fletcher, if angered, had merely to tell the stockholders that Sampson Rock's son wanted to buy the control. Dynamite wouldn't budge them after that, unless it was the kind that his father used, which was the kind Sam did not like. This deal meant work to come, good work, big work. The Austin Iron Company had to be bought. Too much depended on it.

Fletcher answered Darrell:

"I don't expect to make anything on the options. Some of the stock will cost less, but some will cost more. I'll consider myself lucky if the block you need averages under forty-two. And I was not thinking of my commission. I want you to get the control of this company because I feel my future will be safe in your hands, and, therefore, I'll see that you get the stock." He leered ingratiatingly at the New-Yorkers.

The leer, with its suggestion of a summer-hotel waiter's confidence in a well-served patron's generosity, exasperated Sam even more than the willingness to do dirty work for money had done. Indifferent to what it meant for the deal to miscarry at this stage, he said, angrily·

"You might as well understand right now and here that I won't do business that way."

"Oh!" smiled Fletcher, still misunderstanding Sam's youthful impatience. "I've studied men, and I know I won't suffer if I leave the value of my services to you."

"Mr. Fletcher," said Sam, decisively, "I wouldn't give you a cent—"

"Not one cent over the half million for the sixty per cent. and twenty-five thousand dollars commission for you," interjected Darrell, quickly, as though he were finishing Sam's sentence. "It's enough. You can take it or leave it."

"Jack"—Sam turned to Darrell with a frown—"you must not—"

"No," said Darrell to Fletcher, "that's the limit. Now let me look again at these blue-prints of the proposed—"

As the manager rose quickly to comply with Darrell's request, the Westerner whispered to Sam, fiercely: "Hold your horses, will you?"

And Sampson Rock, Jr., held his horses—that is, his tongue. He was annoyed at being forced to control his feelings by the importance of this deal, not in its financial aspect, but in its bearing on his future manner of life. Rather than self-disgust, it was a sort of irritation. But he would not tolerate any underhanded methods, nevertheless.

It is the first step that is difficult. But when it is down-stairs it seldom strains the leg muscles.

"Mr. Rock," said Fletcher, laying before Darrell the blue-prints of the projected record-breaking blast-furnaces—another dream of his which he had elaborated to the point of complete plans and specifications—"I'll treble the value of this plant with a little capital. Nothing but the boom in the trade enabled us to pay that two per cent. dividend last January. Now, if I report the truth, and nothing but the truth, which is all I am supposed to do, it will make them shiver when they realize how precarious the dividends are. I don't have to lie. I wouldn't do it, not for the presidency of the Steel Trust. I've told them what I've told you dozens of times, till they dodge when they see me coming. I won't tell them any more."

"Were you going to tell the truth in the report?"

"I was going to tell them that, if I had had my way, they wouldn't have received that two per cent. dividend. I wanted the money for improvements. But the company had money in the bank and owed little, and they went crazy when they saw a profit after so many hungry years. If I hadn't given in to the clamor for a dividend I'd have lost my job."

"And now you've decided on complete and detailed veracity because — " The slight sneer on Sam's lips was as a subtle solace to his own stifled virtue.

"Because now, if you will do as you say, it will be possible to do the work that ought to be done here. Austin iron is the best foundry-iron in the world, and it ought to be known as such, and it ought to bring a corresponding price. With enough working capital, we can sell all we can make, and we can deliver when and as we promise. If the present stockholders won't do it they must step out of the way and let somebody else try. It's got to be done sooner or later; and the sooner the better, for I'm not growing any younger. That's the way I feel."

Sampson Rock's argument! The sincerity that rang in the little manager's voice impressed Sam, but before he could say anything, Darrell and Fletcher were at it again, until, at midnight, Darrell rose and said: "We'll advance you twenty-five hundred dollars for preliminary expenses. Of the total twenty thousand shares you must get options on at least twelve thousand. We won't buy a share outright until we are sure we can get the majority. It's against my principles to bid up prices on myself. Moreover, we have to consider the additional capital that must be raised. Don't use a brass-band while you are getting the options, and keep our names out of it."

Sam said nothing.

"And my commission—"

"Twenty-five thousand dollars cash, as soon as you have the options safe; the difference in the price you pay and the one we offer you will be your additional profit. But don't be a hog. Get the stock. We'll let you in for a block of whatever new securities we may issue at the same price we pay, and we'll carry it for you for two years, at six per cent. interest. Don't have to take it if you don't wish to. Your future salary and position we shall leave for future discussion, after we are in control. If this isn't satisfactory, say so now. We don't want to waste any more time over the matter."

"It's satisfactory," said Fletcher, after a pause. It was not, quite. Reality seldom equals vague anticipation. There were one or two things he had neglected to mention, as, for instance, that the cost of materials had gone up since he made his estimates on the cost of the improvements. But that was the New-Yorkers' lookout. Mr. Fletcher was looking out for Mr. Fletcher. Therefore, Mr. Fletcher asked for some written trifle, a memorandum, to avoid misunderstandings later.

"You'll get it to-morrow. In the mean time, Sam, give Mr. Fletcher twenty-five hundred dollars."

Sam silently took the money from his wallet and handed it to the little manager. Fletcher, ostentatiously not counting it, carelessly put it in his vest-pocket. Then he extended his hand to Sam. Sam took it and smiled, when the manager said:

"I hope you'll find this a profitable venture, Mr. Rock; I know you will."

"I hope so," answered Sam, quietly. "Good-night, Mr. Fletcher."

Early the next day Darrell and Fletcher again went over sundry details, and the little manager received his written trifle—an agreement to pay five hundred thousand dollars for twelve thousand shares of Austin Iron Company stock, fifty thousand dollars on receiving the options and the balance ninety days later, Mr. Fletcher's commission to be twenty-five thousand dollars. Then Darrell and Sam went to look at coal lands. The Austin Iron Company's coal-mines were more than enough for its wants, but Darrell thought it well to pick up any other bargains there might be in the neighborhood. He told Sam:

"We can form a subsidiary company with a capital stock big enough to—"

"You ought to stay in Wall Street!" laughed Sam.

But when they casually broached the subject of options on coal lands to the owners thereof, they learned that a Mr. Morson, a Northern gentleman of nice manners, resistless energy, and some ready cash, had a few days before secured long options on the principal undeveloped tracts in the county as well as on most of the producing mines. He was a very fine gentleman, and the people had hopes that something would happen. They had cherished such hopes since the war—Sam again saw a Rip Van Winkle population—and their hopes had withered. But now the hopes were greening anew. If Northern capital came down to this blessed country they would all prosper.

"That's the Old Man," laughed Sam, and Darrell nodded admiringly. Anything that his father could do to make these people acquire the habit of work, if not the love of it, to make them prosper, would be in the nature of a miracle. To galvanize into life a land asleep, to increase the wealth of the country, to fight, to overcome obstacles.

"We will pay Mr. Morson the compliment of assuming that he has overlooked nothing bigger than a five-cent piece," said Darrell. "I think you had better hypnotize Robinson pretty quick, or your father will leave nothing to you except a glow of unselfish joy, Sammy."

And Sam, who saw the goal near now and more alluring than ever, replied, happily:

"On to Richmond!"

It is the first step which is difficult. But when it is down-stairs. . . .

XVI

THEY had letters of introduction to several people in Richmond, but the first man they called on was Joseph Leigh, first vice-president of the Roanoke & Western. Mr. Leigh was as nice as he could possibly be to the only son of the Roanoke's master.

"Your father wrote me you were coming and would travel over the entire system. We've been expecting you, Mr. Rock. Captain Rogers, superintendent of our Western division will be very glad to place himself at your disposal, and in two weeks you'll know the road as well as he does, or better—almost as well as your father. Anything in the way of a special train, and so forth, you have only to let us know what you wish to do, Mr. Rock. Captain Rogers will see to it."

"Thank you. I haven't fully decided. I think we'll stay in Richmond a few days," said Sam.

"I'm too busy myself"—Leigh spoke regretfully, but at the same time with an air of exclusive devotion to the railroad—"to have much time for social pleasures, and I'm really almost as much of a stranger here as you. But I'll have Judge Abercrombie put you up at the Dominion Club. He is a great admirer of your father's. He is the Roanoke's confidential attorney—"

"Is he generally known as such here?"

"No, indeed!" laughed Mr. Leigh. "He is one of our political leaders, with senatorial ambitions, and it would not do to be a corporation man. He knows everybody worth knowing in Virginia, and is a very able and discreet man. As for myself, I need not say my time is entirely yours, Mr. Rock, at any and all times. Excuse me half a second." And he turned to a clerk who had just come in with some documents. The vice-president read them over very quickly, perhaps not displeased to work in the sight of the only son, and gave short, sharp instructions to the waiting clerk, with a decisive air, almost military.

Sam could not help being impressed by the atmosphere of this office and the manner of these men in contrast with the happy-go-lucky methods of what Virginia Central officials had come to his observation. Here the machinery ran smoothly, like machinery under control of an efficient engineer. He turned to Darrell, and the Westerner, divining what was in the youngster's mind, smiled acquiescingly. This was Sampson Rock's office and Sam was Sampson Rock's son. The thought gave Sam a vague sense of ownership, and it stimulated his desire to take an active part in his father's business.

Shortly afterwards they left Mr. Leigh to call on Judge Abercrombie, Mr. Leigh volunteering to inform the Judge by telephone of their intended visit.

The confidential legal adviser of the Roanoke, who knew everybody in Virginia worth knowing, and all the politicians to boot, was delighted to meet young Mr. Rock and his friend. He showed it facially. To make sure, he also said it twice. He would consider it an honor, as well as a pleasure, to have them make his office their office and his home their home during their stay in Richmond. He was a handsome man, well preserved, with a tendency towards dignified oratory.

Sam thanked him, and explained that their move-ments would be too uncertain for them to think of trespassing upon his hospitality.

"I'm sorry," said Judge Abercrombie, with the simplicity of real tragedy.

"And we, naturally, even more," Sam assured him. He was again impressed by the persistence of his father's far-reaching influence. As in the office of the Roanoke's vice-president, there was in this room, with its walls one solid mass of law-books and lawyer's tin boxes, a subtle atmosphere that told of Sampson Rock's power. Sam felt almost as if his father were present in the flesh. These men displayed not so much deference, but attentiveness; they were soldiers listen-ing to the general-in-chief who would tell them what position they should take on the battle-field. Always when this phase of Sampson Rock's business came before him, Sam felt that there was inspiration in the work itself. There was no time to lose. Sam said:

"Judge Abercrombie, I'm here on a little business trip with Mr. Darrell. We have just come from Austin."

"Oh yes."

"Have you seen Mr. Morson lately?"

"I had that pleasure last week," answered the law-yer, cordially. "He is a very interesting man, Mr. Rock, and very devoted to your father."

Sam smiled. His father's lieutenants were so loyal that each spoke well of the other. How did the Old Man manage to do it? Surely, not alone by paying big fees! Half at random he said:

"You probably know what he has been doing in Austin County?"

Judge Abercrombie permitted himself a non-committal smile, and, in a rather careful manner, carelessly said nothing. There was, of course, nothing to say— both if Sam were informed and if he were not.   ⟋

"At all events, I wish you would look after the legal end of a little matter that I may or may not carry through," went on Sam. "But this is not a Roanoke affair, nor one in which my father is interested officially. The selection of these particular words came easy. Sam knew what he wished to do.

The lawyer bowed a trifle formally, and said, "I am at your service, Mr. Rock." The salvation of the South would come from Northern capital. The salvation of Southern gentlemen of the learned professions would come from Northern captains of industry of enterprising habits. This made him smile cordially as he added:

"If I may ask—"

"I hope to be ready in a few days. By-the-way, sir, do you happen to know Colonel Robinson, of the Virginia Central?" Leigh had said the lawyer was able and discreet.

"Very well," replied Judge Abercrombie—"very well, indeed." The plot thickened. The deal might grow. If it did, the fee similarly would take on weight. These Northern capitalists were very curious; very frank one moment, exasperatingly reserved the next. In due time he would know more.

"Mr. Darrell and I would like to meet him."

"Whenever you wish. He is in town now."

"The sooner the better." The very great interest with which his words were heard gave to Sam a feeling of confidence. That interest he owed to his father. That confidence made him feel that he would be able to go through life without ever having to sacrifice directness in his business dealings in order to attain his ends. It was not the Sampson Rock of the ticker, but the Sampson Rock who did things, who was his father now.

"Colonel Robinson and your father, Mr. Rock—" began the lawyer, with a sort of deferential regret.

"If it embarrasses you in the slightest to introduce me to the Colonel, Mr. Darrell not being my father's son, perhaps—" He paused. Here was another obstacle.

"Not at all," denied Judge Abercrombie, looking very brave and very loyal. "I consider it an honor to be included among your father's friends. I regard him as one of the greatest men we have to-day in this country, and I've known many distinguished Americans in my time, Mr. Rock. I would there were more like him." The lawyer managed to look both affectionate and strictly judicial.

"I'm naturally glad to have you think so, Judge Abercrombie," said Sam, with a grateful smile. A fleeting glimpse of his father beside the ticker flashed across his mind. The stock-market was merely an incident; it was the man at work, improving railroads, establishing efficiency, the fighter of the modern battle of business, the man who commanded thousands of other men. Sam said, briskly:

"At all events, it would be just as well to have Darrell meet the Colonel first."

"The fewer people who know that Mr. Sampson Rock's son is here the better," put in Darrell. "Above all, beware of the reporters." He smiled, but Sam saw that he was in earnest. That made him frown. His father's reputation helped, but it also was inconvenient, at times. The name on a hotel-register could interfere with important plans.

"You must let me put you up at the club, gentlemen," said the Judge. "Colonel Robinson is there every night. But you must not misunderstand me, Mr. Rock, and thereby do an injustice to Colonel Robinson. He is a gentleman by birth and breeding, a very charming man socially. But his railroad interests have clashed at times with those of your—of the Roanoke." He looked as if it were not so much poor Robinson's fault, but the Virginia Central's.

"I understand, perfectly," Sam assured him.

"Suppose we dine at the club to-night?" suggested Judge Abercrombie.

"You are very good. We should be delighted." No time was being wasted. To see what manner of man Robinson was, and then to act; this was pleasing. The lawyer, who was watching him attentively, felt certain young Rock must be in his father's confidence, and marvelled never to have heard Sampson Rock speak of his son. A fine-looking young fellow who looked kindly, as all young men should to whom the cost of kindliness cannot be prohibitive. He would ask Leigh about young Rock. For reasons of his own—and, no doubt, supremely wise — Sampson Rock did not choose to appear directly in this new and mysterious, but probably very important, deal. For one thing, the cost of getting what he wanted would obviously be much cheaper; but he had sent his own son instead of an agent. The lawyer was even then looking into the titles of the coal properties, and Morson had also enjoined the utmost discretion.

"By-the-way, Judge, are you familiar with the Austin Iron Company's property?" asked Sam.

"Ye-es," replied the Judge, meditatively. "It is owned practically by local capitalists. I know all of them. It has never fulfilled their expectations. Why it is not a success I do not know."

"Do you know Mr. Fletcher, the manager?"

"No; but I can easily learn all about him."

Darrell began to fidget.

"Well, he thinks he can get the majority of its stock for us. Mr. Darrell, who is an expert, thinks the property would pay well with a better plant, and I do too. We'll take it—Mr. Darrell and I—jointly, if we can get it now at our own price. But Fletcher may find it a little difficult to get as much as we want, and I think we shall have to ask your help. But we shall discuss this later."

Darrell, who had been staring at a corner of the room, biting his lips from time to time, turned to Sam and said, calmly:

"I think it would be well to have Judge Abercrombie see the company's charter. We really don't know whether it is possible to issue bonds to provide for new working capital." He looked at Sam meaningly.

"I shall examine it at once," said the lawyer.

"Telegraph Fletcher to make haste, Jack. I don't want to stay in Richmond forever. If you don't mind, we shall write Fletcher to address his letters to us in your care, Judge."

"Consider this your office, Mr. Rock."

"Thank you. We've taken up enough of your time. Oh yes, we have! To-night at the club; about seven?"

"At your pleasure. I shall be there from five o'clock on."

"Au revoir, then, Judge."

As soon as they were in the street Darrell turned to Sam and asked, with much solemnity, "Will you kindly tell me in words of one syllable why you had to tell Abercrombie that we were after the Austin Iron Company?"

Sam looked at his friend a moment and then laughed. "To tell you the truth, Jack, it came out of itself."

"Oh, I thought you liked the Judge so much you wished to buy stock from him—the same stock he will proceed to buy as soon as your back is turned. I'm glad it wasn't an irresistible burst of generosity." Darrell nodded to himself as if in relief.

"But it struck me immediately afterwards that it would be better if he thought we were after coal and iron than after the railroad itself. Our trip to Austin right after Morson began to look too devilish mysterious."

Darrell looked at Sam with interest. Then he asked: "And you thought that all by yourself? Well, now!"

"That's all right," retorted Sam, confidently. "It's better for him to make a few dollars out of Austin than to interfere with the real article. We probably will need legal advice, and by talking about it now we show we have perfect confidence in him. I tell you, he's worked for my father. Now he'll work for me."

"Look here, Sam; you mustn't imagine you are the ninth wonder. Your father's name helps you more than anything else short of millions in cold cash would."

"I know. And it makes it difficult, if I want to get anything for my own self."

"Precisely. You let me handle Robinson—"

"I want to deal fair—"

"If he needs a wet-nurse, he's no business to be president of a railroad. His place is in an asylum for the feeble-minded. What are you going to tell him—

that you want to buy the control of his blooming streaks of rust at any figure he'll name? I see him marking down the price to sixteen cents a yard."

"I don't know what I'll say, but—"

"The first thing he will ask himself is why you should want to buy Virginia Central stock at all. Being Sampson Rock's only son, he will suspect at once—"

"Yes," frowned Sam. He saw no beautiful direct plan of dealing.

"The only decent excuse you could have is for me— *my* coal and iron syndicate—to have an interest in the road upon which our prosperity depends. But for Sampson Rock to buy one share of Virginia Central stock means absorption by the Roanoke. He'd succumb to that argument like a thousand of brick, I don't think!"

"We'll have to get it." Sam spoke determinedly. He frowned, staring groundward, thinking of ways and means to buy Robinson's stock honestly, fairly, decently. The work itself, the doing of it, that was the thing. "We'll have to get it," he repeated, "somehow!"

"By business methods or by real, pleasant, lady-like loquacity?" Darrell asked it with exaggerated anxiety.

"We'll get it," replied Sam, without a smile, "like gentlemen."

XVII

AT dinner that evening Judge Abercrombie told them that Colonel Robinson was greatly interested in the development of suburban real estate and needed money—needed it, he had heard it whispered, quite urgently. But, the lawyer added, with sudden caution, he had many friends and quite a "following."

"He always needs money. He is in a million schemes, and none of them does as well as it ought to because he always lacks sufficient capital. He seldom loses heavily, but he never makes much. Usually other people take it off his hands at cost or a little below, and they make a good thing out of it. He is one of God's optimists. He sees the future all sunshine. His eyes look so intently upon his latest hope gleaming in the distance, made real by his imagination and his optimism, that he does not see the rough road up which he must walk before he can grasp his glittering desire. One of God's own optimists, sir, and he imparts his optimism to many people!"

Judge Abercrombie seemed pleased. Sam concluded it must be with his rhetoric, which he thought was really very nice. He knew some men who were just like Colonel Robinson. Doubtless this was one of the dogs in the manger, one of the incompetents that exasperated Sampson Rock. Sam was forced to admit that such exasperation was not strange. But the strong should be merciful. At the worst, Colonel Robinson was but a child at play beside men at work. He asked, indulgently:

"Which is the latest glittering desire, Judge Abercrombie, the Virginia Central or his suburban properties?" It seemed to him a man should have a definite aim and stick to one thing. A diversity of desire was demoralizing, according to Sampson Rock; and Sam now agreed with him.

"He has talked of nothing else but Capital Park these past six weeks. He wished me to have an interest in the company."

"And you?"

"I did not, Mr. Rock," smiled the Judge. "I am a poor man."

Sam felt vaguely this was a hint. The Judge was a nice chap. Sam was well disposed towards him. He said:

"So am I. We'll have to see if we can't stop being that—together, Judge, eh?" To name the exact date and the figures would have been poor taste. The use of the plural conveyed the promise nicely. The implied partnership showed personal affection. Sam really had not thought of all this, but after the words were out he was rather pleased at the effect on the lawyer, who replied:

"My dear young man, I should feel much easier for my family if I thought you would really keep in mind a poor old Southern lawyer in your deals." Judge Abercrombie said it quizzically, subtly, intimately, with a humorous smile—and yet there was an undercurrent of earnestness in the voice. In his eyes, for all their would-be whimsical expression of gratitude, there smouldered an irrepressible hope. And Sam perceived the gleam and his own importance to this gray-haired lawyer. For the way the thoughts ran in the gray-haired lawyer's mind was this: Sampson Rock, Jr.; that is to say, Sampson Rock, Sr.; that is to say, money; that is to say, gratified ambitions—perhaps even the United States Senate. The United States Senate—that is to say, reasoning backward, gratified ambitions; that is to say, money. It ended there—in money. He was not "mercenary," because money means one thing to one man and to another something else. Dollar-signs can spell so many kinds of words—epithalamiums, for instance, and fierce war-chants and political orations and grateful truths—also lies. Mere money-hoarders are few. Sampson Rock, who had it, did not sigh for more money—only for more time; there were so many things to do, and life was so short. To his son money was barely commencing to take on a meaning. But already there was a different hue to his thoughts, a glitter faintly metallic.

Therefore, Judge Abercrombie loved the young man. That was no exaggeration; it was merely a reflex action: for he loved himself and his family and his laudable ambitions, and was an optimist; also sixty-eight years of age.

They were at their coffee when one of the waiters told the Judge that Colonel Robinson had arrived at the club. Shortly afterwards the Judge took Darrell with him and sought the Colonel.

"Good-evening, Colonel; I trust I see you well?"

"You may safely trust your sight, your honor. How is my learned brother?" Colonel Robinson smiled, evidently pleased with himself, his digestion, his finances, his friends, the Judge's appearance, and his own witty way of speaking. He was a tall, straight, handsome man, with a florid complexion, snow-white hair and "imperial," and clear, clean, blue eyes. Over the left eyebrow he carried—almost you might say he wore—a sabre scar. It became him. He knew it. His military carriage was deliberately meant to match the scar—the autograph of the war god, he probably called it.

"I wish to present to you my very good friend, Mr. John Darrell, of New York, Colonel Robinson."

Colonel Robinson stood up, erect, impressive, a Southern gentleman, a soldier—and an optimist. He bowed very gracefully. Darrell's bow was not quite so graceful. Colonel Robinson said, "Mr. Darrell, when I say I am delighted, I do no justice to my feelings."

"I myself am more than glad to meet you, Colonel Robinson. And you must allow me to express the hope—"

Colonel Robinson bowed again.

"Sir, consider it fulfilled, whatever it may be." He extended his hand with a sort of dignified cordiality that somehow imparted to his action a sort of sense of unusual favor, compelled by Darrell's winning ways. He looked straight into Darrell's eyes as Darrell shook the out-stretched hand firmly.

"A very nice man!" thought Colonel Robinson.

"Funny old cuss!" thought Darrell.

"Mr. Darrell, sir, in the classic language of his Excellence of South Carolina—" And Colonel Robinson looked anxiously at Darrell. Would Mr. Darrell blast all his hopes by a negative?

"I'm not proof against your eloquence," replied Darrell, with much seriousness.

The Colonel beamed, his one ambition in life having been gratified.

"Waiter!" he said, snapping his fingers sharply. His very impatience was a subtle compliment to Darrell.

"I leave you in good hands, Mr. Darrell," said Judge Abercrombie, rising to go.

"And Colonel Robinson in better," said the Colonel. "But, surely, Judge, you—"

"I have a friend in the dining-room—"

"May I not be his friend also, Judge?"

"Thank you; we shall join you directly."

"I beg that you will give me that pleasure, Judge." He looked after Abercrombie lovingly.

"I have been travelling over your road lately, Colonel Robinson," began Darrell, explanatorily.

"Then, sir, you have my sincere sympathy," said the Colonel, with decision.

Darrell smiled uncertainly, because Colonel Robinson looked so serious. The Westerner went on:

"I think it has a great future. It is my firm conviction that a new era of prosperity is dawning for the entire South." He was vaguely plagiarizing from some land-boomer's prospectus. "Some friends of mine have been thinking that there ought to be money in the Austin County coal and iron mines."

This was a pleasant surprise to the Colonel—his road tapped, or was supposed to tap, that section. It meant this man's money would help the road. But if Mr. Darrell or his friends had capital to invest, there were other opportunities for them to do so. Colonel Robinson knew them; he was the president of other companies than the Virginia Central Railroad.

"Money?" almost sneered Colonel Robinson, as if a child had spoken of a half-dime in connection with four bushels of diamonds, Kohinoor size. "Money? Millions, sir! But"—he would be frank, at any pecuniary cost to the president of the Virginia Central, who stood to win much from such an investment by

Darrell and his friends—"but of course it is slow work —very slow, sir. Our people are not educated to the strenuous life of the North. Virginia, sir, to-day offers the grandest opportunities to capital and intelligent enterprise ever vouchsafed to man since the beginning of time; nor are the opportunities confined to one section. They are everywhere. In this very city, the capital of this grand old State, I can see magnificent returns to the investor—and at the same time, Mr. Darrell, absolutely beyond all risk and peradventure, ten thousand leagues beyond the least possibility of a loss."

Colonel Robinson was frowning, almost as though he had caught Darrell doing a great wrong to Darrell's best friends by being wilfully blind to the contents of the Richmond Golconda, above the open door of which anybody with half an eye could read the huge placard: "Help yourself.—T. Robinson."

"I may say to you, Colonel Robinson, confidentially of course—"

"*Of* course," assented Colonel Robinson, tranquillizingly.

"That I am seeking opportunities for investment. But I don't want little things. I'd like something worth while, something big."

"Cer-tain-ly!" acquiesced Colonel Robinson. His manner showed that he had known that much from the first merely by looking at Darrell's face, and also that he himself never bothered with small affairs. In his own section Colonel Robinson was a big man. He represented, to his poorer fellow-Virginians, the Money Power—capital and enterprise. But often, when he read in the New York papers about the latest Northern captains of industry and the stock-market magnates, and their deals and their winnings, he felt his own insignificance with a vague regret. His people thought him a money-maker. He allowed them to think so, but in his heart of hearts he knew he was not. His ideas were good, but the results were never commensurate with his hopes nor with the hopes of his associates. But his soul, for all that, was ever a hot-bed of hope. How the hopes grew!

"But," continued Darrell, "to be perfectly frank—"

"Let us irrigate, Mr. Darrell, sir." The Colonel's quick but ingenuous interruption made Darrell smile slightly. Irrigation meant good temper, and that might make perfect frankness almost palatable, which unirrigated frankness not always was. The Colonel held up his glass and said, with an affectionate respect:

"To your very good health, sir! And now," he went on, with the air of resuming the conversation where he and none other had left off, "though there is much profit to be found in the development of iron and coal properties—much money, Mr. Darrell"—Colonel Robinson conceded at least one hundred millions readily and impressively—"yet there is the element of time to consider. It is well that one should reap the rewards of one's labors, instead of one's grandchildren doing it after one is cold clay. And, moreover, you have the instability of the iron trade to consider. As the great Carnegie, of library fame, has aptly observed, it is a case of feast or famine. There is no happy, no golden medium. I know people, most estimable people, who owned iron-mines and thought they were gold-mines, and waited years and years—and they are still waiting —for somebody else to develop them. Do you know what an iron-mine is? *The graveyard of hope!* But"— the Colonel, having sternly buried all iron hopes, past, present, and prospective, permitted a slight but affectionate smile to illumine his face—"a constantly increasing population is one of nature's grand and wise laws. The love of family is implanted by the Supreme Creator in the heart of man. Grow and multiply! That is a divine command, and, by gad, sir! it is easy to follow in this glorious climate. We have no race-suicides in this garden-spot of the earth. Therefore, I say"—he paused to shake a rigid forefinger at Darrell—"I say, *Real Estate!*"

There are many speakers who have the hypnotic faculty. Colonel Robinson had it. His own words always hypnotized him; the psychological effluvia struck inward. Darrell's look of interest made a warm glow come over the auto-hypnotist. He rang the little bell and said:

"Waiter, tell William it's for Colonel Robinson. As I was saying, Mr. Darrell, Richmond's population is growing by leaps and bounds, and with it the wealth of the cultured classes. The first thought a young man has when he contemplates matrimony is a home. The birds build nests on the trees the moment they begin to think of a family. But a young man of refinement can't make a house of nine straws and seven horse-hairs in a leafy bower. Therefore, if the young couple must have progeny that shall grow into useful men and beautiful women, why, the young couple must have a nice house. It is nature's eternal law, which is reducible to beautiful poems, but also to dollars and cents. We must not talk business here, but this is a hobby of mine. Say when, Mr. Darrell."

"My, this is fine," said Darrell, smacking his lips. He felt he had taken the measure of the old chap and wished Sam would come. He was not selfish.

"You may well say so, sir. There is not, alas! very much of it extant. The fact that I have not concealed this golden secret from you shows that there is no North and no South, only a common country." He smiled, lest Darrell should take him too seriously or talk politics. The Colonel wished to be airily jocular, but the words ran away with him.

"As I was saying, Mr. Darrell, when a business is based upon something so beautiful and so substantial as the love of home—that grand old Anglo-Saxon word for which there is no exact equivalent in any other language—then, sir, it is merely a case of folding your arms and letting your bank account grow with the growth of the city. The greatest, the most solid fortune in America, that of the Astors, was made by real estate. It was suburban when they bought it; it is now in the heart of the city. The population of Richmond in the year 1875 was, in round numbers—"

Judge Abercrombie and Sam approached them.

"If you will excuse me, Colonel Robinson," said the lawyer, "I'll leave my friend in your care. I promised to take Mrs. Abercrombie to Mrs. Lyman's musicale."

"She is well, Judge? She will see Mrs. Robinson there. My very best compliments. Can you not tarry a fraction of a second? Waiter!"

Sam bowed to Colonel Robinson, and said to Darrell:

"Jack, are you aware that we have—"

"I'd rather break the engagement than leave Colonel Robinson until he bid me. Colonel, my assistant, Mr. Rock," said Darrell.

"Assistant nothing," said Sam.

"I'm trying to teach him how to be a truthful mining engineer," Darrell confided to Colonel Robinson.

"An excellent profession," said Colonel Robinson,

with an almost affectionate encouragement to the young man. "I'm glad to meet you, sir. And I hope that you may exercise it in this State."

"It is not my profession," Sam smiled. But he did not wish Robinson to be misinformed.

"Not yet, but you wait," and Darrell laughed.

Judge Abercrombie was looking intently at his watch, which, after his absorbed scrutiny, he held to his ear and listened, frowning—in order not to seem to hear Colonel Robinson should Colonel Robinson ask inconvenient questions about Sam's identity. He put the watch in his pocket, and, rising to his feet, said:

"I'm very sorry, but I must be off post-haste. Darrell, I'll see both of you boys to-morrow." He looked at Sam to explain by a meaning glance that his familiarity was forced upon him. "Good-night, gentlemen."

Colonel Robinson, excusing himself from the guests, walked with the Judge to the door.

"Your friend Darrell is a very charming man." The very tone in which he said this was full of unuttered questions.

"Yes. He is associated with important capitalists in New York who are chiefly interested in mining and industrial enterprises. He is a mining expert, a very famous one. I hope we can induce him to invest a few millions in mines in this State. He controls considerable capital, not only in this country but in England."

"Indeed! Who are his—"

"Colonel, Mr. Darrell, through his reputation and his own resources, has only to allot to the members of his syndicate their respective participations and the money is forthcoming at once. I think he is not only a very able but a very nice man. I introduced him to you because I wanted you to know gentlemen whom I am very glad to know, and I wanted him to know you because you know of so many opportunities for investment in this State. I did not bring Darrell to the club to talk business to you. But I regard it as a solemn duty to interest such men in our State."

"I am very sorry you can't be with us, Judge," said Colonel Robinson, and he returned to his new friends.

"You were saying the Astor fortune was made out of buying real estate," said Darrell, barely allowing time for the Colonel to sit down

"Yes, sir; by buying suburban real estate and waiting for the city to grow up. The growth of Richmond is certain; it is inevitable. But, as I said, there is no need to work for your unborn grandchildren. The unearned increment is a loathsome and un-American way of making money. In other words, anticipate the future and help it to come quickly. ' Assist the growth; encourage it; by gad, sir, force it! That has ever been my motto. A few friends—life-long, personal friends, who believe as I do—have associated themselves with me in securing what is beyond doubt the most valuable tract of land in Richmond—Capital Park. We shall develop it as a high-class residential park, carefully restricted, with beautiful scenery, beautiful surroundings, magnificent avenues, quick and efficient transportation. It is altogether an attractive proposition, and, apart from the financial phase of it, it has a distinctly patriotic side."

It was, indeed, an attractive proposition to Colonel Robinson. He would not do things on a half scale. His executive ability consisted in giving orders to subordinates and assuming that they would be diligently and skilfully carried out. His plans entailed lavish expenditures. Such land and town schemes had been highly profitable in the North and West. There was no reason why this should not prove equally successful in Richmond—that is, none that Colonel Robinson could see. He had read and lovingly studied numerous prospectuses and advertisements. He would give orders to subordinates. Hence his speeches to Darrell.

"I quite agree with you, Colonel," said Sam, with evident sincerity.

"Your street-railway service—" began Darrell, politely.

"Of course"—the Colonel smiled to show such a thing had not escaped him—"we have completed the surveys and obtained the right of way and consents, and are about to secure the franchise for an electric road from Capital Park to the heart of Richmond. Perhaps, unless your plans prevent it, you may afford me the privilege of showing you Capital Park?"

"We gladly accept your invitation," said Darrell. "We came down partly on pleasure and partly on business, and if an opportunity offers we may avail ourselves of it. To have your company to-morrow will be a pleasure. Now, the Austin coal properties look to me like a very good thing. But I am assured the transportation facilities are scarcely adequate for—"

"If you will guarantee the tonnage I will guarantee the transportation," said Colonel Robinson, impressively. These Northern people would talk business in a church, not to mention a club. The Colonel himself would not. He really was sure of it.

"It would be a good thing for your Virginia Central if the coal-mines were developed."

"We would bear such an increase in traffic with

philosophical fortitude," assented Colonel Robinson with his humorous seriousness.

"I built the Mesa Grande road in Arizona from the Lomita coal-mines to the Southwestern and Gulf main line; we gave them enough tonnage to put their preferred stock on a dividend-paying basis. But their rates did not show that they were grateful to us. There were lots of promises before we developed the mines. But when the tonnage was safe, they lost their memory. What we ought to have done was to have bought Southwestern and Gulf stock to give us representation in their board. When we realized this, the stock had trebled in price owing to the profit they were making out of us. And then we were forced to build our own railroad at a very heavy expense."

"Well, sir, Virginia Central stock at this moment is one of the grandest bargains ever offered to a blind and unsuspecting world," said Colonel Robinson decidedly.

"It has been rather weak, lately, I understand," put in Sam. "About forty, I think?" He looked inquiringly at the Colonel. The price that morning had touched thirty-five again. Colonel Robinson, with an air of being above petty details, as, for instance, a difference of five dollars a share in the price of the stock of his road, said: "About there, more or less. I think my friends are buying it at every opportunity." Of his friends, fully twoscore had been asking and writing and even telephoning for explanations and barely a half-dozen had promised to buy, if it went any lower. The latter were friends who did not wish to buy suburban real estate, but were willing to say they would do what Colonel Robinson could not object to, in order to show they were loyal; such as, for instance, promise to buy stock in another Robinson company.

"It's pretty well held in Virginia, I suppose," said Sam.

"The stock is held pretty well over the entire country by conservative investors. Our bond-holders are mostly English, you know."

"Do you think it is cheap at forty?" asked Sam.

"Is a gold dollar cheap at forty cents?" asked Colonel Robinson.

"Yes, but you can't always make people believe it. They'll swear it must be a counterfeit," laughed Sam.

Colonel Robinson remembered the pusillanimous and impatient inquiries that had poured in during the last few weeks. He agreed, almost angrily:

"That is very true. People are apt to confound suspiciousness with conservatism. Silly men who know me and the road actually ask me if I think their investment is safe! It is incomprehensible to me"—he shook his head despairingly and abandoned all hope of ever understanding it—"how people pretending to ordinary intelligence fail to recognize the self-evident truth when they meet it face to face. They simply don't know it when they see it." He shook his head in sorrow; then in pity; the men were blind; blindness is a terrible affliction.

"But," said Sam sympathizingly, "after the stock turns out to be a bonanza, you will have the satisfaction—"

"But no gratitude. I sometimes feel like relinquishing my management of the road and devoting myself to—"

"But you couldn't do that," said Sam. "Surely, you are not serious? Why, they call it Colonel Robinson's railroad." Sam looked eagerly as he leaned forward slightly the better.to hear the Colonel's answer.

"That's what they call it," assented Colonel Robinson grimly, "whenever something goes wrong, through no fault of mine. It's my road, then — oh yes! They expect miracles and expect them every five minutes!" Then he smiled and he went on pleasantly: "I should like to have you take luncheon with me here to-morrow afternoon and afterwards we might drive to Capital Park. That is, of course, if the weather permits and such a thing is agreeable to you." He had dismissed the Virginia Central from his mind. The leaves of the trees in Capital Park were dollars. The Colonel almost heard them jingle in the passing breezes. There were millions of leaves and the wind was blowing briskly. They were ever so much nearer than Austin County. The railroad was an old vexation and Capital Park was his baby, the sweetest ever.

"Nothing could possibly please us more, Colonel Robinson," said Darrell.

"Nothing," echoed Sam pleasantly.

Then the Colonel told them stories.

XVIII

THEY met at Colonel Robinson's office the next morning by appointment, in order to "talk business," as Darrell had put it. Colonel Robinson silently hoped they would buy Capital Park Improvement Company stock, and Sam had hoped, also silently, that he could buy Virginia Central stock. What the Colonel audibly hoped was that they had enjoyed a good night's rest. They hoped he felt as well as he looked. He did. Smiles.

There was a pause. Robinson was about to end it with a premeditated jocularity when Darrell said:

"Colonel, we shall return to New York in a few days. As I told you last night, we have been looking into the Austin County coal-fields and we think there's money in them." Darrell abstained from mentioning the Austin Iron Company.

"There certainly is," acquiesced the Colonel. He still hoped they would see how much more there was in real estate and suburban trolleys. "You are making no mistake."

"We are not," assented Darrell, calmly, "unless the transportation facility should continue inadequate."

"Continue?" echoed the Colonel, arching his eyebrows in polite surprise.

"Surely you don't think you could handle a much bigger tonnage with your present equipment?"

"As I said before, you get the tonnage and we'll move it." The Colonel said it tranquilly. His tranquillity would have impressed them had they not known the road's condition, physical and financial. The Colonel then waited for more.

"I hope you will," went on Darrell. "But, even assuming that you will be in shape to do so, we should like to feel that the Virginia Central is friendly to us." To Sam, Darrell was indirect. There was no frontal attack. He was intimating what was not so.

"Friendly? Of course we'll be friendly! We'd help you out of pure, unadulterated selfishness." The Colonel smiled unselfishly.

"What assurance are you willing to give us that you will put yourself in a position to handle the traffic we'll give you?"

"My word," answered Colonel Robinson, simply. He looked Homeric.

Darrell bowed. This play-acting made him smile— his own as well as Robinson's. He looked at Sam and almost winked, but the youngster's face was too serious. Sam took his friend's glance as a cue for him to say something. Thereupon Sam said, with much positiveness:

"Colonel Robinson, I consider the outlook for that section of the country very bright indeed if the railroad could be brought up to date. All that is needed is capital. I think we could help the Virginia Central—"

"If the Virginia Central will help us," interjected Darrell.

"Having been considerately prepared for the worst," said Colonel Robinson, with a genial smile, "suppose you gentlemen tell me exactly what it is you desire?" The president of the Virginia Central Railroad looked at Mr. Darrell as if he welcomed the gladsome opportunity to do exactly as his friend wished, no greater pleasure having yet been discovered by this world's experts in happiness.

"A schedule of rates," replied Darrell — a trifle pugnaciously, Sam thought—"that will enable us to figure on sure profits, thereby facilitating my work of floating a big coal and iron company. The first thing that any capitalist will ask about is railroad rates."

"My dear Mr. Darrell, isn't it a trifle premature to talk of a coal tonnage before you own a single—"

"Before we buy a foot of land in this State we've got to know what the railroad will do for us."

"As I've already said, sir, when you show us the tonnage I will show you satisfactory rates." The Colonel looked business-like. He was very versatile.

"Colonel," said Darrell, bluntly, "we want rates from your road that will make our mines pay. Out West the railroads back up infant industries with actual cash and long credits. In this section the procedure is different, I believe. See what the Great Southern is doing for the Buffalo Creek Coal Company."

"Yes," interrupted Colonel Robinson, angrily, "it is being milked by the coal company which is owned by the president of the Great Southern and his friends in the directorate of the railroad. The railroad stock pays two per cent. dividends and the coal company twelve. The railroad insiders own very little of the railroad stock and *all* of the coal stock." Colonel Robinson did not wish to offend these gentlemen nor to hinder the urgently needed industrial developments along his line, but he would not permit erroneous impressions as to the way his road was willing to do business.

"I did not know that," replied Darrell, apologetically. "I had merely heard that the railroad did all in
its power to help the Buffalo Creek enterprise."
"So it does." Colonel Robinson said it with a grim
smile.
"Of course, we had no idea of asking such a thing.
We want to get out Austin County coal at a profit, and
we want all the aid we can get until we are firmly on
our feet. We have to create a market for that coal.
You realize that, don't you?" Sam was vaguely
irritated by Darrell's talk. It gave him a feeling of
impatience rather than of indignation. The whole
truth could not be told to Colonel Robinson, but, of
course, no unfair advantage would be taken of the
Colonel's ignorance.

"Yes, sir. It is undoubtedly so." The Colonel's
air as he looked at Darrell was one of felicitation—on
Darrell's grasp of the situation and its exigencies.

"We'll have to spend a fortune in advertising—all
kinds of advertising. I want to get the government to
use it on the trial trips of the new war-ships and give
that fact the widest publicity. There are other coal
companies already laying pipes to get the same advertisement. It's a fine, quick-firing coal and ought to win
on its merits. But merit needs pushing and pushing
costs money. I don't mind telling you," said Darrell,
impressively, "that options on all the producing mines
and on several thousands of acres of coal lands in
Austin County have already been secured."

Sam admitted to himself that Darrell had very carefully not lied, and that if they secured good rates and
facilities they would make the new and greater Austin
Iron Company a success whether Sampson Rock secured
the control of the Virginia Central Railroad or not. He

did not feel as indignant about it as he had been at Sampson Rock's misleading truth-telling in Wall Street. He was impatient to finish this preliminary palaver and eager to ask Robinson's price for his railroad stock. Robinson must know they were in earnest and had big plans in mind. He blurted out, impatiently:

"And Mr. Darrell and I would like to buy out the Austin Iron Company; not for a syndicate, but for ourselves."

Darrell flushed violently and did not trust himself to look at Sam. But the Colonel opened wide his eyes. Then he said, with a successful attempt at composure:

"I had suspected something of the sort, gentlemen." He smiled with a quiet sort of mysteriousness, as a man who habitually knows everything but is the incarnation of astute taciturnity. It was very plain to Sam that the Colonel's soul-crises over matters of veracity were not violent.

"We want low rates," said Darrell, quickly. "We will give you the tonnage, which you need pretty badly. You establish your tariffs, but we will guarantee you a minimum the first year of fifty thousand tons more than you carried last year, and we expect that you will give us—"

"Our road has never given rebates," interrupted Colonel Robinson, with austere solemnity. But his heart began to beat with hope. Darrell's speech, with its promise of new business, was as a lungful of fresh air to a drowning man. It showed in his eyes. Sam observed it and mistook the gleam for the last of the resistance. He concluded that the Colonel wished to yield and at the same time to save his self-respect.

"Then you enjoy the proud distinction of being unique among railroads of this great and glorious country, made great and glorious by its railroads," Darrell said, amiably.

"Never mind all that," said Sam. "Colonel, if we are going to get out a tonnage that will mean plenty of work to the inhabitants of Austin County and to the railroad, do you think it is fair we should do all the sweating? What do you say to an increase of fifty thousand tons the first year, one hundred thousand the second, two hundred thousand the third, three hundred thousand the fourth, and so on to five hundred thousand tons more per year than the Virginia Central ever carried before? What do you say ought to be done by the railroad?"

That was so much more than the Colonel had dared to hope that he was tempted to think these men were merely talking for effect. Men who could do such things were too powerful not to be able to force the railroad to do everything short of losing money. Yet there was only one railroad into Austin County, and to build a new line from Austin to either tide-water or some point on another and more complaisant road was an expense too great to incur by the coal and iron company. These men had given him information—to be verified merely by ascertaining the extent of Mr. Darrell's resources in the way of cash and reputation in New York—which would enable him to cheer the pusillanimous holders of Virginia Central stock. They would be told of "important developments," and would thank the sleepless president of the road for his efforts in the road's behalf. With more tonnage, moreover, bond dealers might be less unreasonable. Robinson habitually thought not of the present, which was apt to be cloudy, but of the future, which always was rosy with the incandescence of aureate hopes. To-day was not cloudy.

"You can count on me, gentlemen," he assured them, with much benignity. He carefully avoided looking triumphant or otherwise, showing that he was thinking of himself and of the fact that the Virginia Central was the only road into the Austin coal-fields. He was not in their power. Give and take—that was the science of business. There was no need to think of what he might possibly give; but he saw very vividly and distinctly what he would take.

Sam, more from intuition than from any mental analysis, divined a part of what was passing in the Colonel's mind, and he said, suddenly:

"Not one cent do we spend in Austin County or anywhere else along the line of the Central until we know what to expect from the railroad. Of course, you wouldn't squeeze us"—the Colonel put on a look that emphatically denied such a crime—"because you wouldn't kill the goose that laid the golden eggs; besides which, we would never put ourselves in a position to be squeezed. Iron-bound contracts or nothing. But will you give us adequate facilities—"

"Certainly," interrupted the Colonel, earnestly. "Of course." And he smiled a trifle pityingly.

"You haven't them now, and before you spend money to buy cars and engines you naturally will make certain of our ability to do as we say. We don't want to build another road. It would cost less to buy twenty-five or thirty thousand shares of Virginia Central stock. It would give us," finished Sam, who himself desired now very carefully not to lie, "representation in your road."

"It certainly would," assented the Colonel, cordially. "A most excellent idea." He did not feel cordial. The greatest man in the world would not listen to a "bluff" with real cordiality.

"If you buy thirty thousand shares, Sam," said Darrell, in a cold-shower voice, "it will tie up a million dollars. That's fifty thousand dollars a year loss in interest, or just about the profit on two hundred and fifty or three hundred thousand tons of coal."

"It would prove a fine investment, sir!" The Colonel said it with conviction. He might be able to issue treasury stock and sell it to these people, who would by no means control the road thereby. He looked sternly at Darrell until the thought struck him that these men might have designs on the road as well, and thereupon looked encouragingly — that there might be further revelations.

"I have no desire to invest in railroad stocks," said Darrell, decisively. "It's out of my line."

"Colonel," put in Sam, abruptly, "your road needs money as much as the Austin County mines do. You haven't the equipment now, but we might be able to help you get it. But before taking any steps in the matter of pledging ourselves to buy the stock or bonds that you would have to issue to raise the money needed, we can't be rank outsiders. The stock is now selling around thirty-five, and many people think it is pretty high at that. I am no expert on values of stocks, but I know that after we've put in money into coal and iron here, and your road's in better physical shape, the stock will be worth more. Therefore, suppose you get us options on a block of the stock held by those of your acquaintances who, you say, are grumbling because the stock isn't paying dividends?"

"You mean you will buy—"

"No; I won't buy any stock outright; but for an option on, say, fifty thousand shares at a price a little higher than the stock may be bought for to-day in the open market, I'm willing to pay whatever you think is fair."

"For example?"

"For fifty thousand shares at forty I'll pay two hundred thousand dollars. That's for a year's option."

"Two hundred thousand dollars," said Darrell, "will drive a mighty long tunnel—"

Colonel Robinson smiled blandly and shook his head, both of which vexed Sam. He said:

"Gentlemen, all I can say is: Go ahead and develop the mines and the Virginia Central will help you to the best of its ability. As for the option, why, the stock will sell much higher before the year is out. The open market is before you."

"Without such developments as we have in mind, you must realize that the stock's chances of selling at higher prices are remote."

"I decidedly realize nothing of the sort. We have been doing business a week or two and—"

"Yes, and—" Sam checked himself. "We must have time to promote our companies, though we already know what we can do. I don't want to gamble in railroad stocks and I have no desire to invest money in them when I want to work here in Virginia developing the resources of the State. But, of course, if you don't see your way clear to pledging the Central to help us—"

"Pardon me, sir, if I interrupt you," the Colonel said, with much dignity. "We want more business and we'll do all we can to further your desires. But although I might promise much now, I can't pledge my railroad to go into bankruptcy to help companies that, so far as I can see, do not exist as yet even on paper." •

SAMPSON ROCK OF WALL STREET

"So far as I am concerned," said Darrell, coldly, "they will remain on paper unless we can reach a written agreement with your road in the matter of rates. Suppose you prepare a schedule for us and—"

"We don't want to lose time," Sam interjected. "The iron trade is booming. You don't think it is possible for us to buy options on a block of stock from yourself or your friends at a price sufficiently above the market-price to show our faith in Austin County resources, and at the same time discount some of the increase in value our mining operations would bring the stock?"

"Not one share of my holdings is for sale at any price, and I have steadfastly advised my frends to hold theirs. I cannot compel them to hold. But I do not think they would accept any such absurd price as forty dollars a share, nor would they childishly allow any strange capitalists to deprive them of their voice in the management of their road. Moreover"—the Colonel said this with a friendly smile, for he would not close the door on developments that would make him a very rich man—"I do not think that the voting power of fifty thousand shares would enable you as directors of the railroad to vote to yourselves, as directors of the coal company, rates that would bankrupt the road in a year or two." He had seen their plot and he was not angry. He was tolerant and, yes, amused. But, then, everything is fair in business.

"Then no coal lands for us," said Sam, with much decision.

"That is for you to decide, gentlemen." Colonel Robinson said this calmly. Of course, these men would go away — and would return and talk rates. Both sides would yield—one side a few inches and no more—

255

at the psychological moment. The other side, realizing the uselessness of trying to get more, would be content. Darrell confirmed his suspicions by saying:

"Colonel, will you think over this matter, and just try to put yourself in our place, and also consider fairly how much it is worth to your road to double your tonnage from Austin?"

"I have thought. We won't cut off our nose to spite our face. But we have to live. Millions for defence, but not one cent for—"

"Rebates!" finished Darrell, smiling. He rose to go. "Of course our talk has been in strict confidence."

"Of course." Colonel Robinson aimed at the engineer a rebuking look of surprise. But Sam, who saw the look, was not impressed with the Colonel's histrionic ability. He felt certain Robinson would tell everybody that a new era of prosperity was dawning for the Virginia Central. Nevertheless, he shook hands warmly and said he would call again as soon as he returned from a few days' absence on a personal business that unexpectedly called him away.

As soon as they were out of hearing of the Colonel, Darrell halted, looked at Sam steadily a minute before he spoke. Then he said:

"I'll bet there never was your equal in this world for sheer, unadulterated—"

"You win, Jack," said Sam, with conviction.

XIX

FROM time to time Sam endeavored to defend his tactless truth - telling, which had succeeded in making Robinson less willing to sell his Central stock, but it was a half-hearted defence at best. He could not claim as his own a fanatical devotion to the truth. He had not told the entire truth to the Colonel, and he recognized that such a thing would have been impossible, or at all events highly impolitic. To tell less than the whole truth, granting there was no loss of self-respect in the proceeding, might be pardoned if the fractional veracity had been judiciously selected. This latter was Darrell's contention, made all the more irritating in that no honest reply could come to Sam's mind. He had no desire to be an altruist; he did not feel called upon to lead a crusade against wealth while there was one unsuccored pauper in the wide world. He might not admit it to himself, but, for all that, his hatred of mendacity was now qualified. It was lying for money that he hated. He did not think it the part of a gentleman ever to lie. It was even more than cowardly—it was useless. He had tried to be honest and veracious in his dealings with Robinson. He had succeeded in being honest, but only to the extent that he had endeavored not to defraud. Absolutely truthful he had not been, and all he had gained was the con-

257

sciousness that his half-truths had shown how absurd complete veracity would have been.

This feeling of impotence to be completely one thing or the other filled him with a sense of exasperation. He had experienced a check; his progress towards a goal, that hourly became more pleasing as he thought of the manifold meanings of his definite arrival at it, had been impeded. As his resentment waxed hotter, he thought less of himself and his honorable intentions and more of Robinson. There was no doubt of it, the president of the Virginia Central was one of the dogs in the manger whose mission in life was to convince strenuous philanthropists that the end, after all, justifies the means. Indeed, the desire to get Robinson's own stock—or rather enough shares to insure the possession of the control of the road itself—came to him; an ardent wish to supplant a phrase-drunken visionary by a taciturn but highly efficient railroad manager, a chap like Rogers of the Roanoke working under Sampson Rock. Withal, he had not the shadow of a wish to pay other than a fair price for Robinson's stock, and even more than a fair price if only Robinson could be induced to sell out at once. When this had crystallized in his mind, the juvenile inconsistency of it all, the indifference to the money - cost in a purely business transaction—an indifference which plainly arose from his ignorance of the value of money—struck him humor ously. He laughed, and said to Darrell:

"Jack, I am all you think, and more, too. But let us give Robinson another chance."

"I think you'd better stick to the iron company and leave the man's work to your father."

Sam flushed because Darrell looked very much in earnest, but he smiled good-humoredly as he replied:

"Maybe you are right, Jack. You go to Austin and stir up Fletcher and I'll take a little trip over the Roanoke. That will give Robinson time to think it over."

"Yes, I expect he will do a heap of thinking this next week or two, if you allow your father to work undisturbed."

The same thought had been in Sam's mind, and with it the not altogether pleasant realization that he had become an accomplice of the great stock manipulator in his unedifying task. The work that his father was doing did not now have the same power to arouse indignation and the instinctive opposition that had caused their great misunderstanding. It could not, even without causing a deterioration in the moral fibre, for the reason that he now realized the utter futility of straightforwardness and complete veracity. He did not think of the difference between instigating in person attacks on Robinson's credit and taking advantage of similar attacks made by some one else. The unwavering desire to pay a fair money price was as the light of an antique alabaster lamp, poetical, but dim. It made motives shadowy and intentions flickering. By going away now he would let events shape themselves. Nothing could possibly happen in his absence that would make his task any more difficult than it was now, and he would have time to think of Robinson and plan a course of action even while he acquainted himself with the railroad, the development of which was his father's sole motive-power in business. Patience would not come hard after realizing that it was absolutely necessary.

Darrell went to Austin, uninstructed and in good humor, while Sam, under the tutelage of Rogers, division superintendent and famous railroad expert, made an "exhaustive trip" over the Roanoke. He saw his father's road from the observation-windows of the president's private car, looking through the eyes of an expert who pointed out nothing but the excellent work done and doing under the supervision of the modest Mr. Rogers. Never had Mr. Rogers suggested improvements that Sampson Rock had not promptly telegraphed from New York, "Go ahead." To make a fine road for a man who did not want and would not have any other kind, Rogers told Sam, was like being in heaven. The result—of Mr. Rogers's suggestions and Sampson Rock's financial bravery and resources —was before Sam. The Roanoke was making money. It would make much more. Factories were going up —many of them on paper, but none the less impressive for all that—along the line of the railroad; the population was increasing; the people were prosperous and working as never before; real-estate booms were heard of here and there; farms were paying, money was circulating freely, and all about him, besides the agricultural activity visible from the windows, Sam could see new cars, new locomotives, new stations, construction gangs at work on sidings and switches—the tireless spirit of Sampson Rock omnipresent.

Unconsciously Rogers, in his explanation of the outwardness and inwardness of what they saw, did much to change Sam's point of view towards his father's business methods. What Sam saw excused much. It took the sting from many reproaches, it made the suffering of the individual a matter of less importance until vague regrets seemed more natural than heart-wrung tears. As he studied the Roanoke under the tuition of Mr. Rogers, he wrote to Fanny—long letters containing very little of himself and very much about the road and the work and the inspiration of the work, so that Fanny rejoiced and answered. accordingly, and he wrote again. In his wish to interest her, he intensified his own interest until he was full to overflowing with a resolve to devote his life to doing such work as his father had done. He most certainly would be with Rogers when Rogers was intrusted with the modernization of the Virginia Central. He wrote at length to his father—enthusiastic descriptions of what he had seen as well as many echoes of the modest Rogers's expert utterances. Ten days later he went back to Richmond.

Darrell would not return from Austin until the following day, and Sam called on Judge Abercrombie.

"I am, indeed, glad to see you, Mr. Rock." The Judge scrutinized him caressingly. "Your trip," he ventured, tentatively felicitating, "certainly seems to have agreed with you. Did you enjoy it?"

"Very much. It won't be my last trip."

"Rogers is an able man," Abercrombie said—"a very able man. Your father, I think, has a genius for recognizing talent."

"I like Rogers." Sam confirmed his father's judgment. "By-the-way, have you seen anything of Colonel Robinson lately?"

"Oh yes. He has been very active—and very voluble." The Judge smiled. "Perhaps I should have said loquacious. He has been telling everybody that very important developments were pending, and has written to his London agents—so I have been reliably informed—of great plans for improving the road and getting the facilities to handle an approaching increase in traffic. To his more intimate friends he has hinted that the coal-fields of Austin County—"

Sam frowned. Judge Abercrombie went on, a trifle deprecatingly: "I suppose some of the people whom Mr. Morson saw must have given him an inkling of the deal. At all events, the Colonel went to Austin last week. His coming back and his loquacity were synchronous."

There was a silence. At length Sam, with an effort that was not apparent to Abercrombie, suggested, calmly, "I think you had better write to my father about it."

"I have done so. This morning I received this telegram:

"'Thanks. Keep us fully informed. Discourage belief that options will be exercised. Continue searches and arrange final papers.—MORSON.'"

Sam's feeling of relief that his indiscretion had not upset his father's plans made him overlook the instructions as to the discouragement of the coal-land owners' hopes, the latter properly being for effect on the over-optimistic Robinson. He was concerned with his own Austin Iron Company deal and was anxious to learn what progress had been made by Darrell and Fletcher. When he left Richmond, Austin shares had been quoted at thirty-five to forty, but that morning he had seen the latest quotation in the broker's office which adjoined the hotel. They were from thirty to thirty-five. He had wondered, curiously rather than indignantly, how the drop in the quoted price had been achieved. Fletcher's versatility might have taken a new turn and possibly had helped to offset Robinson's oratory.

Rogers, the able and modest superintendent of the Roanoke's Western division, was waiting in the hotel lobby for his pupil. At the sight of Sam the able superintendent put on a grateful smile:

"Mr. Rock, I don't know how to thank you."

"For what?"

"For the raise."

"What raise?" Sam was puzzled and looked it. His ignorance made him rise in Rogers's estimation. It proved to the superintendent that young Rock was in the confidence of the great Sampson Rock. It behooved him to cultivate his young benefactor.

"My salary has been raised a thousand a year. New York orders." Rogers's delight was distinctly visible to the naked eye. It was not alone the increase; but the superintendent had tried to make a good impression on the master's son and had succeeded. Success cheers because it is the most insidious form of flattery —self-flattery.

"Well, I am glad of it, Rogers," laughed Sam. "You deserve it; but I am not guilty."

"It is very nice of you, Mr. Rock, and all I can say is—"

"I tell you I didn't do it. Such letters as I wrote to my father were entirely about personal matters."

"Well, it happened as soon as we got back," said Rogers, in a pleasantly controversial tone. "Wages have been advanced ten per cent. all along the line." Rogers looked at Sam as though he expected fresh contradictions, which would be entirely useless, for he had told Sam how business was increasing and how the morale of the operating force was improving. "It is a stroke of genius on your father's part—you notice "— Rogers smiled a significant smile at the denying Sam— "you notice I say *your father*—to anticipate voluntarily what was bound to come in a few months, after a lot of meetings and resolutions and discontent, and no gratitude when the raise did come. This will please the boys and it advertises the road's prosperity. The boys all think they owe this to you. In fact, I've told them—"

"Then untell them," said Sam, decisively.

"They'd still believe it was you, no matter what I said to the contrary," said Rogers. The men had learned that Rogers had suggested it to young Rock and young Rock to old Rock and old Rock to President Leigh, all because of Rogers, who knew the men would work better for him and thus it would help the Roanoke—and Rogers. "Your father wrote Leigh to make it appear it came from the Richmond office without instructions from New York. He wants results and not personal popularity. That's why we swear by him, even if he didn't begin as a brakeman," he finished, enthusiastically. The one thousand dollars a year increase in the Rogers income was conducive to hero-worship, but apart from that Sam himself could not help a feeling of admiration for his father. He shook hands with the hero-worshipper and sat down to read the Richmond papers, which devoted some columns to the Roanoke's action.

It was not until three days afterwards that Sam read in the same papers that there were "ugly mutterings of discontent" from the employés of the Virginia Central and the Great Southern roads, but particularly the Virginia Central. Also he read that Mr. W. P. St. John, the well-known traffic manager of the famous Allegheny & Ohio River Railroad, had decided not to accept the general managership of the Virginia Central, an offer he had had under consideration for some months. This, the papers added—each curiously enough using the identical words of the others—had greatly disappointed the hopes of the more progressive element among the Central stockholders.

Darrell reached Richmond at noon, accompanied by Fletcher, who came to attend the annual meeting of the Austin Iron Company. Late that afternoon the little manager went to Darrell's room at the hotel—Sam's name not being on the hotel-register on account of the reporters. Fletcher's face was composed enough, but his eyes sparkled impressively. He addressed himself to Darrell.

"It happened exactly as I told you it would." Pausing a few seconds to allow that to sink in, he went on: "That closing down of No. 3 came at the psychological moment. I spoke freely to them and told them we had to raise money and probably buy our own cars. Colonel Robinson tried to get them to pledge themselves to raise a half-million by an issue of bonds, but when Westlake asked him how much he would subscribe for, the Colonel said he'd take as big a slice as the next man. The next man happened to be old Morton, and all he said was: 'I pass, Colonel.' That really ended it. Why, they couldn't raise half a million cents in half a million years." He paused triumphantly

"Well?" Darrell spoke impatiently.

"The Colonel would have it that they didn't need half a million dollars, and I said we didn't need it if the Central gave us more cars and carried a little of our paper just to encourage an infant industry, which every railroad did. To cut a long story short, they voted to make repairs out of earnings, and I said, 'Then, gentlemen, no dividends for five years, and I say five years because I'm naturally a hopeful sort of cuss.' Robinson said, very sarcastic-like, that it would not take that many years to find a less hopeful manager, and that there was no reason why dividends and repairs couldn't happen at the same time. I said I'd pay the expenses of the search for the man who could work wonders by putting in thirty hours out of the twenty-four, and besides be his own chemist, bookkeeper, mining engineer, and cook, and that my resignation was in their hands, to take effect whenever they said so. That took the wind out of their sails." He looked at Sam, conqueror-like, but Sam asked him, quietly:

"How did the accident to No. 3 happen?"

"How? Because it was due to happen. It's a miracle we didn't get it earlier."

"Aha!" muttered Sam. Perhaps it was merely good luck. He desired the Austin Iron Company more than ever, since he had decided to witness with his own eyes the regeneration of the Virginia Central under Rogers, as soon as the control of the Central passed to the Roanoke.

"You don't think I did it on purpose, Mr. Rock?" asked Fletcher, with a sort of politely amused look. "It's just as I've told you. I've had to take all sorts of chances, because my people pushed me and were keen for more dividends. They got what they deserved It's the old penny-wise, pound-foolish policy. It doesn't pay."

"Getting down to business, what did you do about our matter?" asked Darrell, coldly.

Fletcher very impressively took a little memorandum-book from his pocket and read aloud from it: "Nine thousand three hundred shares. But they must have their money this week, and the option is good for thirty days only in most cases. On thirty-six hundred shares I've got sixty days. When I saw that all we needed to cinch the control was eight hundred shares, I didn't fight for the six months' time."

"Our terms were based on six months—" began Darrell.

But Sam broke in; he felt that he had the control, and the terms of payment concerned him least of all:

"I'll pay you the twenty-five thousand dollars I promised you now. And keep on trying to get as much more of the stock as you can. Suppose you turn it in to me at cost, plus five per cent. commission to yourself?"

Darrell smiled, because he understood Sam's eagerness and rather liked the gambler-like decision. But Fletcher figured rapidly. He had made a handsome profit on the nine thousand three hundred shares he had already secured, and would make more. He saw a broad avenue before him, suitable for rapid locomotion and paved with gold. In the distance, dimly, he descried the Fletcher mansion and a mob of future admirers listening to the most interesting talker in the world. This was the road to fame and fortune. He literally burned to work for his new masters, who had presented to him on a golden salver the opportunity that made him a great engineer and a rich man. He blinked his eyes in order to awake.

"It suits me. But more than anything else I want to see you get the company and make things hum," he said, with a happy laugh. "I'm beginning to get gray hairs waiting to start."

Sam wrote out a check for twenty-five thousand dollars to Fletcher's order, and gave it to the little manager silently. He changed his mind and spoke, in a kindly voice: "This is the first, Fletcher. I hope it won't be the last; but that depends upon you." He turned to Darrell in time to detect the ghost of a smile on the Westerner's lips, and said: "Jack, I'm going to send some telegrams. Excuse me a few minutes, Fletcher. Just talk matters over with Darrell, will you?"

Darrell accompanied Sam to the door.

"What's on your heavy-weight mind, Sam?"

"That I'm going to need a heap of money and need it quick. Now that we've got the iron company, I'm going after.the real article. I'll be back in a minute."

He telegraphed to Valentine to deposit to his credit at the Metropolitan thirty thousand dollars, and to his father he sent this message:

"Have drawn on Metropolitan National Bank to order of Darrell for five hundred thousand dollars. Please see that the money is forthcoming. Have found immensely valuable property. Darrell puts in as much as I. Am sure you will approve my action.—SAM."

He went back to hear the discussion between Fletcher and Darrell, conscious of a rather mild excitement at having burned his bridges behind him. He had decided what his own future should be, and the prospect pleased him. It was not long before the answer to this telegram came:

"Certainly not. Stop draft at once. Come home.—S. R."

Sam frowned; then he laughed and wrote, Darrell looking over his shoulder as he did so:

"Too late to stop anything. Have had best advice. You are getting off cheap.—SAM."

Darrell said, seriously: "Take out that last alleged witticism. Perhaps you'd better do as he says and go back."

"Not yet," retorted Sam. "Leave the Colonel *now?* What are you thinking of?" He gave the answer—unchanged—to the waiting boy, and said: "Please have this go at once. You can keep the change if you hurry up."

The messenger earned his money.

Fletcher had carefully but gleefully figured that not more than fifty thousand dollars cash would be needed for the next fortnight, and, having dismissed the matter of the options from his mind, was grandly building the model iron plant of the South for his new master. His enthusiasm pleased Sam. Fletcher had quadrupled the capacity and decupled the net earnings when another telegram came for Sam. It was brief:

"Return immediately.—S. R."

He passed it to Darrell, who said, seriously: "I told you perhaps you'd better. Anybody else would have wired the Judge to have you examined by a commissioner of lunacy."

"Yes?" said Sam, absently. He rose and, walking to a window, stared at the sunset for a full minute. He went back to the table, sat down, and wrote slowly:

"If necessary sell half my mother's bonds. If you don't I shall telegraph the bank to do so for my account. Draft must be honored. I mean business.—Sam."

"Let me see it," said Darrell, quickly, as Sam was about to give it to the boy—the same boy that had earned his money before. He read it and looked at Sam, making no motion to return the message. Sam looked at Darrell and extended his hand. Darrell shook his head dubiously.

"Sam, you don't need that much. Why don't you—"

"I think I'll need it before I'm done, and I'm taking no chances."

"Then take it down yourself," advised Darrell, returning the telegram. "I think you'd better send it from the main office, next block. We'll all go down. Fletcher, get a hustle on with the rest of the stock and keep in touch with me."

They left the room together. In the lobby they met Colonel Robinson, who bowed amiably and was about to speak to them when he saw Fletcher in their company. His face thereupon took on a look of dignified austerity and he passed on.

The dogs in the manger of the business world, the industrial incompetents who must go to the wall—they need not be killed, but they had begun to irritate Sam as he compared the Roanoke with the Virginia Central. Now that he owned the control of the Austin Iron Company and he had seen how Rogers worked, and understood what could be done in the way of improving properties legitimately for the benefit of the entire community, he perceived more clearly than ever before what work meant. It was not pleasant to think that anybody or anything might come in the way of a man with honest intentions and an ideal.

They were at dinner when Sam heard again from his father.

"We'll save it for dessert," smiled Sam.

"No; read it now," said Darrell.

" Draft will be paid. Don't do it again. Come home at once.—S. R."

"No answer," Sam told the waiting boy.

"What are you going to do?" asked Darrell.

"I'm going to wire my thanks and a promise to be more economical next week, when I may draw again, and I am—" He paused and stared fixedly at a corner of the dining-room. Darrell followed his gaze, saw nobody in the corner, and said:

"Wake up, Sammy. What is it you are going to do?"

"I'm going to get Robinson's stock. It might as well be done now as later."

XX

THE Richmond *World*, on the next morning, published a ten-column exposé of the iniquities of tax-dodging corporations which waxed fat—and correspondingly wickeder—by sucking the life-blood of the helpless people. Legalized leeches, the paper said they were, who if they were but trodden upon by the righteous foot of aroused civic pride and the relentless heel of common honesty would exude stolen millions from their insatiable pores. There was a stirring appeal to the righteous foot of civic pride, and the peroration was a single word in big, black letters—"DISGORGE!" It might have been jaundiced rhetoric, worthy of a Metropolitan Champion of the People at a cent a copy, but it was clear that the paper's indignation would last an entire "campaign" against the tax-dodging corporations. All the railroads were accused of vampire practices on the people, but the *World's* "incontrovertible statistics of graft," and "mathematical measurements of the thefts, past, present, and contemplated," concerned the Virginia Central alone. The others' turn, the paper darkly threatened, would come later, dishonorable precedence being given to the Virginia Central because it was the most brazen offender of the lot.

Sam and Darrell read the article together.

"Say, that galoot can sling ink, all right, can't he?" said Darrell, laughing.

"THE ROANOKE IS ACCUSED, TOO' POINTED OUT SAM"

"The Roanoke is accused, too," pointed out Sam. There was a trace of self-defence in his tone.

"Of course. Why leave out the Roanoke? It would have been stupid, and I don't suppose—"

"It might have been Leigh or the Judge," interrupted Sam.

"It might," said Darrell, dryly.

"Why not?"

"Why not, indeed? They live here and they know the newspapers."

Sam did not answer. He did not like Darrell's insinuation that the *World's* virtuous campaign had been planned in a Wall Street office. But he admitted to himself rather dispassionately that Robinson·was difficult to deal with by direct methods, and not everybody possessed the patience to sit down and calmly study ways and means whereby to persuade an inefficient railroad president not to continue to obstruct the march of progress. He himself felt a great desire to say to Robinson:

"Look here, Colonel, sell me your stock at a good, fair price, because you have neither the ability nor the capital to do what is needed."

But that merely would wound the Colonel's vanity; it would turn the anger engendered by the telling of such a truth to such a man into sheer, asinine stubbornness. As a matter of fact, Sam's disgust at his father's business methods, even at the outset, had probably been æsthetic rather than ethical; more the shudder at eating beside a man who masticated audibly or misused his knife than the protest of an aroused conscience. Yet for all that his point of view had changed and was changing, Sam felt that the Colonel should not be financially slain by the efficient foe of inefficiency, who was even then training his long-range artillery on the unsuspecting Robinson. In deciding, as Sam did, to give the doomed man one more chance, he was conscious of a magnanimity not altogether business-like, for some of the money that he would offer might perhaps be better employed on the improvement of the road itself than on the increasing of Robinson's bank account. He must learn from Abercrombie the precise condition of the Colonel's finances, in order the better to judge to what extent he might be magnanimous without being too great an ass. Besides which, he did not have money enough to buy the Colonel's stock outright.

The lawyer received him with much cordiality, and almost immediately began to talk about the *World's* attack on the Virginia Central.

"It's the first shot. Wait until the real firing begins."

"Have you seen the Colonel this morning?" asked Sam. He had no desire to see the malevolent machinery actually at work. He merely wished to know if Robinson's mood was more receptive.

"Oh yes! He deplores the obsolescence of the code duello, but talks horsewhip. To-morrow, I understand, the *World* will have something to say about the franchises the land-development and trolley companies are trying to obtain from the city by dishonorable methods. I think our friend will consider dynamite more adequate than rawhide." The Judge's humorously pitying smile told Sam whence the inspiration of the articles came.

"It doesn't seem quite a fair game, Judge," Sam said, thoughtfully, "but I will admit that Colonel Robinson is a little difficult to convince by other methods." His own dealings with the Central's optimistic president had come to naught. His more than puerile tactlessness had been because he had not then had clear ideas on what he desired to do. The ideas had since been undergoing clarification.

"He is all you say, Mr. Rock."

"How can such a man have been president of a railroad?"

"Well, he was younger and more active after the war, and his social connections were of the best. He did well enough in his day. But that was before competition came and before we awoke to the value of our natural resources when scientifically developed. He is an anachronism in trousers and a goatee. He is a good talker and was once able to raise needed capital— before he had demonstrated his inability to do systematic and intelligent work. Even now, many people consider him a good railroad man because they have never seen a man like Leigh, of the Roanoke; I don't mention your father, because *he* is in a class by himself. Colonel Robinson has this week lost his best lieutenant, George Witherspoon, who has been appointed superintendent of the Roanoke's seaboard division."

Sam's mind jumped to an office in Wall Street where a man with a thousand eyes and ten thousand hands was at work, his gaze fixed on the ticker-tape, reading characters that meant not dollars, more dollars, but far greater things—a man at work, in love with work— big work—doing it calmly, scientifically, relentlessly; not thinking of doing it as soon as certain fine points of ethics had been cleared, but *doing it*. And Robinson. .

"Major Witherspoon was the most popular man in the Central," continued Judge Abercrombie, blandly, "and from what I hear, the men—his old operating force—are talking of striking unless wages are raised and certain conditions are changed. Since the Roanoke raised wages the Great Southern has been forced to promise an advance to begin September 1st. As for the Central—"

"Oh! So that's what the raise meant?" mused Sam, aloud.

"I only know what it will mean if the Central does not do likewise. Also what it will mean to its treasury if it does. An increase in its operating expenses is no laughing matter."

"I suppose my father knows about this agitation?"

"Oh yes. Your father knows everything that is going on in this State having any bearing, however remote, on his own or any other railroad. As a matter of fact, even if I didn't write to him every day, he would know from the New York papers. They've all been receiving long despatches from their Richmond correspondents. You see, this railroad agitation has also a very interesting political end to it."

He smiled. The Roanoke's credit was better than that of any other big corporation in the State and its purse-strings were tied the loosest. He was its chief adviser in political matters. He was in the pleasant position of actually not being able to help the Roanoke without at the same time helping his own personal political aspirations. For how could the politicians, the big bosses and the little local leaders, feel grateful to the liberal Roanoke and not feel under personal obligations to the captivating agent who brought what caused the gratitude—no checks, cash only? If he had but known Sampson Rock earlier in life, or if Sampson Rock had only owned the Roanoke longer!

But there was still time. Some of the best-known Senators were octogenarians. William Abercrombie, who was only sixty-one, smiled.

"Judge," said Sam, after a pause, "you are aware that Colonel Robinson knows about our projects in Austin County?"

"Of course. I can't find out how it leaked out. But the *World's* article should help to offset it."

"Darrell tried to secure a pledge of low rates and better facilities."

"Oh!" The Judge shook his head sorrowfully. Darrell should have left it to the Honorable W. Abercrombie. But the Honorable W. Abercrombie was loyal to Mr. Rock and their friends; wherefore the Honorable W. Abercrombie apologized for Darrell's oversight by talking about Robinson. "It's just like him. Instead of welcoming his road's one chance of salvation, he immediately beheld instead a marvellous change in his personal fortunes and at once proceeded to talk about it. He simply couldn't help it, Mr. Rock. It is curious that all born optimists are supremely selfish, and their glowing visions of the future are those of extremely short-sighted people. Perhaps optimism is but a sublimated form of selfishness, eh?" He looked philosophical. Presently he became mildly indignant. "Why, he has been trying, the last few days, to borrow hundreds of thousands of dollars on notes. He already looks upon his real-estate schemes as actual dividend-payers and regards his incorporation papers as gilt-edged collateral. But the banks—"

"What about the banks?" asked Sam, for the lawyer had paused.

"The banks," answered Judge Abercrombie, with a touch of deprecatory villany, as it were, "are not of the same opinion. I should not be very much surprised if some of the Colonel's loans were not renewed—especially if Virginia Central stock continues to decline."

"The stock probably will," said Sam, with a far-away look in his eyes.

"Do you really think so?" Judge Abercrombie asked this with a lively interest.

"I don't know," answered Sam. "It looks as if nothing except what is disagreeable is going to happen to Colonel Robinson." He saw that Abercrombie's judicial mind was inclining ticker-ward and that he must presently suspect what he had not yet thought of suspecting. That would not do. Abercrombie's enlightenment must come, if at all, from Sampson Rock. "I never bother much with the stock-market, Judge, but I should say, speaking seriously, that the stock is rather low to go short of it now. It's had a pretty bad break. You and I are not the only people who know the road's shortcomings."

"I suppose not," agreed Abercrombie, thoughtfully.

"At all events, I shall watch the accumulating misfortunes of the Colonel with some degree of personal interest."

Judge Abercrombie smiled appreciatively at the quiet humor of the young man's phrase, thereby crediting Sam with Machiavellian subtleties. Sam perceived this, but there was no need to deny anything. Exaggerated regard for the opinion of the world was a form of vanity that Sampson Rock, for one, did not have.

"I'll wager a big red apple that this sequence of inexplicable calamities will in due time make the banks superstitious—even those of which Colonel Robinson is a director. Indeed, I think that two such banks will this very day inform the Colonel that they should like more collateral, and if possible they would prefer to pass the privilege of holding the Colonel's paper to other banks."

The Judge himself looked Machiavellian. It made Sam rise—further conversation would have made him a full-fledged accomplice—and say, "I promised Darrell I wouldn't stay long."

"If there is anything you can suggest—" began the lawyer, with a subtle flattery.

Sam shook his head, without heat, and said, very politely: "My father might; but I could not—not to *you*, Judge. Good-day, sir."

Judge Abercrombie smiled gratefully. The young man had complimented him very nicely. He was now sure of the confidence and personal regard of Sampson Rock's only son and heir, who, Morson had informed him, was as the apple of the Old Man's eye. A very nice young man.

The conversation had turned Sam's thoughts to New York, to Wall Street, to the office of the finder of work for idle hands to do, and the distributer of prosperity for somnolent States and largess for faithful servitors, and inexplicable misfortunes for dogs in the manger. As he walked back to the hotel, his gaze on the ground, he saw his father with his keen eyes fixed on the tape, watching the battle—the modern battle of business, the modern struggle for life. . . . It was like watching a boa-constrictor coiled crushingly about the writhing prey. The process of swallowing—slow, but so sure!—would presently begin. . . But the boa-constrictor lengthened itself until it was a hundred, five hundred, a thousand miles, and then split in two—thin, twin snakes of metal, eighty pounds to the yard—steel rails! . . .

A hard game it was—to the victim who was swallowed because he would not listen to reason. It was youthful ignorance that had made it seem easy to play it otherwise that epic day when he entered the boa-constrictor's den on the return from the trip around the world. It was not possible to meet business people anywhere who did not think of money. And it came to Sam that this universal sordidness was not so ugly as it looked at first blush; it was natural that men should think of their own stomachs before they thought of other people's stomachs, and also that some palates were more fastidious than others and required more expensive food. Fletcher was a good little chap; yet he was for himself. He would work hard at Austin, and he really hungered to see a model plant; but—Henry F. Fletcher, general manager! Judge Abercrombie, a man to be trusted with millions, a man of ability, of loyalty—yet the Roanoke's lobbyist, with political aspirations of themselves praiseworthy, and as such a man who would be an incorruptible patriot; yet doing his dirty work blithely because it meant the sinews of his political war. Colonel Robinson, a pleasant, well-meaning man, inefficient because he lacked the relentlessness of the born executive manager; utterly unfit to run a railroad, and yet one of "God's optimists." He was constitutionally a non-money-maker, and yet to make money was all he was thinking of, so that it was difficult to deal fairly with him, because the more the philanthropist offered to do, the more the well-meaning, would-be money-maker wanted.

A pedestrian jostled him out of his walking trance, and Sam considered the problem immediately before him. Robinson's stock and the stock of other local holders he must get, because then he could say how important a share he should have in the Great Work. In Wall Street, in Virginia, the world over, everywhere, it was the same: people wanted money, and, moreover, hated to share an unexpected profit even with the man whose work, or whose prescience, or whose knowledge of the march of events alone made that profit possible. He must get that stock and pay more for it than Sampson Rock or anybody else not in the secret of the deal would dream of paying. Then there could be no bitterness, no wails, nothing worse than the whining self-reproach of the average ignoramus, "Oh, why didn't I know this stock was going higher!"

He and Rogers would work together in the regeneration of the mismanaged Virginia Central. The sooner the control was secured, the sooner the work would begin.

That very day a battle royal raged on the floor of the New York Stock Exchange. The press despatches from Richmond, anticipating matters slightly, had it that the stern authorities of Virginia had decided to bring suits to compel the full and speedy payment of back taxes by railroads and other corporations doing business in the State. The amounts were not specified, but "it was said" that "millions" were involved. The news reached Gilmartin, and he rewrote the items. His style may have lacked distinction, but the intimations of disaster were literary masterpieces in their way. They even conveyed the impression that the writer knew the worst, but could not bring himself to tell it in all its naked hideousness, out of pity—the philanthropy of a man who was short of Virginia Central stock and understood the psychology of fear!

Then Sampson Rock did his best—and his worst. He distributed scores of selling orders among scores of brokers. Some of them were given directly, others circuitously, several reaching brokers from Richmond correspondents—no detail was too insignificant to overlook. The entire capital stock of the Virginia Central Railroad, it seemed, was offered for sale, urgently, without regard for price—the action of panic-stricken holders the country over who not only feared but must actually *know* the worst. Other stocks were similarly pressed for sale. It was not a selling movement; it was an avalanche. Shortly before noon the news reached the Board Room that a receivership for the Virginia Central had been applied for—which, indeed, it had, by an obscure firm of Richmond lawyers, who had received instructions to do so, accompanied by a telegraph money-order from New York for one thousand dollars and the promise of more to come if they made enough noise. The instructions did not come from Sampson Rock, but from a professional gambler who was short of the market and used crude methods. But it helped Sampson Rock, for, on the receipt of the news, orders to sell Virginia Central poured in from other people than Sampson Rock, people who understood now why Virginia Central had been so ominously weak for so many weeks: the rats had been leaving the sinking ship; that is to say, the insiders had been selling. Therefore the outsiders sold now—with the exception of Sampson Rock, who began to buy as soon as everybody else began to sell.

The market staggered, reeled crazily as though about to collapse utterly, for there was other bad news, other rumors, insistent, sinister — this man was in trouble, that firm was about to go under, another corporation would have to give up a hopeless struggle against insolvency—until the black shadow of panic brooded over the Street and in a thousand gambler-hearts the chill of suspense froze the blood.

That was Sampson Rock at his best—or his worst. A confidential clerk, with long sheets of paper before him, jotted down sales and purchases and names of brokers and of stocks—not only Virginia Central, but a dozen others which the Old Man was using as projectiles to batter down what stood between him and the control of a discredited road. On these sheets he could see at a glance where his troops were and what they were doing, and when there were too many at one point and must prudently retreat, and where he could venture to throw a few thousands more. A hundred times in an hour he made the fifteen-foot trip between the ticker and the tally-sheets, and listened to fifty telephone messages, and heard reports from Valentine and from Dunlap, and gave more orders.

His own pet, Roanoke, had, of course, suffered with the rest, but while he sold it quietly with his left hand he bought it ostentatiously with the right, so that men who watched perceived unmistakably that Roanoke, though weak, had friends and must not be attacked too recklessly. This enabled Rock to reduce his home garrison without over-great risks. Gilt-edged investment stocks were as weak as the worthless, even weaker at times—those times that Sampson Rock himself sold them for effect. But in Virginia Central his attacks were fiercest—savage onslaught after onslaught, whenever it looked as if it might rally, using to the utmost the great human factor of fear. Tirelessly he hammered the doomed stock, and under the impact of his blows the price went down to thirty-three, to thirty-two, to thirty-one, to thirty, to twenty-nine. Then it was that everybody else sold. And then it was that, while he commanded six brokers to keep on selling, he instructed ten to buy it, and to the last one of the ten he told, by word of mouth, in the private office— a tall, smooth-faced, delicately built young man, almost a boy, whose mind was as a machine made of polished steel and smoothly oiled:

"Eddie, go over to the Board and buy Virginia Central for me. Don't wait for bargains. Buy it steadily. Follow it. Don't bid it up at any time, but don't let up. Keep close to the sellers and take all that comes. Don't draw attention on yourself, but let as little get away from you as you can."

The stock closed at thirty-one that night, the entire market somewhat above the lowest prices of the day, but very feverish and unsettled. The slaughter had been "appalling," according to the commission-houses, whose customers had been duly slaughtered to enable one man to give a hundred thousand men the chance to sweat in coal-mines yet unopened and blast-furnaces yet unbuilt. But that one man had recovered from the battle-field most of the solid gold bullets he had fired, buying back at little or no loss the blocks of various guiltless stocks he had sold to depress one particular guilty stock. Also, after Dunlap's clerks had worked late into the night, he found he had sold and repurchased two hundred and thirty thousand shares of various stocks and was "long" only of Roanoke and Virginia Central. Of the first he had perhaps nine thousand shares more than he had owned in the morning. But of Virginia Central he now had eighty-seven thousand shares. He needed seventy-five thousand shares more. He had not done quite as well as he had expected. Evidently the floating supply was smaller than he had supposed. All had been forced on the market that a decline could force. The rest he must get by paying more for the stock than the foolish holders would think it was worth. They would think this because they would know only what the road could earn under such a management as Robinson's.

The upward campaign would begin in earnest as soon as he had bought at private sale whatever stock could be picked up in Richmond—the bull campaign that was to make people sell because they would fondly imagine they were selling half-dollars at sixty cents. They would think that in another month.

XXI

THE letter that Sam received that evening from his father was not long, because Sampson Rock wrote it with his own hand and he was too busy to spend much time in autograph missives. He wished to know what Sam was doing, and ended with:

"I hope you are having a nice time and are learning something. If you've found something good I'll help you, but don't be too reckless with your own educational expenses. Don't write, but come back and tell me.

"YOUR LOVING FATHER."

Sam himself had no desire to answer by mail, but neither did he wish to return to New York just yet. He felt certain the Old Man had not secured enough Virginia Central stock, and it was only a question of a few days before he would send Morson to Richmond to gather up what certificates could be bought there. Then the price would begin to advance on the Stock Exchange on the final clean-up. All of which would render Sam's task the more difficult.

Darrell reported that they had sixty-eight per cent. of the Austin Iron Company's safe in hand and that people were beginning to talk suspiciously.

"We'll have to form a syndicate, I suppose, to reorganize the company." Sam looked at Darrell for confirmation.

286

"Of course. And nobody can help you in that like your father, Sam."

"Nobody can," assented Sam. He thought a moment. "It's part of the general development scheme."

Darrell nodded. The Virginia Central deal interested him only indirectly in that it would help the profit on the Austin iron enterprise. He told Sam:

"We'll sell the stock to the new company at par, taking first-mortgage bonds in payment and a bonus in new stock. More bonds will be issued for working capital and enlargement of the plant, and, as your father said, the Virginia Central might guarantee the bonds. We'll be on velvet then, and—"

"Jack," said Sam, "I am more interested in seeing the plant enlarged and modernized and in watching Rogers perform his wonders on the road while we leave the financial end to the old gentleman. I want to see for myself how a railroad is changed from a tin pot into a dividend-payer. This is a matter of years, and so the velvet does not appeal to me just now."

"It does to me, very much, seeing that I am old and feeble-minded. Kindly consider *my* feelings in the matter, kid."

"Oh, you be hanged!"

"Maybe I will. But I have a duty to perform towards the future Mrs. Darrell. I'm sure she'll be extravagant, and I am one of the kind that can't deny them anything. You are about to graduate from the kindergarten. Very soon it will dawn on your startled understanding that you'll have use for the filthy lucre, microbes and all. I repeat dispassionately that your game is to squat beside your poor father and soak up sense while your back molars grow.

Of course, having been at it nearly a month now you know a heap. Your picnic is nearly over and now comes the ennobling sweat—now that you'll have to raise money. If you are a labor-saver, you'll just let your father write a half-dozen letters to his particular friends. Do you know why that's all he'll have to do? Because those particular friends have always made money whenever they've answered his previous letters and enclosed their little checks. *You* may be satisfied with one per cent. cash and ninety-nine per cent. glory, but not so the friends. One per cent. and no risk is good, but forty per cent. and no risk is better. The forty for mine. I'll even take my chances on making it fifty, to show there's no hard feelings."

"Supposing *you* tried to float the new company?"

"I guess I could do it. But you'd get better terms from your father, who will probably waive his commission so that you may learn business by playing at it with the calcium-light beating on your lovely, upturned face. *My* friends wouldn't waive anything, except the chance to make your share as little as possible, being despicable creatures who want to get the dust quick and plenty. *Sabe?* I lean towards Sampson Rock, Esquire."

"I want you to make a good thing here, of course, Jack; you know that. But why can't I be satisfied if we make a big plant of the Austin Iron Company?"

"In the name of the Prophet, figs! If I were Sampson Rock's only son, every time I felt like making money I'd look in Bradstreet's and then I'd fill with scorn at the sordid world. Money? Nasty thing! What's it good for? Yachts? Game preserves? Country houses? Automobiles? Fifth Avenue shacks? What are such things to me? I might, of course, want to run a gentleman's farm and raise things on it, and if the money held out I might incorporate a society of one for the encouragement of the histrionic art."

Sam smiled perfunctorily. He said, thinking of Robinson's obstinacy: "Jack, did it ever strike you that it is a hard job to make people believe you're not an ass when you tell them you want to do something else besides making money?"

"Not an ass, exactly, Sam — do not be hard on yourself; just a lunatic." Darrell smiled. Then he went on, seriously: "Sam, you are a nice chap, but you are young. The only foolish thing your father has ever done, that I can find out, is to have let you wear short dresses too long. He might better have made less money and wasted a quarter on a barber to cut your curls when you were twenty-one. Let me tell you right here that it's nothing especially creditable to you that you don't care about making money. You've never had to make it; you've had it made for you and it's meant nothing. It suddenly bursts upon you that playing marbles is not exciting. You decide on adult games. What happens? Money-making is vulgar. The real stake is not the plated loving-cup but the glory of the victory. Everybody else wants both, but you are better than the others; so you'll donate the cup to some thin-blooded, flat-chested teetotaler. Everybody is selfish, but that doesn't mean that everybody will spike the other runners to keep them from having a fair show at the cup. You've been pottering around for a week doing something else besides playing polo, and one moment you think one thing and the next another. You are full of the excitement of the game, but I shouldn't wonder if you are a little ethical society all by yourself. In the mean time, while your father is getting there, you're having what you call a soul-crisis. You remind me of a 'lunger' I knew in Colorado Springs once. That's what he had while he was thinking of the righteousness of working in a gambling-house, that being the only job he could get that he was strong enough to fill. He was in doubt whether it was not nobler to return penniless to the bleak East and die, painfully, but with an immaculate soul. It took three coughing-spells and the sight of a blank certificate all ready to be filled out by an impatient doctor before he 'seen his duty and done it.' He owns the joint now and is almost fat. Do you want my serious and disinterested advice?"

"Let's hear it," said Sam, cautiously.

"All right, Scotchy. Well, then, return to New York, tell the Old Man what you've done—casually observing that yours truly is in this deal with you, as an evidence of good faith—and suggest that you want to form a new company to take in his coal-lands and our iron company. He'll do anything you ask when you further assure him that you are resolved to make your headquarters in Richmond and learn practical railroading as well. Then get the best men you can hire and tell them to go ahead and do their best. They will understand what you mean, to wit, dividends; and don't get a soul spasm. Let them alone. After two or three years you will hike back to New York, your desk alongside of the old gentleman's, and just absorb. By that time you will be married. You will let your children go to public school. It doesn't make any difference if they go in an automobile as long as Micky Reilly can show your oldest that money doesn't always prevent black eyes. When they grow up, don't let them be mining-engineers. Far better to go into poetry. You can publish their sonnets at your expense and suppress the edition, thus doing your duty as a fond father and as a public-spirited citizen. At the age of seventy-five you will expire to slow music, much lamented by the men who helped you to become beastly rich so that they themselves might not be beset by the temptation of great wealth; and you will join poor old Jack in the happy hunting-grounds where we can swap long yarns, and never go near the stock-tickers in the basement."

"Good shot," laughed Sam. Darrell was a better and more level-headed fellow than his manner of speech indicated. He went on, falling into the same manner of speech: "Then, first we will increase our holdings of Virginia Central in Sydney's office, and then we will give our genial friend Robinson and his friends a last farewell chance. Then back home to fall on the paternal neck to inform him that we have the deciding vote and won't he please be nice to the mob, also to Darrell."

"Get a gait on! Let's tackle Robinson at the club to-night," said Darrell, "and have it out."

They were smoking placidly when Colonel Robinson sauntered in. His manner, as they simultaneously rose to greet him, was a trifle constrained. But Darrell was as jovial as usual and Sam smiled pleasantly.

"What's the news, Colonel?" asked Darrell.

"I understand," answered Robinson, with a rather cold politeness, "that you have been getting options on Austin Iron Company stock?"

"Yes; options, instead of buying the stock outright," answered Darrell, amiably. "You see, I still have hopes of coming to some agreement on rates. What do you say, Colonel; am I too optimistic?"

Robinson looked suspiciously at Darrell, who looked particularly conciliatory, then at Sam. Darrell was the man to do business with. His New York correspondents had written that Darrell was a well-known mining expert and mine-owner, with ample resource of his own and excellent financial connections in New York and London. Mostly he had gone in for copper and silver mines. As for stock-market affiliations, he had none so far as they could learn. But many of his friends were big operators, and he, like most of the Westerners with money, probably plunged in stocks with wild and woolly recklessness. They all did.

The important thing to Robinson was that Darrell had money and connections. That point became doubly important since the banks so suddenly began to display deafness to oratorical appeals for renewals of notes. Some of the verbal promises to join the Colonel in the Capital Park enterprise had been cancelled, the unstable friends having become evasive in their explanations but obviously determined not to contribute the cash. The decline in Virginia Central stock had come at a most inopportune time, for lifelong banking friends, strangely enough, now insisted on the margins being kept up. Still these New-Yorkers did not know his tribulations. Therefore he answered Darrell with a sort of humorous inflexibility·

"I say what I said before. We'll do the best we can. But on rebates we are immutable as the Rock of Gibraltar."

"I left my dynamite and drills home," laughed Darrell. "We'll drop the matter and leave Austin and its coal and iron in undisturbed repose for another century or two."

The Colonel knew the rhetoric was for effect; in American, "bluff." He said, calmly:

"That is for Mr. Darrell to decide. But my advice is to carry out your plans. It's to our interest to help you."

"That's what I think," interjected Sam. "In fact, I've been thinking that perhaps you would like to have a share in our syndicate."

"I shall be glad to consider that when your plans are sufficiently perfected to enable me to judge. Not that I am not obliged to you for the opportunity," he finished, graciously., He had troubles of his own and was willing to receive help. Give help he couldn't, but he was willing to say he might do so. It didn't cost anything.

"Well," said Darrell, slowly, "since we came here conditions in New York have become less favorable for a big industrial promotion. The stock-market has been weak, and until the present liquidation is over and forgotten, capitalists will sit tight. I myself think that in the fall conditions will be more propitious. Colonel, if you will not take it amiss, I will say frankly that the inadequacy of the facilities given by your road is so well known that it will handicap us."

"How, sir?" frowned the Colonel.

"Everybody knows that your road needs money and that you couldn't raise it in New York—"

"I certainly could, Mr. Darrell." The Colonel was visibly annoyed.

"Yes; on terms that are much worse than giving rebates to the Austin Coal and Iron Company. And I read in the paper that London had been a steady seller of Virginia Central stock for some days. That doesn't look as if the English were over-anxious to help."

It was all true; but the Colonel put on a look of immeasurable dignity and was about to speak when Sam said to Jack, obviously to mollify the Colonel:

"The whole market has been very weak. All stocks are down."

"Virginia Central broke thirty," put in Darrell, controversially.

Colonel Robinson frowned. "It is the consequences of over-speculation. We've never felt called upon to do more than to operate the Central to the best of our ability, leaving the stock-ticker to direct the policies of other roads. The decline in our stock is due to attacks by professional gamblers. Some day the bears," he finished, darkly, "will find out to their sorrow that they cannot sell with impunity what they do not own." He looked like the menace of an after-life of torment for the bears.

"In the mean time they are gathering up the ducats in bushel-baskets." As Darrell said this the Colonel thought he had the look of one of those Western plungers who were startling Wall Street with the magnitude of their play.

"Do you happen to be short of it, Mr. Darrell?" asked the Colonel. Then, with a smile, that the question might be robbed of its rudeness: "If so, I hope your basket is spacious, sir."

"Not yet," replied Darrell.

"They are overdoing it. They always do. Wall Street is peopled by fools and sheep," said Sam, with profound conviction. "The easiest thing in the world is to beat them at their own game. They are so cock-sure of their wonderful cleverness that a man with a little modesty and some cash can always extort tribute from the ticker-fiends."

"He thinks so because he hasn't lost yet," said Darrell to the Colonel, with a smile of fatherly tolerance at Sam.

"I'll bet there is a big short interest in Virginia Central and that it would be easy to run up the price. I've a great mind to—" He checked himself, and stared meditatively at the Colonel.

"Sir, I know nothing about the stock-market," said Robinson, not quite veraciously. But on the other hand, he spoke with an austere dignity that was a rebuke to all disciples of the devil. He then finished: "But I should think the short interest in it is enormous! The country is prosperous. It is only in Wall Street that there is any depression."

"You are right, Colonel Robinson," said Sam. He arose and began to pace up and down the room, frowning at the floor. Robinson looked at him in mild surprise. Darrell leaned over and whispered: "Colonel, if he plans a stock-market coup, I advise you to come in with us. On my honor, I assure you I'd not only risk every cent I own—and it's more than a dollar and a half—but I'd put my friends in. He'll make enough in a week to pay for the Austin coal-lands."

"Who is Mr. Rock? Is he any relation of—" Robinson had not before connected him with Sampson Rock. They had taken care he should not.

"His mother left him a multi-millionaire several years ago; and since he came back from an extended tour of the world I've taken him under my wing."

"Indeed? Is he so well to do?"

"Colonel," said Darrell, simply, "I am rated a millionaire and I can draw my check for six figures now without stirring from this chair, or having to sell any of my investments. But alongside of my friend I'm a pauper. Do you know what his money is in, mostly?"

"No, sir."

"Government bonds, which he won't sell because of loyalty to his mother."

Sam paused before Colonel Robinson, still frowning.

"Colonel," he asked abruptly, "how much Virginia Central stock do you control personally?"

"I cannot answer that question." Robinson said it stiffly.

Sam affected to misunderstand the Colonel, and he said: "I mean, approximately."

The Colonel hesitated. The recollection of the newly developed unfriendliness of the bankers made him say, dubiously: "I am the largest individual holder." It was no time to resent such questions.

"All right. Then you'll profit more than anybody else," Sam told him; and the Colonel silently hoped so. "A hundred thousand shares?"

"No. I think — yes, fifty thousand shares, or a trifle over." He and his kinspeople controlled about fifty-two thousand shares.

"Very well. Now I won't ask you to join us in a pool, because—" He paused. The Colonel shook his hand in majestic decision and volunteered, coldly:

"I do not approve of Wall Street methods. Too many railroads in this country are run by the ticker."

"That's all right. Some of those same roads pay dividends and sell above thirty. Look here. I'll give you fifty dollars a share—"

"My stock is not for sale."

"I haven't asked you to sell it to me, Colonel Robinson. If you will give me a thirty-day option on your fifty thousand shares of stock at fifty dollars a share, I will pay you—"

"It is no use to talk about such matters," interrupted the Colonel, decisively. But he began to breathe quickly. Succor might come from an unexpected quarter. It was welcome from any quarter, celestial or infernal—anything to make the banks regret their unseemly unfriendliness.

"I want to get your stock where it won't come out," explained Sam. He frowned in his earnestness. Almost he felt that he was grasping that block of stock, the possession of which would start him and Rogers in their work of regeneration. "I'll give you two hundred and fifty thousand dollars cash for the option."

"It's no use. You have my promise that—" A quarter of a million in cold cash would help a great deal. That made the Colonel check his rash speech.

"I'll take your word, Colonel," Sam assured him. "But life is an uncertain thing at best How do I know what your executors would do if something happened to you? This isn't cold-bloodedness, but I'm risking a heap. The stock is thirty. The option is at fifty—"

"The stock is worth—" began the Colonel.

"What it will fetch," retorted Sam. "Does fifty dollars a share seem too low?"

"It doesn't seem—it *is* too low, and, moreover, I don't wish to sell."

"Make the option price sixty," said Sam. The Colonel understood from that that all the young stock-gambler desired was to keep this stock from coming into the market while he was punishing the shorts, a praiseworthy and deserved castigation. But he shook his head. Sam said: "This is my last word on the subject. The cash price for the option I won't raise. It's two hundred and fifty thousand dollars cash. But you can make the price at which you would sell the stock sixty-five dollars a share. That's more than fair. It's thirty-five points more than the market price, and that's over a million and a half more. The fifty thousand shares won't give me the control of your road, and if all I wanted was to get that much stock I wouldn't pay sixty-five, would I? Look at the transactions in the stock lately. Of course, it's trading—speculators buying and selling the same stock over and over again. The longer that keeps on the more likely they are to get real stock from holders who are frightened by the drop in the price, and if such stock comes out in quantity it would take a million derricks to hoist the price five cents a share. I want your stock fixed so that it won't come out on the market. After I give you the two hundred and fifty thousand dollars cash and you give me the option, I want to fix the rest of the stock held in Virginia by your friends and foes, but at no such fool price as sixty-five. Tie up that stock so it won't come out for a month or six weeks and we'll give the bears the time of their lives."

Sam's face was flushed and his eyes shone eagerly. His hands were clinched—and each clutched the stock certificates that would enable the regeneration of the tin-pot railway to begin apace!

Darrell looked at Sam curiously. But the Colonel shook his head dubiously. At first flush this seemed a plan to oust him from the control. But sixty-five a share meant three and a quarter millions of dollars. That would enable him to do as he pleased. It was too big a price to pay for stock by people like the Darrells if they wanted to secure representation in the directorate of the road for unworthy motives — such, for example, as favoring themselves as shippers of Austin coal and iron. It must be a stock-market plan, as daring as it was simple. He was not pledging himself to anything. Long before the stock could sell in the open market at sixty-five—the bonds were barely above seventy—he could protect himself. The banks were fidgeting; so was the Colonel's honorable soul.

"Look here, Colonel, you must help me to tie up all the stock here. Then you leave the rest of it to us in Wall Street. We'll make them remember Virginia Central as long as they live. After we get them where we want them we'll announce our big coal and iron company, and Darrell and I will try to do what we can in the bond matter. Maybe we can help, if—"

"We will, if you will give us decent rates," said Darrell, harking back to his muttons.

"Good Heavens, Mr. Darrell, is that an obsession?" The Colonel smiled jovially. Sam's heart gave a great bound. He felt that the battle was won.

"Shall Jack give you a check now, Colonel?"

"Not so quick, young man," smiled Robinson. He shook his head; it was the last ditch.

"No time to lose. I want to go back to New York to-morrow night if possible. I'll telegraph my brokers for detailed information as to the technical condition of the stock. But I know I am right and I can put it up—if I am not flooded with long stock from Richmond. In the mean time don't waste time to deny malicious rumors. They help."

"You won't be flooded," the Colonel assured him, amiably.

"I don't intend to be," retorted Sam, decisively.

"Now you and Jack get options on all that's floating around here, and—"

"Look here, sir, you understand that I don't wish to sell my stock?" Robinson tried to look adamantine. He did not succeed. The "sequence of inexplicable calamities," as Abercrombie called Sampson Rock's tactics, had unnerved him.

"I understand that, if the option was exercised, you would get three million two hundred and fifty thousand dollars cash in a month, which is a terrible affliction." Sam laughed, a trifle excitedly. He had not told any untruths and he had offered the Colonel a fortune in order to be permitted to do the great work and do it at once. It was as gentlemanly a way of doing business as was possible, in view of the hopelessness of telling the truth, the whole truth, and nothing but the truth. He had not taken advantage of his knowledge of Robinson's financial straits. He had not even been tempted to do so. And as his mind, working quickly now, dwelt upon that, he felt a glow of self-congratulation. He did not care what his father would say about the high price. He actually felt glad that he was paying a big price. That was a pleasurable expiation.

"Colonel, suppose we sign papers to-morrow morning?" Sam looked as if it were all settled.

"Sonny, am I in this deal?" Darrell asked this in a remonstrating tone of voice. The Colonel looked at Darrell with a quick uneasiness.

"Sure."

"Stung again!" said Darrell resignedly. The Colonel smiled uncertainly. He had not been anxious to do business in the dark, but the thought of the two hundred and fifty thousand dollars cash—and, if it came to the worst, of the three million dollars more in a month — had been assuming a more pleasant aspeet.

"You pusillanimous idiot!" laughed Sam. Then Providence pushed him a few hundred miles nearer the goal.

XXII

"HOW do you do, Colonel Robinson?" said a short, stout, very dignified man who had just come in. He wore a long, white beard, and under shaggy, frowning brows two sharp eyes gleamed with a sort of general hostility. They did not gleam very intelligently; the hostility very obviously did not include the owner of the eyes.

Colonel Robinson rose rather eagerly. Perhaps he was glad of the opportunity. He was beginning to suspect that he was cornered by temptation; and he did not feel very robust.

"General Winfree, I am right glad to see you, sir. Won't you join us, General?"

The Colonel presented his friends to General Peyton B. Winfree and to the General's companion, Major Tolliver Moreland. The General was pleased to be almost gracious. The Major shook hands with a sort of restrained eagerness. He had heard that Mr. Darrell was very wealthy—heard it from a friend to whom Robinson had spoken of the "important developments."

"I trust your trip to New York was satisfactory, General," said Colonel Robinson. He looked at the old warrior with an affectionate hopefulness. Everybody in Richmond knew about the trip that was to make Winfree a rich man if only a few vulgar New York millionaires took the General's view of the value of a certain waterpower at Winfreesboro. General Winfree himself was inclined to think that his trip was in a class of itself, next to which came Columbus's first voyage of discovery, the search of the Golden Fleece, and Alexander's expeditions.

"Yes and no, Colonel Robinson," replied General Winfree, with an air of not only narrating, but making, history. "Northern capitalists are willing enough to supply the wherewithal. Oh yes! But they realize the temporary financial impotence of the South and they exact the last drop of blood; and the carcass as well." The heavy mustaches moved up and down thrice; he was sneering.

"Oh, not all Northern capitalists, General Winfree!" said Sam with a sort of conciliating dissent.

"I should be overjoyed to make the personal acquaintance of the shining exceptions that your words would imply exist. They have kept out of *my* way with complete success, young sir. To me, politically," he went on, with an air of great magnanimity, "there is no North, no South, no East, and no West. But in business the ways of the North are not the ways of the South. And I thank the Almighty that they are not," he finished, without the air of magnanimity.

"I have not had as much experience in business as you, General Winfree," said Sam, "but I do not find much difference in capitalists anywhere. All of them want to make as much money as they can. Darrell here has had many dealings with British capitalists, and he will tell you that London is as bad as New York. Some people have money to buy with and others have property to sell. The point of view is bound to differ."

"Speaking about London reminds me, Colonel Robinson," said General Winfree, temporarily overlooking Sam's impertinence in his eagerness not to forget to repeat bad news; "I've just seen in the evening papers that the Virginia Central bondholders' committee have received an adverse report from their expert." It was news to the Colonel, though not unexpected. The General looked almost happy at his success.

"The stock sold in New York to-day at twenty-seven and seven-eighths," put in Major Moreland, to show that, though he was not loquacious, he was entitled to a respectful hearing whenever he spoke. "Somebody must have known the news before the papers got it." He nodded. Almost he implied he knew who the somebody was. He haunted the local brokers' offices and knew the quotations of stocks and cotton just as though he were a plunger instead of a piker—the brokers were so unreasonable in the matter of margins! He was the kind that buys mining stocks to get rich, as per advertisements—a mental miser that loves to fondle imaginary gold coins.

"What could you expect from a man of Williams's breeding?" asked Colonel Robinson with a show of indignation. It was news he did not like to get at this time and place. General Winfree looked at him suspiciously. The Colonel went on, hotly: "An ass, sir, a corrupt and malignant ass! But we don't need foreign capital." Colonel Robinson frowned: he himself would supply the Virginia Central's needs from his privy purse. His frown and his attitude showed plainly his determination to do so. That had been his autohypnotic trance these many years—before this same public, in this same club. All poses in time become habits.

"You need any kind of capital you can get," said

Winfree with a decisive irascibility—it had been simmering since Sam's audacity. "All that your stockholders care about is that you make the road pay dividends. And the way to do it is to improve it, and to do that you need money. And you've got to get it—the sooner the better." General Winfree nodded to himself. He agreed with General Winfree, the unsurpassed logician.

"General Winfree," said Colonel Robinson with much dignity, his ruddy face several shades ruddier, "I do not think the stockholders of the Virginia Central have any fault to find with the road or with the management. It has been my sleepless endeavor, sir—my sleepless endeavor—"

"The repetition of the word *sleepless*, Colonel Robinson, in connection with the stockholders, is, as you might say, quite *apropos*." And General Winfree laughed disagreeably. He himself had been jarred by bankers. Sam's face flushed and he looked quickly at Darrell. The Westerner, from force of habit, looked twice as stolid as the Sphinx. He understood what Sam thought.

"I've just travelled over the Virginia Central," interjected Sam, calmly, before Colonel Robinson could retort, "and I see nothing to make any reasonable man lose sleep. It's not the management's fault if the country through which it passes is not more productive. In my opinion it has a great future." Colonel Robinson looked pleased, and was about to speak when General Winfree said, so politely that the sneer was doubly effective:

"You are, of course, a large stockholder in it, young sir?"

"Not yet. Are you?" Sam remembered how boys

goaded other boys into doing foolish things. Curious were the tools that Providence placed at the disposal of men who would do big work! But there need be no philosophizing about it. Time urged.

"Yes, sir. I am sorry to say that I am."

"Well," said Sam, "you needn't be. I'll take your holdings off your hands any time you say so."

"And I stand ready to do likewise, General Winfree," said Colonel Robinson with stupendous dignity.

"I do not propose to sell when the stock is at the lowest price of months—stock that I purchased on the assurance that it would prove a valuable investment." From the General's manner he owned a million shares. The sin of Colonel Robinson, who had given the assurance, was beyond characterization in a gentleman's club.

Before Colonel Robinson could retort that if the General had sold out a few weeks before he would have made a fair profit on his two hundred shares, Sam said, with a smile:

"I thought not! But I'll tell you what I'll do—" His hearers were disagreeably made aware that the young Northerner with the clean-cut features and gray-blue eyes was taunting General Winfree, who habitually browbeat half the State of Virginia—"I'll buy all the Virginia Central stock you own at ten dollars a share more than the highest price at which it sold on the New York Stock Exchange to-day. And I don't care a continental whether it's one share or one hundred thousand!"

"That's a pretty broad assertion, young sir," said the General, his brows frowning and his lips quivering. "The spoken word of an adolescent stranger rather curiously excited—"

"General Winfree," interrupted Sam, very calmly, "I may be young, and I lack the phlegmatic temperament that I notice all elderly people have, but my word, sir, is as good as if I were a hundred years old and a philosopher, because I can back it up with good hard cash. And money talks, you know, in all languages."

Colonel Robinson looked at Darrell a trifle uneasily and Jack said, very slowly, almost drawlingly:

"I guess if General Winfree wishes to dispose of his stock in the road managed by my friend Colonel Robinson, he will find us ready to do as you say, Sam."

"General Winfree, your play, sir," said Sam, bowing politely, but looking as though he were trying to repress a smile.

The General thought that possibly Robinson had secured new allies. He sputtered: "I think, of course, that the stock is worth more than thirty dollars a share." At this price his holdings showed him a loss of nearly two thousand dollars. He had overstayed his market. The realization of it did not make him more amiable.

"Then you have a splendid opportunity to make a fortune by buying more and holding it for a rise, which I think is bound to come sooner or later. Colonel Robinson will tell you that I am not a stockholder in his road, but I believe in it, and I have the courage of my convictions enough to agree to take one hundred thousand shares at forty dollars or fifty dollars a share—"

"What?" shouted General Winfree.

Major Moreland said nothing. He stared fascinatedly at Sam. Here was a king-gambler, a man of real

money.   In the turbulent rush of the golden torrent he
—Tolliver Moreland—might be splashed!   He did not
know how, but he would stand near by and never dodge.
Was this stock going up on the mysterious developments Colonel Robinson had even more mysteriously
hinted at?   He listened with his very soul as the
young man continued:

"Provided you have the stock ready at 10 A.M. to-
morrow. Colonel Robinson, that will show some of
your Southern friends what some of your Northern
friends think of you."   And Sam held out his hand.
Colonel Robinson shook it, not over-enthusiastically.
The affair was degenerating into a verbal brawl; and
besides, that was not the wise way to secure the stock
the Northerners said they needed in their stock-market
deal.   Darrell and his young friend were strangers and
would be gone to-morrow.   But Winfree would remain
and his tongue with him; also his notion that eloquence
consisted of a succession of explosions, and arguments
of invective.   And, what was worse, many people in
the state took General Winfree at General Winfree's
own valuation.   Colonel Robinson began to feel sorry
he had not taken Darrell's check—certified.   It was
more than the stock was worth.

"You ask an impossibility, sir, so delicately expressed that I am lost in admiration," said the General,
witheringly.

"General Winfree," replied Sam, with an air of making an effort to remain calm and respectful before age,
"I am not in the habit of speaking merely to hear
myself.   It would be an asinine thing for me to offer to
buy stock from you at forty that I can buy for thirty
in the open market, and possibly for less to-morrow,
though I hope not.   What I had in mind was stock

held by the people who know Colonel Robinson and are not satisfied with his management. Therefore I said, and I repeat, that I will buy all the stock that you own, General, at a price sufficiently above the prevailing market-price to show I believe in doing justice to whom justice is due. Do I make myself sufficiently clear?"

"Do you mean to say," put in Major Moreland before General Winfree could reply, "that you will pay fifty dollars a share for one hundred thousand shares of Virginia Central stock?" The young man had said forty *or* fifty. He affected not to have heard the lower alternative figure.

"Yes, provided—" began Sam.

"Of course there is a proviso with the courage of the convictions. Of course!" sneered General Winfree. He did not know what the young man's talk might mean. When in doubt, he sneered. Many people thought him a very wise man. He agreed with them. Thinking of his reputation now made him nod twice, sapiently.

"Of course; yes, sir, of course. Provided"—Sam spoke deliberately because he knew what he wanted— "it is stock of people who are dissatisfied with the way my friend Colonel Robinson is managing the road."

"We are all friends of Colonel Robinson's, sir, whom we have known and admired for more years than you have spent on God's green footstool. For that reason, sir, we devoutly hope that what you say of the road's future may be fulfilled," said Major Moreland, with a sincerity that was beyond all question. He went on, deprecatingly, "But then, doubtless—er—ignoramuses who, as you say, may be discontented, however illogically, with—ah—the road's earnings and the talk of labor troubles and inability to float the bonds, and they—" He paused. He was quaking inwardly. The stock might go up in the future; to-morrow, cloudy and cold. Here was money in sight; to-day, fair and sunshine.

"Send them around," said Sam, exactly as though he were convinced not one would accept his offer and that Colonel Robinson's detractors would be silenced forever more. "I'll be here for some days yet."

"You doubtless would make that offer in writing?" pursued Major Moreland, as he thought, diplomatically. His question was a verbal pinch to himself to determine whether he was asleep or awake. It was too good to be true.

"If Colonel Robinson doesn't object," said Sam, with a touch of deference, "I am willing."

The Colonel fidgeted, and replied, deprecatingly: "I cannot object to so gratifying an exhibition of confidence in me, which, from its very unexpectedness, touches me deeply. But I really think, gentlemen—"

"General Winfree, might I speak with you one moment? If these gentlemen will pardon me—" And Major Moreland rose. The General and the Major retired to a remote corner and talked very earnestly, from time to time the Major shaking his head at some low but vehement words of the General.

Sam leaned over and whispered to Colonel Robinson: "This is the best way to tie up the stock. They brought it on themselves. Before they come back at me you must promise to give me the option on your fifty thousand shares. Then I'll rush back to New York. Jack, give the Colonel your check for two hundred and fifty thousand dollars now. Go into the other room while I wait here. No time to lose, Colonel. Wait till these people see how the stock will recover. They'll sing a different tune, and nobody can blame you. You will find that the same bond-houses that wouldn't touch your bonds will also be sorry. Think of your Capital Park and of my Austin Iron Company. No time to lose!"

It was only vaguely that Sam felt Winfree and Moreland, the most indiscreet men in the world, would be most discreet in getting the stock he wanted. Nobody would suspect these men's principal; that was clear and that was enough. Hope filled his heart. Twice he clutched the air nervously. It made him look like a gambler to Colonel Robinson, one who took big chances, but whom fortune favored.

Darrell seized the opportunity and deftly took the Colonel into the next room. He wrote out the check and gave it to the Central's president before Colonel Robinson could say his name. With two hundred and fifty thousand dollars in his pocket, the worst that could happen, thought the Colonel, would be to lose his fifty thousand shares and gain three million dollars for himself and his family if the options were exercised. And there was always the open market before him in which to purchase the stock. He knew his relations would be overjoyed to sell their holdings at even less than sixty-five dollars a share. Promises made in bursts of enthusiasm could be kept now. And, if the options were not exercised, the stock would advance in any case on the Darrell development of Austin coal and iron. That he was helping stock-gamblers was colorless; that he was helping Colonel Robinson was like the sunshine—golden.

He took the check carelessly, from force of habitual pose, and went back with Darrell just as General Winfree and his self-appointed accomplice were sitting down again beside Sam.

"Perhaps Mr. Darrell," said the General, in the tone and manner he would have used had he been charged to deliver a challenge, "will make me an offer to buy at fifty dollars a share all the Virginia Central stock I can deliver to him?"

"My price was forty—" began Sam.

"*Or* fifty, you said," interjected Moreland. He smiled. "You certainly said it, whatever you may have meant." The Major looked pleadingly at the young man. He subdued himself and proceeded to look contemptuous. The philosophy of the change of expression was so subtle that Moreland felt a thrill of pride.

"Very well. Mr. Darrell will, anyhow, if you can deliver enough to silence the anti-Robinson faction once and for all," replied Sam, with the good-nature of a man who is overcharged at a café after a "killing" at the race-track. It was the diminishing distance between himself and a big block of Central stock that animated his thoughts and words and his very gestures. He felt that his exultation must not show. He concealed it by his manner. It seemed natural to him. Almost within his grasp was the prize. That kept him from thinking of other things.

"There is no anti-Robinson faction, sir, and I object to your unjustified and frequent use of that expression!" shouted General Winfree, irascibly. "We are all, sir, friends of Colonel Robinson, as he knows without my saying it."

"Excuse me; I shall not use it again. I thought there was such a faction." Sam smiled, not at all penitently.

"No, sir, there is not. We cherish a warm regard for all of Virginia's great and loyal sons, sir." He glared at Sam—for effect on Robinson. The General often permitted himself to think that Peyton B. Winfree was not only great and loyal, but also courtly and astute—very decidedly astute.

"I am delighted to hear it, General. And now, how much Virginia Central stock from Virginia's other loyal sons will you deliver to us, sir?" Sam almost repeated his flippancy, because, though he had indeed meant it as a goad, it seemed to exasperate Winfree to the verge of purple apoplexy. But the old man, by a great effort and a quick kick from Major Moreland, contented himself with sneering:

"More than you will probably care to see."

"Mr. Darrell," interjected Major Moreland, with a smile he could not keep from tinging with apprehension, though he also meant it as a prudence-dispelling taunt, "may only have been jesting, General Winfree." Jack was the older man. Moreland made him responsible. Besides which, Colonel Robinson had hinted that Darrell was "good for millions." The young man was a stranger, and Moreland suddenly remembered that Robinson was one of God's optimists. But Darrell looked the more responsible.

"Jack, make the offer in writing," said Sam. Major Moreland drew in his breath. He heard the roar of the torrent. The little waves clinked. He stood near the shore. He *must* be splashed! Thinking of the golden bath kept him from thinking of any ulterior motives these Northern sports might have. That's all they were—gamblers, reckless, with the gambler's ignorance of the value of money. Some of the new stock-market millionaires often bet a fortune on a horse-race.

Paper and ink were brought to the engineer, who had been thinking about it, and he therefore was able to write, with an impressive appearance of spontaneity, which accorded with Moreland's theory of the Northerners' recklessness:

"I hereby agree to purchase from General Peyton B. Winfree not less than fifty thousand and not more than one hundred thousand shares of the stock of the Virginia Central Railroad at fifty dollars per share, ten per cent. of the price to be paid on presentation of the certificates at the Southern National Bank of Richmond, Virginia, an additional ten per cent. thirty days thereafter, and the balance of eighty per cent within sixty days from this date. In the event of my failure to pay the second instalment, the first instalment is to be forfeited, and if both the first and the second instalments shall have been paid and the final payment is not made on or before the date specified, all previous payments shall be forfeited to General Winfree, the stock in the meanwhile to remain in escrow with the president of the Southern National Bank until the final payment is made and to be returned by him to General Winfree in the event of the failure of said payment to be made. This offer to hold good until twelve o'clock meridian on May 15th. It is further understood that this applies exclusively to stock which shall have been in possession of the present owners for at least three months previous to May 15th.

"JOHN A. DARRELL."

Darrell read it aloud. Sam said:
"There you are, General."
"Your generous and philanthropic offer, sir, is full of 'provisos' and 'ifs' and 'buts,'" said General Winfree, disagreeably. It had upset a very naïf plan of his.
"Did you think we were going to pay fifty dollars a share for stock that you could buy to-morrow on the New York Stock Exchange for twenty dollars a share less? This binds you to nothing, and it covers all your

stock and Major Moreland's and your other friends who have held it more than a few weeks. Put in 'and associates,' Jack, after General Winfree's name. That lets in everybody in Richmond and vicinity."

Darrell so wrote, and Sam said: "Colonel Robinson had better witness this document. The phraseology may not be legal, but it will fully hold. It is backed by the word of Mr. Darrell, which is as good as his bond"—and Sam looked straight into General Winfree's eyes, as man to man.

"I am sure that makes it absolutely to be depended on, sir," put in Major Moreland, cordially. "But I do not think our conversation should become public."

"Certainly not," affirmed the General, fiercely.

"As you please," said Sam, carelessly. In their eagerness to make money, Moreland and Winfree would tell the owner of the stock many things, but not the truth. This thought aroused no indignation in Sam. He was too eager to get the stock.

Moreland nudged General Winfree. The old man put out his hand to Sam, very formally, almost as if reluctantly. Sam shook it without any apparent feeling whatever, and said:

"And now, sir, let me say the last word. When we came to Richmond we had not the slightest idea we would make you such an offer. It is not a business like thing, on the face of it. But when we came here we also did not know Colonel Robinson, excepting by his reputation, and, now that we know him, we like him. This, and my belief that better days are coming for this State, and coming soon, will explain my action."

"A feeling we all share with you, gentlemen," said Major Moreland, in duty bound. He thought better days were coming for the Morelands.

It made a pleasant feeling go all around. Moreland was living in the blissful, dollar-studded future; Colonel Robinson was already tiding over his troubles; Sam saw the stock he needed coming towards him in hordes; Darrell thought the buying-agents had been selected by Providence, but that Sam had managed it very well. If anybody else but a rich and reckless boy had made the same proposition, the device would have been too transparent.

Shortly afterwards the party broke up. Sam shook hands very warmly with Colonel Robinson, who had been very thoughtful. Was it a trap? Colonel Robinson felt certain that Sam liked him, which, indeed, Sam did, now. Did these Northerners really want the Virginia Central stock to make a big plunge in the stock-market? The Colonel realized that they had completely tied up the Virginia-held stock by this manœuvre, at a relatively small cost. If the entire stock-market had not been so weak, and if Williams's report had not been adverse—and in his heart of hearts he had known it would be both adverse and honest — the Colonel would have suspected buying for control; and with that control he would not part, because it meant more than money; it meant the prestige of the road's presidency and a life-long habit. But, on the other hand, many of his friends took the same view that General Winfree did of his management, and he must have the Virginia holders friendly to him if he would keep the control. There had never been any serious organized opposition to him. Before elections he always promised—promised anything. But now the obstinate and narrow-minded bankers at home and everywhere else refused to lend money to the road—and to its president. That thought helped to club his doubts into insensibility.

At the door of the club Darrell said to him:

"Colonel Robinson, I think you will hear less grumbling in the future. If by any chance the General should produce enough stock to make the youngster's deal more profitable than we now hope by reducing the amount that an advance would bring on the market, we shall do what is right by you. But it seems to me only fair to say that we look to you to do the right thing by us in Austin, in the matter of rates and facilities."

Robinson smiled weakly. "Still at it! I think you always get what you want. You may count on the Virginia Central to do what is right." He really felt some relief. It looked, from Darrell's persistence, as if there was no more to the Darrell scheme than they said. At the worst these men might get lower freight rates than they should, but the Central was in no position to pick and choose, and he had the cash, which meant relief—which was precisely what Darrell had meant he should think.

"That's what we are banking on," said Sam, with one of his pleasant, boyish smiles. It made Colonel Robinson like him. After all, these people would develop the coal lands and the Virginia Central would prosper. He himself had often spoken of the same buried millions in Austin County, and once he even tried to form a syndicate to buy all the mines along the line of his road. He had seen coal and iron booms come and go. He would rather gamble in suburban real estate. After all, whatever might happen to his road and his stock, these men would enable him to build the most beautiful suburb in the South. It was a good price, sixty-five dollars a share. Almost he wished they would buy his stock outright. He was getting old, and so were

the cars and locomotives of the non-dividend-paying
Virginia Central; and the temper of many of his friends
and fellow-stockholders was not improving with age...
There were many trees in Capital Park, beautiful trees;
and the leaves were gold coins and the breeze blew
briskly. . The music kept him from hearing the
whispers of suspicion. And sixty-five dollars a share
was a good price. It had been a shrewd bargain. . . .
It blew a gale.

XXIII

IN Richmond the news of the "panic" in Virginia Central, as the sensational newspapers called Sampson Rock's drive against the stock, helped Major Moreland. It had been meant to help Sampson Rock. The thought of making money—real cash—made the Major the most active man south of Mason and Dixon's line. He personally interviewed scores of holders whose names and addresses he secured from the transfer clerk of the railroad company, and he deputed General Winfree to spread consternation among Colonel Robinson's stanchest friends — whose stanchness was not proof against the diminishing number of dollars in the market-price of their investment. The newspapers were reckless in the matter of space and dwelt at length on the labor troubles that were sure to come. The banks developed a habit of telephoning to Robinson at all hours to hear about the bond issue, which first New York and now London bankers had refused to touch— also in the matter of certain notes nearing maturity. All the machinery of the misfortune-factory, set in motion by Sampson Rock, worked overtime, until Colonel Robinson rejoiced in his own wisdom in giving the option on his holdings even to stock-gamblers. Had they been more business-like, less plunger-like, he would have suspected so many things that he might not have jeopardized his holdings and the presidency of the road. But the men were ticker-operators first and railroad managers a distant second. In that distance Colonel Robinson found safety and comfort.

Sydney had called Darrell on the long-distance telephone, and Darrell in reply had instructed him to buy as much Virginia Central at from twenty-nine to thirty-two as he was game for, also assuring him that the margins would be propped up to his entire satisfaction. Darrell's credit was good, and in addition he transferred all his ready funds, save five thousand dollars, by telegraph from his bank to his brokers. It gave Sam a little over two hundred thousand dollars with Sydney, and that night the brokers telegraphed that the young man was "long" nineteen thousand shares of Virginia Central, much of which had been bought at the low prices, so that the average on the "line" was only thirty-two and one-half. Darrell telegraphed back that they would return to New York in a day or two.

Major Moreland had slangily assured General Winfree that the rich but arrogant Northerners were "their meat." Personally the Major did not permit himself any convictions on the subject save one—that he stood to make money. The time he spent with the scattered owners of Virginia Central stock was well spent. Nothing might come from the deal; it would be very sad; but already his prestige had been raised to the pedestal of a great capitalist, for even the reflected glory of gold can exalt. He used various arguments to cajole his friends and acquaintances into giving options on their holdings, greed sharpening his wits marvellously. Curiously, one of his whispers was that world-famous men —whom he knew as he knew so many other world-famous men—wanted to make sure they would not be "squeezed" in their short sales of Virginia Central on the New York Stock Exchange, and therefore sought options on the stock at thirty-five or forty—or forty-five, as he said to those who smelled a mouse—which was far above the market-price, and indeed the intrinsic value of the shares. Stock-gambling was an expensive luxury, and it behooved staid business men to supply the luxury—at a price. That he would get fifty dollars for the same stock he did not feel it necessary even to suggest—it would have been highly unbecoming in a staid business man. However, all he was able to secure was about thirty thousand shares.

Darrell had gone to Austin to consult with Fletcher and obtain detailed statistics of the company's resources and undeveloped property, and Sam spent most of his time with Judge Abercrombie, busy with the Austin Iron Company options which were coming in driblets. Sampson Rock was pulling the wires that made Virginia Central stock rise and fall within a range of three points—from thirty to thirty-three—but was getting very little "real" stock on the "drives," because the supply from the sunny South on which he had reckoned was not trooping tumultuously into his open bag, and, moreover, he did not know that A. Sydney & Co. had bought twenty thousand shares that should have been his. The reason he did not know it was that he could not suspect Sam. The market was unsettled, the public afraid to buy enough and the professionals afraid to sell too much. He had not quite ninety thousand shares —the easy and profitable ninety thousand shares—but before he began to put up the price he waited for market conditions to crystallize, as he knew they must. When they should be ripe, Virginia Central would go up "naturally"—because the rest of the market would go up first. Before it did so, Morson would visit

Richmond. But it was well to let the market become dull in the mean time.

General Winfree, speaking for Major Moreland, asked Darrell at the club — rather offensively because he thought it masterly strategy, precisely as Sam had done—to waive the minimum of fifty thousand shares and take the thirty-three thousand they already had secured—belonging, he said, to himself and "a few friends." Major Moreland had nearly two hundred names on his little book; they did not seem many to him. After a sneer or two from Winfree, the ingenuous Darrell, with obvious reluctance, gave him a check for one hundred and sixty-five thousand dollars. The reluctance pleased the General almost as much as the check. Colonel Robinson had already given the written option on his fifty thousand shares, and ten minutes after paying Winfree, Sam told Darrell to send a draft for one hundred thousand dollars to Albert Sydney & Co. with instructions to buy more Virginia Central, very carefully.

He had the stock. The Virginia Central was theirs— his and his father's. Strictly speaking, the stock would be the Roanoke's. But, after assuming that the Roanoke's was his father's, Sam, thinking of the life-work before him, began to feel a proprietary interest in the "Greater Roanoke"—which would last as long as he lived. He even began to study the unsuspecting Rogers to determine for himself if the work of modernizing the former Robinson road should be intrusted to the Roanoke's best division superintendent.

Sam's last order made Sydney think. Mysteries are no laughing matter in Wall Street. Sydney watched Virginia Central with soulful attention, studying the "trading"—the buying and the selling of it—very closely, until he began to see unmistakable signs of absorption, very careful, very adroit, so skilfully circuitous that he could not discover by whom nor for whom the stock was being so quietly picked up. It began to look to Mr. Albert Sydney as if he had unwittingly aided in this same adroit absorption.

"I might have known they were using Jack as a blind. Of course, it's Old Man Rock! That boy is no idiot. He fooled *me !*" After which glowing tribute to Sam's genius Sydney bought one thousand shares of Virginia Central for his own personal account that he might share in the good thing—the nature of which he did not even faintly suspect—and immediately felt more courage. He telegraphed to Darrell:

"I am now carrying twenty-two thousand shares. Would like to see more margin. When do you return?"

But it was Sam who telegraphed back:

"Don't worry about margin. Will be home this week. Buy three thousand more.—S. R., Jr."

And Darrell also sent word:

"Do as instructed. Keep your pores open and your mouth shut.—JACK."

That day Sydney bought three thousand more, completing the twenty-five thousand shares. Notwithstanding his suspicion, if it had not been that Virginia Central enjoyed one of its strong spells that day, selling at around thirty-five, the broker would not have slept, for he properly assumed that if the deal, whatever it was, fell through, the stock would be worth very little. The potential loss on the twenty-five thousand shares was too big for comfort, even though he knew of course that Darrell and young Rock were "good" for any possible drop.

Even while Sam was on his way back, triumphant with the knowledge that at a risk of six hundred thousand dollars he controlled one hundred and eight thousand shares of Virginia Central, Mr. Sampson Rock had begun once more to buy the stock slowly, but steadily, selling only enough to check over-rapid advances. He telegraphed to Judge Abercrombie to report the frame of mind of Virginia Central stockholders in Richmond, and Abercrombie telegraphed back:

"All the property obtainable in this vicinity safely located. Bulk held at fifty cents or better. More may be forthcoming above that figure, as faith in management severely shaken by failure English deal. Suggest you await the arrival of your son.—W. A.".

The last sentence made Rock frown. What had Sam said? How indiscreet had he been? Sam had left Richmond, and Abercrombie evidently knew more than he could have learned from the phraseology of Rock's telegram. Had Sampson Rock delayed overlong the effort to secure at private sale the stock held in Richmond? Private negotiations can never prevent suspicion, and he had left them for the last. He would drive to cover a few shorts before another assault. He had sent for Dunlap.

"Dan, you'd better run up Virginia Central three or four points. Buy all you can carefully, but keep it under forty if the short interest is bigger than we figure. Any houses here, that you know, carrying Virginia Central?"

"Yes; Albert Sydney & Co. I was going to speak to you about it when you sent for me. They are lending quite a wad of it."

"Sydney?" mused Rock. ، "Who are they? For whom do they do business?"

"I don't know. They are a quiet firm. They have no big account that I ever heard of. I asked Sydney if they had much of it in the office and he said no; but he is lending Jim Greeley five thousand shares, and I saw him in the loan crowd lending it in five hundred share lots. I counted twelve thousand shares in all."

"What sort of a man is Sydney?"

"Oh, nice sort of chap; never has much to say. He is one of the governors of the Exchange, you know."

"Who are his partners?"

"Only one—A. P. Wheeler, who was his cashier for years."

"I'd like to see Sydney, Dan. Tell him to come over."

"Sure. I say, Sampson, he is—" began Dunlap, in a warning voice. He would not have Sampson Rock insult Sydney by unworthy offers or impertinent questions. The average man is apt to doubt every other man's tact.

"I know," interrupted Sampson Rock. The governors of the Exchange were all honorable men; and some of them were intelligent. But they were men, and therefore had tongues to answer questions with.

"All right. I'll send him. He is a pretty square fellow, Sampson."

"How do you do, Mr. Sydney?" said Sampson Rock, very politely, ten minutes later. "Thank you for coming over. It's only fair you should, because I'm so much older, you know. Mr. Sydney, I should like to give your firm some confidential business. I am certain you can do it." Sampson Rock would trust Albert Sydney & Co.'s integrity and discretion to the extent of millions. That was quite evident from Sampson Rock's manner.

"We should be very glad to do it for you, Mr. Rock, said Sydney, simply. He knew the Old Man by sight and had long admired him for his abilities and his versatility.

"I have been told that you've been somewhat active in Virginia Central lately?" The versatile Rock looked mildly inquisitive at the broker.

"We have done a little in it; yes, sir. But I can't say we've been active, exactly."

"Have you any special information on it that you can give me without violating any confidences?"

"No, sir. I have no information about it one way or another. We had some orders from customers and we executed them."

Rock's eyes did not leave the broker's face. But Sydney was looking back calmly, as though he would not for worlds withhold facts from generous Mr. Rock, who was going to give him a profitable confidential business.

"Have you any opinion of your own on the stock?"

"No, sir. I can't say that I have."

"Well, you must have watched it lately. If you had any of it yourself which showed you a nice profit now, would you sell it, simply from what you've seen of the trading in it?"

Sydney hesitated. He very much desired the Old Man's account—it was good, safe business, and there might be satisfying crumbs at banquet-time. But he could not forget Sam's injunction. Perhaps the boy was working unknown to, or even against, the Old Man. More likely he had bought on the Old Man's advice. If Mr. Rock had bought some for a turn, there was no need to say he suspected steady, but quiet and therefore important, buying. He answered:

"It would depend on what I thought the rest of the market would do."

"I see," said Sampson Rock "Now I would like you to buy for me to-morrow, at the opening, five thousand shares of Roanoke, at the market, but don't climb for it. And please clear it." He rang the bell for Valentine, and told him: "Mr. Sydney will buy five thousand Roanoke for me to-morrow. Give him a check: account R."

"Very well, sir."

"I may want you to sell some Virginia Central for me, Mr. Sydney, very carefully."

"Yes, sir."

"Your office is still long of it, I take it?"

"Quite possibly. But whether it is or not, Mr. Rock, you needn't fear for one moment that we—"

"I don't, Mr. Sydney; not for one moment. I'm very glad to have met you."

"Thank you, sir. I want to say, Mr. Rock, that if we should happen to sell Virginia Central to-morrow or buy Roanoke it will not be because—"

"My dear chap," said Rock, quite amiably, because he now knew Sydney's purchases of Virginia Central had not been for any possible opponent, which was all that might have made Sydney's buying important, "if I thought you were that kind of a man, do you suppose I'd have sent for you? I knew all about you before I told Dunlap to ask you to come here. Have you ever had any orders from Mr. Dunlap?"

"No; not that I remember."

"Well, you will hereafter."

"Thank you, Mr. Rock."

"Don't mention it. And, I say, Mr. Sydney, if you should hear any gossip about Virginia Central, or Great Southern, you might let me know, if you will. And about Roanoke, too." And he smiled.

Sydney also smiled—appreciatively—the idea of his telling Rock anything about Roanoke!—and answered:

"I certainly will. Good-afternoon, Mr. Rock."

That night while Sampson Rock was at his club he was called to the telephone. Sam was speaking from Washington.

"Hello, Dad! This is Sam. How are you?—What? —I said, how are you?—Oh, I'm fine!—How's the market?—What?—I can't hear—How's V. C.?—Do you think it's going up now?—I only wanted to know if you'd swept up all the loose stuff that was floating around.—I'm going to stay here until to-morrow to meet some of Darrell's friends.—About the five hundred thousand dollars?—I'll tell you about that when I see you. Take care of yourself, Dad. I must go now; they are waiting for me. Good-bye."

A minute after he rang off Sam sent a telegram to Sydney:

"Buy as much more of our specialty as you can without getting heart disease. Will be in New York Thursday."

Sydney on the next day bought twenty-five hundred shares of Virginia Central for Sam, paying up to forty and one-half for it. Dunlap reported this to Sampson Rock, who frowned and devoted his attention to putting up Roanoke from ·seventy-five to seventy-seven. It closed at seventy-six and three-quarters, and Virginia Central at thirty-nine. The rest of the market was also strong, but Roanoke was the leader.

At the club that night Sampson Rock and a number of his associates held an informal council of war. They agreed that the market ought to go up, and each man agreed to take care of his own stocks. Sampson Rock was not loquacious, but they knew he would do as much as the most optimistic of them promised to do. Before he went home he had formed a pool to advance Roanoke. The Virginia Central deal he kept to himself and the three men who always went in with him in all his deals. They knew what he was about to do with the Virginia Central and the Roanoke. He did not require any advice or any money from them. When he did he said so, and their checks were quite as prompt in coming as their advice. That same evening Morson left for Richmond. Sampson Rock would give him three days. That was enough time for such a man, who knew what such a master desired.

The stock-market opened strong and developed a very pronounced rising tendency as the day wore on. But not all manipulators were as skilful as Sampson Rock, who made Roanoke rise to eighty during the first hour. In other stocks the artificiality of the subsequent advance was so obvious as to arouse not enthusiasm but scepticism and suspicion in wise minds. One of the wisely incredulous minds belonged to Gilmartin. He called on Rock to learn if the Old Man also was wise.

"Mr. Gilmartin, I'm very busy to-day," said Rock, curtly. It made Gilmartin feel very angry at Rock and sorry for Gilmartin. He wasted no time, but asked, point-blank, the usual question:

"What do you think of the market, Mr. Rock?"

"Up!" answered Rock, from the ticker. Gilmartin's heart did the reverse; it sank.

"And Virginia Central?"

"Somebody's buying it." Rock was studying the ticker unblinkingly.

"It looks to me like short covering," ventured Gilmartin.

"Quite likely."

"I—er—Mr. Rock—you've been so good to me I don't want to bother you when you are so busy. But—er—do you think I ought to cover?"

"Cover? Ah!" And Rock, staring at Gilmartin, suddenly looked as if he remembered. "Great Heavens, man, didn't you cover on the break?"

"N-no, sir."

"You are a fool!" Rock told him, irritably. "You had a fine profit. Did you want to make a million?"

Gilmartin felt that Rock had made one by not being avaricious. But poor Gilmartin's beautiful paper profit had been gnawed away by the ticker's teeth, and there seemed no likelihood of its being restored by the same gnawing fiend incarnate. Gilmartin despairingly began to defend himself:

"No, sir. But the stock was worthless—"

"The stock was *not* worthless. No stock of a railroad that's not in a receiver's hands is. Did you expect to buy it in at two or three dollars a share?"

"You yourself said the road—" Gilmartin was at bay.

"And you yourself were a hog! That's the truth of it. The road's unchanged; but the general market is in far stronger condition than it was when I spoke to you." Gilmartin looked so sincerely wretched that Rock laughed. He took another look at the ticker.

All was going well. He therefore turned to Gilmartin and said, cheerfully: "Never mind, Gilmartin. You are like the rest of the world. You always want a little more than you are entitled to. Cover your Virginia Central. It may not go up right away, but the rest of the market will carry it along. If there's any loss, tell Valentine to charge it to me. And tell him I said to buy you a couple of hundred Roanoke. It's seventy-eight and one-half now. It ought to go to par. I'm not ready to tell you more now, but there's something going on. You'll get the news when I'm ready, and don't ask questions."

"Increased dividend?" irrepressibly said Gilmartin, voicing both his suspicion and his new golden hope.

"Don't ask me questions! Next time you do it will be the last." He rang the bell for Valentine, and said:

"Buy two hundred shares of Roanoke for Gilmartin. I'm very busy, Gilmartin. Come again later. And if you do any more guessing, don't print it."

Gilmartin left him, half-dazed. He almost hoped, like the veriest lamb, that his paper profits of about five thousand dollars, which had dwindled to a few beggarly hundreds, would come back. Only this hope kept him from thinking seriously of suicide or murder. As it was, murder had been done, Sampson Rock having thoughtlessly eviscerated Gilmartin's hopes. The new potential treasure-trove of Roanoke, given to him by the same sanguinary Rock, only half-comforted the victim of Virginia Central's illogical rally. Therefore, in his news-slips he wrote that the rise in Virginia Central was due exclusively to the determination of one clique of professionals to compel another clique of professionals to cover. Since the road remained the same and the management unchanged and the company's need of funds still unrelieved, as soon as the two cliques were done fighting each other the price would probably go back to where it should, if intrinsic value alone were considered, which was far below thirty. He wrote this in the hope that the mob would believe it. Such a belief would restore the vanished profit and the golden independence.

Of Roanoke he said that important developments were in progress calculated greatly to enhance the value of the stock. Prominent insiders made no secret of their belief that the stock would sell at par by reason of the value-making deal, concerning which it was premature to speak, though there was every prospect that the plans under consideration would go through. He also published the road's recent earnings because they showed increases, just as he had given the Virginia Central's because they showed decreases. Of other stocks he did not write optimistically. He preferred rather to make money on the down side, through Virginia Central, which he considered owed him five thousand dollars, than on the up-track with Roanoke. It was a human enough prejudice. He even bitterly bemoaned his ill-luck, and blamed everybody but himself for not having converted the elusive paper profit into good hard cash when the opportunity was before him—for having wanted more—more—more—at the wrong time. That was his only sin—not wanting more, but wanting it at the wrong time.

Roanoke quickly rose to eighty-two. The entire market was strong and active—so strong that many shrewd people, whose theory of the stock-market was based on mechanics and cynicism, became suspicious. The bull manipulators had begun to find considerable professional selling on the advance and very little response from the public. More to stimulate the rest of the market than because he desired fire-works, Rock put up Virginia Central two points by the purchase of only nine hundred shares. The scarcity of offerings was so obvious that it showed the floating supply had been absorbed by some one. It let loose many rumors; among others, one that the Great Southern was after it. It was a false step, that day's rise in Virginia Central. But not beyond recovery. After all, the Street was not sure of it. But it made Sampson Rock's work a trifle more difficult.

XXIV

THE bears began to sell Roanoke tentatively and Rock let them do it without the slightest concern. Whatever they sold now they would have to buy back later; therefore the more the merrier, for if they sold at eighty-two and bought back at eighty-four or eighty-six, the difference, though slight, would be pleasant. But there suddenly developed scattering buying of Virginia Central that he could not account for. It might mean nothing, but he knew that an order to buy ten thousand shares of the stock, which one of the plunging professionals might easily take it into his reckless head to give, would make the price rise sensationally, and that would not do at all—not yet. Competitive buying is all very well when only a few thousand shares more are needed and the price is consequently of little importance, since the average cost is already practically fixed. He had barely ninety thousand shares, and he disliked to reduce his holdings by selling should such buying develop. He heard with displeasure the rumor that the Great Southern was after the Virginia Central. It was untrue, of course, but, if enough people believed it, Virginia Central was bound to rise inopportunely. It would also make those who had Virginia Central stock hold it with the tenacity begotten of a fresh and blossoming hope—and Sampson Rock had striven to make that same hope wither.

Even now, a fresh slump in Virginia Central would do much good. Such a thing would be contrary to the general market's tendency and thus be doubly ominous. That slump would come when Morson, in Richmond, would give the word. The people in Virginia who had not sold when the stock was thirty would sell if, after touching forty, the price began once more to decline. They would figure that on the second slump it would make a lower record than ever. Sydney would get some big selling orders and instructions to execute them very carefully. That would make Sydney's customers think about the wisdom of holding their Central stock.

The *Epoch*, however, came out the next morning with a long article on the first page, saying it had the highest unofficial authority for the statement that the Great Southern had bought the controlling interest of the Virginia Central road. The writer took great pains and much space to show how very valuable the Virginia Central was and how its acquisition would make the Great Southern the most powerful railway system south of Mason and Dixon's line. The *Epoch's* Richmond correspondent was a complaisant and diligent man, and, having been asked by his New York paper to ascertain if any big blocks of Virginia Central had quietly changed hands recently, was able to learn enough about General Winfree's manœuvre and to surmise enough of Robinson's financial condition to telegraph back that a local syndicate had corralled some stock and had turned it over to parties unknown. At the New York end of the wire a few changes were made in the despatch, among others to substitute "Great Southern" for "parties unknown," and "huge block" for "some stock." The "huge block" supplemented by what the Great Southern people had "quietly picked up" in the open market gave Roanoke's rival "the control." The writer added that President Robinson had "significantly" declined to deny or confirm the report.

It was quite obvious that, by the deal, the Roanoke fell back definitely into second place—it never had been indisputably first. But that was not the reason Sampson Rock's irritation was so great when he read the article. Before the market opened he gave his brokers orders to sell one thousand shares of Virginia Central every eighth of a point from forty-two up—and also to take back the same stock, on the downward reaction, at a quarter of a point below each broker's selling-price. In Roanoke he gave supporting orders, one thousand shares every eighth of a point down, from eighty to seventy-five. The stock had closed at eighty-two. That should be more than ample, since Rock knew the story was a canard and he was at peace with all the other big capitalists who might fight with sixteen-inch guns.

The concern of the bull clique—which had "inspired" the article by the simple device of telling the reporter they had heard the news in confidence, but that it was sure to come out in a day or two—was chiefly with Great Southern, and the stock rose six points, being duly assisted by the clique brokers. Virginia Central tried to rise in sympathy with its absorber's advance, but the weight of Sampson Rock's sales, as well as some by friends of the Great Southern, insiders who knew the report was untrue, and therefore bought Great Southern while they sold the other, kept Virginia Central from doing more than flutter feebly in its effort to soar. As for Roanoke, it went down to seventy - nine and seven - eighths and went back to eighty-two. It was a fizzle—the sensation—so far as Virginia Central was concerned, but the failure of the jobbing clique did not lift Sampson Rock's ill-humor. He could not punish the Great Southern crowd because he, like themselves, was committed to the bull side. He tried to telephone to Richmond early, but there was an electrical storm south of Washington and the wires did not work well. He telegraphed to Morson to lose no time, and asked for details of what had been done in the negotiations for the purchase of the locally held Virginia Central stock. It was Judge Abercrombie who answered, his message being delayed in transmission:

"Your son has full details.—W. A."

His son had no business to have full details nor Abercrombie to know that there were any details whatever. It was therefore precisely the worst moment for Sam's triumphant return, a few minutes after Abercrombie's despatch.

Sampson Rock, Jr., was in fine spirits, and looked it. "Hello, Governor!" he shouted, happily, from the door of the office. He loved his father for what he had been and for what he would be. A worker of wonders, a prestidigitator of dollars; but a builder of railroads, a giver of work, a general, and—his father. The worker of wonders might be vexed at the philanthropy of the ignoramus, but the father should sympathize with the game as played by his son. And, moreover, there was the Great Work—the development of the coal-fields, the enlargement of the iron-works, the modernization of the obsolete Virginia Central—a *man's* task! . . .

"How do you do, Sam?" said Sampson Rock. His ticker-hypnotized eyes lighted up; the boy looked well, happy, affectionate. They shook hands.

"Did you have a good time, Sammy?" Rock smiled, though the ticker was whirring away furiously.

"You bet! How's the market?" It was unfortunate. Sam approached the ticker. "Great Scott, forty for Virginia Central!" He turned and said, irrepressibly: "Bully for you, Dad!" The stock was not so far from the price he had paid Winfree and Moreland.

"What details have you that Abercrombie says you had? What have you been doing in Richmond?" asked Sampson Rock, sharply, almost reproducing the staccato speech of the ticker.

Sam turned quickly. Sampson Rock was frowning, probably only from force of habit. He looked, for all his frown, unenlightened. Sam replied, calmly:

"Exactly what you told me to do."

"What is it? What?" questioned Sampson Rock, impatiently. He was still annoyed by the miscarriage of his calculations. He had planned deliberately, and had considered every contingency carefully. The plan should have gone through without a hitch and he should by now have acquired fully two-thirds of the one hundred and seventy-five thousand shares of the Virginia Central by means of the campaign of depression, exactly as he had planned to do. The Southern holdings of the stock had not come out, for all that the road was discredited at home and Robinson was up to his ears in the slough of financial despond. He now expected that Morson would telegraph bad news—that is, suspicious stockholders and a tight grip on the shares.

"You told me," said Sam, conscious that he was not

acting or talking as he had meant to act and speak, and yet somehow unable to blurt out the whole story without preamble, "to get facts the next time I spoke to you about your business." He paused. Then he finished, a trifle defiantly, by reason of the look on his father's face: "Well, I've got them." He was not thinking of what he had been, nor of what he was, but of what he would be: *He* would reorganize the Virginia Central in due time, and his father would help him. But he felt that his father would insist on a few more years at the railroad kindergarten and the habit of listening, not of speech.

"I didn't tell you to spend half a million to get them," began Rock, irritably.

"I've spent more than that, Dad." Sam smiled. It was not a fatuous smile; rather it was meant to be an encouraging and conciliating grin—to prepare the ground by allaying irritation. But Sampson Rock said, impatiently:

"For Heaven's sake, Sam, don't play at having brains! You discourage me. What have you done? Have you seen Morson? What does Abercrombie's telegram mean?"

"I'm not sure I know what he means," said Sam, with composure, "not knowing what he has telegraphed you." Sampson Rock misread Sam's look. It seemed to him one of empty-headed complacency. It exasperated him. He muttered something that sounded like a dissyllabic oath. Sam went on:

"I found out you had sent Morson after options on all the Austin County coal-lands he could lay his hands on. So I've secured sixty-eight per cent. of the stock of the Austin Iron Company at a little over forty dollars a share."

Sampson Rock actually sighed. It was a half-impatient, half-resigned sigh, an exhalation inarticulate but subtly profane. He shook his head and said:

"That was foolish, Sam. Hang it, the time wasn't ready for it!"

"Yes, it was. The moment the Virginia Central was safe in your possession, that was the time to get the iron company's stock. Of course, people would sell it at forty when it began to pay ten or fifteen per cent. dividends. I should have waited a few years.

"Bosh!" It was a father's reply to a son's youthful sarcasm.

"You don't have to bother with it. I can sell it at a profit. Darrell and I are in this and—"

"It ties up a lot of money." Sampson Rock's fingers were drumming on the table. He did not like to call upon the members of his syndicates until he was certain of success. That way they were content with smaller profits, the risk being slight. The half-million he had paid out on Sam's account was needed elsewhere.

"I told you to sell my bonds."

"Look here, Sam," and the look on Sampson Rock's face was not pleasant, "you must never do that again. They were your mother's. Never do it again. Never dare to think of doing it again. Do you hear me, Sam?" It was Sam's threat about the bonds that had made him honor the draft. He now resented the compulsion hotly.

"Yes, I hear you. However, the Austin Iron Company was only a side-issue, of not much importance. You are going to help me reorganize it. But there was something else."

"Another gold-mine?" Sampson Rock frowned. Then he looked resigned:

"I didn't go into it to make money, but to do a square thing, because I found I would like the work."
Sampson Rock now felt certain his son had committed the unpardonable sin of stupidity—the one thing that Wall Street never has time to forgive—the punishment follows so quickly. He asked, impatiently:
"What is it? Who advised you?"

"You did." Sam looked steadily at his father.

"Go on, you silly—" What Rock now wished to know was exactly how many dollars Sam's inexperience and volubility would cost him.

"If you told me the truth, which I am sure you did, I can sell something for seventy-five that I have bought for less. I have bought Colonel Robinson's stock, fifty thousand shares at sixty-five."

"Fifty thousand at sixty-five?"

"Yes, Dad." Before Sam could tell his father about Winfree's thirty-three thousand at fifty and about the twenty-five thousand in Sydney's office, Sampson Rock shouted:

"Why did you meddle with this matter? Why did you pay him such a damned-fool price? Why—" His face was flushed with anger. It showed also in his eyes, but most of all in the unpleasant dilation of the nostrils.

"You think that's a damned-fool price, do you? I suppose that's because it's only a little less than it's worth and that goes against the grain. I wanted to cinch the control and do it at once and do it like a gentleman. You just try to get any stock in Richmond for less." He felt a sense of hot resentment that blotted out the thrilling vision of the Great Work.

Fury flooded Sampson Rock's soul to overflowing. Obviously Sam had talked not wisely, but too much.

SAMPSON ROCK OF WALL STREET

The fifty thousand shares from Robinson was not enough, and the task of getting the balance of the majority at a low price had deliberately been made more difficult by his own son. The news had been given to the world through a megaphone—from his own office. And the son had taken a million dollars from Sampson Rock's pocket and stuffed it into Robinson's.

"Ugh!" snarled Sampson Rock, his hands clinched. "Why in hell did you think you had brains? Why did you meddle? Who gave you authority to buy—"

"I did it," said Sam, doggedly. "That's all there is about it. And now—"

"Yes, you did it! You are a Napoleon of finance! You ought to open a school for teaching people how to do business! You might possibly tell me, while you are about it, where you are going to get the money to pay for it. Not from me!"

Sampson Rock was a practical financier, wise, cool-headed, steel-nerved, and lightning-witted. He had wanted what Sam had in his possession; he could use it even now to advantage. In thinking of the deal he had thought only of results; and of results not in more dollars for Sampson Rock but in increased tonnage for the Roanoke. In the end it worked out in more dollars, anyhow. But also he had been overworking for years, and he was human. He had wanted the stock, but he wanted to get it himself in his own carefully planned way—the way to which he was accustomed. He would have changed his plans in the twinkling of an eye had the need arisen; but even then that would have been a change effected by himself. It was not stubbornness, nor wounded artistic pride, nor the high price paid, nor egotism•that made him angry enough to refuse Sam's option. It was a little of all these, but mostly it was a curious twist in his character. He was very fond of oysters, but he would not eat them unless they came to the table on a shallow white dish, very cold, but without cracked ice.

A very wise man knows that even wiser men are capable of saying foolish things at times. But Sam was not in a very wise mood. He retorted, stubbornly:

"If you want it, you'll have to pay me seventy-five dollars for it and treat the minority decently. If you don't I'll keep it myself. And if I find I can't swing it by myself, I'll see if somebody else won't help me, here or in London. All that road needs is brains and hustle, and men that have those can be hired."

All his anger at the oysters which had come to the table on the wrong dish vanished. Sampson Rock was conscious of Sam's boyish determination—and conscious of treachery from his son, his only son, the heir to his money and his work. Again a problem far more momentous than the absorption of the Virginia Central confronted him. He rose and began to walk up and down the room, snapping his fingers behind his back, thinking of the future of that son of whom he had begun to have hopes. Perhaps the boy had been merely hasty; that came from inexperience. He had been indiscreet; that also might have come from inexperience. He might not be a hopeless ass. He might yet learn.

Rock halted in his walking abruptly and said to his son, with an effort to speak kindly:

"Never mind, Sam. We'll see what we can do to repair your folly."

"Folly nothing!" retorted Sam. "I know better. Before you can sell your own Virginia Central stock to the Roanoke you'll have to buy mine at my price, and you know it. If you don't, you ought to realize it as soon as you can. I haven't told you all." The obstinacy that settled on his face was not at all the pertinacity of an intelligent man.

"Don't talk that way to me, you jackass!" Sampson Rock's face flushed hotly and he spoke loudly.

"I take after you, and you don't realize it yet," said Sam, defiantly. "Leaving aside all question of right or wrong, suppose I tell you that I've listened to you and I've taken your advice and, in becoming a business man of your type, I tell you right now and here that you'll have to buy Robinson's stock from me at seventy-five, and more stock besides at the same price, or you won't carry your deal through? What do you say to that?"

"He was looking at his father unblinkingly, his face a trifle pale, his jaw set firmly, his hands clinched as though they were clutching the control of the Virginia Central and the power that went with it. There was something distinctly unpleasant about his expression. And yet he was once more thinking of the Great Work; and he wondered if, left to himself, he could not make Rogers transform the Virginia Central while Darrell looked after the Austin Iron Company

Sampson Rock drew in a deep breath. He looked steadily at Sam, but said nothing. Of a sudden he turned and walked to the ticker. He passed the tape through his fingers. The market was quiet; the early excitement had subsided. His previous orders, given in expectation of a flurry, had not been executed; there had been no occasion for the elaborate preparations, it now seemed. The early orders would be ample for any contingency likely to arise before the market's close.

He would leave the office and go somewhere, out of sight of Sam, whose looks, whose words, whose very presence irritated him beyond calm utterance. It was not a stock-market problem he wished to think about, but one far more important for a man with an only child—far more important and very much more common. He was calm now, but Sam would upset him again with his next sentence. He would not give Sam the chance. It was better for him to leave the office than for Sam. Everything in this room reminded him of his work. It made him think the work would die with him. There was no heir to his work.

It is always the human factor that spells failure as well as success.

He avoided looking at his son. Of a sudden he rang the bell for Valentine.

"Valentine, tell Mr. Dunlap to cancel the selling orders in Virginia Central. The supporting orders in Roanoke stand as given out this morning. I'm off for the day."

"Yes, sir. In case—"

"I'll be at the Ardsley Club. But don't bother me unless it is something very important."

"Very well, sir."

"I say, Dad—" began Sam. He was frowning. The occasion called for calm discussion.

Rock held up a silencing hand.

"You've said enough for one day. I don't want to hear another word from you. You may possibly succeed in realizing that your meddling with my business will cost me several hundred thousand dollars—"

"Can't you think of anything but money when you talk to me?" cried Sam, fiercely. "Listen to what I have to say, and then—"

345

"Not now, damn it, not now!"

Gilmartin entered unannounced. Rock had told Valentine to send the reporter in the moment he showed up. He had some Roanoke news to give out, to discourage what selling might be prompted by the *Epoch* article.

"There's no reason why the Virginia Central deal can't go through as originally planned," said Sam. He controlled his feelings and spoke very earnestly, unaware of the reporter's presence. "I can't see why the Roanoke—"

"I know you can't see. You can't see a lot. But I tell you it won't," said Sampson Rock, decisively. But even as he spoke he knew it would. He would make the best of a bad bargain. He would exercise Robinson's option, but not until he was certain he could not do better. He would telegraph for Abercrombie to come to New York at once. Nevertheless, the father's problem of the son and heir remained. It could not be studied in this office at this time.

"This talk of yours is not going to make Roanoke sell at par," began Sam, with a weak attempt at conciliatory humor.

"It isn't going to sell there now, thanks to intelligent interference."

"And your great plans for changing the State of Virginia so its own mother wouldn't recognize—"

"Oh, you—"

Gilmartin, whose heart had skipped on an average three beats out of seven while he was listening, had a flash of wisdom—and promptly stepped outside. Then he rattled the door-knob and peered into the office before entering. He precisely succeeded in checking the Old Man's expression of opinion about his only son.

346

"Good-morning, Mr. Rock." Gilmartin's heart was not skipping beats now, but it was going very fast.

"What do you want?"

"They said you wanted to see me."

"They lied. I don't."

"Do you care to say anything about the *Epoch* story that the Great Southern—"

"What the deuce do I care what the Great Southern does? Why don't you ask Winters? He's the president of it."

"It will hurt the Roanoke, won't it?" said Gilmartin. The next moment he shuddered at his own temerity. It was a waste of fear, for Sampson Rock merely scowled and said, impatiently:

"No; why should it?"

"I—well, everybody says—"

"Everybody is always right," interrupted Sampson Rock, sarcastically. Gilmartin had never seen the Old Man in such a mood. Even without the evidence of his ears he would have known the Roanoke deal was off, from the Old Man's manner. The Old Man had tried and failed. Failure might possess the charm of novelty to the great and successful Sampson Rock; but it had not made the great and successful Sampson Rock amiable.

"Doesn't that mean the Roanoke deal you told me about is off?" asked Gilmartin, regardless of consequences. There was about four or five hundred dollars profit in the two hundred shares the Old Man, in a more amiable mood, had bought for him the day before.

"You certainly have a nerve, Gilmartin," said Rock, with an admiring sneer. "You'll be running my business for me next week. Since I have no secrets from you, Gilmartin, you might as well begin at once. I'll leave you in charge of my son. He needs a nice, discreet man for confidential adviser. I won't be home to dinner, Sam."

"Wait a minute, Dad!" exclaimed Sam, hastily.

But Sampson Rock went out. Captain of finance though he was, he slammed the door.

Sam approached the ticker almost mechanically. He was still dazed by his father's anger and his own resentment, and puzzled at the unbusiness-like refusal to hear the whole story. His father might have haggled as to price; and Sam would have turned the option over at cost. But anger at having to pay a fair price—that did not accord with his new conception of Sampson Rock's character and business hopes. His father had ninety thousand shares of Virginia Central and Sam one hundred and eight thousand—that was more than enough. And the deal; the doing of the thing—that was the thing, not the money. Was the deal definitely off. If so, what was to be done? He racked his mind for an answer. None came.

The thought of the possible loss of his money never occurred to him. It was how to develop Austin County's resources, how to make the Virginia Central as good a railroad as the Roanoke. With money he could do it—his jaws were tightly set as he thought—but he was without capital. He must induce his father to help. He began to say to himself now what he should have said to Sampson Rock—what he would say that night at home. His father would listen; he felt certain of it. The Great Work could not be sacrificed. He would compel Sampson Rock to help, for the Virginia Central *must* be changed into a second Roanoke! He drew in a deep breath, his eyes fixed on the tape unseeingly.

•

XXV

"MR. ROCK," said Gilmartin, courageously, as he approached at one and the same time Sam and the ticker, "could you tell me anything more about the matter?"

Sam turned to the reporter.

"About what matter?" he asked. "I've just come back from the South." He saw the look that irrepressibly flashed in Gilmartin's eyes, and, remembering whose son he was, he added, calmly, "I am interested in an iron property down there."

The evasion was too obvious; but Gilmartin did not again betray himself. He remarked, casually, with a faint air of being in the confidence of Sampson Rock, Sr

"Do you know, I felt certain that the Roanoke would gobble up the Virginia Central." He looked at young Rock sympathetically, making the Roanoke a family affair, and its failures a matter of personal regret.

"Yes?" said Sam, very politely. One thing was for him to disagree with his father; another to help his father's foes by telling anything to reporters. He add ed, to throw this hound off the scent, "What would the Roanoke do with the Virginia Central?"

"What?" echoed Gilmartin. "For one thing, it would cut the gizzard out of the Great Southern! To check the Great Southern expansion in competitive

349

territory alone would make Roanoke sell at par."
Jupiter, head-god and railroad expert, had spoken.
If Sam's ignorance was feigned he would now realize
its uselessness. If it was real he would be enlightened.
Attempts to deceive were vain.

"Roanoke will do that some day, anyhow," said
Sam. He elected himself the mouth-piece of the stock-
market, and confidently added, "With or without the
Virginia Central."

Gilmartin was tip-proof by now. He said, as if
soliloquizing:

"The question is, can the Roanoke get the Virginia
Central?" He frowned, strainingly, as if he were trying to read the answer in his own brain.

"That's the question," acquiesced Sam, very amiably, because he saw his way clear enough now. "Yes,
Mr. Gilmartin, *that* is the question. And you'd better
ask it of Colonel Robinson. He's a very truthful man.
Ask him if he will sell his holdings." The spirit of
Sampson Rock passed into him uninvited; it simply
came. It made him finish: "Even at one hundred
dollars a share."

Gilmartin, not fearing the youngster, ventured, "If
the Great Southern offers him more than the Roanoke,
I'll bet he—"

"Don't bet, Mr. Gilmartin, unless you are absolutely
certain you will win. But there is no absolutely safe
bet in this world. I used to think there was; but
horses are so uncertain! I don't know whether the
Great Southern can gather up enough Virginia Central
stock to give it the control, but I am inclined to doubt
it. I think if they try they will soon tell you that
yours is no safe bet." Sam was speaking with a sort
of ingenuous wisdom—the wisdom of a rich man's son

playing at business. It was almost sinful to take advantage of this boy, Gilmartin thought. But business was business, no matter who played it. He was no eleemosynary institution, even if he was a reporter, for on the two hundred shares of Roanoke which the boy's father had given him there was a nice little paper profit. Should that profit be taken? The answer depended on the deal, its success or its failure. He would not overstay the market in Roanoke as he had in Virginia Central. He said:

"Then you don't think the control of the Virginia Central has passed to another road?" His manner invitingly showed that he himself did not believe it had.

"Not that *I* know of," answered Sam, from the ticker, without looking up, as he had seen his father speak. "But, really, I don't think it's such an important matter. The Roanoke," he explained, thrilled with the beautiful, misleading words that came to him and gave him a sense of loyalty to his father and of progress in the Great Work, "has got along very nicely without the Virginia Central so far. I've just gone over the Roanoke. It's in fine shape."

It was as plain as day to Gilmartin that the Roanoke crowd had tried to get the Central and had failed, to their great chagrin and financial damage. Now, unless the Great Southern had secured the Virginia Central, it probably would do to sell Virginia Central stock short again. But it was as certain as anything could be that to sell Roanoke short now was the twin-brother of getting money for the asking. He saw very distinctly what wisdom consisted of. He was poor, and it was no seventh heaven worrying about the rent. This was the 20th of the month, too.

"Thank you, Mr. Rock. Good-morning."

"You must not say I said anything," said Sam. He felt it wise to look uneasy. "I don't think my father would like me to speak to any one about Roanoke. It's a very fine stock, you know. I think it will go to par." It was his very obvious over-eagerness to impress Gilmartin that made his words unconvincing to the reporter. He was a pleasant-spoken youngster, and so deep—about half an inch. Gilmartin felt himself so much cleverer than Sam that he liked Sam.

"I hope so." He spoke very gently and reassuringly. "Of course, Mr. Rock, I sha'n't repeat anything you've told me. If I hear anything of interest I'll come in and tell you."

"That will be very nice of you, I'm sure,' said Sam, with a grateful smile.

"He's pie," thought Gilmartin. "I'll cultivate *him*." He told Valentine to sell out his two hundred Roanoke and waited for the report of the sale. Rock might be angry when he read what Gilmartin would print about the Roanoke, and Gilmartin was taking no chances. Captains of finance might "welsh" just out of spite. The stock was sold at eighty-one and five-eighths. With the memorandum of the sale safe in his pocket and the promise of Valentine to send him a check, he hastened away, not to print his suspicions, but to see Samuel W. Sharpe, the great bear operator, for Gilmartin now had information to sell as well as to print. The selling came first. He was a journalistic parasite, whose industry in gathering market gossip alone made anybody employ him. He knew that the average speculator did not desire facts, but gossip—"explanations" of market movements, past, present, and to come, such as might furnish not reasons, but excuses, for gambling blindly—and he supplied it. He was successful. Respected nowhere, he was tolerated everywhere. The other financial reporters laughed at his insensibility to snubs. But perhaps that very thick hide gave him the *entrée* into nearly every office in the Street, big or little. The wise rich found him cheap; the foolish poor were impressed by his omniscience.

"I have a big thing for you, Mr. Sharpe. The Roanoke has been trying to get control of the Virginia Central and has failed. The Rock crowd were so sure they had it that they started to put up Roanoke on the strength of it. They are loaded to the guards with it. And now the whole thing's off."

"How do you know?"

"Mr. Rock admitted it to me."

"Then they have it safe." Being a "big man" himself, Sharpe knew his fellows and had no illusions on the subject of veracity.

"No, no! Don't be too suspicious and don't think I'm that much of an ass. I heard him say so to his son when he didn't know I was in the room. I saw young Rock afterwards. He told me the Roanoke did not have the Virginia Central, but that neither had the Great Southern. He didn't know he was saying anything out of the way. I know Mr. Rock expected to put the deal through this week and that it's all off now. Robinson wouldn't sell his holdings. He has refused one hundred dollars a share. If somebody else hasn't got the Virginia Central, it ought to be a good thing to sell that, too, for the Rock crowd will have to unload what they've got, now that they've found they can't get enough to control. But there surely can be no question about Roanoke being sure money on the short side."

Sharpe did not deign to answer, but walked quickly to his desk, took up the telephone and called up 7777 Cortlandt. On his face was the usual fierce frown. He was a financial free-lance, a soldier of fortune whose brain was a great army. A "trader" on a large scale, his foes called him, but he was more than a mere plunger: he was a stock-market strategist of the first rank, who often made a million dollars on the offensive keep ten millions on a long and desperate defensive. He was ready to fight at the drop of the hat and to gamble on the blink of an eyelid. He chronically frowned, be-cause his financial life was never unmenaced for a single minute; it was an uncomfortable existence, his— to the other big operators. The most powerful leaders on the bull side are never powerful enough to do with-out allies. Sharpe, as a bear, needed none. He was the spirit of the stock-market embodied in a hyena. In his triumphs he snarled; in his good humor he sneered. If he laughed, sardonically, it was at the smallness of the gun with which he sometimes battered down a seeming Gibraltar. Not even the thought that his accumulated dollars represented the coined terror of the multitude made him smile. He was suspected of loving his horses. Accused of it point-blank one day by this same unwise Gilmartin, he denied it with passionate profanity. But that was a pose. He did love his horses—and his enemies' money.

"Hello? Mr. Winter, please—Hello?—Who is this? Tell Mr. Winter that Mr. Sharpe is on the 'phone— Winter?—Yes—Has the Great Southern got the con-trol of the Virginia Central?—Never mind that! Have you or haven't you?—Have you any of the stock at all? —Very well—I understand Rock tried to get it for the Roanoke and failed—Know anything about it? H'm!

—Who told you? Then it will do to sell a little—Sell what?—Virginia Central?—You are old enough to know what to do—Yes, I'm going to sell some—Of course, Roanoke; do you think I meant house-furnishing goods?—The market ought to have a reaction anyhow, —How much?—Five thousand?—Very well; the first ten thousand will be joint account—you keep your hands off it—I don't care what your friends do—Sure, tell them in twenty minutes—How did you make out with your bull movement in Great Southern?—I'm sorry you did not see me first, before doing such a fool trick—Stick to railroad management hereafter—Certainly not!—On the contrary, *put up* Great Southern— This is the very time to do it. It will make it look as if you had something up your sleeve; yes, and also some brains higher up—Of course—And, for Heaven's sake, tell your broker not to begin on Great Southern until Roanoke starts to slide for keeps. Yes—Good-bye!"

He started, in his quick, stealthy way, unpleasantly like some feline animal's, towards the ticker and perceived the fascinated Gilmartin, who had listened to the conversation of the famous stock-gambler with the conservative and respected president of the Great Southern.

Sharpe's shaggy eyebrows came together and he snarled: "What are you doing here?"

His eyes took on a cold, menacing look. It was an habitual trick of his to disconcert people who would make money through and out of him—a form of hypnotism not unlike that practised on their victims by certain beasts of prey, Oriental bullies, and prize-ring champions. But Gilmartin was too excited by the scent of the coming dollars to heed it.

"Old Rock has gone for the day," he said, very quickly, "and there's nobody in the office. This is your chance, Mr. Sharpe. You know how he works. Probably his supporting orders are not for more than ten thousand shares in all. Why, if this deal is off you can smash the stuffing out of Roanoke!" He all but saw the smash, in his excitement. Sharpe was a wonderful stock-market general, the Phil Sheridan of the ticker.

"Rock is a clever man," said Sharpe, half to himself. Then wholly to Gilmartin: "He's almost as clever as you, Gilmartin. And you know you're a wonder."

The lust of gain made Gilmartin not only impervious to Sharpe's sarcasm, but preternaturally quick in divining Sharpe's doubts and suspicions, also brave as a lion or an equal of Sharpe's. He retorted, quickly:

"And you've got both of us beat a mile! See here, Mr. Sharpe, I don't want to know what you are going to do with my information, or even if you are going to use it or not. I only want you to sell some Roanoke for me. You always wish me to bring you what news I get."

"All right, Gilmartin. You just write what you've told me and publish it in twenty minutes; not one second before. I'll sell five hundred Roanoke for you at once. Let me know promptly anything more you may hear."

Gilmartin started for the door, wasting no time in expressions of gratitude or farewell phrases. Sharpe took up a private telephone that hung from the wall near the ticker, and said:

"See how Roanoke is and what buying orders are under the market. Be quick!"

He walked quickly into the adjoining room where a

confidential clerk at an upright desk kept the memoranda of his operations. There were at least a dozen telephones in this room, each in its individual booth— so that the man at the other end of each line might hear only what was meant for his ears. Sharpe called up one of his numerous lieutenants. He spoke quickly, sharply, almost chopping off the ends of his words:

"Hello? Go over to Virginia Central and see what you could get for five thousand shares if you had them to sell."

He walked back to his office as the bell of the telephone by the ticker rang. The man he had sent to the Roanoke "post" was reporting.

"Well? What? A thousand every eighth down? Where is Dunlap? Hurry back and sell five thousand. Don't give them away, but get them off quickly."

The confidential clerk tapped on the open door and Sharpe returned to the telephone-room to hear his lieutenant's report.

"What is it?" He spoke impatiently, so that by his voice the broker at the other end of the wire knew his chief was frowning. "What? Three hundred at forty-eight and one-half and two hundred at forty-eight? Nonsense! There must be more wanted. A hundred at forty-five? The specialists are lying to you. Very well. I'll let you know."

His scowl took on an expression of anger and malignity. Jimmy Hopetoun said there were no buying orders in Virginia Central excepting four hundred shares on the specialists' books. It was a trap, and the taint of the deceit exasperated him as though it were an insult to his brain and to his unerring instinct. The Great Southern had not bought the control of the Virginia Central; the Roanoke crowd had tried and failed; therefore Rock had a lot of the stock on hand, and was shrewd enough to conceal the fact by taking no steps to keep the price up, as a less able man would have thought it wise to do in order to market his now useless holdings. Instead, Rock was encouraging short sales by obtuse traders; *they* might sell enough to give him what market he wanted, or at all events enough to make them suffer and thereby reduce the final costs of the retreat to Rock. Sharpe was pulling nobody's chestnuts from the skilfully concealed fire; but by-and-by he would start that same innocent-looking and ostentatiously unprotected Virginia Central going down. He would distribute a few impressions among his susceptible and over-eager followers. If there was no trap the stock would break wide open and the followers would make money. If there was one, he would lose none.

He read on the tape: "RK 1500, $79\frac{1}{2}$; 2000, $\frac{3}{8}$; 500, $\frac{1}{4}$; 2000, $\frac{3}{8}$; 500, $\frac{1}{2}$." It held fairly well. Other brokers than Rock's, evidently, had buying orders. He took down the wall-telephone and, without lifting his gaze from the sliding tape, he spoke into the transmitter: "Sell ten thousand more, carefully, but quickly. Yes, Roanoke!"

He stepped back to the ticker, and leaning an elbow on a corner of the little machine, watched the tape unblinkingly. Presently there came: "RK 1000, $79\frac{1}{2}$; 100, $\frac{3}{8}$; 1500, $\frac{1}{4}$; 1000, $\frac{1}{8}$; 5000, 79; 1700, $78\frac{7}{8}$; 1000, $\frac{3}{4}$; 1700, $\frac{5}{8}$; 2000, $\frac{1}{2}$."

He had sent his message to the stock-market and his words were heeded. Other stocks hesitated; then they began to follow Roanoke. The room-traders, vulture-like, scented easy money and flocked to the Roanoke post. They asked for no reasons; they sought no explanations; they perceived with their own eyes that the selling was more aggressive than the buying; therefore the dollars were at the bottom of the hill, not at the summit; now they began to help Sharpe, unaware that they were helping anybody but each man his own bank-account. As the price yielded their hopes became certainties, and they sold more confidently, with the confidence of men who might fire a load of bird-shot into an election-night crowd in order that at least one shot would lodge in one man.

Sharpe went to his desk and telephoned to his chief confidential broker—the man to whose advice and restraining influence so much of Sharpe's success and reputation as a great stock manipulator and a marvellous judge of market conditions were due.

"Hello, Jim! I wish you'd offer down Roanoke for me without losing much stock. I have a few thousands out. Very well. Pool? That's all right; it will go down just the same, pool or no pool. You don't think so? Well, just you watch it and see. I understand Rock is not in his office. Find out, will you? If he isn't, do your worst and have a man to report his return. I hear he wanted the Virginia Central and there was going to be a great hurrah. Well, he didn't get it—What's the odds who's in the pool? It's going down—They can't buy the entire capital stock, can they?—Get busy, Jim."

He rose frowning; he did not like Jim to disagree with him. The news of the strong pool—James Allsopp knew nearly everything that went on in Wall Street—did not bother him, because he knew that Rock's pools were always blind pools, the management of which was left entirely to Rock. He rang up little

Hopetoun, the best disseminator of "tips" on Sharpe's staff, the most skilful preacher of the gospel of discontent in the Street.

"Jimmy, Roanoke is going down. The boys can safely help it along."

It was enough; the boys made money following him, until they overstayed the market. It saved him commissions in some of his bear campaigns.

With Jim Allsopp's manipulative orders and Hopetoun's freely distributed tips the big Board Room began to boil. Roanoke was the storm centre. About that post a hundred greed-maddened men were shrieking—buying and selling, making money and losing it, at the top of their voices. And the price of Sampson Rock's pet stock began to give way, slowly at first, obstinately, stubbornly, like a very powerful man fighting a crowd, and then a little faster, but still too slowly for the mob that had scented money and were fighting to get some of it. It was down to seventy-seven when Gilmartin's news came out on the news-tickers, as well as on the pink slips taken into the commission-houses by messenger-boys, who darted in shouting "Rush!" and bolted away again like mad on their way to another office to startle. And what the Street read—and believed, because the tape corroborated it—was:

"There is the very highest authority for the statement that the deal for the acquisition of the Virginia Central by the Roanoke, on which the recent rise of the latter was entirely based, has fallen through. The deal was expected to carry Roanoke to par. The frantic selling by the overloaded insiders started the break. The control of the Virginia Central, whose strategical value and possibilities of development are well known by railroad financiers, will not pass to the Roanoke, but to another road, probably the Great Southern. The plans of the Roanoke management were comprehensive, but the control of the desired road was indispensable. This was not obtainable. It is said the inside pool bought one hundred thousand shares in anticipation of the successful completion of the deal. It is undoubtedly that stock which is now being sold."

Every trader who was neither blind nor deaf was now selling Roanoke and buying it back in fear of a rally and selling it again because it did not rally, until the road to great and sudden wealth instead of being a precipitous mountain-path, became a toboggan-slide with millions in gold eagles at the bottom and shovels and horses and wagons close by. And in commission-offices, the men who were long of the same stock saw the toboggan-slide—only that at the bottom they also saw the yawning chasm into which they might dump all they owned in the world and to the chasm it would be as a grain of sand; so they merely let a few hundreds or a few thousands drop. That is, they sold their stocks and cursed; and then they shuddered at their narrow escape, for the price was going lower and lower, towards the bottomless pit.

Of a sudden an adventurous trader discovered the defencelessness of Virginia Central and began to sell it, without thought and therefore without fear of a trap—the trap which was not exactly the trap Sharpe had expected, but was nevertheless a trap for bears, by reason of the small available supply of the stock.

Sharpe had smelt it from sheer force of habit of suspicion or his wonderful instinct as a trader.

XXVI

DUNLAP, at the very outset of the attack, telephoned to the office. When Valentine told him that Mr. Rock was not in he returned to the Roanoke "post" and superintended the defence in person. But as the skirmish began to develop into a pitched battle he again telephoned to Valentine that Mr. Rock must be found at all hazards.

Dunlap could protect the Rock stocks against ordinary drives by misguided traders, but this onslaught might mean more; it might be that something serious had happened somewhere — some cataclysmal news that would tax Rock's resources and abilities to the utmost. The stock was coming from so many sources that he could not be comfortably certain it was all short stock from the room-traders. Much of it undoubtedly was, and, knowing that they would have to buy back as likely as not from himself, he took it freely, with an ostentatious, good-natured pity. But his acting was wasted on Sharpe's lieutenants and on the traders in whom the scent of near-by money had aroused a Berserker rage. Hastily distributing substantial buying-orders among his most experienced brokers, Dunlap rushed to the office.

Valentine and the telephone operator had called up Rock's house and the clubs and Ardsley and one or two offices—every place where Rock might possibly be—all without success. Nobody had seen him. Dunlap, rushing hither and thither in the office but never keeping away from the ticker longer than forty seconds at a time, saw that, notwithstanding his doubling of many of the Old Man's supporting orders, Roanoke continued to decline. He hesitated. Was this Sampson Rock's own work for mysterious reason not yet confided to his old friend and chief broker? Rock sometimes did things first—inexplicable, mystifying things—and explained afterwards.

In various offices, members of Rock's Roanoke pool also wondered. Sampson Rock's manipulation was not always as clear as crystal, and they concluded that the Old Man was shaking out somebody—whom or why they could not tell. They paid him the compliment of thinking of him in the same class with the elemental forces of Nature. But Dunlap dismissed the same thought as soon as it occurred to him. Sampson Rock was not doing this; it had gone too far; the stock was too genuinely weak.

Sam had gone to Albert Sydney's office to find Darrell, but Jack was out and Sam asked that they tell him to come over to the office. It was a good time to reassure the broker, and therefore Sam said:

"Mr. Sydney, I am going to give you a lot of business, I hope." He added, smilingly: "And I'll see that my father does, too." There was no telling when Sydney might come in handy.

"Many thanks, Mr. Rock. We'll do our best for you." The broker did not mention to Sam that he had already received some orders from Sampson Rock. By-and-by, when the two Rocks compared notes, they would see that Albert Sydney was a discreet broker, a man to be trusted.

"And our margin arrangements will be more satisfactory in the future." Sam was made aware by the look on the discreet broker's face that Mr. Albert Sydney was taking the expression of a hope for a definite promise; and the great deal had not been consummated.

He left Sydney and walked back slowly, thinking, trying to see his way clear. When he reached the office Dunlap was rushing from the ticker to the telephone and back to the ticker; to Valentine and back to the ticker; to the window and back to the ticker. The moment he saw Sam he shouted, eagerly:

"Where is your father, Sammy?"

"Gone up to the Ardsley Club."

Dunlap was a fluent swearer—very. Also his face, in his excitement, twitched so curiously that Sam looked at him — with amazement rather than with alarm.

"What in hell am I to do?" shrieked Dunlap, oblivious of the half-dozen pale-faced customers who took no pains to conceal the fact that they were quiveringly listening to his every word. "Valentine, call up the Ardsley Club and get Mr. Rock on the wire."

Sam's heart began to beat more quickly—excitement is a contagious disease.

"What's the matter?" he asked.

"Roanoke, seventy-five!" called out a swarthy, black-bearded little man who sat on a high stool beside the office-ticker. A flaxen-haired boy was busily marking the prices on a big oaken quotation-board.

On hearing the price, Dunlap said, "Much stock coming out?" and without waiting for an answer rushed to the ticker to see for himself. What he saw for himself made him swear again, and Sam walked up to him, took him by the arm, and led him into the inner office, the elder man's excitement making him not calm so much as tensely alert.

"Come here with me, Dan," he said.

Dunlap was not frightened at what had happened thus far, but he was exasperated by what might yet happen. He yelled at Valentine, "Telephone to—"

"Now," said Sam, sharply, "what is the matter?"

Dunlap had run to the ticker at which Sampson Rock should have been looking at that very moment.

"Great Scott, seventy-four and one-half; one quarter! Sam, I don't like—Virginia Central, forty-two—forty!"

"What?" shouted Sam. That quotation touched him.

"Look at it, seventy-four for Roanoke, seventy three and three-quarters! I can't stand this pace unless— Where's your father?" He glared at the cashier, who answered:

"He isn't at the Ardsley Club. I've had it on the wire four times. I have told them to send a man to the station to meet him and have him call us." Valentine imparted this information self-defensively; he must not be blamed for Rock's inopportune disappearance. He went out to telephone once more.

"There's something wrong! I ought to be in the Board Room. Why isn't he here?" Dunlap's eyes were fixed fascinatingly on the little paper ribbon. The ticker was whirring away madly, excitedly, as if it rejoiced in its death-dealing task.

"Look here, Dan, the old gentleman went away angry because somebody else scooped in all the Virginia Central that was floating around in Richmond—"

"Why didn't he tell me? Why did he have to go

away? When did he go? What does he want me to do? What—"

"It's my doing."

"You damned fool!" Dunlap glared at him. "What do you mean? That you told somebody we were after—"

"Keep cool, Dan!" advised Sam. He felt so cool that he could add, jocularly: "And you'll live longer. Of course, I didn't tell anybody. I—"

Valentine rushed into the room. He told Dunlap, speaking very quickly, "The Eastern National is calling up for—"

Dunlap's oaths—he seemed unable to do anything but swear—made Sam keep cool. He understood that the situation was growing serious. What he did not know was that the bank was calling for additional collateral on one of the firm's loans, not because of high-minded conservatism, but because President Winter of the Great Southern Railroad was a close personal and stock-market friend of President Green of the Eastern National Bank, and had made a friendly suggestion or two about any big block of Roanoke stock the bank might be lending money on. It was Green's duty to safeguard his depositors' funds.

"They say," went on Valentine, hurriedly, "that they understand the Virginia Central deal is off and—"

"What business is it of theirs? Who told them there was a deal?" Dunlap looked furiously at the cashier. Valentine merely asked, in reply, "What shall I do?"

"Give them what they ask, damn them," said Dunlap.

If one of the banks from which Sampson Rock was borrowing millions began to show anxiety, there was no telling what the other banks, friendly enough in normal times, would do presently, especially as Dunlap, in Rock's absence, must keep on buying Roanoke without orders, to keep the price from disappearing utterly.

"*Seventy-three for Roanoke!*" came from the other room. The swarthy little man by the ticker had, with malice prepense, shouted it at the top of his voice, and they heard him through the closed door.

"Valentine, who's got my bonds?" asked Sam. "You or my father?"

"We have. We cashed some of the coupons yester-day and—"

"How much Roanoke can I buy with them, Dan?"

"There's a million of them, governments," explained Valentine, brightening visibly. "And about three hundred and fifty thousand dollars of railroads. Mr. Rock always invested the interest for you, Sam, and would never touch them. It's a standing rule."

Dunlap stared at him and then turned to Sam.

"That's so; you've got—" He looked at Sam dubiously. Then, with a sudden decision, "Well, there's no time to lose!" He ran to one of the telephones on the long table and said: "Hello! Hello! Buy ten thousand Roanoke, not above seventy-five. Hurry up!"

IIo drew a breath of relief and said to Valentine: "Take the bonds yourself to the Marshall Bank and borrow the limit on them. Then notify the Eastern you'll pay them off." Valentine knew what to do and how to hurry, especially now when the Eastern was to know that Dunlap & Co. had money to burn. He left on a run.

"Dan, I have the Virginia Central stock. I've options on eighty-three thousand shares—thirty-three thousand at fifty and fifty thousand at sixty-five.

That stock is all in escrow in Richmond banks. How much's the Governor got?"

"Ninety thousand—ninety-one, I think. It's over ninety thousand."

"I wanted him to pay me seventy-five for mine and he wouldn't. He was mad as blazes, and he said there would be no deal. But there must, now."

"There must," echoed Dunlap. His eyes were fixed on Sam's. He was not thinking of the future, nor of financial subtleties, or railroad development, but of the unnerving present.

"And I've twenty-five thousand besides at Albert Sydney & Co.—"

"Then you are the man—"

"Yes; that's one hundred and eight thousand shares, and with the Old Man's, and what there must be in London, it doesn't leave much floating around, so that—"

"Great God! What a squeeze! If your father were only here! Where is he, anyhow? There goes Roanoke again!"

Roanoke, which had begun to rally, was once more declining. A rich but intelligent accomplice of Rock's had telephoned for his dear friend, and Valentine had unwarily told him that Mr. Rock was not in the office and he couldn't say where he was because he did not know. They were looking for him. Therefore the accomplice promptly sold five thousand shares — the amount of his holdings in the pool—and then prudently sold short five thousand more. Having carefully waited until his orders had been executed, he generously told one of his friends. The market like that and no Sampson Rock in his office? Sampson Rock must be dangerously ill.

The friend had friends. Sampson Rock's illness grew more dangerous with each repetition. It was inevitable. In its travels the inference became an assertion, and the illness ended in what the serious illness of all great stock operators always ends. Millions cannot fend it off or prayers keep it away. And a few hours ago Sampson Rock looked so strong! And now Roanoke was so weak!

When the rumor that Sampson Rock was dead reached the Stock Exchange there was a moment's hesitation—it showed the intelligent suspiciousness of the brokers. And then the real, the furious, the panic-stricken selling of the Rock stocks began. It was the Street's mighty tribute to Rock's great abilities as a railroad strategist—and to his enormous commitments as a stock-gambler.

It was as though the flood-gates of the stock-market heaven had burst wide open. It was the deluge, and everything gave way before it!

XXVII

BUT it was not alone the men who actually owned Roanoke stock that were selling it, fearful of pecuniary disaster, now that the masterful guiding-hand had been wrenched from the helm by death. It was also the professional speculators, who held no shares, but were frantic with eagerness to fill their pockets with dollars, whether the dollars thus plucked from the grave of a great railroad man were the blossoms of death or not, so long as they were dollars. To the extent that they succeeded in driving down the price, to that extent would the real holders, trusting in the superior knowledge of financial ghouls, part with their holdings—the "real goods"—and then those dollars would be merely the blossoms of fear, perhaps not very nice flowers, but the banks would receive them, and the shopkeepers would take them, and out of the losses of some the wives of the others would be made glad and gorgeous; and the education of children be paid; and houses bought and establishments maintained; also economies enforced in less fortunate households. If the price were hammered sufficiently to cause genuine panic-stricken selling, there was no telling what would happen—with Sampson Rock dead and his associates taken by surprise.

Dunlap, as he saw the huge blocks of Roanoke hurled madly at the market, was silenced. Then he said:

"My God, Sam, we'll have a panic here if— *Where's your father?*" He had begun with a whisper and ended with a shriek. Sam was keenly conscious of a sense of danger—a not fully understood danger; but the menace of it made his blood tingle and brought a certain watchfulness of mind that made him think not only clearly, but quickly—almost with the mind of his father. He had his father's courage without his father's experience. His face was a shade paler, but his jaw was thrust forward, and he was frowning. He knew that he had money of his own.

"Dan"—he spoke quickly, but distinctly, and in a measure he was thinking aloud—"my father never would have allowed this to happen. To prevent it he would have bought all the Roanoke they sold, and more, too. And Virginia Central—if we buy fifty thousand shares now we'll have more than there is to go around. I paid sixty-five for the Robinson stock, because he wouldn't sell it any cheaper. Understand? Now telephone to my father's friends to buy Roanoke and those who were in the deal to buy Central."

"I—I—my buying is Dunlap & Co. If your father doesn't approve I'd be responsible, personally. It might mean losses he wouldn't care to shoulder, and I'd be in a—"

"Go on, hang you!" said Sam, between his clinched teeth. The opposition roused him to a pitch of fury. Somebody was trying to injure Sampson Rock. That meant Sampson Rock, Jr. That meant self-defence; and *that* meant blind anger.

Dunlap blinked his eyes and closed his fists spasmodically—not at Sam, but at the overwhelming responsibility, painfully aware now, for the first time in his life, that he did not have Sampson Rock's full confidence and that Sampson Rock was an unusual man. But the stock was going down too rapidly, too ominously. The short interest, having had no chance to cover, must be enormous; to wait longer was, to say the least, to present several hundred thousand dollars to the ghouls as a reward for destroying several millions. Sam might not realize the various questions involved, but there was nothing else to do but to obey Sam's orders. The boy had grasped the elemental necessities of the situation. Still, Dunlap hesitated.

"It's with my money. I am giving the orders," said Sam. "Go ahead!" And he pushed Dunlap out of the office. Valentine collided with the head of the firm.

"They're all telephoning to ask about Roanoke and if it's true Mr. Rock—"

"Tell them Mr. Rock says to buy Roanoke. *I* am Mr. Rock," interrupted Sam, fiercely, impatient at Valentine's helplessness. "Go, Dan! Don't you hear? And you, Valentine!" In his heart there was nothing but a desire to fight the unseen enemy—fight to win, and not to establish the truth of abstract principles.

Dunlap ran and Valentine hastened back to the telephone. Sam *was* "Mr. Rock." If any fault was found at the obsequies, he could prove he had not lied. And fault certainly would be found if he did not answer the telephone messages, for the uncontradicted cry was heard above the bedlam noises of the Stock Exchange:

"Sampson Rock is Dead and Sharpe is on the Rampage!"

They had been enemies, and Rock was dead and defenceless and Sharpe was alive and raging. And

Sharpe had money and brains and a devilish disposition; and Sampson Rock's broker's office was like a broken engine, still running—but running without an engineer, jerkily, erratically, on the verge of a final smash.

Dunlap's buying—he took twenty thousand shares of Roanoke in less than two minutes—and the buying of Rock's friends, who now realized with chuckles of admiration that the grand Old Man had connived at the artistic simulation of a panic for the common weal of the Rock crowd—in order to buy the pool's complement of stock at bargain prices—checked the decline. The traders, urged by Sharpe and the lash of greed, hurled themselves against Dunlap, but he held his ground stubbornly, his face showing that he felt the wall behind his back. With Rock to command him, he would not have fought a defensive but an offensive fight, which is the best defence. But to hold his own until the commander-in-chief arrived, that was all he· hoped to do, all he fought for. Let the commander-in-chief turn resistance into pursuit; let the commander-in-chief do anything, so long as he came back to command.

Sam, impatient with the slowness of the rally, unaware that the tape, owing to the volume of transactions, was minutes behind the market, seeing Roanoke at seventy-four—in the Board Room it was actually selling at seventy-five and a half—was made furious. He ran to the outer office.

"Valentine," he shouted, and did not know that he was shouting, "buy Roanoke until I tell you to stop!" He would not stop until somebody howled for mercy and howled unmistakably.

Valentine came out of his cage, but Sam yelled at him, "Go back and do as I tell you, or by—"

"You've done enough, Sam," Valentine assured him, with a white face. "We'll pull out—"

"I don't want to pull out! I want to teach these dogs something!"

"Sammy," replied Valentine, "if you don't do anything rash, you'll make a lot of—"

"I'll make more if I buy more," he interrupted. He had not before thought that he stood to win big stakes. The realization of this now fanned the flame. How much he would make, or in what precise fashion, he did not know. Risk his own money? He would have risked it all, unhesitatingly, now; even if his father had been a pauper. To gain his golden independence, to punish those who would stab his father's turned back, who would upset the ideals of the Rock family, to punish and to win—above everything, *to win!*—all of this made Sam say, fiercely: "Go ahead. Buy till I tell you to stop! Use my bonds, all of them, and my father's as well." He needed money. He did not know how much there was available now, in the office. He would assume there was a great deal. There *must* be a great deal. And he would use it. He said, sharply, "Get me Albert Sydney on the 'phone."

"Use the 'phone on your father's desk," advised Valentine, non-committally. "I'll get them on that wire for you."

Sam rushed back to the private office and waited impatiently for an answer to his call. Sooner or later his father had said Virginia Central would sell at seventy-five or eighty—just before the Roanoke took over the control. It might as well be soon. It might as well be now. For he and Sampson Rock controlled the Central and he and Sampson Rock were the Roanoke!

SAMPSON ROCK OF WALL STREET

"Hello? Mr. Sydney? In the Board Room? This is Sampson Rock. Tell Sydney Mr. Rock says to buy—What? No, I won't wait. You tell him at once!—Keep away, Central—What? Oh, is this you, Sydney? This is Rock. I want you to buy all the Virginia Central you can. You'll find there isn't very much—We have—Corner? No. Take all they offer you—Don't pay above eighty—Yes, eighty! A few thousands ought to do it. I tell you, we have it safe in the office! Above eighty you can let them have one hundred thousand shares if need be, and below seventy-five buy all they will sell you. Certainly not; we don't want any panic—I know all that!—Oh yes, the Roanoke will take it over!—We have much more than the majority.—My father's busy.—Dead? Somebody else will be the corpse!—Sure!—Don't lose any time. This is your chance to show what you're good for. Goodbye."

As Sam rose his gaze fell on the row of telephones on the long table. They were private lines, mostly to confidential brokers. This Sam knew. What he did not know was that those same confidential brokers had called up time and again in the last half-hour and, receiving no answer to their calls and seeing Dunlap's face and hearing the terrible rumor, had sold Roanoke short — to be on the safe side, for if Sampson Rock was not in the office with the market in such a condition Sampson Rock must indeed be where he never again would answer telephone-calls.

Sam did not know the name of the broker. He called to Valentine:

"Come here, quick! How much Roanoke did you buy?"

"I—er—" the cashier's face betrayed him.

"Not a share! You ass! Whose 'phone is this?"

"Meighan & Cross."

Sam took up the receiver. "Hello!" he shouted. "This is Mr. Rock. Buy five thousand Roanoke at the market. Quick."

"That's for my father," he told Valentine. He pointed to the next instrument. "Is this some other broker?"

"Yes. But you mustn't—"

But Sam was speaking into the transmitter: "Buy five thousand Roanoke, right away. Yes—at the market.—Hurry up!"

He did not ask whose telephone the next was, but spoke—another five thousand shares to buy—and passed on to the fourth.

"Not that!" interjected Valentine, quickly. "That's to Commodore Roberts!"

"So much the better. This is not for my father, it's for myself," said Sam. "Hello? Commodore Roberts? This is Sam Rock, Commodore. Very well, thank you. —I called up to tell you.—Nonsense, he's as much alive as I am. I think you'd better buy a little Roanoke. No, sir. This is my own deal—my first offence—I've got the Virginia Central where I want it now and you might make some money just to please me. Don't thank me, because I expect you to reciprocate some day very soon.—You'd better hurry.—I've got a big coal and iron proposition and— Yes, sir. Thank you! Good-bye."

Sam rose. His face was flushed. Valentine looked at him with as much respect as surprise, and Sam enlightened him:

"He's going to buy ten thousand shares of Roanoke, and he'll go into my iron syndicate."

He approached the ticker and shouted:

"Seventy-eight—seventy-nine—seventy-eight and a half — seventy-nine — a quarter — eighty, by Jingo! *Eighty-two for Roanoke—!*"

A clerk rushed in for Valentine, who was wanted in a hurry outside. One of the telephones on the long table rang. Sam answered it.

"Hello? Yes. Send the reports to Valentine. Sure. It's going to par. In about five minutes."

The farthest bell rang and Sam ran to it.

"Yes? What, Dan? No. Better keep on buying. Commodore Roberts will buy—I just had him on the 'phone.—He's buying ten thousand shares.—Sure.— Give it to 'em good!"

He walked restlessly to the outer office in time to hear the swarthy man by the ticker shout, "Roanoke, eighty-five!"

Valentine rushed to Sam, his face joyful: "It's enough, Sam. You stand to make—"

"Look at this Virginia Central!" shouted the swarthy man, excitedly: "Fifty-seven; sixty; sixty-three; sixty-seven! Jinks! All hundred-share lots—sixty-eight; sixty-nine; seventy; sixty-five; sixty-eight; sixty-six; seventy-one!"

It was a crazy market; merely to see the tape maddened with the sense of tragedy.

Gilmartin, his face livid, rushed in.

"Where's Mr. Rock?" he panted. He perceived Sam and asked, gasping, "Is—your—father—dead?"

"Not yet," answered Sam, calmly.

"Roanoke, eighty-six and five-eighths; five thousand at eighty-seven; a half; eighty-eight; eighty-nine; ninety; ninety-one; ninety-two!" The swarthy customer's hands were shaking as he guided the cascading tape into the long, upright tape-basket. The air was full of excitement. He did not have one share of the stock, but he saw a big fight and was thrilled without understanding.

"Not yet!" repeated Sam, with an excited laugh. Several people entered hastily. One of them, a stout, bespectacled young man, with a bundle of papers in one hand and a pencil in the other, asked, with a genial smile:

"Where's Mr. Rock?"

"Here!" answered Sam, promptly.

"I'm from the *Planet*. There's a report that your father is dead. He poised his pencil ready to jot down, smiling, an exasperated denial or a sad affirm ative.

"Nothing in it," interrupted Sam. The reporter wrote nothing, but smiled more broadly and was about to speak, when:

"Roanoke, eighty-seven; eighty-six; eighty-five!— She's going down again," shrieked the swarthy man.

The other customers stopped smiling. One of them went pale—he had five hundred shares of Roanoke and had prematurely bought a country-place with his paper profits. The profits were oscillating, and his heart was set on that Westchester County farm.

"Valentine," said Sam, loudly, "tell them to buy me ten thousand more."

"He's in the other room, Mr. Rock," called out a clerk from behind the wire partition.

"You give the order then." He remembered Harding. His father had said he was a good broker. Sam approached the clerk and whispered: "Give the order to Harding. Buy ten thousand at the market, but not above par. You understand?" He meant Harding to understand he must bid up the stock to par if possible on the purchase of the ten thousand shares. It was the way his father gave orders to Harding. It was a very good way.

"Yes, sir," the clerk assured him, importantly. Sam's commands had been executed by Valentine, even by Mr. Dunlap himself. The clerk had no other thought than to please young Mr. Rock, who was certainly a wonder—and the Old Man's only son and logical successor. He therefore quickly telephoned to Harding's office, and then he whispered to his next-desk colleague and chum:

"Sam's got the Old Man beat a mile at this game. He is a corker!"

"V. C., seventy-three; seventy-eight; seventy-five; seventy; seventy-seven; eighty!"

"The stock's cornered! I knew it!" yelled Gilmartin. The other reporters pricked up their ears, excepting the stout *Planet* man, who continued to smile broadly and wrote, "*Corner.*" That meant a big story. He said, "If you will give us the disgusting details—"

Sam did not heed him; he laughed and said: "Oh no, Mr. Gilmartin! No, indeed. Nobody wants corners nowadays. But it's a nice stock and—"

Sampson Rock, his face livid, so that it made his gray eyes look almost black, burst into the office. In his hand was a copy of the *Evening Planet*, on the front page of which, in huge red letters, was the heading:

SAMPSON ROCK

REPORTED

DEAD

BIG PANIC

DEEMED POSSIBLE

IN WALL STREET

The rumor of the demise of the great captain of finance was given and the panic-stricken selling of the Rock stocks—Roanoke below seventy—was described as the tribute of stock-gamblers to the king of them all.

At the sight of Sam, Sampson Rock halted abruptly. Oblivious of strangers, he said, thickly:

"This is your work—*yours!*"

The look in his eyes was not pleasant. But before Sam could say anything, Rock started towards the ticker.

Sam had seen conflicting emotions in his father's look, but also ignorance of the turn in the tide. And, remembering the danger from which they had emerged in his father's absence and his own probable winnings and Commodore Roberts's promise, he replied:

"Yes, this is *my* work."

He spoke with confidence, but in his eyes there was a curious defiance. It would take more than words to pry open his clutch on the Virginia Central.

"Ninety-three for Roanoke!" shouted the swarthy man by the ticker, with a note of personal triumph in his voice—as though he and none other had routed the born enemies of the office.

"What?" shouted Rock. He pushed the swarthy man unceremoniously out of the way, nearly making him tumble from his high stool.

"'V. C.,'" read Rock, aloud, "'seventy-eight—eighty-two—eighty-five—eighty—' What the—" He ran the tape through his fingers to make sure it was not a mistake and to see how the rally had been effected—in his absence.

It had been a crazy market—boys playing at engineers; but, wittingly or not, it had been a great stroke

—unfortunately over-enthusiastic; the machinery not well oiled and a part here and there strained, but, on the whole, successfully lucky.

He turned to Sam, his eyes overflowing with interrogations, but, as if against his will as a human being, his habit as a ticker-maniac drew his eyes again to the tape. He had returned. He could check or drive, he could direct. He called to the cashier without looking up:

"Valentine, get me Dunlap on the 'phone at once!"

"Yes, sir," said Valentine, turning to a clerk and motioning to do as Mr. Rock had commanded. One of the office-boys whispered to Valentine, and the cashier approached the Old Man and said: "Mr. Rock, Mrs. Collyer is in the end room—"

Sampson Rock did not hear him; his mind was full of the retreat of his enemies, ignorant of whether what looked like punitive fusillading came from his own soldiers or from the exigencies of a badly frightened short interest. Which of his friends had conducted the defence? Or was it Dunlap alone? How much Roanoke had they been forced to take? New conditions had been created. Perceiving that his father had not heard, Sam told Valentine:

"Show Mrs. Collyer into the private office."

A moment later Mrs. Collyer, her florid face chalk-white, a copy of the *Evening Planet* in one hand and in her eyes the fear of death—followed the harassed-looking Valentine into the big customers' room. She paused at the threshold and shouted after Valentine, who was going through the door of the partition which fenced off the clerks:

"Sell mine! It's below seventy. You mustn't let it go any lower! Hurry! Hurry!"

She was not counting on her fingers. She did not wish to count. The thought of what she would have to count, as soon as Valentine reported, made her forget that Sampson Rock was dead.

She had been unable to get Dunlap's office on the telephone. Always "Central" said the number was busy. The last time "Central" volunteered the information that there was great excitement in Wall Street and that she had heard that somebody was dead. Mrs. Collyer, uneasy rather than alarmed and fully prepared to hear that Roanoke was climbing at the rate of a thousand dollars a minute, had started to come down. But Fanny caught a glimpse of the big head-lines in the "extra" which a shrill-voiced newsboy was urging the world to buy, and Mrs. Collyer read her death-warrant. Rock, she knew, was dead; and of Roanoke she had two thousand shares. Rock was dead; poor Rock! Roanoke might be zero by now. Poor Rock, but poor, poorer, poorest Mrs. Collyer!

Of a sudden her nervous glance fell on Rock standing by the ticker. Since he was alive, not dead, and she was alive, but also dead, she more rackingly than ever thought only of Roanoke: that is to say, of herself.

"This is your work, Sampson Rock!" she said, with a half sob.

Rock looked at the clock. It was too late to do anything more in the market. There was therefore no occasion for excitement. He pointed to Sam, sternly, and replied, curtly: "No; *his!*"

"*You*, Sam?" she said, with a sharp, indrawn gasp. She looked at Sam's face, which of a sudden had been endowed with the petrifying power of Medusa's.

"Yes, ma'am," said Rock, walking towards Valentine's little window in the brass-wire partition.

"Roanoke, ninety-five — ninety-six — ninety-eight!" shouted the swarthy man, who now turned to discharge a look full of malignity and triumph at Sampson Rock's back.

"What? NINETY-EIGHT?" screamed Mrs. Collyer. The blackness of the long arctic night enveloped her. She stretched her arms out as though to keep herself from falling. Then there was a blinding flash and the cry was torn out of her dazzled soul: "I didn't tell you to sell, Mr. Valentine! I didn't! I didn't!"

Dunlap, red-faced, his collar torn off him, a fragment of his cravat dangling from his neck, his coat ripped in a dozen places, with marks on his face as of fist-bruises, ran in and shouted:

"Where's Rock?"

"Here," said Sampson Rock.

"No; here!" interjected Sam, sharply. "Dan, go back and buy—"

"Ninety-seven, five thousand at ninety-eight; thirty-five hundred at ninety-eight and a half; six thousand at ninety-nine! PAR FOR ROANOKE!" shouted the swarthy man. "Hooray! Hooray-ay-ay-ay!" He was not carrying a share of the stock, but he was heavily long of the excitement of the battle.

The other customers were again smiling—one was dancing in an abandon of delight; he had bought the country-place with the profits on his five hundred shares; the floor of the office was the velvety lawn; snow-white sheep would keep it close cropped, as they did in England.

"Hooray!" chorused the other customers, looking at him. Then they looked at Rock and became mute.

"You needn't go back, Dan. Harding did it, I'll bet, with that last order," said Sam, his face flushed, his eyes gleaming triumphantly. The confident manner in which he spoke of the broker made Sampson Rock look at him curiously. The problem of the heir seemed walking fast towards a satisfactory solution. This revived the sense of humor. He said nothing, but his lips twitched.

Gilmartin and the other reporters approached Sampson Rock, and Gilmartin asked:

"Mr. Rock, we'd like to know—"

"There he is," interrupted Rock, pointing to Sam.

The newspaper men looked with interest at the young man who—they were reading their own "stories" of the day, before they had written one line—had suddenly become famous as a financier. The *Epoch* chap had already decided to make Sam the winner of twenty-five million dollars as the result of the day's work. The *Planet* man's smile, though broad, had a congratulatory quality to it even if his off-hand estimate was only ten million dollars. His was really a conservative paper in financial matters.

"You may say, gentleman," said Sam, with a frown —a trick of his father's that, like other tricks, seemed to have developed in Sammy in a few hours—"that the controlling interest of the Virginia Central Railroad has been acquired by Mr. Sampson Rock—"

"Junior!" interjected Sampson Rock, Senior.

Sam looked at his father's face; it was expressionless. He nodded acquiescingly at Sampson Rock, and went on, gravely:

"—in the interest of the Roanoke & Western Railroad Company."

Sampson Rock looked at his son. Then he smiled.

It was a sort of resigned chuckle. He turned his head away so that Sam could not see the smile. The sense of humor was full-grown again.

"At what price?" asked Gilmartin.

"Mr. Sampson Rock, Jr., will give out a statement for publication after three," quickly said Rock, unsmilingly; this was business.

Gilmartin could not wait. He rushed out to get the skeleton news on the news-ticker and on his slips; he would return later for the full statement—and for forgiveness. Maybe Rock would be magnanimous. It was an epoch-making deal. The victor might want everybody to feel happy. He might desire kindly comment from the newspapers. Gilmartin was ready to meet him half-way. He was even ready to tell Rock that the reason why he had sold out his Roanoke was to keep Rock from losing when the stock began to decline. Moreover, Rock had lied about the deal. But Gilmartin would forgive even that. It all depended on Rock.

"It's ten after three now," said one of the reporters, looking at the office clock. The ticker was still printing transactions—it was so far behind.

"Closing!" shouted the swarthy man at the ticker, climbing down from the high stool. "Great day, wasn't it?" he observed, to another customer, loudly enough for Sam to hear. He himself had not made any money, but he knew the man who had made that great day so great, and also had made millions. In his graphic narrative to friends later he always referred to the man as "Sammy." The country-place buyer nodded and went out to telephone to the real-estate man to go ahead; no haggling.

"Come back in an hour, won't you?" said Sam to the newspaper men.

"Can't you give us the disgusting details now?" asked the *Epoch* man. "Mine is an afternoon paper." "Yes; it's a very fine paper."

"You read it every night and take it home to your wife, I know," laughed the fat reporter, who knew other Napoleons of Finance and several politicians. "What we want now is the disgusting de—"

"No," laughed Sam, "but if you gentlemen hadn't killed my father I don't think Roanoke would have sold at par to-day. You had a 'beat' when you murdered him. But he knows now what to do any time he wants to put up one of his stocks—just die in the *Planet*. Be nice and come back in an hour, won't you?" And with a pleasant nod, as though he and the "press representatives" were old friends, he followed his father into the private office.

"I say, Dad"—he began. Then, as he saw who stood beside Mrs. Collyer, listening, wide-eyed, to Dunlap: "Fanny!"

The spirit of the fight was over. He had done the right thing, but he was not altogether certain he had done it with a proper regard to the commercial side of the proposition. He had made Roanoke sell at par, perhaps over-precipitately. But he had sold his Virginia Central holdings to his father's road, after all. He himself was ahead of the game, and it was a bully fight, anyhow. And he was glad to see Fanny now—who stood there, smiling, still excited by Dunlap's rather technical version of Sam's victory. Her obvious interest in his affairs so pleased him that, as he smiled back at her, a great tenderness came over him. He held out both hands and said:

"How do you do, Fanny?"

"How do you do, Sam?"

SAMPSON ROCK OF WALL STREET

All his letters to her, the development in his character and the progress of his business education, which she had traced in his letters, at first so full of himself and later so full of his work; a growing belief that she would share in his victory, that she had shared it, that in working for himself he was working for her—these things flashed across her mind. Her eyes were moist as she pressed his hand. A sense of ownership stole over her: this Sam, this man, this hero, was to be more. . . This was her victory! And, as she thought what the victory meant, she blushed.

Dunlap had left Mrs. Collyer by the window and was now talking vehemently to Sampson Rock. At the mention of his son's name by Fanny, Sampson Rock turned and called:

"Sammy?"

Sam was speaking to Fanny. "I'm fine, Fanny. Did you get my letters from Washington? You'll owe me about twenty, but I'll get even. What is it, Dad?"

"Come here, will you?"

Leading Fanny by the hand, Sam approached his father and asked:

"Well?" His face was serious, so changed, so different, that Fanny looked wonderingly at him. Then the same feeling of pride and joy of ownership came over her. She looked as though she were unaware he was still holding her hand and smiled at Sampson Rock. She must smile at somebody.

"Now, what about Colonel Robinson's option?" There was a kindly curiosity in Sampson' Rock's eyes.

"It's for fifty thousand shares at sixty-five, good for six months. That, I figured, would give me time to negotiate with you—or somebody else, in case you were unreasonable about it. And the reason I paid as much as I did was that he isn't such a bad old chap. I didn't have the heart to beat him down, though he certainly was a dog in the manger." Fanny smiled approvingly. "Besides which," Sam went on, meditatively, "it was his bottom price, though he was very hard up and he knew that I knew it. There's so much work to do that I didn't want to lose much time."

It was Sampson Rock's turn to smile. He was in a forgiving mood.

"And then," continued Sam, "I had bought thirty-three thousand shares from General Winfree, who rounded up about all there was to be had in the State. If one share escaped him and he knows it, he'll drop dead. They are all out for the dust, everywhere." He smiled as he thought of the doughty General's look when he should read the New York papers—and the price of Virginia Central. "I agreed to pay fifty dollars—ten per cent. down, ten per cent. in thirty days, and the balance in sixty days. That was cheap, I think."

Sampson Rock raised his eyebrows, but said nothing. This made Sam go on calmly:

"Of course, I had previously bought twenty-five thousand shares through Sydney & Co.; that stock doesn't average much over thirty-five. That was the cheapest stock I bought. It wasn't quite fair to you, but I made up my mind that if you weren't fatherly about it I'd turn it over to you at cost. All I wanted was money to try experiments with, in case you developed parsimony. But, since you look so very paternal, I suppose that you are willing to pay a fair price—enough to reduce my average on the whole— What?"

"I'll be—ah—Where did you get the money for

that?" asked Sampson Rock. His eyelids had narrowed and he was looking intently at his son.

"Before I got the five hundred thousand dollars from you I gave a mortgage on our house to Darrell, who agreed not to record it unless the deal fell through and you refused to help me out. I had to protect him in case I died suddenly. It's a terrible handicap in business not to have ready cash at times and to have to borrow it when you can't tell a soul why you want it." He looked at his father steadily, and for all his humorous manner he unconsciously tightened his grip on Fanny's hand. The pressure thrilled her.

Sampson Rock rose and, from sheer force of habit, walked to the ticker. The little machine was printing its usual record of "bid and asked" and "high and low" prices of the day, of academic interest only. Sampson Rock turned to his son and said in an even voice:

"Sammy, you are an ass!"

"Sure. That's how I got the Virginia Central stock. That's why I had trouble with Dan at first, and why I put Roanoke to par when I got mad because they had killed you and they thought there was nobody to fight for you. I don't know how you will make out with Roanoke in the future, when I may not be here. You will probably make more money. When it comes to that, I guess I'm an ass. But consider; I'm your son."

"No, I'm your father, Sammy," said Sampson Rock. Then he laughed, but suddenly became serious again. Fanny's hand moved nervously. Quick as a flash, Sam turned to her and said:

"Hear that, Fanny?"

"Yes; I hear it," she whispered.

"Then—"

She felt her face burn. She was grateful when Sampson Rock said:

"Sam, I'm afraid I'll need you to supply some gaps. Awfully sorry to take you away from Fanny." Sampson Rock smiled at her apologetically.

"It will only be for a little while," said Sam, reassuringly to Fanny.

"Mother," said Fanny, glad of an excuse, "we must be going."

Mrs. Collyer came down to earth.

"Do you think I'd better hold for one hundred and ten, Sampson?" she asked Rock. She had given all up for lost and had now a forty thousand dollar profit. Should she make it sixty thousand dollars, to offset the earlier agony?

"Ask Sam," replied Sampson Rock. "He's running this deal."

"I'll let you know before the market opens to-morrow," Sam said. Sampson Rock laughed appreciatively. Fanny looked at Sam and he smiled back, boyishly. She turned away her eyes and Sam looked at his father, who asked, hopefully:

"You don't happen to know how much Roanoke approximately you bought, do you?"

"No. What's the odds? I think Dan bought thirty thousand—"

"I know how much *I* bought," broke in Dunlap.

"I don't know how much Valentine bought," said Sam. "I told him to keep on buying till I told him to stop."

"Of course—" began Dunlap.

"Yes; you've made• him a white-livered coward. Ask him! I told Meighan & Cross to buy five thousand, and this telephone"—pointing to the guilty instrument—"another five thousand, and this one, another five thousand, and Harding, ten thousand. I haven't seen their reports. I specifically told Valentine that those purchases were for your account, Dad. What Dan bought around seventy-two and seventy-four was for mine, with my money. But if you want to divide profits on yours, I'll be forbearing. Mine, I'll keep." He smiled, quizzically.

"Twenty-five thousand. Thank Heaven for that. I feared you had bought the whole capital stock." Rock sighed in humorous relief.

"And I strongly advised Commodore Roberts to buy, and he said he'd take on ten thousand just to please me. He also promised to join my Austin iron syndicate, and—"

"Great Scott!" Sampson Rock burst out laughing.

Valentine came in.

"There's a mob outside to see you, Mr. Dunlap. I guess it's the shorts in Roanoke and Virginia Central. The afternoon papers say Virginia Central is cornered and—"

"Go easy with them, Dad," said Sam. "I'd rather not make a cent than—" He paused and looked uncertainly at his father.

"Of course not, my son," said Sampson Rock, in a matter-of-fact tone. Then he added, jovially: "There's glory enough to go around. You've made enough, although the Sydney purchases were rather Wall Streety. Go, Dan, and cheer them up. Tell the Roanoke shorts we'll fix the settling price after we figure out how we ourselves stand, or they can take their chances in the open market to-morrow. Don't lend a share. As for Virginia Central, the Roanoke will pay seventy-five dollars a share. So must they, plus a little commission from those who sold it short above sixty-five."

"Sam's done pretty well, considering," smiled Dunlap. Fanny's face was radiant. There was a suggestion of pride not less than contentment. In her eyes was a light that came from other things than excitement. Mrs. Collyer's lips were parted breathlessly. She was at the great Mint, looking at the machinery which coined the hopes that soared into the eagles that did not.

"Yes," retorted Sam, looking at Dunlap, "considering that you were scared stiff, I have done pretty well." He turned to his father and said, briskly: "As soon as the novelty of your resurrection wears off I want to say something to you. There's no time to lose."

"Oh, rest on your laurels for a week!" laughed Sampson Rock. In his glance there was satisfaction and unmistakable affection. Sam was glad to see it. It meant easy sailing in the future. It insured the success of the Great Work. He said, in a tone of raillery that had a serious undertone:

"I'll strike while the iron is hot—Austin iron—and I want to pay for the stock with what profits come from saving your esteemed life to-day. Also, I might as well have the options on the coal-lands that Morson treacherously secured before I reached Austin. I want you to see Darrell to-morrow and help us organize the—"

Sampson Rock threw up both hands. "Don't shoot! Take all I have! Leave me only these clothes and a tooth-brush!"

"You might as well do it, Sampson," put in Mrs. Collyer, with a felicitating smile. She looked first at Rock and then at Sam—the same smile to each.

"Very well, Sam. Bring Darrell, and we'll talk it over."

"There's no talking to do. You are here to listen. Remember, I am to make my headquarters at Austin while Rogers gets in his fine licks on the old Central. He'll have the job of his life."

"While waiting for your train to leave, suppose you let me introduce you to some of those victims of yours who are waiting tremblingly outside?" Dunlap jauntily left the room to act as Grand Chamberlain.

Fanny, realizing that the men had important business before them, said: "Mother, what is home without you? I don't think there are sleeping accommodations here." She made an attempt at a smile, but in her eyes there was a determined look. Sam did not see it, because he had not looked at her since he began to talk business with his father.

Sampson Rock took advantage of the society look of penitence which Mrs. Collyer put on and deftly escorted her to the corridor. Sam accompanied Fanny. There were several people standing outside the door of the office and before the elevator shaft. Three newspaper photographers aimed their cameras at Sam.

"Hey!" he shouted. "Don't you—"

The cameras clicked. One of the photographers calmly said: "Just once more, please, Mr. Rock."

"No use, Sam," laughed Sampson Rock, not unpleasantly. He was without personal vanity, but Sam was his only son. "They all carry accident policies. This is what you get for being famous."

"Look pleasant, Fanny," laughed Sam. She turned away her head unsmilingly.

"Here's the elevator. Down!"

"Good-bye, Sampson. Sam," said Mrs. Collyer, shaking her finger while she blocked the door of the elevator, "don't forget, my dear boy, before the market opens to-morrow—"

"Going down?" asked the elevator man, in a resigned voice.

"Yes," Mrs. Collyer told him politely. "Now, Sam—"

Sam was listening to his father. But he turned and said:

"Very well, Aunt Marie. Good-bye, Fanny. I'll be up to the house—ah—soon." He added, a trifle apologetically, "Just as soon as I possibly can."

"Very well, Sam," said Fanny, quietly. She saw that he was already talking to his father, who smiled as he listened with paternal interest. She caught the word "Austin." She bit her lip and turned to her mother. The gate slammed and they shot downward.

"At a hundred and twenty-five," murmured Mrs. Collyer, absently, "it will be—I'll ask Sam."

"Mother!" whispered Fanny. There were tears in her voice; her eyes were dry and very bright, but they looked tired. It was not until, after a restless night, she saw the morning papers and the long "stories" of the great *coup* and Sam's picture that there came to her eyes the tears that were the price of her victory— the same papers that made Sam smile before he began to talk to his father about the Great Work, at the breakfast-table.

THE END

Made in the USA
Columbia, SC
19 February 2025

54114654R00226